To Helen,

TOMORROW
WAS BEAUTIFUL
ONCE

with best wishes,

Amy Circll

1.9.25

AMY ORRELL

TOMORROW WAS BEAUTIFUL ONCE

Elsewhen Press

Tomorrow Was Beautiful Once
First published in Great Britain by Elsewhen Press, 2025
An imprint of Alnpete Limited

Elsewhen Press, PO Box 757, Dartford, Kent DA2 7TQ
www.elsewhen.press

British Library Cataloguing in Publication Data.
A catalogue record for this book is available from the British Library.

ISBN 978-1-915304-65-0 Print edition
ISBN 978-1-915304-75-9 eBook edition

Designed and formatted by Elsewhen Press

For my husband, Simon,
and my parents, Ann and Andrew.
Thank you for always believing in me.

January 2150
London

The room had been grand once. Doric columns held aloft a high ceiling where the last traces of ornate plasterwork and cornice clung perilously to the cracked surface. Dips and bulges were transformed into a lunar landscape as they caught the evening light pouring through sash windows. Miraculously, the glass was intact.

A raised voice echoed from an adjoining room, followed by rapid footsteps. Alice burst through the doorway, sending a cloud of dust swirling through the light shafts, and careened towards the window as though she might throw herself through it.

"Come on!" admonished the man following in her wake.

"You can't just kill people, Howard!" she cried. Her hands gripped the edge of the window frame, blanching her knuckles white. Her breath clouded the glass and her eyes strained to watch figures crossing the bridge in the distance.

"We won't *be* killing people, Al." Howard's voice was firm and he squared his broad shoulders, but the look in his eyes, had Alice been watching, betrayed his inner anguish.

"Technicalities! It's genocide." Alice spun round to face him. "How can we live with that?"

Howard inhaled deeply, dusty air catching at his throat. He raised his hands, imploring his colleague to understand and accept the circumstances that had funnelled them down this path. "The difference is…" He paused as the image of a child flashed before his eyes. Bonnie. She was laughing as she ran, not looking while her feet carried her into the path of a car. She was five now, but in the world that Howard sought, she would have died aged just two. He shook his head, clearing away the curve of her smile from his mind. "The difference is…"

1

"You can't be responsible for killing people who never existed."

The voice flowed from the shadows.

"Bloody hell, Jack, you scared me." Alice clutched her hands to her chest and squinted into the gloom.

The drift of dust parted, admitting a younger man into the light. He paused by the edge of a desk where an employee key card and a few sheets of yellowed paper offered clues to the building's bygone history. Jack lifted the card and wiped the grime from its surface, trying, but failing, to make out the face of a woman who had worked there seventy, maybe even a hundred years ago.

"Once we've accomplished our goal, this conversation, our decision, the 'deaths', will never have happened." As he spoke, Jack replaced the key card on the desk, exactly where it had been, covering its own imprint in the dust. "If we destroy the technology at its inception and prevent time travel from ever becoming a reality, then time will return to the path that it should have followed. We're all agreed on that outcome, at least."

Alice shook her head. "How can you be so calm about this?"

Jack's gaze washed over her to the bridge beyond. He pushed a few strands of sandy hair from his forehead and his grey eyes fixed on some point in the distance that only he could see.

"Jack, you're a Cronod. Sorry," —she flushed— "I mean Mixed-Era." He didn't respond and Alice wondered if he'd heard her. "This will wipe out your kind," she persisted.

"Alice, you know that's not true." Howard frowned and stepped forwards to touch Jack's shoulder, thinking again of the duty he had once shirked. He had tried to atone for it since, to be the father Jack had never had. "Jack has a place in Gaia, along with the other invited Mixed-Eras."

Jack grimaced. "People of Mixed Era Origin..." He spat out each word. "I think Cronod is more apt, don't you? Anyway, I won't be needing that place."

"What?"

Jack took in his friend's broad face. Howard's features, once strong, were weathered by years of difficult decisions. Jack shuttered the trace of remorse that threatened his resolve and delivered the words he had gone there to say. "I've been selected for the mission."

In the silence, a sliver of plaster broke free from the ceiling, shattering when it hit the tiled floor. Its impact broke the gulf between them.

"Are you crazy? It would be a suicide mission. Your only chance to survive this is in Gaia."

Jack pictured Gaia, a biosphere that, once sealed, would be immune to all changes in time. Once its doors closed, they could never again be opened. "Surviving is not the same thing as living," he replied. "And anyway, this is a suicide mission irrespective of your parentage. Someone's got to do it, and I've got as good a reason as anyone."

The blood pounded inside Howard's head as the weight of his failure became clear. "When did you volunteer? Why didn't you tell me?"

"Because you'd have tried to stop me," said Jack simply.

The three stood for a moment, each locked in the world of their own thoughts.

Jack broke the impasse and, leaning forwards, took Howard's hands in his and pressed them. He turned to the figure in the window. "Alice."

She nodded in reply.

Jack turned and left the room.

§

April 2150

Jack shifted his weight against the raised head of the trolley bed, turning away from the bank of monitors that intermittently beeped as they measured his vital signs and brain function. Periodically, the muscles in his face and body spasmed.

Jack glanced at the room around him. Small details betrayed the fact that this was no hospital; the fluorescent strip bulbs were from a bygone era, the walls were grey with dust, and the dark corridor outside was eerily silent. It was one of a handful of medical laboratories that Earth Revolution operated, hidden in disused buildings in London's former commercial centre.

The room was too brightly lit and Jack paused to rub his eyes. It wasn't an ideal setting for marking papers, but this would be his only chance. He adjusted the position of his iHolo and selected the last essay he would ever mark.

As a research historian, Jack rarely taught. But his expertise in the field of Transient History made him an asset to his colleagues at the university. The last two weeks' teaching had been unexpected and, in all honesty, inconvenient. But once Jack saw the lecture topic, he'd been unable to resist. He hadn't been required to set an assignment, but he'd done so all the same. He huffed out a soft laugh, thinking how if his mission was successful, the essay's subject would cease to exist.

Modern European History: An Outline of the Key Events Leading to the Temporal Stalemate of the Twenty-Second Century. It was written by a first year, just eighteen or nineteen years old, born into a world where shifting realities had become the norm. Jack's eyes raced across the words, following the letters' rise and fall, knowing already what they would say.

That given Europe's fragility at the beginning of the 21st century, the diatribe of the far right needed only a spark to engulf that continent in flame. By mid-century, great swathes of the Middle East, Asia, Central America, and Africa were uninhabitable, the global temperature-rise forcing the dispossessed into a mass northern migration. The far right, no longer able to deny the scale of the crisis, changed the narrative: this was the "Great Flood" of our time, proof that God favoured Europe and would gift the planet to those He deemed worthy.

Jack's stomach twisted, the passage of time failing, as it always had, to lessen his response to those dark times. Perhaps it was inevitable that the pressures of a swollen population would claw away at the established ideology, toppling the belief that there was "One World For All." Yet the speed at which support for the displaced fell away, traded for a dangerous new, protectionist stance, remained a source of shame. Migrant families were forced to fight for equal footing, and in March 2070, thousands gathered at the European Parliament to demand citizenship rights in their adopted countries.

Jack's mind conjured images of the peaceful protest turned sour; bodies strewn across the concourse, one of the fallen covered in blue fabric with yellow stars – a banner torn defiantly from a broken flagpole. The altercation between protestors and police might have been smoothed over, but Neo-fascists within the crowd that day seized their chance and opened fire, their hatred claiming the lives of more than five-hundred men, women, and children. One day's protest became four years of war.

Meanwhile, experimental physicist, Dr Noah Kingsley pushed forward his work on time-cast technology. Little was known of the illusive inventor, but there were dozens of theories and Jack knew them all. Some presented Kingsley as power hungry and vainglorious, whilst others held that his goal was humanitarian, a quest to turn back time and arrest the destruction of the planet.

Jack's gaze lifted from the essay. He stared into space. Time travel had marred his life with its ability to injure and undermine. Could such darkness have been borne from good intentions? And would it make a difference to him if he discovered that it had? The truth had vanished along with Kingsley, when he and his research were seized by the Republic, but Jack hoped he would learn it.

Jack flicked his finger and the essay vanished. He laid the iHolo down and closed his eyes, unsure to what extent his rising nausea was due to the history laid out before him, or the treatment he was undergoing – a pre-emptive dose of hypocampozine. His hands involuntarily tensed into fists and he grimaced, white-knuckled, until the pain passed. The drug was proven to lessen the effects of time-travel sickness, but since the average person was rarely affected, and the medicine itself had unpleasant side effects, few people bothered with it.

Unfortunately, time travel sickness affected almost all People of Mixed-Era Origin – Cronods, as they were commonly known. For them, the medication hurt like hell. Cronods rarely cast through time, but Jack had chosen to; he couldn't afford to arrive in a hostile environment suffering blinding headaches and disorientation while his frontal and temporal lobes fought one another to overcome the conflicting messages of multiple timelines.

He wondered how his students would respond if they knew what he was about to do. Amongst young adults, sympathy for climate refugees was high, but would they sanction an attempt to alter eighty years of history? And how many of them might prove to be victims of that change?

A hundred and fifty years earlier, London had been the beating heart of the country where millions of people flowed daily along its streets, rivers and underground like blood through the body's veins. Then came the pandemics of 2020 and 2028, and the heart went into cardiac arrest. Nervous Londoners began to search out a safer existence away from the crowded apartment blocks, offices, and crush of the inner-city transport network. By the time the diseases were vanquished, new norms of home-work life had been established and smaller, safer, regional centres had won the business and backing that they had long-time courted.

The challenges of those pandemics were a minor precursor to those posed by climate flux, and the government's politically hostile environment proved no match to that generated by nature in collapse. Vacant commercial buildings might have housed thousands in desperate need, but the government was unmoved: property would not be requisitioned, the rights of owners would be protected and real estate would not be devalued.

Climate refugees were forced into the gap, the unseen cracks and rifts of the city, whilst tourism for those rich enough to afford it resumed. But their simmering anger only needed a spark, and news of the massacre in 2070 unleashed an outpouring of anger and weeklong riots that left great swathes of buildings as smouldering shells.

Years later, the tourists, though fewer in number, had slowly returned. But the decaying buildings of the commercial district remained empty, standing as tomb-like monuments to the history of London's working past. Though, as Jack knew, a few still housed secrets within.

The light overhead flickered then cut out. The hairs on the back of Jack's arms tingled and stood on end as the beeping of the heart monitor rapidly accelerated. A crash of lightning sent his hands to his temples and he cursed as pain seared through him. The walls vibrated as a second shock wave hit the building and a low moan escaped through Jack's clenched teeth. He panted shallowly as the pressure crescendoed and then ebbed away.

Everyone hated temporal storms – which were occurring ever more frequently – but Cronods experienced them as an internal, physical pain. Jack thought he'd become better at blocking out the discomfort, but the sweat beading his brow and his racing pulse belied his belief.

There was a knock on the door and Howard entered. "Can I come in?" he asked, not waiting for the reply. Once inside, however, he paused awkwardly at the foot of the bed.

"Have you come here to hold my hand, Howard?" Jack teased.

"Don't joke." Howard bit back the emotions threatening his composure. "If I had my way you wouldn't be here at all."

"I'm sorry." Jack took a deep breath and exhaled slowly, focusing on the cannula and wires running to his arm. "I can't allow myself to go there, Howard. I can't waver now."

"I know. I'm not here to try and dissuade you." He moved round to the bedside and smiled grimly. "There's something else; I came to give you this."

Jack's eyes flicked up, refocusing on the envelope that his friend drew from his pocket. His stomach twisted as he recognised the looped writing on the front, his name. Howard held it out to him, but Jack didn't move to take it.

"Your mother wanted you to have it, when…" Howard paused, considering the irony, "when the time was right."

Jack took the envelope and ran his thumb over the writing. The monitor flashed a warning light when his heart skipped a beat. "How long have you had it?" His words felt ragged.

"A couple of years, she gave it to me just before she…" his voice trailed off. "Look, there were things she wanted to explain herself. She may have regretted some of the choices she made, Jack, but you weren't one of them. She loved you." Howard felt the inadequacy of his statement, felt Jack's eyes probing his, wanting so very much to accept the truth in his words.

Howard considered those eyes which were so like Mary's. They reflected the same hurt that he had seen in hers all those years ago. He wondered, once more, whether he should have tried to change time. Undone the decision he had made thirty years earlier and lived a different life. But what about Joanne and the kids? What about Bonnie? The image of his granddaughter ran through his mind, laughing as she jumped on the bed, laughing as she chased him in the park, laughing as she ran out into the road…

"I need my life to count for something," said Jack,

interrupting Howard's thoughts. "I need something, just *one* good thing to come from it."

"Jack, you are already that and more!"

"Not for her."

"And that belief is why you gave up your place in Gaia and volunteered to go back?"

It wasn't really a question, and Jack knew it didn't require an answer. Howard sat in the chair beside the bed, bringing his eyes in line with Jack's.

"There's a reason I didn't give you the letter sooner; I'm afraid that after reading it you'll think badly of me. I kept putting it off, but it seems I've run out of time. I'm sorry."

A crease formed between Jack's brows as he searched his friend's face and discovered him aged since they'd last met. He wanted to ask what Howard meant, to be told in person what he needed to know. But there were too many questions for the moments that remained.

The chair scraped the floor as Howard slowly stood up. This large man, a powerful figure throughout Jack's life, looked suddenly smaller, diminished. "I loved your mother, Jack, and in spite of myself, I loved you."

A nurse knocked at the door and entered.

"It's time for the last dose now, Mr Elliot." She smiled and held the door open.

Howard took the cue and headed to the exit. "Good luck, Jack." He smiled unsteadily, a dozen words frozen on his lips.

"Howard? I—"

"Read the letter, Jack."

Jack held his gaze until the door clicked shut, cutting him off, from this life, from this time. He sighed. "And so starts the clock."

"I'm sorry?" asked the nurse.

"Nothing," Jack replied, and with forced jollity added, "Shall we?"

The woman smiled reassuringly. She had a kindly, motherly sort of face that instantly instilled trust, and for a moment Jack felt the urge to confess all his fears to her, certain that she would understand and sooth away the darkness. She leant down to adjust the cannula and the hairs on Jack's hand rose at her touch. Another crash of lightning rocked the room, compressing the air within and forcing it from Jack's lungs.

"Poor love," the nurse soothed, brushing the hair from Jack's forehead as a mother would to a child. "The storms have been bad today." She sighed with resignation, reached to adjust the drip, and vanished.

"No!" Jack cried.

The air thickened around him. He squeezed his eyes shut and, rocking slightly, began to count.

"One... Two... Three..."

Was this a test, he wondered, to have to witness this on the eve of his mission? "Eight... Nine... Ten..."

To have to witness this life, this soul, that never was. The knowledge that he would be one of only a few people to know she had ever existed weighed on him and he was faced with the harsh reality that he would be responsible for this same act a million times over. Not just People of Mixed Era Origin, but those whose lives they'd touched in countless unknown ways.

"Twenty-nine... Thirty... Thirty-one..."

He'd been a witness before to the erasure of lives and the crushing moments that followed as the timelines readjusted.

"Forty-one... Forty-two... Forty-three..."

They were always the worst part. He'd once watched as a mother wept for that long, cruel minute, rocking back and forth empty arms which had, moments before, been holding a child. As the minute concluded she, too, disappeared, to continue the alternative life she was living elsewhere. Only Jack remembered the child she had once loved and mourned in another thread of time that was now lost.

"Fifty-eight... Fifty-nine... Sixty."

The air thinned, returning to its usual fluid state.

"OK, hold still," said a deep, male voice.

Jack opened his eyes and took in the latest reality.

The nurse was tall, with pecan skin and an accent that hinted at a childhood in the Republic. He hummed quietly as he bent down to check the cannula and adjust the dial on the drip. "Nearly there now," he smiled. "Oh! And thanks for the tip," he added cheerily. "My kid will love that." He made a note on Jack's chart then left the room.

A conversation about Windsor Castle washed in and out of the memory of a kindly woman brushing the hair from his forehead. Two versions of time, struggling and failing to be one. Jack fought the swimming sensation and rising nausea. This time the medicine was not responsible.

"Yes, I promise, I'll take it easy for the next few hours," Jack repeated.

"Okay, well good luck with that research project of yours," said the nurse as he opened the door to leave.

"Thanks." Jack forced a smile.

The door clicked shut and Jack began to pull on his clothes. The training of the past few months had changed his body; less lean, and more muscular than it had been. Though, as Howard had helpfully pointed out, a far cry from the physique of the usual characters charged with saving the world. Unlike superheroes, however, who guarded the planet from supervillains, Jack sought to defend it from mankind's own folly. And who better to understand that folly than a historian?

Pioneering time-travellers had believed that through limiting their interactions with the past, their presence would go undetected, but even slight changes generated temporal flux – a destabilising force that rippled forwards and played havoc with the weather. Unaware of the connection, Republican leaders had authorised the use of time technology to alleviate some of their more pressing issues, strengthen their authority and silence their opposition. Their actions unleashed devasting storms as the timelines readjusted.

The connection between temporal storms and time travel would never have been known, if not for another unexpected consequence of playing with the past: the emergence of a new people, those whose parents came from different times and eras. As the use of time travel increased there was a surge in births of People of Mixed-Era Origin.

When the first Mixed-Eras came forwards to protest changes to the past that they, and only they seemed aware of, they were scorned as conspiracy theorists, their claims denounced as preposterous. But as their cry against time atrocities grew louder and was joined by Mixed-Eras in positions of power and status, the scientific community began to sit up and listen.

Eventually, research revealed that a genetic abnormality in the hippocampus meant that the memories of Mixed-Eras could not be rewritten, only added to. Remarkably, people like Jack were able to recall multiple, alternative timelines, their layered recollections known as polymorphic memories. The newspaper that broke the story referred to Mixed-Eras as 'chronological oddities', which in turn spawned the nickname, Cronod. It was commonly used, but rarely politely.

But as this incredible discovery gained acceptance, a terrible truth was revealed: the Republic had used time technology to travel back in time and alter the outcome of hundreds of votes on conservation and energy in favour of fossil fuels. Far from enabling mankind to avert the course of climate change, time travel had in fact accelerated the rate of Earth's destruction.

Jack stepped from the building into the shadows of the unlit street. To the south, the moon's reflection glinted on the watery flood plain that was once the South Bank. He wondered whether families would soon again stroll its walkways to be entertained by street performers, visit the Tate Modern, or simply enjoy the view of the city from the south side of the river. Jack had never done any of those things, but he'd read about them.

He slung his backpack onto his shoulder and pushed his hand into his pocket, where his fingers curled around the envelope inscribed with his name. He began to pull it free, then changed his mind. Did he even want to read it? What could it tell him, that wouldn't feel too late to hear? Slowly, Jack forced himself into a walk, focusing on the feel of the pavement beneath the soles of his shoes.

Without time travel, Jack could not exist, but at what cost did he and others like him walk this earth? He had been given an opportunity, a chance to make amends for the damage time travel had wrought, and he'd seized it with both hands. Some might call it his destiny, but his mind, filled as it was by polymorphic memories, rebelled against such a concept. As far as Jack was concerned there were simply choices and consequences. He had made a choice, and he would accept the consequences. Whatever they might be.

§

13th August 2073

Thames Barrier, London.

Dr Noah Kingsley had already checked the conduits twice, but nonetheless he checked them again, ticking each one off against his list. He missed the team of engineers who had worked for him in the Republic because now he alone was responsible for it all. Every alteration had to be catalogued precisely, with rigorous checks before it could be tested. A tiny flaw in his calculations would render the results void, and if he failed to adequately shield the atomic clocks from the surging electrical field, then the past week's work would all be in vain.

He had barely slept for days as he worked and reworked each one of his measurements, but now he was buoyed up by the frisson of possibility, the chance that this time it *might* succeed. He sealed shut the capsule's door and carefully flicked each of the machine's switches, before moving to the far end of the warehouse, his footsteps echoing dully across the vast space. He pulled down the head piece of the heat-resistant proximity suit – a precaution that he hoped would not be put to the test – and ran his finger down the list of calibrations on the screen in front of him. Everything was set.

Noah lifted his head and triggered the countdown. His gaze flicked between the capsule straight ahead and the numbers descending on the screen. His eyes narrowed when the countdown neared its end. As the dial hit zero, the overhead lights sparked then extinguished, plunging the warehouse into darkness. He hadn't seen what he had hoped to – a brief vanishing of his prototype machine – but Noah wasn't defeated yet, not until he took readings from the atomic clock inside.

He grabbed a torch and hurried forwards to grasp the handle on the capsule's door, noting that the metal felt hot to the touch. That was new. He heaved the door back and removed his hood to better read the digits on the clock. There was no discrepancy. The capsule had not left its temporal path of origin.

Exhaustion, no longer held back, threatened to rise like a flood and consume him. But seasoned by decades of discipline, Noah did not lose control. He carefully unzipped the proximity suit and hung it over the back of a workbench then pinched his tired eyes with forefinger and thumb, swallowing back his disappointment. He made a brief entry in his logbook before powering down the machine, double checking each switch as he turned them off one by one.

Noah slipped through a side entrance, down a narrow corridor, and unlocked the fortified door at the end. He pushed it open, at once feeling the rush of warm air against his skin, and the distinctive smell of oil and mud that hung about the Thames. He walked to the river wall and leant heavily against it, his mind already beginning to fill with potential alterations, small changes to the calibrations that might make a difference next time.

He laughed at his own inability to stop and raised his face to the sun, allowing its heat to warm his dark skin, noting the changes in wind direction as the hot, damp air caught at his beard and tousled the long white hairs that sprouted from his brows. If he closed his eyes he might, for a moment, fancy himself back in the South of his childhood, where the languid brackish water held a wealth of treasures, from sumptuous shrimp and crawfish to deadly snakes and gators.

He sighed. No child would now know how it felt to grow up, fishing and exploring the bayous; they were all lost beneath an ever-present high tide.

Noah turned his face towards the Thames Barrier, which was raised, as it always was these days, working in tandem with the larger barrier further downstream. His features hardened, the fleeting joy of distant memories already forgotten as he began once again to turn the numbers over in his mind.

§

April 2150
Aldgate

The original plan was for Jack to cast from Brussels, where Howard worked for the European Confederacy of Time Travel, but during the past month, on-site security had been increased. Visitor clearance was almost impossible to obtain. In the UK, however, Howard had access to the London factory, where a shipment of capsules was due to leave that day. The manufacture of time capsules was hazardous, and the abandoned London underground network had provided an ideal safe housing for their construction. The tunnels also allowed for a 'faulty' capsule to be redirected beneath the city's streets.

In a crumbling building opposite the derelict entrance to Aldgate Station, Jack waited for word that the capsule was ready. The contents of his backpack were spread across the bed, and he ran his fingers across the surface of each object, mentally checking it off the list in his mind. He replaced each item in the bag, slowly and methodically for the third time that night.

Waiting made him uneasy. The tension was palpable and sleep would not be forthcoming.

Jack liked certainties – they were the antithesis of temporal flux – but for thirty years, his life had held little he could depend upon. He considered the world that he hoped to make and imagined the comfort of knowing that the past was unchangeable and only the future was yet to be written.

He zipped up the backpack, replaced it on the chair by the door, and sat back down on the edge of the bed. His eyes fell again on the envelope on the bedside table. He stared at it for some minutes then, with a sigh, pushed aside his unease and reached for it.

He pulled himself up the bed so his back rested against the wall, his arms on his raised knees. He traced his name with his finger and recalled a time when the fluid handwriting hadn't caused his breath to catch in his throat or his mouth to run dry. Birthday cards: he remembered one or two, and the way his mother always looped the J around seamlessly into the second letter of his name. He'd been in awe of that as a child, at a time when few adults, let alone children, continued to value the inherent art in the formation of writing. He ran his finger under the fold of paper, easily breaking the glue seal that had dried years before and pulled out the letter with trembling hands.

November 5th, 2147

Darling Jack,

I know that if you're reading this, then I've let you down in a way for which no apology will ever suffice. But then I know you wouldn't accept my apology, so for what it's worth, and while my mind is clear and able, I am offering you an explanation.

I was like you once: righteous, head-strong and as-sured of my ability to make a difference in this world. I wanted children one day, I really did, but not to raise them in the world that you and I were given. Oh Jack, how I wish the world were different, and I the mother you deserved. None of it was your fault.

I told you, I think, that I worked for Earth Revolu-tion: it gave me purpose and a reason for hope. I knew the missions were dangerous so I hid my in-volvement from my parents, and I tried to hide it from Howard, but he knew, I could never keep anything from him. We were engaged, you see. Did you know that, Jack? Did he tell you?

He begged me not to volunteer for that last mission and he almost succeeded. I loved him desperately, but I couldn't see how the future we craved could ex-ist in the world we had inherited. So, I accepted a mission to return to 2070 to extract the right-wing politician, Kayson Hart.

I was tough back then, Jack, please don't laugh! Though I don't suppose you can imagine it. Hart's *family wealth stemmed from fossil fuels, and he was hugely influential amongst the far-right and centre-right factions of the EU Parliament. He'd played a role in defeating every emergency environmental act put forward since the end of the 21st century and we believed his knowledge could be pivotal in allowing us to pinpoint the precise moments in time that, if changed, could preserve the planet's future.*

But the mission didn't go to plan. Hart wasn't where records said he'd be, and I made some difficult decisions in order to get close to him. I thought I was succeeding, but he was playing me. If I had captured him, then the sacrifices would have been worth it. That's my greatest regret, Jack; I could have borne it all, the torture, his forcing himself on me, if I had only managed to bring him back.

I escaped when the first shots were fired outside the Louise Weisse building. I was there, Jack, in Strasbourg on 29th March. Perhaps I'd have done better to try and stop the massacre? Though others had tried and failed. In the chaos, I escaped and managed to return to my own time. I hadn't brought Hart, but instead brought the guilt of my failure, my shame, and you. I brought you.

I'm so sorry Jack, this must be hard for you to hear. I didn't want you to know your father's identity, to know what kind of man he was, to try to seek him out, or to risk your own life to change the course of mine. I know you would, Jack, because that's what I would have done once too. But I know you want the truth, you deserve the truth, and to hear it from me.

I know you blame T-Tech for robbing us of the life we should have had. You think that time travel itself destroyed my mind and led to the nightmares that incapacitate me. Possibly, knowing that your father was from another time, you believed yourself responsible for all that I suffer? But it wasn't time travel, Jack, and it wasn't you. It was just a man, and the lengths man will go to, to protect their own interests.

The nightmares and hallucinations that I suffer are the result of amobarbital, which Hart dosed me with. Luckily for our cause, it's not always effective as a truth serum, but for a few people the side effects are severe and long-ranging. It's why I always held you at a distance, Jack, even when I seemed myself. The doctors said I couldn't be trusted not to harm those I loved, the same way I have harmed myself. I would never knowingly hurt you Jack, but there's so much time that I have no memory of, consequences that I cannot account for. I couldn't take that risk: you are my reason to live, to go on. If I'd hurt you, Jack, there would have been nothing.

When you were born, I asked Howard to take you and care for you, and I know part of him wanted to, for my sake, but he couldn't do it. The life we'd had was lost to us and it was unfair of me to try to bind him to the ruined fragments that remained. So, my parents took you and there, at least, I knew you'd be safe and loved. Howard promised to watch out for you, but he left not long after and I thought it was for good. I don't know what changed five years later, but I believe he's been a part of your life since. He's come to see me a few times, maybe more often. I find it hard to remember, and I wasn't always myself when he was here. I do know that he spoke of you these last years when I haven't been able to see you. He said I'd be proud of the man you've become; he said you're like me. I hope not too much like me.

Don't try to change the past, Jack, like I did, it only ends up hurting too many people. This world is not as I would wish it but use what you can in the here and now to try to forge a better future. That is all we can do. It is what I should have done.

I am so sorry that I wasn't there for you, but please know that I have and always will love you.

Mary

Jack stared blankly into the space beyond the bed, his

mother's voice an unsettling echo from the past. *Mary...* she hadn't called herself mum for years, she'd relinquished that title, or right, sometime around his tenth birthday.

This letter was written a few months before she'd died, and it had been in Howard's possession since then. *We were engaged, you see...* Inwardly he kicked himself. How had he not seen it? He'd always accepted that Howard was an old friend of the family, never thought to look for anything more. What was it Howard had said? *I loved you in-spite of myself.* The man that Jack trusted most in this world had failed him and failed his mother when he'd walked away. Betrayal twisted his insides, fighting against the established recognition of the friendship and affection that Howard professed, and that Jack felt in return. Howard had come back, after all. But why? Out of love for Jack's mother, or guilt and obligation?

Jack pushed his thumbs into his temples, trying to suppress the throbbing sensation growing in his head. In an alternative thread of time, he might have been Howard's son, his mother would have been happy and he would have been loved. That was where his mother was wrong. Her parents had assumed the responsibility of raising the child, but they struggled to see beyond what he represented: the loss of their daughter.

From the age of one, Jack had everything necessary and essential to his development save that which mattered most: love. He'd learned to be undemanding and self-sufficient early on and was naturally wary of the interest shown by his mother's friend who had visited on his fifth birthday. It had taken years for Howard to fully win the trust of the child with the guarded grey eyes.

Jack stood up and walked the few paces to the window. He pulled back the blind and peered into the gloomy street. Fragmented beams of light from the nearby Tower reflected off the remains of the Aldgate Station tube sign and the few remaining glazed windows of long-abandoned shops. The major tourist attractions were well lit at night, their bright facades dimming into invisibility the crumbling metropolis surrounding them. Tourists travelled the City Monorail, sweeping safely and securely from one listed monument to another: Tower Bridge, the Tower of London, St Paul's Cathedral, Westminster Abbey. There had been scarce enough funds to repair the war-damage to these buildings, let alone construct the monorail. It had been a source of national pride to do so, so much of the nation's identity was bound to the bricks and mortar of those edifices, but nothing was left for the thoroughfares and neighbourhoods that warfare had decimated.

Jack's gaze fell upon a series of pockmarks in the station's frontage: scars of the fierce fighting the city had seen. *Don't try to change the past like I did...* Jack shook his head and laughed, then spun suddenly, shouting into the empty heart of the room. "Well, it's a bit late for that advice, Mary!"

He stared into the space, defiant, but no ghosts appeared to challenge him. His tensed body relaxed, and he shook his head again, this time at his own folly. What would happen to Mary's life – his mum's life – after the mission was completed? He couldn't begin to guess the ways in which time travel had touched the lives of people born in the last few centuries, but it was possible that she would still exist, would still meet Howard, and, without her doomed mission into the past they would marry and have a future together.

Howard and his family would now be arriving at Gaia. If not for that safe haven, Howard's own daughter and grandchild might be erased from history. Howard wasn't certain that the physics would hold up on the massive scale to which the dome had been constructed, but it was a risk he and the others had to take. If it worked, it would be held like a bubble in time and space, a life support to those inside.

But it was also a prison. Once the biosphere was sealed it must remain so, or the occupants would be subject to adjustments made to the time continuum. Some Gaians,

21

such as Cronods, could exist only in that refuge, but others might exist in both temporal planes: one within Gaia; the other walking freely in the latest reality – a world without time travel. It made Jack's head hurt to think about it.

Jack sat back down on the bed and picked up the pages of the letter. The name of his father glared out at him. He flicked open his iHolo and instructed a search for Kayson Hart. A variety of articles confirmed what his mother had written about the history and character of the man, but it was the photographs that stopped him in his tracks. The similarities would have escaped him if he hadn't known to look for them, but now they were quite evident. In himself, Jack saw an echo of Hart: the square set of his jaw; hair parted at the same place, falling forwards at the front; even the same creases traced a path across their brow. This obscene man who had helped to destroy the planet was, without doubt, his father. Jack felt sick.

I know you want the truth. Did he? Would he have changed his current course of action had he known the truth sooner? Either way it was too late. Jack considered the irony of his mother's concern that he might seek his father out, to try to alter events, or even to take revenge. Soon enough he would find himself in the same world as his living, breathing father, but any actions he took against Hart would last only as long as it took for his mission to be completed. Bastards, Jack reflected, always seemed to get away with it.

As far as he knew, Kayson Hart was on the continent during most of the Civil War and the likelihood that their paths would cross was extremely remote. Perhaps that was just as well, for it removed the risk of being distracted from his mission in order to make Hart pay, even if just for a moment, for all of the suffering he had caused.

Jack flicked the iHolo shut and put it, along with his mother's letter, in the rucksack. He lay down on the bed, facing up at the ceiling and resumed the wait.

§

13th August 2073
Southbank

Madeeha lay with her body flattened to the roof panels. Her clothes were dirty shades of grey and stone that blended well with the rooftops of the city and a hood was drawn over the soft curls of her ebony black hair. The spy-heroes of films she'd seen as a child were always dressed in black for reconnaissance work, but if you didn't want to be picked off by drones, black was best avoided.

She had lain still for nearly an hour now and the cold had leached from the concrete into her flesh so that the need to move tugged and frayed at her concentration. She checked the time again and scanned the rooftops on the opposite bank of the river. Threads of anxiety clawed at her mind; Suraya had never been this late before.

At just eighteen, Suraya was one of the youngest of LEFA's recruits but had already proved – as Madeeha had known she would – an invaluable asset. Liberal Europe For All. It was what they believed in; what their parents had believed in. But allowing her baby sister to walk amongst the enemy went against the promise she'd made to their father to protect her and keep her safe.

Of course, it had been impossible to stop her; Suraya had always been stubborn and impulsive, and Madeeha's seniority of eight years meant little when it came to authority. In a different world, Suraya could have been anything she wanted, from a politician to an athlete or an actress. Her self-possession and powers of persuasion were matched by her ability to move gracefully, with the fluidity and beauty of a dancer. She captivated people. Her role, these past few months had been doing just that, but in the heart of the scorpion's nest. The key to the dance was to befriend, beguile and extract information from Republican agents without getting stung.

Madeeha – Maddie, as she was generally known – could never have assumed the same role as her sister. She was open and honest, never artful; fierce and courageous, but averse to unnecessary risk. She could be endearing, but never dazzling; she was the earth to her sister's fire. For as long as she could remember her role had been to tend the fire and ensure that the flames didn't burn out of control.

Since she had gone undercover two months ago, Suraya had met Maddie and exchanged intelligence at 7pm every Wednesday, signalling her location from Victoria Embankment, before Maddie took a circuitous route, mindful of drones and prying eyes, to reach her. It was now 8.45pm. Maddie nervously bit at her fingernail.

She considered the risk of sending a message but, should Suraya be in a tight spot, it might just make things worse. Recent rationing and food shortages had led to an upturn in the number of Surveillance Network Agents, commonly known as Snags. Everyone felt the bite of hunger, but Snags gleefully cashed in on others' misfortune.

A sharp metallic clang from downriver rapidly brought Maddie to a crouch, adrenaline pumping, searching the sky for drones. She scanned the rooftops with her binoculars but couldn't see any movement. She crawled to the eastern edge of the building and peered over the parapet to the street below. All was still.

She held her breath, eyes straining into the dark. A shout sounded nearby. Her stomach twisted, wondering if it was her sister. From the next building she might get a view of the river. She lowered herself over the edge until her feet found the narrow ledge below, inched sideways until she reached the fire escape, then swung herself round onto the rungs which led to the ground. Her footsteps clanged softly on the metal as she sped downwards, and she prayed the noise would go undetected.

Maddie hit the ground and sprinted towards the river. Jumping onto the bonnet, then roof, of a parked van, she leapt through the broken first floor window of a burnt-out restaurant. She wove through the soot-strewn tables to the hallway staircase, and raced, sure-footed despite the dark, up towards the roof. She paused at the exit to listen before easing the door open, then made her way to the building's edge and scanned the scene below. The view offered nothing more.

More shouts – something wasn't right. She strained to make out the voices.

The sky flashed blue.

§

2150

Aldgate

Heavy pounding on the door awoke Jack with a start. His phone was ringing and there was shouting from outside.

"For God's sake, Jack, wake up!" the voice was desperate, pleading.

Jack, heavy with sleep that had come too late, stumbled to the door and unlocked it.

Alice almost fell into the room. "Jesus, Jack, I've been calling for the last twenty minutes. We've got to go now!"

Jack, suddenly awake, grabbed his jacket and bag and was pulled into the corridor and down the stairs at a run.

"What's happened?"

"There's a mole," Alice replied, puffing as she ran. "The capsule was almost intercepted at Embankment. Not sure if it was British agents or the Republic."

They ducked into the entrance of Aldgate Station, weaving around debris and jumping the ancient turnstiles.

"Not that way!" Alice yelled as Jack began to descend towards the eastbound tunnel. "We've changed site...can't risk the old one...not sure how much they know." She indicated the staircase leading down towards the Hammersmith and City Line and tried to catch her breath. "We need to cast as soon as possible."

"Where is it? No offence Al, but I'll move faster alone." He shrugged apologetically.

Alice nodded. "It's at Barts, Whitechapel. I'll let Feynman know you're on your way. I'll join you before the calibrations are finished."

Jack didn't wait for further details but broke into a sprint down the steps and into the dark tunnel. The journey above ground would have been quicker, but the area was now undoubtedly full of drones. He tapped his watch and a soft light, just sufficient to see any obstacles, infused the passageway. If he hadn't feared exposure, he could have tripped the circuit and ridden a maintenance carriage, but the electric current might be detected from the surface. Instead, Jack concentrated on keeping his footing as he sped, full pelt towards Whitechapel.

He didn't need to exit at the station this time. Earth Revolution had, decades before, excavated their own tunnel off the Metropolitan Line to the basement of Barts, from which they were able to salvage antique, but nonetheless, valuable medical equipment and supplies. As he approached Whitechapel, he slowed his pace and looked for the shadow that revealed the siding. About fifty metres down he came to a locked door and tapped it gently. An intercom to the side crackled, "Instead of controlling the environment for the benefit of the population…"

"Perhaps we should control the population for the benefit of our environment," Jack replied, completing the passphrase.

The door slid open to reveal Dr Feynman. "Thank God you're here!" she exclaimed as she relocked the door. "Where's Alice?"

"On her way." Jack caught the look on Feynman's face as they hurried towards the stairwell. "Sorry," he added.

"Well, let's just hope we can make the cast before the bastards get here."

"It's the Republic then?" Jack asked.

"They're all bastards in my opinion," she replied ruefully.

They reached a bright-lit room on the second floor and joined a small team of doctors and physicists who were scrambling to connect wires and monitors around the time capsule. Feynman double-bolted the door behind them.

Jack raised an eyebrow.

"Just in case," she responded, pulling a pencil from her shirt pocket as she crossed the room. "Come on, sit here, let's hook you up. Time's tight now."

Jack stepped across the trailing wires and wriggled into the seat at the heart of the capsule; the rare metals needed for their construction meant that they were cosy to say the least.

Feynman twisted her hair behind her head and secured

it with the pencil, then began to attach probes to Jack's temples. "The plan had been to code the capsule's return to us, but we can't risk whoever's on their way getting hold of it and tracing your journey. So," Feynman paused, "we've set a self-destruct."

"Oh. Great."

"It will only be triggered once you open the door," she continued. "After that, you will have precisely five minutes to get the hell away."

Jack raised an eyebrow. His fingers gripped the armrests, hiding how they had begun to shake. He nodded and focussed on steadying his breathing whilst Feynman's team programmed the coordinates for the cast.

Time casting: it made him think of a fisherman with a rod and line, aiming his hook and float into a river through which time flowed without end. It might once have been called a launch, back in the day when capsules carrying astronauts travelled through linear space, and time travel was the stuff of science-fiction.

"Dr Feynman?" One of Earth Rebellion's soldiers beckoned urgently. She and Jack turned to the young man standing in front of a bank of security monitors. "Look." He pointed to the siding off the tube line and Jack could make out four or five figures moving cautiously towards the camera.

"Shit." Dr Feynman's slow exhalation filled the silence in the room where all activity was suddenly frozen.

"They've got Al," whispered Jack. If the room hadn't been silent no one would have heard the barely audible words.

All eyes focussed on the struggling figure on screen who, despite the fuzzy image, could only be Alice.

"They'll kill her before she lets them in," said Feynman. She turned to Jack, her face pale but determined. "If you're successful, this will never happen. So," she announced, re-engaging the room, "let's make this work."

The team resumed their tasks with a ferocious concentration, but Jack's eyes remained fixed on the monitor. He watched the fuzzy figure recoil then fall to the ground, and slowly became aware of the distant clank and screech of metal being forced and bent. The soldiers heard it too and armed themselves. With a nod from Feynman, they unbolted the door and headed out and down the stairwell.

Feynman locked the door again then checked the readings for the capsule. "Mike?" she asked.

The physicist was urgently tapping numbers into the control panel on the capsule's door. "It's almost there, just trying to fine-tune the precise cast location."

From the distance, down below, they heard shouts and guns exchanging fire.

"Strap yourself in, Jack. Andrew, fire it up." Feynman was decisive in the face of adversity.

The capsule thrummed while the electrical charge built up: every generator left in Barts had been hooked up to it and the accumulating power made the air thick and agitated. Feynman swung the door closed. Jack braced himself. Through a small window she signalled a thumbs-up. He nodded in reply.

"Ready, Mike?"

"I haven't had enough time to calibrate the location." The man shook his head, whilst furiously punching in code. They both jumped as a bullet shattered the glass in the top of the door, spraying fragments over the equipment. The screaming from outside was alarmingly close.

"If we don't go now, there won't be time to erase the cast data." Feynman spoke forcefully and took a step towards the control hub.

"He might end up lodged in a wall..." warned Mike.

A body crashed back against the door. "Fucking go!" yelled the figure outside, firing back at his assailants.

"We'll take that risk." Feynman hit the ignition then aimed a gun at the control hub.

The last Jack saw was the door exploding inward.

Searing pain coursed through Jack's head as white light flooded the capsule.

Jack fought to steady his mind, to contain it, whilst the temporal displacement attempted to strip the layers of it away. He had the sensation of being both immense and minute at the same time, a leaden weight, yet insubstantial, and nausea flowed through him in waves. It had been a mistake to select a Cronod for the mission, he thought, but it was too late, and their discovery meant he might be their only chance.

Don't try to change the past... Don't try to change the past... His mother's words echoed around his head... *Change it for the better... change it...*

§

13th August 2073

Southbank, London

Jack came to as the vessel lurched sideways. He shut his eyes and breathed deeply, trying to settle his nausea. His mind felt surprisingly clear. Maybe the medication had done its job after all. He tapped the small display to the left of his head, causing the capsule to shift again. Wherever he was, he was not on solid ground.

He thought he heard sounds and held still… Nothing.

The monitor flickered into life, bringing up a map which seemed to suggest he was in the Thames. Not ideal, thought Jack, whose glance at the window revealed only darkened sky. He wasn't submerged at least. He zoomed into the map to discover that he was on the Southbank, near to the remains of the Millennium Bridge – one of the earliest casualties of the fighting. At low tide, the riverbed became exposed, which might explain both his location and the shifting movement.

Jack brought up the diagnostics panel and requested a life-sign scan, but the screen flickered and went dark. He hoped that his position, down on the riverbed, would at least screen him from the nearest buildings. If Feynman's team had had more time, they could have ensured that the cast landed on the north side of the river, well away from prying eyes. Feynman.

The image of her flying backwards as a door imploded flashed through Jack's mind.

In the pause, something struck the capsule. Jack froze. From a distance came jeering shouts.

"Shit." Jack unfastened himself and tore away probes and sensors, looping his backpack over his shoulder as best he could in the confined space.

The voices from outside seemed to be arguing but weren't close enough to make out. Small objects intermittently struck the metal as if those who cast them were standing well back, testing the foreign object for instability. Unsurprising, given that the vessel had probably

31

materialised in front of them. Jack shifted, to try to see out of the small window, causing the capsule to rock slightly, grinding the ground below. The voices hushed and Jack again risked moving his face towards the window.

Footsteps… Then an eye pressed against the glass met directly with his.

"There's fuckin' someone in 'ere!"

More jeering and footsteps as bodies moved closer.

"It's a bloody spaceman innit!"

Laughter.

"Nah, reckon' it's the fuckin' Republic," responded the closest voice.

"Well let's get 'im out then, could be a nice reward for turnin' 'im in, and 'is spaceship's gotta be worth a bob or two!"

The gathered voices crowed consensus.

Jack's mind raced as he considered his options and getting caught by scavengers wasn't one of them. He strained to listen to the voices, trying to determine their configuration around the capsule; there were six, maybe seven men outside and it was best to consider that they were armed. Most were out front but at least two were somewhere behind him. The self-destruct would activate as soon as the door was opened, and he needed to be efficient to get clear of the blast zone. He would use ultrasound to disable them and escape whilst they were disorientated. The detonation of the capsule would ensure no one was left to track him.

"'E's movin' around in there! Welcome back to Earf spaceman…Yoo-hoo!"

Laughter mixed with the ringing of metal as an iron bar met the side of the capsule.

"Stop fuckin' messin' around, Rusty! It won't be wurf as much if it's broken."

Jack pulled the sonic taser from his bag; it should take out everyone in front, giving him space from which to target those behind. The capsule shifted again as the scavengers, armed with a crowbar, began their attempt to prise the door open.

Jack adjusted his grip on the taser and raised his right foot. Taking a deep breath, he pressed the door release and kicked hard, sending the nearest man flying backwards to the water's edge.

"Fuckin' bastard!" roared his friend.

The closest figures surged forwards and Jack fired the taser. The beam fired wide on its highest setting and Jack's assailants crumpled, clutching their heads at the searing intensity.

Jack turned to take aim at those behind him but came crashing down to his knees with pain. The hairs on his arms raised on end and conflicting voices fought for dominance in his head…

*Who're you? … **BANG!** … Welcome to Westminster, well, what's left of it … **We're losing him!** … Coffee? … **No, there's a heartbeat** … So glad you can be a part of this … **Howard, let him go** … We have one base here, for the time-being … **No, damn-it, Jack! Breathe!** … We move around regularly, to avoid detection … **Breathe!***

Jack vomited. He gasped as he was wrenched from the ground and pinned against the side of the capsule.

"Feisty one, eh?" the scavenger called Rusty sneered. He lifted Jack's feet clear of the mud and pushed hard into Jack's throat with a tattooed, muscular arm.

Jack struggled, fighting to draw breath, but the giant stood immovable. On the ground in front of him, the tasered men began to regain control of their bodies.

Rusty nudged the closest one with his foot, "Wot d'you fink, Clint? D' we turn 'im in? Or d' we make 'im pay for 'is little stunt?"

Clint heaved but didn't vomit and, groaning loudly, pulled himself upright. "I fink the little shit should pay," he spat.

"I'd rather get the money for 'im," protested a diminutive scavenger with beady eyes.

"Well, you would, Ratty." Clint shoved him back and the men descended into an argument with those who favoured cash above revenge.

Jack's vision blurred. His lungs were on fire. His

hands, slippery with sweat, tried to grip the gargantuan arm and relieve the pressure on his neck. How much time left until the capsule detonated? He caught a small breath as Rusty changed his grip and spotted the taser, half buried in the mud of the riverbank. None of the scavengers had spotted it. He tried to speak.

"Wha's that? Cat got yer tongue?" Rusty eased back slightly.

"I said," Jack hissed, "watch out."

The gathered men laughed, and Rusty increased the pressure on Jack's throat. Jack's vision darkened and his limbs turned leaden as he released his hold on Rusty's arm and shakily double-tapped his watch. Rusty glanced down just as the flare of light blazed out, dazzling him, making him drop his prize.

Jack ducked past the giant and threw himself forwards into the mud, freeing the taser, flicking it to 360 degrees and firing. Fighting the pain that flooded his body, he scrambled to his feet. Half staggering, half running, he propelled himself into the water. The ripples reached his thighs and he plunged forwards.

The air erupted into blue flame.

§

The explosion was unlike any Maddie had ever seen. The air crackled and thrummed as the shock wave billowed and unfurled, knocking Maddie over.

"Suraya!" Maddie screamed into the churning air. She fought to find her feet and flew back to the stairwell, certain that her sister was at the heart of the blast. She stumbled down the steps, through the building's entrance and out onto the pavement. The pounding of her heart matched her feet as she tore down the Southbank.

"Oh no, no, no!"

She skidded to a halt just before the blackened and scorched paving slabs gave way to a rift into which the railings dripped glowing metal. The water of the river sucked and hissed as it flowed back onto the muddy riverbed, dispersing and dissolving clumps of sooty deposit. Maddie edged around the crumbling concrete.

"Raya?"

Smoke stung Maddie's eyes and seared her throat. She coughed and retched at the acrid taste it left in her mouth. She pulled her top over her mouth and nose and shrank back from the blast crater until the air began to clear. The trembling in her legs was so violent it threatened to overwhelm her. She crouched and leant forwards onto her palms, feeling the solidity of the ground, and tried to stem her rising panic with calming breaths. Images of Suraya flashed through her mind, all confident, all smiling, all radiating life. But no one could have survived that explosion.

A low humming noise brought her back to herself. Drones. She was surprised they hadn't appeared sooner. She needed to take cover and quickly, but when she stood, a movement at the river's edge caught her eye.

"Ray?" She ran forwards, hopeful, but faltered when a bloodied man pulled himself over the embankment and collapsed, panting on the walkway.

As the humming grew louder, Maddie pulled her gun and targeted the prostrate figure. "The drones are nearly here. Did you call them?" she demanded.

Head buzzing and the world a blur, Jack pulled himself to his knees and raised his empty hands into the air. He tried to focus on the woman who was neither an official nor a typical Republican. "I'm with LEFA," he croaked, hazarding a guess. The words were barely audible, and the woman's finger tightened on the trigger. "Wait! You cannot…" he struggled trying to remember the exact phrase. "You cannot shake hands with a clenched fist." Jack watched her hesitate before coming to a decision and lowering her weapon.

"We need to move now. Can you run?"

Jack nodded and she grabbed his hand and pulled him to his feet. He stumbled forwards as pain stabbed at his body.

The hum of drones was loud now, and Maddie pulled them into a doorway and raised her finger to her lips. The gyrocopter passed overhead and continued towards the river but others were approaching, their thermal cameras probing the streets for signs of life.

"There's not enough cover here." Maddie glanced towards the looming bulk of the Tate Modern. "But if we make it over there, we can... Hey!" She shook Jack's shoulder.

Jack opened his eyes and tried to smile. "Sorry," he slurred. He glanced down at the blood that was beginning to pool at his feet.

"Shit." Maddie exhaled slowly, unbuckled her belt, then fastened it tightly around Jack's thigh. "Okay... Hey, you listening?" She shook him again. "If you don't move fast, you're dead. If I need to, I *will* leave you. You got that?"

Jack nodded and focussed on the pressure of her hand on his wrist.

"Ready?"

She propelled them forwards and to the right, stopping to pull Jack's arm over her shoulders, hoping that whatever he knew was worth the risk she was taking. There was no light, save that cast by the moon, and she paused within the inky shadow of trees bordering Hopton Street. She pulled out her binoculars and quickly scanned the windows of the Tate.

"Might be lucky," she whispered, moving them on and away from their cover. "Road to the right... Door on the left—"

They were just metres from the glass doorway when the drone appeared. Maddie shot at the door on the opposite side of the street, cracking open the lock. She ran at it, dragging Jack, kicked it open and pushed him inside. She'd barely begun to turn when the drone's laser met its target, vaporising her gun. Maddie gasped. Her palm seared with pain.

It was an MD5, armed with darts to disable fugitives so they could be taken in for questioning. While she weighed up her chances of reaching the doorway without being hit, her fingers sought the micro-explosive concealed inside her jacket. It was enough to take out the drone, although at this range she might not survive. As her fingers curled around it, she pictured Suraya...

The drone exploded.

Maddie flung herself to the ground as fragments rained down. Ears ringing, she stared first at the explosive, still intact in her hand, then at the space where the drone had been. She twisted around to find the wounded man leant on the door frame, his weapon still raised.

"Lucky shot," he offered. He tried to steady himself, but his knees gave way.

Maddie scrambled to catch him. "That drone filmed you entering this building. We've got to move" —she pointed— "over there."

Jack's head swam as he tried to focus on her.

"Hey! You can do this." She hauled him up and through the dust cloud, crossing the road to the glass doors opposite, where she punched a code into the keypad.

Once inside, silence enshrouded them. The clean lines of the lobby, its luxurious chairs and stack of magazines, felt crass in contrast with the world outside, but the layer of dust on the reception desk revealed that the occupants were long-gone.

Maddie helped Jack through the doors behind the desk and into a corridor that led to the service stairwell, but at the base of the steps he shook his head.

"I need..." Jack was panting heavily. "From my bag..."

"We can't stop here." Maddie forced him onwards. "Drone sensors can penetrate this part of the building."

They climbed two flights before Jack's strength gave out. Maddie grabbed the shoulder straps of his backpack, dragged him down a corridor and finally into an apartment. She secured the door behind them, resting her forehead on its cool surface for a moment.

Her muscles ached with the strain of dragging the

man's dead weight, but she gritted her teeth and pulled him deeper into the darkness. Her hands fumbled along the wall until she found a doorway. She heaved the man onto the cold tiles beyond it, then shut them both inside.

"Please," whispered Jack. "My bag." His breathing was laboured.

Maddie pulled a small torch from her jacket and balanced it on the sink, then rolled Jack onto his side so she could ease the straps from his shoulders. The fabric of the bag was bubbled and cracked; the zip sealed shut from the heat of the blast.

She glanced from the blood-streaked tiles to the man's ashen face. Her makeshift tourniquet had failed and blood flowed from the wound, making torn fabric and lacerated flesh appear as one. His chances of making it were slim. Maddie's breath caught in her throat as she pictured Suraya, alone and in pain, injured or dying, and suddenly tears were coursing down her cheeks.

"Med kit... inside... red syringe."

Maddie blinked the tears away and pulled at the fabric, ripping it down through the worst of the heat-seared area, then rummaged through the contents until she found a small medicine pouch. Her hands were shaking as she pulled free a syringe containing a red fluid. "I haven't done this before," she explained.

"It's okay." Jack reached for her hand and held it still, his grasp firm.

Maddie, surprised, watched in silence as he removed the cap from the syringe and plunged it into his thigh. His face contorted, his eyes squeezed shut, and he held his breath for so long that Maddie thought it had stopped altogether. She leant closer to check his pulse and jumped when he finally exhaled. His eyes remained closed, but he found her hand again and squeezed it.

"Thank you," he whispered.

And then he seemed to sleep.

§

14th August 2073
Thames Barrier

Dr Kingsley's eyes glowed with the conviction that at last, he had achieved it. He checked the readings on the screen in front of him. They were no different from those of the last test, but he was certain that he had seen the capsule flicker.

His pulse thudded in his ears as approached the machine. His rapid breathing steamed up his visor. He pulled back his hood and stood facing his creation, anxious to know, and yet hesitant to take the steps that would reveal if he had, in fact, made history.

He placed the palms of his hands together, his thumbs pushing against the hairs on his chin while his fingertips slid up his nose towards the bridge. Had someone been observing him, his posture might have been mistaken for prayer.

Noah, at last, reached forwards and heaved back the capsule's door. He gently placed the sister clocks together and released the breath he had been holding.

The difference was less than a nanosecond, a mere hundred-thousand picoseconds, but that miniscule fragment of time had passed in a temporal realm outside of his own.

The machine had travelled in time.

§

2148

Westminster

Jack walked beside Howard in silence, trying to digest the scope of his friend's plan. It offered a chance to save the planet, but it came at a terrible cost.

Ahead of him, the street's holographic hoardings flickered off, revealing a row of crumbling buildings which had once housed ministerial departments. Cosmetic holographs were used around every tourist hub and would have disguised the devastation successfully were it not for the temporal storms that disrupted the projections and laid bare London's scars.

Jack looked to his left, past the debris of the Foreign Office, to the charred skeletal remains of Downing Street. The hoarding projectors glowed, then blazed back into life, instantly reinstating Great George Street in all its pre-war glory.

The two men entered Parliament Square, passed below the Monorail station, and wove their way through a cluster of tourists. A woman was complaining loudly that she wouldn't have bothered with the journey had she known there was so little left standing. The tour operator politely pointed out that this was just one of many fascinating buildings on their route for the day, while the woman's clearly exasperated husband repeatedly suggested that ruins were 'atmospheric'.

Howard hid a smile that implied that he'd overheard this complaint before. "Why don't they just go the extra mile and reinstate the Houses of Parliament in full, holographic technicolour?" he asked, with a glance at Jack.

Jack looked up at the source of disappointment. The tower known as Big Ben rose from the roof of the House of Commons but stopped far short of where the clock face had once been. The bells, of which Big Ben itself had been the most famous, had been salvaged from the bomb wreckage and allegedly melted down by pro-EU groups, sparking a riot between far-right nationalists and migrant groups. It was suspected, but never proven, that the Republic was responsible, seeking to provoke unrest in the city just when opposing sides had begun to negotiate for peace. Thousands more Londoners had given up and left the city in the wake of those riots, and Big Ben, damaged as badly as it was, had been relegated to the list of restoration projects that would never find funding.

The heart of the government had long-operated out of Manchester, but a few lesser offices remained here amongst the debris of the war, and some symbolic votes were still taken in what remained of the Houses of Parliament. The Prime Minister, Mark Burnham, insisted that the country was better off without the financial drain of Westminster and the endless restoration fees for its decrepit parliament buildings. But the emotional and political pull of the old centre was hard to fully erase.

A few makeshift shelters were scattered over the square, their occupants holding signs urging politicians to "Rebuild London" or "Put British People First." A couple, whose skinny child ran, hair-flying, barefoot and wild between the tents, sat resolutely beneath a sign that proclaimed that, "God Sent the Flood and He Hath Sent the Drought. Repent Thy Sins!" The woman, assuming both men were politicians, fixed Jack with a cold stare, conveying her disgust.

Jack turned to Howard to comment and caught the eye of an elderly man in a long coat and bow tie. He looked familiar, though he couldn't say why. Just in front of him stood a woman holding a sign that read, "Time Is Not a Toy! Terminate Time Travel!" Jack inclined his head in her direction. "One of yours, Howard?"

"No, but we're on the same page. Come on." Howard ushered Jack across the road. "Welcome to Westminster. Well, what's left of it." They passed a refreshment booth where a few tourists stood sipping drinks. "Coffee? It's better than what we have inside."

"No, I'm good thanks."

"I'm so glad you can be a part of this, Jack, your help will be invaluable."

"I haven't actually agreed to anything yet," Jack reminded him.

"You will." Howard stopped and turned to him. There was clearly something more he wanted to say, but the words weren't forthcoming and after a moment he cleared his throat and gestured towards the Palace of Westminster. "We have one base here, for the time-being." He glanced behind them, wary of eavesdroppers. "It's hidden in plain sight within the Department for Temporal Equality."

Jack couldn't help but laugh. "Temporal equality? Does anyone even know what that means?"

Howard shrugged. "We move around regularly to avoid detection," he continued. "We'll probably move the programme from here in a month or two." He glanced up at the sky which had grown dark. "I think we're in for another storm. Better go in. Al's waiting for us, and I want to introduce you to Dr Feynman."

Howard reached the security entrance before he realised that Jack wasn't behind him. He looked back to where Jack stood, staring at the sky, breathing rapidly. "Jack, are you alright?"

Jack felt the hairs rising on the back of his neck and the air around him thickened so that breathing became difficult. A dull pain, that began in his temples, flowed out and around his jaw and brow, before soaring to a blinding crescendo as lightning struck the jagged remains of Big Ben.

Tourists screamed and ran for the cover of the monorail station. Fragments of stone rained down. Jack heard someone calling his name. He stumbled, disorientated, and caught a glimpse of a child, hair flying, being pulled to safety by a man in long coat and bow tie. He tried to spot the child's mother, but the surging pain, more intense than anything he'd felt before, forced him to his hands and knees. He howled into the wind as a second thunder clap shook the ancient buildings, scattering their centuries-old dust to the clouds.

"Jack!"

Jack felt someone beside him, their arms taking his, pulling him to his feet.

"We need to get inside!"

Another crash.

…

Silence.

…

Howard pulled Jack's arm, directing him across the road.

"Welcome to Westminster. Well, what's left of it."

Jack frowned and stared at his friend. "Didn't you already say that?"

"I don't think so." Howard raised a quizzical eyebrow. "Anyway, I'm so glad you can be a part of this, Jack. Your help will be invaluable."

Jack stopped walking and stared at Big Ben. A group of tourists moved towards it from the monorail station, their iHolos raised to capture the view. His head swam.

"Are you alright, Jack? Need a coffee?" Howard pointed at the refreshment booth where a few tourists stood, sipping drinks.

Jack shook his head and breathed deeply, willing the dizzy sensation to clear.

"Mr Elliot?"

A hand grabbed Jack's shoulder and pulled him backwards. He felt something hard press into his back. "What the—"

Bang.

Jack crumpled.

"No!" Howard lunged to catch him. Tourists screamed and ran for the station. Searching the crowd in vain for the gunman, Howard caught sight of a barefoot, skinny child, staring open-mouthed, as she was hauled away by her mother.

"Howard…I…" Jack's eyes closed.

"Oh no. Someone, help! Jack, no…"

There were footsteps. People crowded around. A doctor, somehow already there, administered a syringe of red liquid. Drones hummed above them, circling the area.

Someone was asking questions, but Howard couldn't hear the words. His clothes were soaked in the blood that gushed from the wound in Jack's chest. Medics arrived. They pushed him aside to begin CPR. Jack's hand was still in his.

Howard leaned forwards until their heads touched. "Hold on Jack, we've got you. I've got you, just hold on." Time seemed to stand still.

"We're losing him."

"No!" Howard shouted.

Dr Feynman arrived, her hand firm oh his shoulder. "Howard, let him go."

"The serum is working, but his lungs aren't repairing fast enough." The medic glanced at Howard apologetically.

"No, damn-it. Jack, Breathe!"

"Howard." Feynman squeezed his shoulder.

"Breathe!"

§

14th August 2073

Southbank

Jack awoke with a cry and gasped for breath. Howard was gone and he was shrouded in darkness.

"Howard?" he called. "I…"

He stopped. Hundreds of memories came flooding back, crowding into his consciousness. He became aware of the cold tiles beneath him and pain – not where he expected it, in his chest – but in his leg. In the blackness he reached for the edge of his shirt and explored up and underneath it with his fingertips, feeling the undulation of each muscle until he found the scar. It had been there for two years, and yet it also hadn't.

Two threads of time tugged and pulled at his memories and sweat began to bead on his brow as Jack understood what had happened just after leaving the time capsule. He recalled two versions of the same event: a polymorphic memory. In one memory he had visited Westminster, met Alma Feynman, then left on foot to ponder Howard's proposal. But he also remembered that same occasion where he'd never reached Dr Feynman and had left Westminster, seriously injured, on a stretcher.

Had someone discovered what he and Howard were attempting? Were they trying to remove Jack from the equation by assassinating him in the past? Jack's breathing faltered with the onset of panic. Mentally, he forced himself to take a step back, to view the evidence with an objective, historian's eye. Provided that Howard and his family were in Gaia, they would be safe; any changes to their past wouldn't affect them within the confines of the temporal dome.

Jack wondered if his assailant would try again but took comfort from the knowledge that he would be hard to find. He'd always been a private person – no fan of social media – and in the final week of training his personal records had been wiped, his digital footprint erased. Besides, the forks in his personal timeline, his splintered history, was potentially an advantage. Dr Feynman had suggested that since Jack could recall multiple threads in time, then his death in one might not prevent him from living and completing his mission in another. What neither Feynman nor Jack knew, was how he would cope if his temporal load became too high.

Pain dragged Jack's attention back to the present, and his mission which had almost ended before it had begun. The woman had gone, the room was silent, and he couldn't make out any sounds from beyond it. He felt among the objects that surrounded him until he found a small torch and flicked it on. The light bounced off the sterile white tiles, momentarily dazzling him. He pulled himself upright, leaning back against the wall, then balanced the torch on the edge of the sink. Bloodied towels were piled inside the shower cubicle, and dark streaks across the pearly floor revealed where his blood had been hastily mopped up.

Despite the blood loss and a leg that hurt like hell, his head felt clear, his breathing even. With a grimace, Jack prised back the torn fabric above his knee – dried blood had bonded it to his skin – and wondered at the odds of the explosion's debris cutting his femoral artery. The swollen flesh was an angry red but the wound had sealed over: the serum was working. Another six hours, give or take, and he'd be fit to walk or run if necessary.

He pulled his backpack towards him, feeling the fabric crack beneath his fingertips, then reached swiftly up to feel the back of his head. There was no pain, but he could feel where his hair was singed. Femoral artery aside, he'd been lucky.

Not so for all the bag's contents: his iHolo had not taken kindly to the combination of extreme heat and water; the smart pistol looked as though something had melted internally; and the micro-drone had been partially crushed. There was no sign of his sonic taser, which was probably in the river, or his other handgun – he must have dropped it after shooting down that drone.

He pulled out a packet of energy bars which now

resembled something not unlike coal. Where was the med kit? The fact that it had survived the blast undamaged was miraculous, but it was now nowhere to be found. Had the woman seen its value and stolen it? If she was part of LEFA, she might have gone for back-up. The rebel group would have a lot of questions, and there was no reason for them to believe Jack's story. Jack weighed the value of the med bag's contents against the risk of being detained. Better to make a move now.

Carefully, he placed his possessions back in the rucksack though, blistered and torn, it wouldn't hold together for long. He assumed he was in an apartment and hoped he might find a new bag, as well as something to eat. Holding onto the sink-top, Jack hauled himself to his feet. His head swam and he took a moment to steady himself. A glass sat next to the tap and Jack filled it with cool water and drank deeply. He took the lit torch and put it in his jacket pocket so that the room returned to near darkness, with just a subtle glow that gave shape to the basin and cistern. A couple of unsteady steps brought him to the door.

Jack considered the possibility that someone was on the other side, before gently pushing down on the handle. There was no response and the door was locked. Jack's head inclined slightly, eyebrow raised as he flicked a pin from his wristwatch and inserted it into the keyhole. The door clicked. Jack held his breath, waited, then opened the door a fragment and peered into the hall beyond.

Pink light bounced off a framed photograph on the opposite wall. Jack pushed the door wide and moved closer to examine it. The family depicted was pale and freckled, nothing like the chestnut skinned woman who'd brought Jack here.

He edged down the hallway, leaning against the wall to spare his wounded leg. It brought him into a large, open-plan living space with a lounge to his left and a kitchen to his right. The external walls were glass and opened onto a large balcony where long blinds held back the first blush of morning light. It would be easy for drones to scan this area of the apartment, whereas the bathroom lay behind several thick walls, towards the structure's core. Jack's rescuer had known that, and he wondered how many times she'd taken refuge here.

Jack headed towards the kitchen and began searching for food. The cupboards contained half empty bags of rice and pasta, some dry pulses and a can of tomatoes. The hob was electric, and Jack wondered if it was worth risking the additional heat signature in order to cook the rice, but nothing happened when he tried to turn it on. The fridge was dark, the warm air inside rancid, suggesting that the electricity had been cut. He turned his attention to the drawers where he found a can opener for the tomatoes, too hungry to care that they were cold.

Jack considered each kitchen knife before wrapping one in a tea towel and placing it in the backpack, sliding a second, shorter one into his belt. He pocketed a few other items that might prove useful then headed for the hallway, hoping to find a rucksack in one of the bedrooms.

As he turned into the hall, the entrance at the far end clicked open. Jack pulled back into the kitchen. He drew the knife from his belt. The footsteps sounded once, twice, then paused. Jack had left the bathroom door ajar, and if this was the woman who'd brought him here, she would notice straight away. Just a few hours earlier she had saved his life, but where she had been, and what had happened while he'd been sleeping was an unknown.

Jack listened to the footsteps edge along the hall and considered his words. The faintest metallic scrape and click told him she was armed.

"Hello?" she called out.

Jack pulled a battery from his pocket – he'd found it in a drawer – and threw it high across the room, so that it landed with a thud behind the sofa on the opposite side. The girl stepped forwards, the barrel of her gun peeking around the corner of the hall. Jack braced himself.

"Don't do anything stupid, I'm armed," she warned.

Jack pushed away from the wall and punched hard at

her shoulder blade. She dropped the gun but kicked back, catching the edge of his wounded leg. Jack fell forwards in pain, grabbing her waist and pulling her down with him. She twisted free from his grasp and spun to face him, a flick-knife in her hand. Crouching in a bizarre stand-off, the kitchen knife in Jack's hand, each contemplated the other.

Maddie broke the silence. "Nice way to treat someone who saved your life."

"How would you treat someone who'd pulled a gun on you?" Jack retorted.

"I don't know you," she fired back, "and you're clearly trouble. And how the hell are you up and about already? You were half dead when I left. I assumed someone else must be here." She adjusted her grip on the knife as if she suspected him of some deception.

Weakened by the fight, Jack knew he couldn't take another beating, not just yet. He relaxed his arms and held up his hands in supplication. "Look, I don't want to hurt you."

A slight smile and raised eyebrow implied that she knew she wasn't the one in danger.

"I'm sure you've got questions," Jack continued, "so I'm putting my knife down." He slowly placed the blade on the floor between them. She stood and kicked it away. "I could do with resting my leg," he added, inclining his head towards the sofa.

She nodded but didn't relax her knife arm until he'd gingerly pulled himself up and into the seat.

"I'm Jack," he said, easing his leg up to rest on the coffee table.

She eyed him warily before replying, "Maddie."

A few moments passed before she lowered herself onto the seat opposite his. Keeping her eyes on him, she bent forwards to retrieve her gun from under the table. She tucked it inside her jacket, then finally relaxed her grip on the knife, though she didn't put it down, but leant forwards, arms resting on her knees with the knife held loosely. Present as a warning.

Jack waited, noting the caution in each of her movements. She was younger than him, mid-twenties, but she'd demonstrated that she was an experienced fighter and not someone who would easily be duped. He saw her gaze flick to his leg where fresh blood was seeping from his wound. Jack pulled the fabric back from his injury. Her kick had caught the damaged area, but the wound was already starting to knit back together.

"I've never seen anything like that," said Maddie, her eyes wide in disbelief. "What is this stuff?" She pulled the med bag from her pocket and laid it on the table.

Jack noted, with relief, that it still contained the remaining syringes. "Did you try to sell them?" he asked. "Are you a scavenger?"

"No!" Her eyes narrowed. "And you'll answer my question first."

"Okay, okay," Jack soothed. He paused before explaining, "The serum causes blood cells to replicate, replacing lost blood, while a drug cocktail accelerates healing and tissue regrowth."

Maddie's left hand reflexively moved to her face to touch her cheek bone. "But those kinds of drugs take days to work; it's only been seven or eight hours."

Jack shrugged and looked to where her fingertips brushed against her skin.

She turned her head and ran her fingers through her hair so that it fell further forwards. "So, who are you? Where'd you get something like that?"

"I told you; I work for LEFA."

"No," she shook her head, "I work for LEFA, and we don't have access to anything even close to that." She held his gaze, waiting for something that might resemble the truth.

Jack breathed out slowly. "I work for a secret part of LEFA, only a few in command know the details of our mission."

She waited.

"I really appreciate your help last night," he added. "Things had gone a little awry."

"And that mission is to do what exactly?"

"You know I can't tell you that," Jack replied. "It's classified."

"Well, that's convenient," she quipped. But her hands trembled and her heart raced, wondering if he was connected to what Sarah had mentioned a few hours ago, back at the Hub.

"What about you?" Jack asked, "Where did you go with my med kit?"

Maddie stood up and walked to the window so he couldn't see her face. She peered through the blinds towards the river where she'd found him. If this man really was a senior member of their rebel group, he could be the key to finding Suraya.

She needed to think, carefully, about what she said...

§

Maddie closed the bathroom door, paused, then locked it, just in case. She crossed to one of the bedrooms and used the en-suite to scrub the blood off her hands. Her trousers were soaked in it, so she peeled them off and looked through the drawers until she found a few pairs of jeans. They were a little big but would do. She listened at the front door before easing it open and stepping into the dark corridor beyond. It clicked shut behind her and she made her way to the stairwell, then down towards the office behind the concierge's desk.

She had waited several hours in the pitch-black bathroom, listening to the breathing of the man on the floor, before she had dared to leave its relative safety. It was still dangerous to leave the building, but with no word from Suraya she felt she had no choice but to find out what those at the Hub knew about her whereabouts.

And then there was the man who claimed to be part of LEFA. He needed medical attention, though she wasn't optimistic that he'd still be alive by the time she made it back with a medic. Whatever he'd injected himself with had knocked him out. The bag containing the syringes had a drug name and code which she didn't recognise, so she'd brought it with her in case the information was useful.

She thought resentfully, how much easier it would be if she could trust the phone networks. But they were all tapped, emails hacked, and as fast as LEFA could establish secure lines, government and Republic hackers brought them down. Hackers. Maddie smiled bitterly, recalling the uproar when the story broke that the government had hired convicted hackers – and paid them well – to 'help combat the threat of the Republic'. Everyone knew that theirs was a double-edged sword with which the far right sought to control the population.

She reached the office door and scanned the lobby for signs of any disturbance but found nothing. The night was dark, with just the soft glow from a waxing moon. It was months since the streetlamps in this part of town had last worked and Maddie was grateful for it now as she made her way, fully exposed, across the glass-walled entrance lobby to the doors.

The debris from the MD5 drone had vanished, presumably carried away by others. If its hard drive was still operational, then her face would be recovered from its surveillance footage. Maddie pushed the thought from her mind and concentrated her attention on the road leading towards the river. She couldn't make out any sounds but was certain that there was a faint glow of light: no doubt a containment area, with officials investigating the blast zone where she'd found Jack.

She only had to make it to Southwark Street. From there, she was confident she could move unseen. Her heart pounded inside her chest. She tried to calm it, closing her eyes, breathing slowly and deeply. "Suraya," she whispered, focusing her thoughts before pressing the door-release and stepping into the night.

She clung to the edge of the building as she continued up Castle Yard, then vaulted the railings into Hopton Gardens, hugging the darkest shadows beside the hedge. A quick dash across the road led her to the railway bridge, where she scrambled up the scaffolding and onto the tracks. She felt dizzy with relief and paused for a moment to catch her breath.

The low thrum of drones echoed from the river – she pictured them scanning the blast crater, searching for clues as to what had occurred – but her own route was quiet, the track unused for months. She launched herself into a sprint, across the sleepers towards Elephant and Castle, hidden from curious eyes by the hoardings on either side.

Maddie came to a stop at the bridge that crossed Newington Causeway, close to the old Ministry of Sound building. She'd overheard the older volunteers reminisce about the times they had danced there all night, and had envied them their youth in a time when such things had been taken for granted.

She scanned the streets and buildings either side of the bridge and, once happy that no one was watching, slid down a service ladder next to the arches. She approached the third archway, where a peeling sign read, *Campbell Heating Engineers: Spare Parts, Repairs, Installation Service,* tapped lightly on the door, and waited. After a little while she heard movement, then a muffled voice.

"Is freedom ever really won?" it questioned.

"No," Maddie replied, "you earn it and win it in every generation."

A panel slid back and two dark, age-lined eyes peered out at her. Maddie took a step closer to the door and tapped out a rhythm.

"I's T'ursday, Maddie," responded the voice, its gruff tone softened by a slight Jamaican lilt.

Maddie glanced down at her watch. 00:02. She rolled her eyes and gently tapped out a different rhythm on the door panel.

The man, finally satisfied, pulled back the latches and Maddie stepped into the dimly lit, junk-filled workshop on the other side.

"Really, Leroy?" she demanded, as she watched him slide the latches back to secure the door.

"W'at?" he protested. "It *is* T'ursday." He grinned to himself as he shuffled back towards the bed in the far corner of the room.

Maddie relented. It was impossible to stay mad with Leroy; he was everyone's surrogate uncle, jolly one moment, cranky the next. He was also the first person she'd met when she'd volunteered for LEFA two years ago. Maddie had arrived at this address as directed, a bundle of nerves, to discover a large, elderly man tinkering with a boiler. She'd assumed she'd got the details wrong, then for a horrifying moment thought it might be a trap. When Leroy had stood from his work to get someone for her, she'd panicked and tried to back away…straight into the shelves of spare parts. She'd frozen as pipes, pumps and connectors had rained down around her.

Leroy had looked at her, raised his eyebrows in something she took to be empathy, then turning his gaze to the debris surrounding her, had broken into deep-bellied laughter. "Not to worry!" he'd said, as he'd lowered his ample frame to the floor and begun picking up the parts. Torn between her instinct to flee, and remorse at the mess she'd made, her logical side had won out. She had set about helping him, before a LEFA member appeared to take her down to induction. Maddie sighed; that day was already a lifetime ago.

Leroy lowered himself to the bed with a grunt. The springs creaked under his weight. He looked tired.

"Busy day, Leroy?" Maddie asked.

"Always!" He ran his hands through the tight white curls of his hair.

Leroy had owned this workshop for nearly fifty years and, despite his advanced age, had refused to retire. This had been a boon for LEFA, with whom Leroy, through his nephew, had been connected for many years. LEFA had excavated several underground hubs across London, but their heat signatures had led to their discovery by drone patrols. Leroy's work, pottering with ancient gas and oil burners, as well as modern electric heaters, provided an excellent cover for the heat signature generated by the subterranean base below.

Leroy was the Hub's unofficial doorman, and he wielded his weight as such. It had been at his insistence that LEFA had removed the retinal scanners that had originally granted access to the workshop. Leroy had vowed that there was "no damned way" he'd trust the scans after the Republic had captured an East Hub volunteer and replicated their eyes. Instead, Maddie and the others each had their own pass phrase and a seven-day rotation of rhythms to tap out on the door. Leroy said the rhythms paid homage to his namesake, but Maddie had never found out what he'd meant.

Leroy looked up at Maddie and noted the sweat beading her face. She was tense, her pulse visible, beating rapidly beneath the skin of her neck. "Rough night?" he asked.

"Strange night," she replied. She realised her hands were trembling and tucked them into her jean pockets. "Listen, have you seen Suraya or heard anything from her today?"

Leroy shook his head. "Sorry, hon. Sarah will know." He inclined his head in the direction of the cupboard and gave her arm a reassuring squeeze.

Maddie nodded. She opened the wooden doors and pressed the release button hidden under the lowest shelf. She swung open the back of the unit, revealing a metal security door behind. This one did have a retinal scanner which confirmed her identity and released the lock with a click. As she climbed through and onto the first rung of the ladder, she pulled the door shut, which in turn pulled the back of the cupboard and wooden doors into place. She descended the flight of stairs to a second security door and tapped in the code.

The room beyond was lit by low voltage LEDs but felt bright after the darkened streets of the city. The main room was compact, but big enough to hold several large desks at the centre surrounded by banks of computers and monitors. A couple of tunnels led off to storage rooms, a generator, and a small kitchenette and living area: some volunteers ended up bunking down here for weeks at a time.

Max, a tech engineer, was snoozing on one of the battered armchairs, squeezed into one corner of the control room. An older, fair-haired woman was perched on the edge of the desk watching the bank of monitors. She glanced over her shoulder as Maddie entered.

"Madeeha." She said it slowly, as if she had been expecting someone else. "You're not due in until the morning. Are you alright?" she added, as she turned to the desk and quickly gathered up the papers.

"Not really," Maddie admitted, watching her. "Raya didn't show up tonight and I'm worried. Have you heard from her?"

"No." Sarah paused for a fraction of a moment too long. "Not tonight. But we weren't expecting to," she continued a little more fluidly. "She'll be finding her feet in her new mission."

"What?"

Max mumbled something in his sleep and shifted in the chair.

"What new mission?" Maddie frowned. "Suraya didn't say anything about a new mission."

Sarah sighed. She'd argued with Max about giving Suraya the assignment. Aside from his soft spot for the younger sister, Max had asserted that if anything went wrong, Maddie might be reckless in her response. Sarah didn't disagree, but she also felt Suraya stood the best chance of success.

"Sarah?"

Sarah pushed the papers into a box file. "I…" she glanced up and noticed one she'd missed on the adjoining desk. Maddie's gaze followed hers to a handwritten sheet, listing names. Sarah leaned across, quickly snatched it up and stuffed it into the box with the others. "I'm sorry Madeeha, I can't tell you about her new posting, it's classified."

"But I'm her sister!" Maddie cried.

"Huh?" Max sat up and rubbed his hands over his face. "I was having the best dream…" He yawned widely then stood up. "Maddie, you okay?"

"Raya didn't show for our meeting and there was a massive explosion on the South Bank, a whole bunch of MD5s, and now Sarah says she's on a new assignment but it's *classified*," she spat out the last word. She watched for a reaction and swore that his complexion had blanched a little.

"She's fine, I'm sure," Max insisted. "It always takes a little while to settle into new assignments."

"Max, you can't expect me to—"

"What explosion?" Sarah interrupted.

"I– What?" Maddie spun towards Sarah, her anger rising. "I *want* to know where you've sent my sister."

"Madeeha, you need to calm down. And you're injured." Sarah gestured at Maddie's right hand. "Let me dress that for you and you can tell us what happened. Was it from the blast?"

Confused, Maddie looked down at her hand; the MD5 had vaporised her gun, leaving her palm red and blistered. She wondered how she'd failed to notice, then remembered the injured man back at the flat. "There were casualties," she said.

She felt suddenly drained and allowed Max to steer her into chair. His eyes flicked towards Sarah as he reached for a first aid kit, but he remained silent.

"How many casualties?" Sarah asked. "Did you ID any of them?"

"Why?" Maddie sat forwards. "Was it our operation? Was it anything to do with Ray?"

"No, no, Suraya is fine," Sarah soothed, taking the bandage from Max. "Can you tell us how the explosion happened? Our surveillance cameras have been down today so we're in the dark."

Maddie began to describe the voices she'd heard from the roof and the blast that had briefly turned the world blue. Sarah dressed Maddie's hand slowly and methodically, her eyes cast down, while Max sat in the chair opposite, his weight forward, his thumb rapidly tapping the frayed fabric of the arm. His angst only confirmed to Maddie that he and Sarah were keeping something from her.

"You said there were casualties?" Sarah asked again. She'd finished bandaging Maddie's hand but took her time fastening the end of the gauze. "What happened to them?"

"There were ash piles on the riverbed," Maddie began. "I think they were burned bodies. But they were being swept away by the water when I arrived."

"Did anyone escape alive? Any casualties that were recognisable?"

Max abruptly stood up and walked over to the monitors.

Maddie pictured the face of the man she'd helped... "No," she lied. "If there were, they'd gone by the time I got there."

Sarah questioned her further on the appearance of the blast crater, the identity of the drones and the direction they'd flown from, making notes and marks on a map. "I think we should take a look at the damage ourselves when it's safe to do so. Max, do you think we could get a MD7 down there unnoticed?"

MD7s were the smallest of the surveillance drones, and Max had been working on improving their cloaking ability.

"Maybe," he replied, beginning at once to tweak the machine's code.

Maddie opened her eyes. Damn it, she'd fallen asleep.

Max was crashed-out in the chair opposite. Sarah was sitting with her back to her, head resting on her hand, at one of the desks where a lamp softly illuminated maps and schematics. Maddie watched her for a few minutes but couldn't tell if she was awake or not. She glanced down at her watch: 4:48.

The first aid kit was still sitting on the chair next to her and Maddie gently pulled out bandages, antibiotics, antiseptic and an adrenaline pen and tucked them into her jacket pocket, alongside the syringes of the mystery painkiller. There was a good chance the man was already dead. And then what? She'd have a lot more explaining to do.

She began to shift her weight from the chair, but the springs creaked treacherously, rousing Sarah from her doze.

"Madeeha," she said, stretching her head from side to side. "You were exhausted, we couldn't wake you."

"Sorry, yes, I didn't realise I was so tired."

"Why don't you go rest in my bunk? You'll be more comfortable."

"No. Thank you, I'll head home." Maddie glanced at the desk; the schematics showed Max's adaptations for the drones. "You will tell me if... *when*, you hear from Suraya, won't you?"

Sarah stood up and moved between her and the exit, and for a moment Maddie was afraid that she was going to stop her from leaving. The bulge in her jacket made by the medical supplies felt horribly conspicuous; if Sarah asked what she had, how would she explain the syringes? She tried to clear her mind, focusing on her anger over Sarah's deception so as not to betray her guilt over her own.

"Of course," Sarah said, pulling open the door for Maddie. "You've had a long night. Our comms will be working again soon, and then we'll hear something, I'm sure. Go and get some rest." She smiled reassuringly.

Maddie brushed past her and climbed the ladder up to the workshop. The words, 'we'll hear *something*' did not reassure her.

§

Maddie glanced over her shoulder at Jack, then returned her gaze to the fragments of sky and the Tate Modern building beyond the apartment. "I took the med kit and tried to get to the South Hub," she began. "I didn't know what was in the syringes and figured you might need medical assistance, but there's been some kind of incident south of here and I couldn't get through. Our comms have been down all day and there's nowhere around here to get a secure line. I managed to get these from another safe house though." She turned from the window, pulled out the first aid supplies she'd pocketed, and tossed them onto the sofa next to Jack. "Not that it looks like you need them."

"Maybe not," said Jack. "But thanks."

"So," Maddie continued, the lie taking shape in her mind, "I know that this mission is classified, but it's the same project my sister, Suraya is working on." She watched Jack's face intently, hoping for some reaction to confirm that her hunch was right. "She didn't show up for our latest meeting and in the event that she goes missing, I've been instructed by Sarah to help." Still nothing.

Jack thought back through the endless historical documents that he'd read. *Sarah…* Sarah Fuller? He pictured a woman, in her fifties maybe, who had organised LEFA recruits in South London. The other name meant nothing to him, however, and so it was easy to keep his expression blank as he shook his head. "I'm sorry," he said, "but I don't know your sister. It's not the same mission. I'm working alone."

Maddie sat down facing him. She'd expected as much – all their agents were trained to lie. Undeterred, she pressed on. "She won't be using her real name anyway. She's eighteen, passes for a little older, looks a bit like me, prettier, longer hair…" She took a breath, picturing again her sister's irrepressible smile. "Any information you have on her whereabouts will be required at the Hub. Even if you can only direct me to her last known location, I'll be able to take it from there." The horrifying thought that Suraya might be expendable flashed through her mind. "She has information on a previous mission that needs to be safe guarded," she added, trying to cover all bases.

Jack shook his head again. He needed to maintain his cover until he'd shaken Maddie, and her sudden conviction that he knew something about her sister wasn't helpful. "Look, I'm sorry, but I doubt that even Sarah knows about my mission – it's come direct from HQ and the Hubs aren't in the loop." He caught the fleeting look of desperation in her eyes and thought of his mother. Love, fear, pain: always connected. He sighed. "Honestly, if I knew anything helpful, I would say – it would be the least I could do – but I can't think of anyone who fits her description."

Maddie turned away, frustrated. Sarah had asked so many questions about the explosion, and Max was so agitated, it had to be connected. If only she knew more details, her involvement in the classified case would be more plausible, and he might trust her. There would be other people involved. Other names. "Names..." she murmured.

"Sorry?"

Maddie pictured the sheet of names that Sarah that been in a hurry to hide. She hadn't recognised any of them so would hazard a guess that they were Republicans. "I'm presuming Suraya's run into trouble tracking one of the targets. Maybe Adam Fairfax? Or Mike Harley?" She had a photographic memory and had seen three or four names before the sheet was snatched away.

Jack rolled his eyes before closing them and leaned back in his seat. "No, not my mission."

"Ed Listeman? Dr Kingsley?"

Jack opened his eyes and found Maddie watching him intently. *Kingsley.*

There it was. "Was that where you last saw Suraya? With Dr Kingsley?" Maddie could hear the slight tremble in her voice.

"No..." Jack exhaled slowly. With a slight grimace, he stood up and walked to the kitchen, filling a couple of glasses with water to buy some time. He placed hers on the counter and took a few sips from his own, then struggled onto a bar stool to take the pressure off his leg.

If Maddie had any information on Kingsley, Jack needed to know. The intelligence was either well-hidden, or something had changed, because as far as Jack knew, LEFA was unaware of Dr Kingsley at this point, his previous work for the Republic having been kept off-record. One of the main reasons for the Republican presence in London during the war was their effort to locate him and ensure he fulfilled his 'contractual obligations'. Within the next fortnight, the Republic would find him and all his work on time technology. Nobody knew the precise date that they'd captured Kingsley, but based on his own research, Jack had a hunch it was around the 18th August.

Jack knew the location and entry codes for the Central and East London RSGs – Republican Supremacy Guard bases – his first targets for tracing Kingsley. But if LEFA already had some leads, he might not have to go in blind. He looked at Maddie who sat tense, waiting. "So, what do you know about Kingsley?"

'Fuck-all,' Maddie wanted to say. Instead, she looked down at her feet, a wave of exhaustion washing over her. She tried to summon her strength. Suraya needed her, and she had to discover what Jack knew before he realised that her own knowledge was non-existent.

She stood up and joined him at the counter, perching on the opposite bar stool, and contemplated him, aware of the shift in his attention. What did she know? Only a little about Ray's previous mission. She pictured her dad: one of life's natural philosophers. Didn't he always say that 'admitting the truth can bridge the divide'?

Jack pushed the second glass of water towards her and she picked it up and took a sip. "Truthfully," she began, "I don't know anything about Dr Kingsley, but I believe he's somehow connected to Suraya's mission. What I do know is that until recently, my sister was working undercover at the Republican Ambassador's residence. LEFA suspects the Republic of supplying our government with weapons. Ray was looking for proof; a way to fight them from the inside. Sarah got jumpy when I saw a list of names that included Kingsley, so I think it's all connected."

Jack frowned. "But you said Sarah instructed you to help me?"

Maddie realised her slip. "Yes," she confirmed. "I'm just not party to the details of the mission. But no one understands Suraya like I do, so together we might be able to work out what's happened." She forced herself to breathe steadily, locking Jack's gaze.

Jack felt her eyes hold his, defiant, challenging. She wasn't telling the truth, but then neither was he. If Sarah knew something about Dr Kingsley, Maddie might be able to find out what that was. "Okay," he said at last. "But if Sarah wants us to work together, she's going to need to give you clearance, and tell us what Suraya's found out so far."

Maddie nodded slowly, picturing where Sarah stored her files. Provided she was careful, she could get copies of the information they held. "Of course," she lied. "If I'd been able to get there tonight, Sarah would have filled me in. So, are you allowed to tell me who this Kingsley guy is?"

"He's a physicist," explained Jack. "And a former employee of DARPA."

"The Republic's military-tech place?"

"Yes, the Defence Advanced Research Projects Agency. We've got them to thank for the worst destruction seen in wars over the past two hundred years."

"Two hundred? They can't be that old."

"No, I guess not." Jack smiled wryly. How easy it was to forget that he'd travelled eighty years; he needed to be more careful. "Just feels that way. Anyway, the Republic is looking for Dr Kingsley. He broke ranks with DARPA a couple of years ago, taking his research with him, and they're very anxious to get it back. He's been traced to London. If we can get hold of him and his work first it will give us a massive advantage."

"So, you're on his trail too?"

"Yes," Jack replied truthfully. "It's imperative that I find him first."

"And you really haven't come across my sister?" Maddie asked hopefully.

"No. But if she knows anything about Dr Kingsley, and the Republic has discovered this, then she'll be in some danger."

Maddie faced Jack, but her gaze looked right through him, imagining the horrors that her sister might be enduring. Jack held still and watched the emotions evolve and flow from the depths of her dark eyes across the breadth of her face. His mother's eyes had had that same expressive quality and there had been times when he'd wanted to hate her, tried to hate her, only to be defeated by a look that said more than words had ever done.

Outside, the sun began to edge over the horizon, lifting the shadows from Maddie's face. The hazy light revealed scars whose lacy edges ran from her left eyebrow, puckering the skin at the corner of her eye, before fanning out gently across her cheek bone. As Jack traced the lines down towards her neck, the sunrise burst over the balcony and through the gaps between the blinds.

The rush of gold flooded Maddie's face and broke her trance. She slipped off the stool and returned to the window, where she squinted into the light. "Max will try to send in a drone to view the blast site." She pulled her eyes from the river and turned to look at Jack. "You said what you were doing went awry, but what the hell could cause damage like that?"

"As I said," Jack pictured the makeshift lab in Barts, the time capsule nestled in amongst the power cables, "Kingsley made some pretty scary stuff for the Republic; I just didn't have a lot of warning that it could self-destruct."

Maddie waited. "That's it?" she asked. "That's all you're going tell me after I almost died saving you?"

Jack puffed out his cheeks, expelling air slowly, regretting that in this, she had the upper hand. "Truthfully, I don't think I really understood the…object's potential, only that, in the wrong hands, it could be incredibly dangerous."

"Could be?" she exclaimed. "Did you see what it did to the embankment?" She pictured the dripping metal, the river sucking and hissing as it flowed back across the scalding mud, swirling the ashes into the churning water. "You weren't alone, were you. Who were the others?"

"I ran into some scavengers… Things didn't work out as they'd hoped. Anyway, I'm sure that your drone will shed some light. Do you know what time they'll attempt it? I'm guessing the site has attracted a bit of interest."

"Government will have the site on lockdown, but our drone can cloak. We might get a look later today."

Jack tried to recall the aftermath of the explosion, but it was all a blur. While reasonably confident that nothing suspicious had survived, it was prudent to ensure Maddie gathered what information she could from the Hub before she was given cause to question his identity. If he went to the Hub, his cover would be blown, so Jack was banking on his instinct that she wouldn't want him with her. A few questions would determine if he was correct that Maddie was bluffing about Sarah's instructions.

"Can we go to the Hub this morning?" he asked. "I can get a secure line from there to contact HQ and fill Sarah in on what I know – stop them jumping to false conclusions."

Maddie's stomach lurched. She couldn't turn up with Jack, she'd be excluded from the meeting straight away and whatever trouble Suraya was in would be kept from her. She glanced at him and the frayed fabric of his trouser leg. "It's too far," she said with authority. "I know you're healing fast but walking that distance will set you back." She held her breath, praying he'd agree.

Glad he'd been right, Jack shrugged and played along. "That's probably true, maybe I should stay here. But by this afternoon I should be okay to join you."

"I shouldn't be too long," Maddie said. "I'll come back here afterwards. As I said before, the usual route's blocked and the alternative is more demanding. By the time I'm back you'll be feeling much stronger, and if necessary, I'll have figured out a different route."

"Alright," Jack conceded. "I guess I should rest this leg then." He moved back around the counter and over to the sofas. "Since I probably know more about Kingsley than Sarah does, I'll fill you in on a few things – to help you make sense of the intelligence. If you know what you're looking for, what your sister could know, maybe you can second guess her moves?"

Maddie nodded and sat back down opposite Jack. "Okay, so what *are* we looking for?"

Jack shared what he knew about Kingsley – the projects he'd worked on for DARPA, his possible associates and enemies in London – all the while careful not to reveal details that could only come from the future. It would be months before the Republic's discovery of time travel would be leaked to the world, and the little Jack had revealed was a risk. If he'd read Maddie wrong, if she told Sarah all about him, he might find himself actively competing with LEFA to find his target. But if Maddie was going to help, she needed to know what she was looking for.

Other time travellers had tried and failed before to find Dr Kingsley, and he wondered why he was so sure he stood a chance of success. If he did fail, but LEFA found Dr Kingsley first, that would surely be better than the reality Jack had grown up with. The Republic had to be stopped.

"Okay, time for me to go," said Maddie, emerging from the bedroom in a fresh top.

"Do you know the people who live here?" asked Jack curiously.

"Lived," Maddie corrected. She looked at the photograph hanging in the hall, where four faces beamed out at her. "They were all killed in the Massacre a few years ago, standing up for people like me and my family. My parents were climate refugees." She took a shaky breath. "So, anyway, I figure they wouldn't mind me borrowing their stuff. Here, these might fit you." She handed Jack some trousers and took her jacket from him.

Jack looked from the jeans to the father in the photograph, who smiled back at him from better times.

Maddie pulled on her jacket, teased the borrowed top's hood out and over her hair, then checked on her knife and gun. Leaving the building in daylight, in the shadow of last night's disturbance, felt a little daunting, but she should be alright once she reached the main road.

Jack held out a small round disk. "Please take it."

The tracker was tiny, less than half the size of a penny, and could easily be concealed on her person, but Maddie didn't trust him. He'd listed all the reasons why knowing her location would be a good idea. They were all logical, but something didn't feel quite right.

"I know you can handle yourself," Jack continued, with a slight smile and incline of his head, "but if you run into government agents around the corner, or worse, Republican, then you're not going to be able to help Suraya. I'll need to find you... LEFA will need to find you."

Maddie wondered again whether any footage from the drone had survived: was the government looking for a woman just like her? She sighed and took the tracker, turning the smooth disk over in the palm of her hand. "Okay, I'll take it, but on one condition – if I run into trouble before I get to the Hub then you will go to Sarah, tell her what you've told me, and help find Suraya."

"After I find you," Jack replied.

"No. I can wait. Make sure Suraya's safe first. Please."

Jack tried not to look her in the eye. His main concern wasn't Suraya, or Maddie herself, but that the information he had given her didn't fall into the wrong hands. Whether or not Suraya knew anything about Kingsley he couldn't say, only that Sarah did, and once he knew that information, he would have to break away from the woman now facing him, her dark eyes asking without words for his assurance. She stepped forwards and took his hand and he was surprised at how warm hers was.

"Please?"

He looked up and felt caught. "Okay," he whispered. It was still a lie, but a reluctant one.

She smiled and released his hand, then pushed the tracker into her jeans pocket. "I'll see you in an hour or two."

§

22 Bishopsgate

Suraya bit her lips lest she scream with frustration; she wouldn't give the guard outside the satisfaction. In the darkness, she had felt along every inch of the walls, looking for a vent or shuttered window, but there were none. She could barely tell where the wall ended and the door began, and she wondered whether the room was designed this way so that its occupants would slowly die from oxygen starvation.

It dawned on her that she needed the toilet, but nothing had been provided. Not even a bucket. Did they expect her to pee on the floor? The muscles in her cheeks twitched as she clenched her teeth. She felt for the edge of the metal bench that stuck out from the wall and sat down, crossed one leg over the other and jiggled her foot.

It had all been going so well until the other man, Tobias turned up. But Sarah had been right – Kayson Hart was making some sort of deal with the Republic. Suraya had often heard Dr Kingsley mentioned and gathered that he was a weapons designer who'd deserted his post in Washington a few years earlier. The Republic had been attempting to trace him ever since.

Kayson Hart had been involved for the past ten or eleven months, but Suraya hadn't been able to work out his intentions yet. If she didn't know better, she would say that Hart and the men he met with were allies, but the Republic, whilst not technically an enemy of Britain and the EU, was far from a friend, and one of the few things she knew about her target was that he believed wholeheartedly in European supremacy, with Britain at the forefront. As far as Suraya could see, the likelihood of Hart sharing power with the Republic was akin to his enthusiasm for opening Europe to climate refugees: practically non-existent.

On that score, Hart had certainly asked her a lot of questions. Where in Africa did her family come from and when? Why had they chosen Britain? And how had she made the jump from being a maid at the Ambassador's residence, to working the bar in the Republican Embassy? She had felt uneasy at first, though she hid it well, but he had been quite charming, always ready with a smile.

Suraya might not have matched the profile of Hart's ideal British citizen, but she clearly ticked his boxes when it came to other considerations. Physical attraction, for Hart, was governed neither by his politics nor his bigotry, and as Suraya moved about the Embassy bar, she was conscious of his eyes following her. She had never been much interested in reading the news, finding it endlessly depressing, and she knew little about Hart besides what had been in the dossier provided by Sarah. A selection of photographs lifted from the internet, depicted Kayson Hart surrounded by beautiful women, and this was, she surmised, why Sarah and the others at LEFA command had chosen her for the job. It had worked too. She had smiled and flirted, not overtly, but just enough to bring him to her, where she tried to keep his glass topped up and flatter him into revealing small details that might make a difference.

If only it wasn't for that other guy. Tobias.

Suraya wrinkled her nose with distaste, picturing his crooked teeth and mouth that was too large alongside eyes that were too small, all working together to create an unfavourable face.

She sighed and wondered what the time was, and whether Hart had noticed her absence last night. It was a shame he was on the wrong side – after all, his face was certainly pleasing, even if he was old enough to be her father.

For a moment she pictured her own father, and then Maddie. Madeeha had always been their father's favourite, and Suraya had once sworn there was some kind of plot between the pair of them to stop her from having fun. What would Maddie say if she knew where she was now? Her eyes widened slightly in the dark as tendrils of fear pricked at her stomach. No. Suraya pushed them back squarely to resume her role.

If Hart asked after her... Surely, he would ask after her? If he came looking for her, he would persuade her captors to have her released.

§

Southbank

The door clicked shut behind Maddie and Jack dashed into the bedroom, tugging off his ripped trousers and pulling on the ones she had given him. Ideally, he would wait a bit longer before putting too much strain on his leg, but he thought it would hold up okay. It hadn't hurt at all for the past hour, although, for Maddie's benefit, he'd kept up the act that it was still sore and uncomfortable. He slung the backpack he'd found in the wardrobe over his shoulder, containing the contents of his damaged bag, and quickly headed to the door. His wristwatch lacked the more complex programmes of the iHolo but it was compatible with the tracker. Its screen displayed a basic map with a green line that was lengthening and moving, revealing the path that Maddie had taken as well as her current position.

Jack wanted to stay as close to her as he could without being noticed and headed down the stairwell as she progressed across the entrance lobby. After checking the street outside, and Maddie's location, he followed her out into the city.

Jack knew the streets around here well, but how they would be seventy or eighty years from now. He'd spent weeks preparing himself for the 2070s, studying historical records, town planning reports and wartime maps of bomb damage, but he hadn't anticipated the noises, or the smell, which got worse as he followed Maddie towards Southwark Street.

Piles of rubbish bags were heaped in abandoned shop doorways, many ripped, their contents strewn across the pavements. Dusty cars thrummed back and forth along the road, more cars than he'd ever seen in central London. It was funny how in the quiet of the dawn he'd imagined that this part of the city was deserted, the same way that the apartment block was. Of course, the city had been deserted, but only by those who could afford to. The cars driving past were battered and old, and people had that haunted look of those living in a war zone, doing what was necessary to keep going, to exist. Refuse collection was hardly a priority in a country where resources were stretched to breaking point.

Jack tracked Maddie down the street, curiously studying the people around him and the recycled clothes they wore. Upcycled fashion had been a major trend from the 2040s right up until his own teen years, when smart fabrics had become more readily available. Environmentally responsive fabric made the extremes of climate change more bearable, but not everyone could afford it. Upcycled, vintage clothes remained the uniform of the dispossessed, but also of those who supported and championed their cause. By 2150, wearing a patched pair of jeans was a political statement. Jack looked at those around him and tried to take their measure. Their body language wasn't defiant. Their clothes were nothing more than functional. They were just people trying to get by.

Ahead, Maddie's progress had paused, and Jack pushed himself back against the shopfronts, hoping that she hadn't spotted him. She'd stopped in front of the railway bridge. No, not stopped. She was climbing it. Jack hurried forwards, trying to work out how she'd got up without being seen. The most obvious route was via some scaffolding on the building adjacent to the bridge, but if he followed that way he'd easily be spotted.

A couple of older men eyed him with interest from the doorway of a laundrette on the opposite side of the road. Turning his back to them, Jack checked his watch: Maddie was heading south down the train tracks. He saw now that there was a narrow gap between the building and the bridge, but as Jack edged into it, a hand on his shoulder restrained him.

"Tha's an intrestin' watch you got there," said the man, pulling Jack back towards the street. He was bulky and unshaven, his grip on Jack's shoulder firm. He flexed his free hand, his knuckles cracking each time it balled into a fist. "I expect you'd like to take it off, so I can 'ave a better look."

The men outside the laundrette stepped forwards. One of them was grinning. Shit. Jack looked up and down the road at the approaching traffic.

"I don't fink you 'eard me." The thug's grip on Jack's shoulder increased as he smiled, revealing a large gap in his front teeth.

Beyond the bridge, a lorry exited right from Blackfriars Road and rumbled towards them.

"Oh, this old thing?" Jack asked, pulling his cuff back to show the watch and curling his fingers around the handle of the blade hidden inside his sleeve.

"Don't get funny wiv me," the man warned.

"Not at all," Jack demurred.

The lorry drove under the bridge. Jack drew the blade out and up, slicing the man's arm. The thug howled and drew back to punch. The lorry emerged. Jack leapt up, grabbed the scaffolding and kicked the man hard in the chest, sending him flying backwards towards the vehicle. It swerved to miss him, brakes screeching, bringing it to a juddering halt. Jack hauled himself up and onto the train tracks while those below cursed and shouted at one another, the bleeding man lying, temporarily forgotten, on the edge of the road.

Jack raced down the tracks in Maddie's direction, scanning all around. He thought he'd been careful, but clearly not careful enough, and he couldn't afford to keep drawing attention. Up ahead, her trail paused where the train tracks crossed a large road and, recalling what he knew about LEFA Hubs, he guessed one was nearby. He knew the locations of the Central and East London Hubs. The East Hub, of course, had been infiltrated a year ago by the Republic and its volunteers tortured for information. The exact position of the South Hub had remained a secret, even after the war, it's members no doubt fearful that old scores might yet be settled.

Jack reached the bridge, noting that Maddie's trail led to the railway arches. The mortar here had crumbled away, leaving gaps between the brickwork, and Jack shifted so that he could just make out the top of her head through the crack. He heard her exchange a few words, followed by a tapped pattern of some kind. The slightest gust of oily air told him that the door had opened and Maddie had passed inside.

He scanned the backstreet below and noticed a large, covered loading bay in the brick building opposite. He found the ladder Maddie had used to get down and cautiously descended, making his way quickly to his covered lookout. Once in the shadows, Jack eased himself down on to a wooden crate, stretching his leg out and massaging his thigh. The injured area throbbed and ached from the exertion, but it had held up. Now all he could do was wait.

He studied the door through which Maddie had disappeared. Heating Engineers... Jack raised his eyebrows and gave a slight nod. Clever.

§

South Hub, Elephant and Castle

"Have you 'eard anyt'ing from Suraya?" Leroy asked before he picked up and drained the last of the coffee from his mug.

"Not yet," Maddie said. "But I've got an idea of what she's up to."

"Ah, well dat's good. She's a bit of a rogue, your sister, certainly keeps you busy worryin' about 'er!" He smiled.

"Yeah, she does." Maddie turned and forced her feet towards the cupboard.

"Hey, Maddie?" Leroy called over his shoulder, while placing parts into a holdall. "Can you tell 'em down there I need to go out in a couple of hours? Ask 'em to send up Max to hold the fort?"

"Sure," Maddie called back.

"And can you remind Izaak that he 'as not been up to see his great-uncle for t'ree whole days!"

"Will do."

The cupboard clicked shut behind Maddie. She climbed down the ladder and paused before the lower door, her heart thudding in her chest, sure that her deception was written all over her face. She took a deep breath and released it slowly, reminding herself that if she looked nervous, Sarah and the others would assume it was anxiety for Suraya. Besides, maybe Suraya had been in contact, or was even back at the base?

She peeped through the glass in the door and saw Max working on a drone and a new volunteer, Jenna, monitoring the surveillance footage. She punched in the code and entered.

Jenna looked over her shoulder. "Hey, Maddie."

"Hi. The cameras are working again then."

"Yeah, had them up and running for a couple of hours now," Jenna replied, her eyes back on the screens.

Maddie could feel Max staring at her. Half afraid to ask, she turned to him. "Ray?" He shook his head. Maddie pulled out the chair opposite and sat down heavily, winded by her crashing hopes.

Max pushed his glasses onto the top of his head and rubbed his eyes. His fine black hair slipped through the spaces left by the bridge and where the rims met the arms, flopping back onto his forehead. She'd never asked Max how old he was – she didn't think he was much older than her – but he looked like he'd aged a decade overnight. Maddie watched as he screwed his eyes shut and stifled a yawn. He pulled his glasses back onto his nose and picked up the drone's motor, reconnecting a tiny wire.

Maddie wondered if he really was in love with Suraya. She'd spent the last six months teasing her sister about Max: how he was always quick to open the door for her, check if she wanted a drink, ask how she was or offer his help should she need it. He was kind of cute, in a nerdy way, and Ray flirted back as she tended to do, but to be honest, Maddie had never considered that his affection for her sister was anything more than skin-deep. Though, if he really did care, he'd be as anxious as she was to find out what had happened.

"Max?" she whispered.

He looked up.

"*Do* you know where Suraya is?"

He shook his head again.

"But you know something," she insisted.

Max looked up at the ceiling, avoiding Maddie's eyes. He opened his mouth to speak just as Sarah appeared from the kitchen. He closed it again and looked down at the motor, returning it to the cavity in the drone's shell.

"Madeeha, I wasn't expecting you back so early. I'm afraid we haven't heard anything yet, but I'm sure we will soon." Sarah put her hand on Maddie's shoulder. It made Maddie's skin prickle. "Our cameras suggest that footfall near the blast site is lessening; not long, and then we can send in our drone."

Maddie's pulse quickened, running through the camera locations in her head and praying that none of them covered as far as Castle Yard; she'd need to be even more careful when she returned to Jack.

Max began updating Sarah on his progress, and Maddie took the chance to scan the room for the box files Sarah had been holding the previous night. If not there, it would be in Sarah's bunk room. She couldn't spot it and wondered what excuse she could give for heading into the left corridor; the kitchen and general bunk room was off to the right, and it was only Sarah's bunk and the generator room on the left. "Oh," she said, remembering.

"Leroy has to go out in an hour or two; he needs Max on the door."

"That's fine, I'll be done before then," said Max.

"I also have a message for Izaak, so I'll just…" The sentence trailed off and Maddie stood and walked around the monitors, opening the door behind and stepping into the corridor.

'Corridor' wasn't a good description for a space a little over a metre square, clad on the right-hand side in rough concrete, with one door ahead and another on the left. Maddie tapped very gently on the left-hand door, just in case, and when there was no answer, opened it and went in. The room was just big enough for a single bed, a tiny desk and chair. Shelves above the bed, filled with maps and files, added to the claustrophobia.

Maddie bit her lip as she scanned the shelves, then the papers on the desk. Another list of names had been jotted down on a scrap of paper; a couple circled with question marks. Three mugs of half-drunk, cold tea and a half-eaten sandwich sat next to them. To be fair to Sarah, her life was devoted to LEFA, and the tough decisions for their unit rested on her shoulders.

Maddie crouched down and felt under the bed, pulling out a couple of cardboard boxes. The first one was full of plans for the city's electrical grid, but the second one delivered the file she was looking for. Maddie leafed through the sheets and recognised a few of the names that Jack had mentioned. She pulled out her phone to take photos, but froze when something thudded, back in the control room.

Shit. It would take ages to photograph each sheet, and what if Sarah came to get something? She made a snap decision, pushed the empty file back into the box, slid it under the bed, then grabbed the papers and left the room. She slipped through the adjacent door and closed it behind her. In the back corner of the room, a lad sat with his back propped to the wall in the narrow gap next to the generator.

"Hey Izaak," said Maddie.

He took his eyes off the tablet he was holding for a moment and mumbled back. "Hi."

"You still playing Tremors?" Maddie asked, peering over at the screen.

"Uh-huh."

"Leroy says you're overdue a visit," Maddie admonished and was given a grunt in reply.

Izaak was fifteen. Too young to be given a role within LEFA, but too old to be fobbed off with assurances that everything would be alright, that studying was still important, or that manners still mattered. The world as he knew it had imploded.

Izaak's dad, Ben, who was Leroy's nephew, had tried to get him involved with his work at the Jewry Street Clinic, but Izaak had been wholly resistant. Sensing the impending stand-off, Leroy had stepped in and offered to train Izaak up as a heating engineer. Despite his fears about the Hub's presence, Ben had eventually agreed. Izaak was supposed to spend a couple of hours each day under Leroy's tutorage but, after a promising start, had begun slipping off, preferring to escape into the fantasy worlds of computer games.

In the past few months there had been considerable unrest in the neighbourhood where Ben and Izaak lived, so Izaak had been given permission to stay at the Hub. After a week of Leroy's lessons, making drinks, washing up, and answering the same well-meaning questions over and over, he'd finally discovered that if he stayed in the generator room everyone left him alone.

"I won't be long," said Maddie. She laid the papers down, beyond Izaak's view, on top of the large fuse box and pulled out her phone. "I just can't think in the control room," she explained.

Izaak shrugged without looking up, so Maddie began working through the sheets, photographing each one. She'd almost finished when she heard the outer door click. Heart pounding, she pulled the papers together and turned, hiding them behind her back just in time as Sarah stepped around the door.

"Maddie, have you got a moment to look at the surveillance footage from this morning? Just in case it jogs your memory of last night."

Maddie swallowed. "Sure," she said, but didn't move. Izaak peered up at her.

Sarah raised her eyebrows. "In your own time," she sighed, taking a step closer to Izaak and glancing down. "Same awful game," she commented.

Izaak reddened and flashed Maddie a look of thunder as she took her chance and hurried towards the door, pulling the papers in front of her.

"You passed on Leroy's message?" Sarah asked as Maddie turned the handle.

"Oh...yeah," said Maddie, pulling the door open and stepping out while Sarah reminded Izaak that a bit of help around the place wouldn't go amiss. Sarah would be close behind and Maddie didn't dare risk returning the papers to their box. She hesitated for a moment before stuffing them up under the back of her shirt and tucking it into her jeans. Taking another deep breath, she pushed open the door and went back into the control room, joining Max and Jenna by the monitors.

"Our cameras can see most of the cordoned off area," said Jenna, pointing at a screen. "But we wondered if anything happened around here, something the police might miss?" She turned to Maddie who sat down next to her. "Any clues we can find," she encouraged, "even small, might give us an advantage."

Maddie stared at the monitors, but from the corner of her eye watched the door to the corridor, waiting for Sarah to reappear. The papers felt hot against her skin and she desperately wanted to escape the oppressive glare of the screens in which her own, guilty face was reflected. She tried to think back to the previous night. It already felt so long ago. "The shock wave from the blast travelled a long way," she volunteered eventually, "so it's possible that debris might have—" She stopped short as she heard Sarah's raised voice from beyond the door. "Um, it might have..."

Sarah burst into the room, holding Izaak by the sleeve, her expression somewhere between anger and exasperation. "Maddie, can I have a word?"

Izaak studied the floor intently.

"Of course," Maddie replied, trying to keep her voice level.

"Wait in here," Sarah instructed Izaak, pushing him towards the desks.

As Maddie passed him, she touched his arm and he met the questioning look she gave him. The slightest hint of a smug smile flashed across his face. The little shit. Maddie followed Sarah back into the generator room. Once inside, she turned to Sarah and asked casually, "So what's going on?"

"I'm a little embarrassed to ask you this, Madeeha, but it's a serious accusation." Sarah sighed. "Izaak seems to think that you're hiding something from me."

Silence.

"Well? Would you care to explain?"

"What?" Maddie laughed nervously.

Sarah's face was impassive.

"That kid has been playing way too many conspiracy games," Maddie reasoned. "I'll have a word with Leroy." She moved towards the door but Sarah stood immobile.

"I need to take a look at your phone," she said softly, holding out her hand.

Maddie's hand trembled as she pulled it from her pocket and reluctantly handed it over. She'd always got on with Izaak, why was he stirring up trouble? Was he just pissed-off that she'd disturbed his peace?

Sarah clicked on the gallery app and Maddie's heart froze in her chest. Her mind reeled with excuses, ways to defend herself against Sarah's inevitable anger.

Sarah finished scrolling through the photographs and regarded Maddie, her face weary and disappointed. "Madeeha, you know that these are classified documents, *and* they were in my private quarters." She, too, looked years older this morning.

Maddie had been prepared for her anger, but this was

far worse – she had let Sarah down. Her remorse rose at once, gnawing at her stomach. "I know, I'm sorry. I just think I could find Suraya if I knew some of the details and—"

"That is not your decision to make, Maddie." Sarah rubbed her forehead. "And we have every reason to believe that Suraya is well and following her directions. If we interfere, *then* we could place her in danger."

"Because the Republic want to find Dr Kingsley too?"

Sarah tensed a little. "And what do you understand about that relationship?" she questioned.

"Enough to know that there's no point excluding me from it now," Maddie implored. "I know that HQ would want me to help if I can, and that time is of the essence." She thought of Jack and the advantage that she'd had and now lost. "Please Sarah, just let me help make sure Ray's safe."

Sarah stood still, her face unreadable. "The original documents, please." She calmly held out her hand.

"Look," Maddie persisted, "I know HQ are searching for Dr Kingsley and that they have an agent assigned to find him. Jack – that's his name – and he isn't against my help. Please just call HQ and talk to them. We're not in the loop, but it doesn't make sense to exclude us, and if Suraya's involved it doesn't make sense to exclude me."

Sarah's brow wrinkled. "Where are you getting this from?"

"I…" Maddie paused, uncertain of whether to reveal the depth of her deception.

"It would be better for you to tell me the truth now," Sarah warned.

"Just, speak to HQ, and then I'll explain."

Vexed, Sarah held out her hand. "The documents."

Maddie pulled them from inside her top and handed them over.

"You're detained until further notice." Sarah pulled open the door and left, bolting it shut behind her.

§

Jack glanced down at his watch. It had been nearly two hours now and he was beginning to suspect that something was amiss. At first, Maddie's location had shifted about to a small degree, suggesting she was moving around inside the Hub, but for at least an hour it hadn't budged.

Jack had spent the time studying the front of the workshop with Maddie's binoculars and was certain that a small security camera was hidden in the brickwork above the door. If he was right, then there was no way to approach the arches without being seen. He'd wondered if he could fix the drone and use it to obscure the camera, but he didn't have the right tools and besides, a blocked camera would just draw attention.

His gaze trawled the area, looking for an alternative approach. He noticed pigeons roosting in a recess in the bricks not far above the camera, and others gathered in groups along the length of the top of the bridge. At any one time there were thirty to forty pigeons gathered in the vicinity, and this gave him an idea.

The borrowed backpack was laced with elastic at the front. Jack attached it to the fabric from one of the inner pockets, and a piece of piping from the loading bay, to fashion a makeshift slingshot. He pulled a cereal bar that Maddie had given him from his pocket and crumbled its contents into the fabric pouch. A couple of barrels were stacked to the left of the doorway, giving some cover, and from there Jack might be able to figure out a way in.

§

Max scooped up a spoon of coffee from the jar before realising that he'd already done this. Behind him the kettle whistled gently as it boiled the same water for the third time. "I just can't believe that she'd work against us, Sarah," he argued.

Sarah paced the small space between the wall and the countertop in the kitchen, "I know, I know, but I spoke to both Castillo and Botha at HQ, and neither of them have a clue what Madeeha's referring to. The latest transcript from Suraya suggests that Kayson Hart believes Dr Kingsley is in London, but there's no way Maddie could have known about that. I'm not even sure what Hart's involvement is. Botha's been cross referencing the names, but we're no closer to making sense of it." She shook her head. "And then this man she met? Jack? There's no mention of him, on either side."

"So, he's a Republican agent and it's a cover name." Max shrugged. "Which means that Maddie's been taken in by him, not turned!"

"That's the most likely scenario," Sarah agreed, "but she's refusing to speak to me now. I have no choice but to follow protocol and hand her over to HQ for questioning."

Max turned, picked up the kettle, then put it down again. "I just don't understand why she won't tell you what happened." His voice rose. "Wouldn't that be what's best for Suraya?"

Sarah sighed. "Why don't you try talking to her? She likes you and you have a… a common interest."

Max's face fell. "Is it that obvious?"

"It wasn't, until now."

Max picked up the spoon and prodded the coffee grounds in the bottom of the mug. He pictured Suraya's smile – he wanted so badly to see it again. "I'll try." He turned and clicked the kettle on again, then filled a glass with water and left the room.

Sarah reached over as the kettled thrummed, filling the small space with steam, and switched it off.

§

Maddie looked at her watch again – she'd been stuck in here for well over an hour now. Her fingers turned the tracker disk over and over. Sarah claimed that HQ had denied posting an agent to track Dr Kingsley. She'd also said there was no one in LEFA who fitted Jack's description and he was most likely a Republican or government agent. She had asked for details: how did she meet Jack? What exactly had he said? Maddie wasn't sure why she'd refused to say. Was it possible she had she been taken in by him? Had she aided and abetted the enemy? She turned the disk over again, thinking how Jack knew exactly where she was. If he did work for the Republic then she really had given him a gift. And yet for some reason she just didn't believe it, which was completely irrational given that she knew nothing about him.

She slipped the disk back into her pocket then pushed herself up off the floor to inspect the lock and door hinges. She knew she would be transferred to HQ for questioning, unless she could get out of here first. She heard the outer door open and shut and moved towards the back wall as the bolt slid open and Max appeared.

"So, Sarah's sent you to try now," she remarked sullenly.

"Argh! What has got into you Maddie?" Max burst out. His hands shook with frustration, slopping water from the glass. "Don't you think it would be better to tell us what you know so that we can get Suraya back?"

"Get her back from where?" Maddie jumped at the word. "Where is she?"

"I don't know!" he shouted. "But maybe your *friend* does."

Silenced, Maddie sunk back down to the floor. Max closed the door and, after standing awkwardly a minute, sat down next to her. He handed her the water glass and she took a sip.

"Who is this guy, Maddie? Why are you protecting him?"

She thought back over that morning's strange conversation. "I don't know," she replied at last. "He knows stuff he shouldn't, but I just don't think he's with the Republic."

"And you're basing that on?"

Maddie raised her eyebrows apologetically. "A hunch?"

"Jesus, Maddie!" Max looked up at the ceiling.

"But you won't tell me what Ray was sent to do," she reminded him. "Doesn't trust work both ways?"

Max held his breath a moment before replying. "You know she was working for the Republican ambassador…" Maddie nodded. "It hasn't been easy to get close to the Republicans. We moved her to the embassy to try and find out what Kayson Hart's up to."

"The politician? I thought he was in Brussels, why would he be in London?"

"Exactly. He's been in London for about six weeks now, and we know he's been contacting the Republican Supremacy Guards."

"You think he's a double agent?" Maddie raised her eyebrows. "But he's always been so vocal about European supremacy. Well, white European supremacy," she corrected herself.

"I know," Max agreed, "but he's up to something, and knowing his reputation I don't think it will be philanthropic."

His reputation. The words brought to Maddie's mind stories of accusations and thwarted court-cases going back across the last decade. She felt suddenly queasy. "Why Suraya?" she asked, her voice quiet.

Max screwed up his eyes and bit his lip.

"Max?"

"Sarah and Castillo thought that a woman would have a better chance of getting close to him."

"And you *let them* send her?" Maddie exploded, grabbing Max and thumping him against the wall. "For Christ's sake, she's only eighteen!" Max said nothing. He looked sick too.

Maddie stood and began pacing the tiny space, her mind reeling. Anything could have happened to her in the hands of that misogynistic predator. Anything!

She tried to calm herself and focus on the details. She knew that Hart was in London and that her sister must have seen him; there was some link between Hart and Dr Kingsley which was connected to the Republic; and she knew that Jack was tracking Kingsley – provided he was telling the truth. Sarah had, of course, withheld the details of her conversation with HQ, but she got the impression that they didn't know what the connection between Hart and Kingsley was either. Maybe Jack would?

She could just tell Sarah where Jack was hiding, waiting for her return, and have LEFA take him in. They would find out everything he knew, use it to help find Suraya and bring her home. But what if they didn't bring her home? What if they left her there, asked her to use the information to help further her mission?

Maddie recalled the accusations made in 2068 by Helena Jonas, a young political aide who'd worked for Hart in Brussels. She pictured the photographs that Helena had submitted as evidence for her charge of sexual assault, images that had been leaked on the internet, revealing her bruised face and body. The proposed trial never took place, the reasons for which were never made clear, and Jonas had left the world of politics for good.

Maddie shuddered. No, she couldn't risk Suraya being left in such a dangerous position. A tiny voice in the back of her mind wondered if it might be too late, that Suraya's silence meant the worst may already have happened. She ignored it to focus on her options.

"Max, if you care about Suraya, which I think you do, then you have to help me."

Max lifted his head to look at Maddie. Her expression, of fire and conviction, for a moment rendered her the very likeness of her younger sister. "You know that agents from HQ are on their way to pick you up?"

"Which is why we need to act quickly." She knelt in front of him. "I think that Jack may be able to help, may be able to make the connections that we can't, to lead me to Suraya."

"But what if he's working for the Republic? What if they're on to Suraya and that's why they've targeted you?"

Maddie pushed her hand into her pocket and found the metal disk, warm with her body heat. It had been hours since she'd arrived, easily long enough for the RSG to have dispatched a unit and made an assault on the Hub. "No," she replied, as much to herself as to Max. "He's not with the Republic. But he is currently my best chance of getting some answers."

"Can't we bring him in and question him ourselves?"

"I don't trust Sarah to put Ray's safety first. I'm sorry, Max, but we're going to do this my way."

"And that is?" Max asked a little doubtfully.

"You need to get me out of here. And I need my phone back."

Max regarded her and thought of the repercussions of defying orders. Then he pictured Suraya, the last time he'd seen her. She'd arrived at the Hub for her briefing eating a vile take-away burger, the synthetic meat greasy and limp from the plastic wrapping, and he'd boasted that he did a 'mean home-made burger.' She'd been surprised that he could cook and without thinking he'd offered to make her dinner sometime. The minute he'd said it he felt like an idiot, and had busied himself, looking down at the camera he was fixing in order to hide his blush.

His breath had caught in his throat when she'd laid her hand on his and said, without a hint of irony or the usual teasing tone, that she'd like that. He should have said something else to her, suggested a day even, but he'd been too stunned to speak. She'd gone into the kitchen to see Fuller and Castillo and that was it. He'd had to leave before she'd finished, and that was now a week ago.

He took a deep breath. "OK, how about this…"

§

Jack tossed a couple of stones out into the yard. The pigeons' heads jerked and bobbed around in their direction. One flew down to inspect the small white objects, while the others fluttered with agitated anticipation. Jack took aim with the sling shot, delivering manna from heaven, and thirty feathered bodies took to the air.

Jack burst from the shadows and dashed across the divide, ducking behind the barrels as the last few birds descended in front of the archway doors, pecking and scrapping for the morsels that lay scattered in the dust.

Jack raised his eyebrows and glanced up at the indentation in the brick work, confident that he hadn't been seen. He shifted his gaze to the doorway itself and the next problem of how to get inside.

§

Max felt the simultaneous thrill and dread of his treachery as he re-entered the control room. Jenna had left and Sarah was in her place, watching passers-by on their bank of security monitors. Izaak looked up from one of the dilapidated armchairs, his expression uneasy, perhaps a little bit scared, the consequences of his moment of revenge extending well beyond anything he'd imagined.

"Well, how did you get on?" asked Sarah.

"Uh, well, not great, but she did tell me that this Jack guy sent a couple of messages on her phone. She said he deleted the thread afterwards, but I think I might be able to retrieve them."

"Okay, that might give us some clues about who he's working for. Let me get it." Sarah moved across to the shelves and Max checked his watch, hoping that Leroy would come through for him.

"Here," Sarah handed him the phone and Max made a show of removing the outer casing and inspecting the SIM card.

"I'm going to need my laptop and an external card reader," he lied. "Zaak, I left my laptop in the kitchen, can you get it for me? Oh, and I left the card reader in the bunk room in one of the drawers." Izaak loped off into the right corridor as, on cue, an overhead pipe began to clang. Max slapped his forehead theatrically. "Urg, Leroy! He's waiting to go out."

"I'll go," said Sarah, heading to the door. "Just concentrate on retrieving that data."

As Sarah closed the door behind her, Leroy's voice barked grumpily from the cupboard above.

"Hello? I am *very* late, an' I *hate* being late!"

"Go!" Sarah called up to him. "I'm just coming."

Leroy harrumphed. "About time!"

Above them, Leroy's footsteps stomped towards the door, followed by the scrape of bolts sliding back. "Lock both bolts," he called.

"I can't find the reader. Are you sure it's in here?" Izaak shouted from the bunk room.

"Yes, definitely in there," Max yelled back, as he dashed to the opposite corridor and released Maddie from the generator room. "Try the boxes under the bed," he called. He handed Maddie the SIM card, which she slipped into her back pocket, then quickly put the phone back together and replaced it on the desk. "I'll try to buy you as much time as I can."

"I really don't think it's here!" Izaak shouted, a hint of complaint in his voice.

Max pulled open the door to the stairwell and Maddie went through. "Oh, okay," he called back. "Maybe I left it upstairs. I'll go look." Max pulled the door shut and began to ascend the ladder, with Maddie climbing behind. "Remember, don't move until you hear my cue."

Maddie nodded and held back as Max triggered the door release above.

§

Jack heard a gruff voice shout something from the other side of the door and pushed himself back into the shadow behind the barrels.

The bolts scraped as they slid back and, peering through a gap, Jack made out the ample frame of a man in overalls, a tool bag in his hand.

"Lock both bolts," the man called into the darkness, before stepping into the light and pushing the door to, behind him.

Jack breathed a sigh of relief as the man passed by. He peered back to see that the entrance wasn't fully shut. He dashed towards the door as footsteps approached on the other side. LEFA weren't his enemy, but they didn't know that, and a lengthy conversation wasn't likely to go well. He just hoped the approaching figure wasn't Maddie.

The footsteps reached the door. Jack leaned back and kicked it with full force. The person on the other side flew backwards, crashing into a stand of shelves, their contents rolling and tumbling onto the floor around them.

Max climbed through the opening then froze at the crash and clatter near the doorway. He looked back at Maddie, instantly alarmed.

"Go!" she mouthed, handing him one of the weapons hidden just inside the security door. She took another for herself. Was it the RSG? Had Jack led them here after all?

She pulled the security door shut and winced at the soft click of the lock, praying it hadn't been heard. She could have killed Izaak herself earlier, but he was just a kid, and she wouldn't have him suffer at the hands of the Republic.

Jack knelt to check the woman's pulse then felt the back of her head. She'd hit it hard on the shelves, knocking her out. He recognised her from photographs – Sarah Fuller – though she looked younger than when they'd been taken. "Sorry about that," he whispered, as he pulled her into the recovery position.

A sound from his left caught his attention. In one sinuous movement he reached under his jacket, pulling out his pistol, taking aim at the shelves behind which someone stood. "Come out slowly, with your hands up," he instructed. "I don't want to hurt you." The exploding time machine had rendered the gun useless, but no one else knew that.

Max edged slowly along the shelves. His hands trembled, but his gun was aimed. He wasn't sure what to make of what he'd just seen: Sarah's assailant carefully checking her condition, before placing her in the recovery position. He moved into view. "Who are you? What do you want?"

Maddie barely heard the voices above the thumping of her heart as she inched around the far side of the room. She caught a glimpse of Max through gaps between heat exchangers and coils of wire, but not the other figure. She crouched low and saw Sarah lying on the ground. "Oh no," she breathed, horrified by her own culpability. But Sarah's fingers flexed and her eyes fluttered open. Maddie took a shuddering breath and continued to pick her way over the fallen objects to reach Sarah's side.

Sarah's head throbbed and her vision was blurred. She heard a footstep close by and, moving as little as possible, peered round. Max swam into focus, followed by another figure with his back to her. She saw the gun Max held and looked around for something she could use as a weapon. Above her head, to her left, was a length of copper piping.

From the corner of his eye, Max saw Sarah push herself to her feet. He kept his gaze fixed on the other man, and repeated his question loudly, hoping to cover any noise that Sarah might make. "I said, who are you and what do you want?"

"I didn't mean any harm," said Jack. "I'm just looking for my friend, Maddie."

"Jack?" Maddie stepped out from her cover.

Jack glanced back just long enough for Max to hurl himself forwards, knocking the gun from his hand.

Sarah swung the pipe round, but not at Jack. "You bitch!" she screamed.

Maddie ducked, and the pipe clanged against the shelves behind. "Sarah, please!" She backed away as Sarah advanced. "You don't understand."

"I don't understand that you betrayed us and sold us out to the Republic?"

Maddie pointed her gun at Sarah, who stopped and shook her head with disgust. "He's not with the Republic, please, you have to believe me." Over Sarah's shoulder, Maddie saw Jack trip Max, then raise his fist to strike.

"Jack, no!"

Maddie felt the gaze of all three fall on her. She realised she was trembling, her eyes filling with tears. "I'm sorry, I really am. But I've got to find Suraya. Jack, get off him."

Jack stood up, pulling Max from the floor.

"This is insurrection, Madeeha. Do you think that LEFA won't track you down and stop you?" Sarah demanded.

"I know," said Maddie, pulling away the length of pipe. "Once Suraya's safe I'll turn myself in and answer fully for my actions. I'll share everything I know," she added.

"You will be locked up for this!"

Maddie's face hardened and she held herself taller. "If you hadn't put Suraya in danger then this wouldn't be happening."

"I didn't 'put' her in danger. She *chose* this. And *she* didn't want you to know – to stop her."

"No." Maddie shook her head. "She'd have told me." She doubted the words even as she spoke them, but the thrum of an engine and the crunch of wheels over gravel outside redirected her attention.

"From HQ," warned Max.

Sarah smiled victoriously. "Too late, Madeeha."

Maddie snapped, throwing a punch that toppled Sarah backwards, knocking her out again. "Quick!" she yelled at Max. "Help me move her."

"They're almost here," Jack warned, peering through the crack in the door while the others dragged Sarah out of sight.

"Take them downstairs to 'see me'," said Maddie, "then keep them there as long as you can – lock them in the generator room."

Max, shocked and bruised, nodded obediently.

"Quick!" hissed Jack, edging back into the shadows as Maddie ran to join him.

Max answered the rap at the door, delivering the passphrase, which was duly completed, then pulled the door wide for the agents to step through.

"Wow. You alright?" asked one, peering at the swelling on Max's jaw.

"Uh, yeah," Max mumbled. "We've had a bit of, er, bother downstairs." He led them towards the back of the room. "I'll show you down."

Jack and Maddie slipped out as the agents disappeared from view.

§

Once outside, Maddie grabbed Jack's arm and pulled him towards the main street, dashing across before racing through the back streets and paths that ran between housing blocks.

"Where are we going?" Jack shouted after her.

"To my place, come on."

"What?" Jack ground to a halt.

"Come on!" Maddie pulled at his sleeve.

"That's the first place they'll look for you."

"I know, but I won't be long. There's stuff I need." She stood, hands on hips, panting lightly after their sprint, her obstinate look challenging him to defy her.

Jack shook his head, "Okay, but you have to be quick, five minutes, tops."

"Fine. Come on."

Maddie led him to a housing estate. The blocks of flats were in serious disrepair, their blue fascia boards missing or hanging off, windowpanes broken, and bags of rubbish piled high at every doorway. She led him to an inner stairwell, at the foot of which a pile of signs urged, 'Caution – Demolition Work in Progress'. Maddie didn't pause. She passed the door, hanging precariously on one hinge, and began to climb.

The windows from the stairwell afforded a view across to the neighbouring block, or what was left of it. A mound of rubble and twisted steel sat below the exposed inner walls of room above room, above room. Traces of their former occupants: a band poster, a rainbow painted on a child's blue bedroom wall, a vase of fake flowers tipped over in a doorway, gave a glimpse of the lives that had once been led there.

In Jack's own time, the demolition work had been completed and the buildings razed to the ground, but the financial incentive to rebuild this area of London no longer existed. In the future, Maddie's home was a field of rubble, weeds, and wildflowers.

On the fifth floor, Maddie led him across a walkway and Jack noticed washing strung out from the windows. From somewhere above came the rhythmic thudding of a song's baseline, and carried up on the wind from below, the cry of a young child. "Do many people still live here?" he asked, surprised. "It doesn't look very safe."

"Only those with nowhere else to go," Maddie replied tersely. She stopped at a faded red door. It opened onto a living room, through which Maddie dashed, leaving Jack to close the door behind them. "Keep a lookout," she called from the room beyond.

Jack moved to the window, pulling down the blinds to see outside, but the view revealed very little. He turned instead to the room itself, taking in the worn, mismatched furniture – too much of it – crowded into the small space. An ancient dark-wood dining table and chairs with overly ornate legs were pushed into the corner. Bookshelves, full to bursting, rose from floor to ceiling along the back wall and an oversized three-piece suite in an ugly faded fabric was squeezed in front of an electric fireplace.

The miscellany of furniture, that ought to have been discordant, was somehow brought together by the artworks, cloths and hangings that covered them all, the largest of which hung above the fireplace. In it, woven lines of blue and cream criss-crossed a richly coloured fabric background of burnt sienna, terracotta and ochre. It brought to mind figures in dance. Smaller cloths, draped over the seats, displayed similar colours and patterns, and several small woven baskets, sitting between books on the shelves, incorporated the designs into their vessel forms.

Jack ran his fingers over the cloth draped sofa and was

surprised by the softness of the coarse-looking fabric. The designs were African, though he couldn't say from which country. Most African nations, in his own time, were uninhabitable, their people forced north into Europe and Scandinavia.

A clatter from outside drew Jack to the window, and he peered out to see a child roll past on a scooter. "Are you nearly ready?" he called, conscious of the minutes passing and the short distance they'd travelled.

"Nearly," Maddie called back. "I'll be two minutes." She dashed from the room she'd been in and through a second door which swung shut behind her.

Jack turned to look at the shelves on his right, where photographs sat in front of the jumbled books. In one, a couple stood smiling before a backdrop of terraced hills, a few of them green but most dry and barren. Jack examined their faces, noting the shared likeness to Maddie. Yet her parents, as he presumed them to be, were very different. Her mother was tall with chestnut skin, an abundance of black hair woven into braids around her head; her father looked Chinese and was a good six inches shorter.

Another photograph showed an elderly couple in front of a tiny shop. Grandparents, perhaps. The woman's head was wrapped in a colourful scarf, her face very like her daughter and granddaughter. The man at her side looked Indian, and Jack recalled that there had been many Indian settlers in East Africa at one time. The man's face was well-weathered, staring straight at the camera, proud and defiant, and it was through that, if not his features, that his resemblance to Maddie was clear. Jack returned to the window and peered through the blinds again. Outside the sky was growing dark.

In the kitchen, Maddie searched through the drawers, increasingly irritable as each one failed to produce what she was searching for. She finally found the old phone at the back of the lowest drawer. It was badly battered, with a large crack spreading like a spider's web from one corner of the screen, but it would work. She snatched it and the charger and shoved them into a bag, along with a few clothes she'd grabbed and her and Suraya's passports. She turned to leave the room, then doubled back, retrieving some bottles of water and a box of cereal bars from a cupboard.

She hefted the backpack onto her shoulders then pulled the gun from her belt. She paused before the door. How many times today had her heart raced in fear? She took a deep breath and pushed the door open a crack. Jack had his back to her and was watching out of the window. She advanced towards him, gun drawn.

"The weather's really on the turn out there," said Jack. "So…" He glanced over his shoulder, his breath catching in his throat. "Maddie, what are you doing?"

"Taking control. I don't know who the *hell* you are, so seeing as you need the information I have, it's time to be honest."

Jack nodded slowly. "You're right, I haven't been honest with you, but I'm not the enemy and I do think we can help each other. Now's not the time though. Let's get somewhere safe and then I can answer your questions."

"How do I know I can trust you? I've risked my life for you, but for all I know I'm expendable."

"Please Maddie, I'll explain when—"

The lightbulb flickered, though it wasn't switched on, and Jack felt the skin on the back of his neck prickle. "No, not now," he breathed. He leant forwards as nausea washed over him. The hairs on his arms stood on end.

"What's wrong?" Maddie took a step towards him.

"I'm…urrgh…" Pain seared through his skull.

"Jack! What's going on?"

Jack's legs gave way. Doubled over, he pushed the ball of his hands into his temples, trying to ease the pressure as voices and faces flashed through his mind.

*We just need a bit more time… **Who is that?**… You make it sound so simple… **I recognise him**… Nothing about time is simple… **Get down!**… We can change this!… **NO!***

"Jack? Jack? What's happening?" Maddie crouched beside him and felt his forehead, he was burning up. "I'll get some water."

She ran into the kitchen and filled a glass, turned to leave, and caught a glimpse through the window of the stairwell at the far end of the block. Two figures had just begun to climb it. Both were armed. "Shit."

She ran back to Jack. "We have to go. LEFA's coming."

Jack screwed up his face and sucked in a deep breath, exhaling it for what felt like an age to Maddie, who had opened the door a crack to peer out.

"Jack? We don't have much time."

With effort, Jack pushed himself up off the floor and steadied himself against the shelves.

"Back down the way we came," instructed Maddie, "after that—"

"Vauxhall."

"What?"

"Trust me."

Maddie rolled her eyes and slipped through the door, Jack following, then raced across the walkway to the stairs. She pulled open the door and ran straight into an elderly lady, knocking two shopping bags from her hands which spilled their contents over the dirty concrete.

"Maddie! Didn't your mother teach you not to rush so!" the old lady scolded.

Maddie bent down to pick up her groceries.

"No time," said Jack dragging her away towards the steps.

"I'm so sorry, Mrs Bhaduri," Maddie shouted as Jack pulled her on and down the stairs. They could hear her muttered complaints as they rapidly descended and burst out into the street below, heading for the cover of the railway bridge before pausing.

The pressure was beginning to recede, but Jack still felt off balance.

"What the hell happened to you in there?" Maddie demanded, her face a little frightened.

"It's a…" Jack frowned, then pushed his fingers under

the neck of his shirt and over his shoulder. There it was: another scar. His breath came in short gasps as he tried to block the memories out. They weren't safe yet, they had to keep moving. "It's a long story," he said, looking around to get his bearings. "Come on, this way."

Bewildered, Maddie gave in and followed.

§

It wasn't far to Richborne Terrace, but Jack and Maddie took their time, winding around the smaller streets of Newington and Oval, doubling back on themselves to check that they weren't being followed. They walked in silence, taking cover when the occasional drone passed overhead, and kept their heads down to avoid eye contact with passers-by. A face, casually glancing from a window or door might be innocent enough, but those with something to hide were always fearful of Snags. Snags made their living by selling information, and while their allegiance might officially be to the government, most sold their knowledge to the highest bidder.

Tension and anxiety urged them forwards whilst simultaneously sapping their strength. For Maddie, the morning's events replayed in her mind as they walked, and she longed for a safe house to hide herself in and, for a moment at least, lock the horrors out.

"We're nearly there," said Jack. He glanced back at her, aware of the weapon tucked inside her jacket, every nerve in his body on edge.

Maddie followed him into Palfrey Place – a back alley lined by garages and garden walls, hidden out of sight of the grand Victorian facades. Yet even here, it was clear to Maddie that the people who owned these homes lived in a world far-removed from her own. The streets here were eerily quiet, and Maddie stared at each window, searching for signs of life. She assumed there were still people living here whose jobs required them to stay, such as doctors or teachers, but she knew that those who could afford to live here could also afford to leave.

Maddie quickened her pace to catch up with Jack. "You haven't actually said where we're going."

Jack took a breath. "My grandfather's house."

There was a strain to his voice that Maddie couldn't read. "Oh?" She raised an eyebrow. "Is he still in London?"

Jack didn't answer straight away. He knew that Maddie would picture his grandfather – Robert – as an old man, when in fact, he was just eleven years old at this stage of the war.

Robert's parents, Alice and Peter, had deferred parenthood until late in life, focussing firstly on their careers, and subsequently on the restoration of their house in Richborne Terrace. Robert had arrived as somewhat of an afterthought – something the house required in order to be complete. Nonetheless, as an only child, he was cherished, though some might have called it spoiled.

His parents' advanced age meant that Robert inherited the house young. He moved in with his wife, Sophia, so that their own daughter, Mary, could experience her formative years there like her father before her.

Jack had never been inside the house before, and yet he hated it. It was a typical London Victorian terrace, but rare in that it had never been subdivided into flats. Robert had described it with such pride and reverence that Jack suspected he had more affection for its bricks and mortar than for his own grandchild of flesh and blood. He remembered his grandfather's stories of the war – God knows he'd been told them often enough – and how he had raged against the injustice of leaving the city, his friends, and his beloved house behind to live with his aunt and uncle in the 'arse end of nowhere'.

Jack glanced at Maddie and shook his head. "No, my grandfather left town a while back."

Turning into the terrace, the first thing that struck Maddie was how pretty it was, like something from an historical novel. Then she noticed the broken windows. Her body tensed as she scanned the street and strained to listen for sounds beyond the darkened glass, but none of the damage was new. Looting had been commonplace in the first year of the hostilities and Maddie knew more than one person who traded in stolen goods. She didn't blame them – they'd been living on the breadline even before the outbreak of war – but she wondered if Jack felt the same.

"When were you last here?" she asked.

"Not for some time," Jack replied, stretching the truth.

She looked at him anxiously, but he didn't react when they stopped in front of Number 20, where fragments of glass lay scattered beneath the lowest window. Jack pulled a key from his pocket and climbed the steps to the front door. The idea to bring the key with him had been a last-minute thought, and it had taken some time to find it amongst the mementos of the past that his grandfather had hoarded.

Jack had walked along this road as a small child just once; one of the rare occasions when his mother felt well and had been taken out for the day by her parents. They seemed to think that a trip down memory lane might restore her to herself, and so Jack had been shown the neighbourhood in which his mother had grown up. Like many others, the house had been sold to the government in the wake of the floods, but with his usual mix of sentimentality and bloody-mindedness, Robert had held on to the key.

The sudden wail of a siren and shouting from the direction of Clapham Road hastened their entry to the building. Jack pushed the door open, ploughing aside a pile of dust covered letters. He drew his knife, and Maddie took her gun from her inside pocket.

"Better sweep the building," Jack whispered. "Just in case."

Maddie pointed at the stairs, indicating she would check the upper levels.

Jack nodded in reply and began his sweep of the lower floors. He moved through rooms that he recognised from photographs, though some of their contents were as familiar to him as his grandparents themselves: two vintage armchairs in the living room, their fabric more vibrant than in his own time, a plaster chandelier, and the bronze bust whose cubist design had fascinated him as a young child. Cupboard doors and drawers stood open, their contents tumbled across the floor.

Having checked the ground floor, Jack headed down to the basement which housed a kitchen-diner at the rear and a lounge area at the front. A blind dangled from one corner of the basement window, and fragments of glass were strewn across the sofa. Resting against the wall to the right of the window were the metal bars Jack's great-grandfather had bought just before they left. He hadn't had time to install them – something his wife had never forgiven him for. A bracket on the wall showed where a television had once been, and Jack recalled his grandfather telling him that every smart device in the house had been taken, along with the family's bikes that they'd left inside for safety.

Jack moved into the kitchen where the cupboard doors were all ajar, revealing their bare interiors. A well-stocked pantry would have been a far greater prize than a collection of smart technology. Layers of dust covered everything that Jack passed and he guessed that the house hadn't been touched for quite some time. His body relaxed a little as he headed to the stairs and began to climb.

From above, Maddie screamed.

Jack bolted the steps three at a time. "Maddie? Maddie?"

He found her on the top floor, struggling to open the window. A pigeon flapped around the room, frightened and anxious to be free.

"I'm sorry," Maddie apologised.

Jack helped to push the sash up and the bird made its escape.

Maddie tried to blink away the tears filling her eyes. "It flew out at me… I just, it just made me…" The fear and emotions of the day at last found their way past Maddie's defences, overwhelming her as she tried in vain to keep her composure.

Jack saw that she was trembling, and a pang of guilt twisted in his stomach. She was afraid, he realised. For her sister, for herself. And here he was, using her to his own end.

"I'm sorry, I'm just tired," she said, and sunk onto the edge of the bed.

"It's okay."

"I can't stop shaking." She smiled apologetically, and tears fell, soaking into her top.

Jack stood awkwardly, unsure of whether she wanted privacy or comfort. He joined her, sitting on the bed, and after a moment, tentatively put his arm around her. She buried her face into his shoulder. Jack sat still, holding her as she silently sobbed, feeling the tension in her shoulders gradually ease.

A shard of sunlight burst through the window and Jack watched the particles of dust drifting through it, illuminated one moment, invisible the next. The light, he thought, was like time, which powerfully pushed and flowed ever onwards, and he was just a particle of dust, dancing for the briefest of moments in its glorious warmth before vanishing for good into the dark.

Time passed for once unchecked, and Jack realised that Maddie had fallen asleep on his shoulder. He gently lowered her down and moved to lift her legs onto the bed. The warm afternoon light was soporific and had seemingly hushed the world outside. He watched it pool on the padded seat next to the window, then slipped himself into its path. He would close his eyes and rest, just for a few minutes.

§

2149

Greenwich

Jack pushed open the door and walked a few steps. He paused and looked down at the smooth granite pathway between the cobbles, onto which names of capital cities were inscribed along with their longitude. Running straight down the centre, with Reykjavik and Anchorage on one side, Helsinki, Moscow and Rome on the other, was a band of polished steel. The Prime Meridian. Jack's feet straddled the line, and it struck him as ironic that someone of his kind should be standing across the very line that had helped define linear time and space for hundreds of years. He glanced back at the dome of the observatory and the ancient buildings. What would the men who designed the observatory, the men who once studied here have made of him? A man whose own birth was in defiance of the causal arrow of time?

Jack walked to the railings and leant across them to get a view down the park towards the Queen's House and Royal Naval College. The vast buildings of Canary Wharf dominated the skyline on the other side of the river. If given a cursory glance, the view appeared unchanged in over a hundred years, with the majesty of the neoclassical and baroque buildings contrasting dramatically with the skyscrapers beyond. But as Jack surveyed the scene, tell-tale flickering revealed the presence of holographic hoardings running around the lower perimeter of the park and museums. The projections cut out briefly, exposing the vast and ugly concrete flood defences behind.

Beyond the concrete barriers, the waters of the Thames stretched wide, restoring the Isle of Dogs to the marshy condition it had held millennia ago. Water lapped across the ground floors of Canary Wharf's high-rise buildings. Ducks and seagulls now held residency in place of the businessmen and professional couples who had once lived and worked there. Looking straight ahead, the steel towers that had once held aloft the Millennium Dome were still visible, protruding from the brackish waters. The dome itself had long since decayed and been carried away by the tides.

Jack heard footsteps approaching. He didn't need to look around to know that they were Howard's, they'd spent enough time together in the past year.

"The surge is high today," Jack commented, stuffing his hands deep into his pockets.

Howard joined him, leaning heavily on the railings and taking in the scene. The sun was bright, glinting off the broad expanse of water before them, but a cool wind blew off the river and up the hill.

"What do you think about Eddington's progress?" Howard finally asked, pulling up the collar on his jacket as the wind whipped around them.

"He's not related to the 20th century, Arthur Eddington, is he?" Jack replied curiously.

"You've been brushing up on your astrophysics." Howard laughed with surprise.

"Just trying to get my head around it." Jack shrugged. "But it's a can of worms."

"That's why I leave the difficult stuff to him and Feynman, and no, he's not related that I know of."

The two men turned away from the railings and made their way to the path that led down through the park towards the monorail terminal. Greenwich was the final destination on most tourist routes and in the spring sunshine the park was busy. In the centre of the lawns, a couple of children made the most of the breeze and flew a kite, its colourful body snaking back and forth in the sky.

"The models look promising," said Jack in response to Howard's original question, "but they still require a huge leap of faith."

"We'll get there," said Howard. "We just need a bit more time."

Jack raised his eyebrows and looked at his friend askance. "You make it sound so simple."

"Nothing about time is simple," Howard replied

seriously. "But I do have faith. Your mother had faith too, in our power to change things for the better."

"Did she," said Jack flatly. "I wouldn't know. She never shared her thoughts with me." He sighed and turned his head to watch the children flying the kite. Their mother stood downwind, and he could hear her clapping and cheering the youngsters on. For most people it was such a simple thing – that bond, that love which flowed both ways between mother and child. But something about him had failed to inspire that same sentiment in Mary.

The wind blew stronger. The children laughed and shrieked as the strings tugged at them.

Howard's shoulders drooped and a flicker of guilt ran across his face. He looked up at the expanse of flooded homes and businesses beyond the park. This time they had a real chance to make a difference. "Come on, Jack. With your DNA, our progress has fast-tracked well beyond what we imagined. We can change this, all this!" He waved his hands at the scene before them.

But Jack wasn't listening. The sky was darkening and the children's shrieks turned to screams when the kite pulled the smallest boy off his feet and dragged him up the hill. Jack began to run towards him but stumbled to his knees as pain shot through his head.

"Jack?"

Howard helped him up. He was speaking, but Jack's head was throbbing and he couldn't make out the words. He could see the stricken child and a group of people running to his aid. A figure behind them was moving his way. He wasn't young, and something about his long coat looked familiar. He was wearing a bowtie –

"Aargh," Jack bent forwards, clutching his head. The air was too thick; he couldn't breathe.

The sky flashed white with lightning, its deafening crack sending everyone's hands to their ears. People began to run downhill, children screamed. The pain was blinding, but Jack forced his eyes open, trying to spot the figure again. As if from under water he heard Howard's voice.

"This way, Jack, come on!"

He felt himself being pulled up towards the observatory.

Another crack of lightning split the air.

…

Silence.

…

"The models look promising," said Jack, "but they still require a huge leap of…" He paused and frowned. He glanced back towards the observatory, then down the path that led through the park.

Howard waited. "Of?" he prompted.

"…faith." Jack stopped walking. His body felt suddenly heavy and his head was swimming. "Did I already say that?" he asked.

"Are you alright, Jack?" Howard stepped toward him.

"I…yes, sorry, must be all those statistics, I wasn't…" Jack stopped again as two children flying a kite over the lawns caught his eye. Beyond them a figure was approaching. He looked familiar. "Who is that?" he asked.

Howard looked in the direction Jack was pointing. He took a few steps forwards, but a group of tourists heading up to the observatory blocked their view.

"I recognise him," said Jack. "From Westminster?"

From within the throng of tourists Jack caught a flash of metal.

"Get down!" yelled Howard.

Bang.

The bullet nicked Howard's arm and hit Jack in the shoulder.

"Jack!"

Jack fell forwards. Tourists screamed, some running towards the Observatory, others back down towards the monorail. Howard crouched in front of Jack, his face pale with concern. Blood soaked through Howard's shirt sleeve but he hardly seemed to notice.

Jack craned around, trying to spot the figure in the long coat, but he was gone. "Shit. This hurts." His shoulder was on fire, and he gritted his teeth as Howard balled his jacket and pushed it against the wound, trying to stem the flow of blood.

Shouts sounded as staff from the observatory ran down towards them.

"Help's coming." Howard took hold of Jack's hands as they began to shake.

Jack tried to speak but he couldn't form the words.

"Stay with me, Jack. Don't go to sleep. Jack? Stay awake!"

§

14th August 2073

Richborne Terrace

"Jack? Wake up. Jack?"

Jack awoke with a gasp that made Maddie flinch. Her hand was on his shoulder. She'd been shaking him, telling him not to go to sleep, telling him to stay awake. No, he thought, that wasn't Maddie. His skin prickled with perspiration and he looked around wildly, trying to make sense of the jumble of memories.

Jack made to stand up, but Maddie pushed him firmly back into the seat.

"It's okay, you're safe. Just take a minute." She stood back, giving him space, and watched as he leant forwards and dug the heels of his hands into his temples. His breathing, fast and shallow, gradually slowed and deepened. "Are you alright?" she asked after a time. "Were you dreaming?"

Jack looked up at her. It struck him that her concern was genuine, her dark eyes sympathetic. It would be so easy to confide in her, but it wouldn't be a good idea. "Yeah, I'm sorry, I didn't mean to startle you." He stood. "I'm fine. Excuse me a minute."

Jack knew there was a bathroom on the top floor and found it at the head of the staircase. How long had he been asleep? Too long, given that the light outside was dimming. Jack moved to the basin, splashed his face with cold water and stood a while in the half-light, looking at his reflection in the mirror. He removed his jacket and pulled off his shirt and leaned in to look at his shoulder. The scar had faded a little in the year and a half since the shooting, and yet he could also remember that same year in which his shoulder was blemish-free.

He ran his finger along the scar's rough edges, recalling the pain. It was easy to heal scar tissue in the 22nd century, leaving damaged skin smooth and unblemished as though any number of injuries had never occurred. Jack had chosen to retain his scars; they helped him to distinguish each memory from the increasing number of timelines running parallel in his life.

This was the second attack that had been made on him in the past few years and within the last twenty-four hours, and Jack wondered how many more he might have to face. Howard had been injured this time too, although Jack tried to reassure himself that, no matter what, Howard would be safe within Gaia.

This second attack in Greenwich had put them both on guard; coincidence had been ruled out. He attempted to construct an image of the man in the long coat and bowtie. Few people wore such an antiquated garment, and his presence at both attacks couldn't be a coincidence, and yet the man hadn't been close enough in Parliament Square to have been his assailant. Moreover, the man's advanced age didn't exactly fit the assassin brief. But something about him was familiar beyond those two occasions. Jack stood, staring at his own reflection, willing himself to remember the one thing he couldn't.

Maddie passed the bathroom as she headed for the stairs. Jack hadn't closed the door properly and through the crack, Maddie saw him run his fingertips lightly over his bare shoulder. She caught the strained look on his face, as though he was trying to remember something, and moved closer to watch.

Her heart beat a little faster as she spied, conscious of her intrusion, but he was hiding something, and if they were going to work together, she needed to know the truth. After a while his stillness made Maddie self-conscious and she edged back, making the floorboards creak. She hurried down the stairs, hoping that he hadn't known he was being watched.

Jack heard Maddie's footsteps recede. His mind came back to the present and he looked around the bathroom. He pulled off the rest of his clothes and stepped into the shower which, whilst not hot, at least worked. The cold water pummelled his flesh, removing the sweat and grime of the past day. The wound on his leg had healed well and the scar tissue felt tender only under direct pressure. Jack touched each scar in turn, thinking how they were forming a map across his body, of his memories and misadventures.

Jack dried himself and pulled the jeans back on, then decided to investigate the contents of his great grandfather's wardrobe. Peter's clothes weren't so different to his own, save the absence of reactive fabric and signs of wear and repair. Jack pulled on a plain t-shirt and sweater and smiled to himself, thinking that if Peter had been forced to wear *his* great-grandfather's clothes, it would have been a different story.

Maddie moved around the living room touching the many artworks and sculptures, recognising one or two of the names inscribed within the large gilt frames. She wondered how much money the paintings were worth, undoubtedly far more than the missing holo and smart tech that had been looted. But even if the thieves had known their value, they wouldn't know who to sell them to.

She stopped to look at some family photographs, expecting to see some of Jack. There was a wedding photograph of a couple who looked to be in their early forties, and another of the same couple holding a baby in a park, with the distinctive chimneys of Battersea Power Station visible in the background.

There were further pictures of the same child, who in the most recent one was maybe ten or eleven years old. She picked it up and examined the face. It wasn't Jack, although there was a slight resemblance in the eyes. She looked about the room but there were no other photographs, not even one of Jack. Who were the couple in the photograph? Did Jack have a sister and a nephew?

The contents of a chest of drawers lay strewn across the floor and Maddie crouched down and picked through a collection of letters addressed to Peter and Alice Elliot. She lifted out a school report, dated 2069, for one Robert Elliot, and glanced back up at the child in the photograph.

She startled guiltily when Jack appeared at the doorway and dropped the document back on top of the pile.

Jack didn't comment. He leaned on the doorframe and pushed his damp hair from his eyes, looking about the room, aware of Maddie following his gaze. She was waiting, he knew, for an explanation, but it was better to see what she'd discovered at the Hub before deciding how much to reveal.

He opened his mouth to speak, drawing in breath, and noted the hint of apprehension that flashed across her face. He closed it again and smiled. "I'm starving," he declared. "You?"

She laughed in surprise and shook her head. "Yes, famished, but there's nothing here. I do have a couple of energy bars though." She moved towards the rucksack that she'd dropped on the sofa.

"I think we need a bit more than that," said Jack, "and luckily my family were hoarders."

Intrigued, Maddie followed him downstairs and into the basement.

Jack had heard, many times, the story of his grandfather's return to London in 2074. Robert had been incensed by the loss of his bike, and Alice disturbed by the thought of strangers exploring their home and rifling through their things. She had berated her husband for his failure to secure the property, despite his insistence that desperate people would always have found a way in. His saving grace, according to Robert, had been the cupboards discreetly hidden beneath the staircase, held shut with magnetic catches embedded in the wood. Discovering that their wine collection was intact did wonders to calm Alice's nerves.

Remembering the story, Jack ran his fingers along the woodwork below the staircase, inspecting the surface closely, before pushing the top corner of a panel halfway along. It popped open.

"Oh!" exclaimed Maddie. She peered inside. "I wasn't expecting that."

Jack pulled the door wide, revealing a dozen shelves

stacked high with tins and dried goods and began to study their labels. "Lucky that whoever cleared out the kitchen didn't do a more thorough search," he remarked. "Italian?" He held up some pasta and tinned tomatoes.

"Sure," replied Maddie, who goggled at the rows of supplies, and wondered just how much it would be worth now that food in the capital was being rationed.

Jack handed her some dried spaghetti, olive oil and tinned anchovies. He dug a little deeper into the back of the recess and emerged with a bottle of wine. Jack read the label, "2068, Devonshire Merlot."

Maddie raised her eyebrows, uncertain whether to confess that she'd never tasted wine. Climate change had destroyed most of the New World wineries as well as vast tracts of arable land. The demand for wine meant that prospective vineyards in northern Europe always had financial backing but, politically, they could hardly compete with the need to feed and house the swollen population. The small amount of British Merlot, Cabinet Sauvignon and Pinot Noir that was produced fetched high prices, although it was nothing compared to what the elite were willing to pay for the sparkling wines produced in Scotland.

"Don't worry, it wouldn't be a good idea to drink," said Jack, misinterpreting the look on Maddie's face. "We both need clear heads in case… well, to work through the information you gleaned from the Hub." He sighed wistfully. "Although maybe just a sip? And some for the cooking."

"What? That must be worth at least seventy pounds!"

Jack tilted his head to one side, considering how much it would offend his grandfather. "Then it'll make a great sauce."

Jack moved back into the kitchen and put the ingredients down on the counter.

"Is the electric still connected?" asked Maddie, running a finger through the dust on the hob.

"Let's find out." Jack turned the dial, but nothing happened. He tried a couple of other switches and mumbled something about the fuse box as he dashed back up to the entrance hall. Maddie heard rummaging from above, then the overhead lights and oven clicked on.

Jack ran back down and flicked off the lights. "Not a good idea to draw attention to the building," he explained. "Especially with such ready access," he added, nodding in the direction of the broken window.

Maddie went to look at the damage. "We could put up the bars, but it will make a lot of noise. I'll look for something else to cover it."

She headed up to the ground floor while Jack looked around for pans and filled one with water to boil.

"Give me a hand with this," Maddie called.

Between them, they carried down an enormous oil painting on board, lifted it over the sofa and wedged it between the window and the back of the radiator. Maddie stood back to consider whether its position needed adjusting.

Jack laughed.

"What?" asked Maddie.

He glanced at her open expression. She might have guessed the value of some the artworks, but he could forgive anyone for not realising the value of this piece. "Nothing," he said. "I never liked that one anyway."

Maddie glanced back at the painting as she followed Jack into the kitchen, then realised how dark it was getting. "We're going to need a bit of light. Are there any candles?"

Jack pulled the lid off the pan and lowered a handful of pasta into the bubbling liquid. "I don't know, check the drawers, or maybe in the cupboards upstairs?"

Maddie searched the kitchen and dining room, before finding a couple of holo-candles in one of the bedrooms. She placed them on the kitchen island and switched them on, effusing the room in their illusory warm glow.

She sat for a moment, watching Jack on the other side of the island while he dropped anchovies into hot oil. They sizzled and filled the room with their savoury scent and her stomach rumbled – a reminder that she hadn't eaten anything for the last twenty-four hours. Jack found a bottle opener and removed the wine cork in a single confident movement, proof, again, that his background was very different to her own.

Maddie considered how the war affected everyone, just not in the same way. It made her think of a poem that had been written long ago, in the Pandemic of 2020, in which the author questioned the assumption that everyone's experience was alike – that while everyone was faced by the same storm, not everyone's vessel was seaworthy.

The wine hissed as it hit the hot pan, followed by the tinned tomatoes and herbs. Jack poured a splash into two tumblers and handed one to her. She took it and swirled the dark liquid around the base, smelling its unusual aroma. Something about it reminded her of the blackberries that she and Suraya used to gather around the train tracks as children. She took a tiny sip and was surprised that the flavour was nothing like she'd expected, sharp, yet soft at the same time, and not entirely pleasant.

She frowned slightly and looked up to discover that Jack was watching her. Embarrassed, she put the glass down and pulled over her bag, rummaging around to find the phone and charger she'd taken from her flat, which she plugged into a socket in the centre of the island. She pulled the SIM card Max had retrieved for her from her back pocket, ready to insert it into the casing.

"I took photos of the documents that I thought might help, but this is all I have left of that phone." She placed the SIM card on the work surface. "My old one's seen better days"—she ran a finger across the cracked screen—"but once it's charged it'll work. Unless you've got something better?"

Jack picked up the SIM card and turned it over. His iHolo had an adapter that would have taken it, but first he'd need to repair the water damage. Everything else of use was at the storage unit in Spitalfields. "I lost my phone in the explosion," he replied, "but your old one will do for now."

He handed the card back to Maddie and returned to the hob. "I think this is ready," he said, draining the pasta and tossing it in the sauce. He scooped it into bowls and set them down on the counter, seating himself opposite Maddie.

Maddie took in the scene – the bowls of steaming food, the candles, the wine – and couldn't help but laugh to herself. It was four years since she'd last had a date. This meal with a man she barely knew, who this time yesterday was nearly dead, with whom she'd just assaulted her superior officer, and stolen classified information, was the closest thing in a long time. Surreal didn't come close to describing it.

Jack sat, his fork poised over the bowl of food, and waited for Maddie to take the first bite. She looked about her then smiled, shaking her head very slightly.

"What is it?" he asked.

"It's…" She raised her eyebrows and looked up at him. "Nothing." She picked up her fork and wound the spaghetti around it messily, leaning over her bowl to capture it in her mouth before the strands unravelled. "Oh wow. Did you really make this with just those tins?"

Jack smiled and took a mouthful. It wasn't bad. "And the wine," he added.

She laughed.

They sat in silence for a few minutes, savouring the food and what both knew would be the calm before the storm. As she ate, Maddie stole glances at Jack. His hair had dried to a sandy brown, falling over his forehead when he leant towards his bowl. When he smiled it transformed his face and eyes, their closed and guarded look momentarily rendered warm and open. Maddie thought of her stolen glimpse of him upstairs earlier, his toned chest and arms, and hid a slight blush as she busied herself trying to capture the final strands of pasta. If it had been a date, she wouldn't have minded. She glanced at him wistfully, before the sensation was washed away by her shame for having, in that moment, forgotten the danger that Suraya was in. She cleared her throat and pushed back the empty bowl. "Thank you, that was the best thing I've eaten in ages."

Jack cleared the dishes into the sink and filled water glasses. "You're welcome," he replied, sitting back down opposite her. He drank the last drop of wine from the splash he'd allowed earlier, resisting the temptation to pour more from the open bottle, and examined the glass. The crystal tumblers were familiar and Jack thought he could remember them from his childhood, reserved for special occasions and visiting guests. He felt the weight of it in his hand then set it down, absently running his thumb over the diamond pattern cut into the side whilst watching Maddie. Jack sensed in them both an awareness that this moment offered a refuge, a brief respite that was precious, and neither of them wanted to be the first to disturb it. The candlelight played across her skin, casting shadows from her long lashes that danced about her eyes.

Maddie moved her finger back and forth through the holographic flame, disrupting the illusion as she did so. Holographic technology had taken a leap about a decade ago, with holo-phones and holo-photos starting to become popular. It had been many years since the polluting effects of indoor fires and wood burners had been fully recognised, and holo-fires and candles were commonplace. She wondered how far the technology would develop, whether in the future people would have holo-pets and plants. All the companionship and aesthetic benefits, with none of the tiresome care bills and maintenance.

"Did your grandfather have much holo-tech?" she asked, wondering if there had been holo-photos of Jack.

"Some. Probably stolen."

Maddie reached for her bag. "The only holos I've got are mine and Suraya's passports." She pulled the documents out and opened her sisters. "Here, just in case you do recognise her." She handed it to Jack and watched him closely.

He tilted the passport from side to side, matching the face to the name that had set the day's events in motion.

The holographic rendering showed a young woman who was strikingly beautiful, though heavily made-up in a way that simultaneously disguised and betrayed her youth. He glanced up at Maddie, then back at the holo, thinking that Maddie took after her mother, while her sister had more of their father's look.

Maddie shifted awkwardly on her stool and, as she had done earlier that day, tugged at her curls of dark hair so that they fell across the corner of her left eye and cheek. "Are you sure you've never seen her?"

Jack shook his head and handed the passport back to her.

She leant forwards on her elbows and fixed him with a look. "I know you're not part of LEFA," she stated, bringing their repose to an end.

"No," he admitted.

"But not from the government or a Republican." It was a statement to be confirmed rather than a question.

"No."

"Then who do you work for?"

"A covert group of disaffected politicians and scientists whose aims sit alongside those of LEFA. We're not…currently based in London, but we have ties to Earth Rebellion who keep us informed."

"And this group is called?"

"Better that I don't say."

Maddie raised an eyebrow sceptically, then frowned. "What happened to you earlier, at my flat?"

Jack breathed in and exhaled slowly, delaying his response. He considered telling her the truth but doubted that she'd believe him. He could continue to lie, but with each lie told the traps and pitfalls increased, and besides, for some reason he couldn't explain he was reluctant to lie to her. A selective version of the truth seemed like the best option.

"I told you that the Republic is looking for Dr Kingsley?"

Maddie nodded.

"They need him to finish work on weapons he was

developing for DARPA – long-range sonic missiles, atomic particle destabilisers – but I know that Kingsley's developing something far more dangerous. It's my job to ensure that this technology doesn't fall into the wrong hands."

"You've already told me that," she replied bluntly. "So, what's he working on? What's the connection to that…that seizure or whatever it was you had?"

"Well," Jack ran his fingertip around the rim of the glass. "Kingsley's experimental work can have some side effects. The seizures are the result of being exposed to it."

"So, you've seen his work? You know where it is?"

"My organisation is in possession of some of his tech," Jack agreed, "but we need to secure Dr Kingsley himself."

"So, what is this technology? Why is it so dangerous?"

Jack leant back and glanced out of the window to where the sky had darkened to a rich Prussian blue. From here the night looked enticing, the sky vast and pure, but he knew that changes to Earth's timeline had already increased the atmosphere's toxicity fivefold.

"Jack?"

He returned his attention to Maddie who was waiting expectantly. In her place, he'd have persisted too. "Whoever possesses his technology will have the power to change the course of events to suit their own whims and needs. In the hands of the Republic or the current government that would be disastrous."

"What does that *mean*, Jack? For god's sake," Maddie entreated. "I'm not a child! Just tell me what this thing is."

Jack considered the woman sitting in front of him, sitting tensely with a mix of frustration and apprehension. He looked again at the glass tumbler in his hand, recalling that there was one with a chip in the rim. At what point in time had the damage occurred? He took a deep breath and puffed out his cheeks, coming to a decision. "Alright," he leant towards her, his face serious. "Dr Kingsley is currently developing technology that will allow people to travel through time."

Maddie made no response. She waited for Jack to crack a smile, but he didn't, and as the silence lengthened her eyes widened. "You're serious?" she asked incredulously.

Jack nodded, but Maddie just raised her eyebrows, still waiting for the punchline. Jack ran his hands through his hair and down his neck, massaging either side of his spine where he held his tension. His fingers traced across his skin until they caught the edge of the gun-shot scar, just beneath his collar, and he thought of the pain that time travel had caused him both physically and emotionally. "To be fair," Jack sighed, "I'm not sure I'd believe me either. "

"Right," Maddie blinked. "So, how did your organisation find out about this time machine or whatever it is?"

"At this moment in history, nobody knows about it besides Kingsley himself. We know, from historical records, that he will be captured by the Republic about four or five days from now. The Republic will gain the ability to travel through time, alter the outcome of legislative votes here, in Europe and in the Americas, consolidating their wealth and power over the rest of the world whilst simultaneously accelerating the environmental destruction that will ultimately lead to mankind's demise."

Maddie stared at him dumbfounded.

"Well." Jack shrugged. "That's it in a nutshell."

Maddie stood and took a step backwards, raising her hands as it to ward off the lunatic before her. "I don't know what to say. I think that blast damaged your head."

Jack continued. "Time travel causes extreme stress on the brain, particularly in the temporal lobes. Exposure to multiple time continuums is like, well, a bit like travel sickness, where there's a conflict between the signals from your eyes and ears, only with time travel the conflict between your senses and the parts of your brain that process memory is like a full-scale battle. The human brain just isn't designed to process more than one version of reality at a time."

"And so, when you say you've been *exposed* to it…"

"The 'seizure' as you called it was my body responding to changes being made to my own past."

Maddie leant on the counter, feeling as though she was in some crazy dream. "And your past is?"

"Your future." Jack's eyes met Maddie's. "I was born on October 12th, 2120."

Maddie took a deep breath and pushed herself back from the counter. "Okay," she breathed. "You're totally crazy!" She picked up her rucksack and moved to the foot of the stairs, then remembered her phone and the SIM card. She spun back around as Jack picked them up. "Give them to me."

Jack held them out, and she took a few steps towards him, snatching them from his hand.

"I know it's a lot to take in," he reasoned. "But think about it – the explosion which decimated the embankment? That was caused by my time capsule self-destructing. The serum I injected – you said you'd never seen anything like it. That's because nothing that powerful exists yet. And this place." He gestured to the room around him. "It *is* my grandfather's house, but he's just a child right now." He glanced towards the front window. "And in the future, he really loved that painting that we just shoved down the back of a radiator."

Maddie shook her head and began climbing the steps towards the entrance hall.

"Whether or not you believe me," Jack called after her, "we can still help each other."

She kept climbing.

"I can help you find Suraya."

Maddie paused mid-step but didn't look round.

Jack stood up and moved closer to see her, frozen with indecision, halfway to the front door.

"After the war, the coalition Parliament will investigate the links between the Republican Supremacy Guard and your current government. The Republic did a fair job of covering its tracks, but I know the location of their bases, the names of their agents and passcodes. My primary mission is finding Dr Kingsley, but if Suraya's mixed up in this, then you stand a better chance of finding her with me than without me."

Maddie turned and descended a few steps.

"If I can decipher the documents on your phone," Jack continued, "you'll have a lead on Suraya's location, and hopefully I'll have a lead on Kingsley. If, after that, you chose to proceed alone then that's fine. After all, I have a job to do."

Maddie took another step down. "How do I know you're not just crazy and making this stuff up?" she demanded.

"What, futuristic medicine and cataclysmic explosions?"

Maddie scowled with contempt.

"Not helpful?" Jack asked wryly. He shrugged. "I gave you information on Kingsley that LEFA couldn't possibly have known, and I suspect that it was corroborated by what you discovered at the Hub."

Maddie thought back to her conversations with Sarah, the flashes of information she'd seen as she'd photographed the papers. She shook her head. "Maybe. But that hardly proves that you're a time traveller who's come here to fix the planet?"

Jack relaxed a little and leant back on the counter. "It doesn't matter whether you believe me or not, as long as you get Suraya back and I find Dr Kingsley."

Maddie looked up at the ceiling. She'd thought the day couldn't get any more surreal and now she was considering helping this nutcase. She told herself that she was doing it for Suraya, and that she could lose him as soon as she knew where to look. She took a deep breath and descended the remaining steps to stand in front of Jack. She fixed him with a look that he was beginning to recognise. "If this is a trick…if you cross me, then I will kill you."

Jack nodded his assent and held out his hand.

She shook it.

"We'd better look at those documents then."

Maddie returned to her seat, opened up the casing of the phone, and inserted the SIM card. She stiffened slightly as Jack took the seat next to her.

He pulled his chair back a fraction. "Sorry, it's not the biggest screen."

Maddie glanced down at the phone in her hand. He was right, it wouldn't be easy for them to look at it at together. "Here," she said, handing it to him, and standing up. "I'll look for something to write on. We should make a list of anything important, plus there were a few things I didn't get to photograph."

While Maddie searched the room for paper and pen, Jack began to work his way through the images. There were reconnaissance photos which confirmed what he already knew about the location of the Republican bases, although they afforded more detail about their security than he'd had access to in the future.

He zoomed in on a shot of several men standing together on a pavement. Whilst blurred, he recognised one of them as Tobias Keller, a Republican agent who'd been convicted after the war for the torture of volunteers from LEFA's East Hub. He didn't recognise the man standing next to him and the third figure had his back to the camera, although there was something familiar about the way he was standing that Jack couldn't put his finger on.

Maddie sat back down with some sheets of paper and a pen. She looked into space for a moment, then began writing a list of names.

Distracted momentarily from the photographs, Jack watched with fascination as the pen's nib wound back and forth, the list of names emerging effortlessly in Maddie's cursive script. Her writing was beautiful and he realised he was surprised. The plague of digital media had done much to erode the inherent art of handwriting, and few people in the 22nd century took time to hone this traditional skill. Until now, the only other person he knew who took such care writing had been his mother. She'd grown up with the privilege of an expensive education and ample leisure time, free from the burdens of financial worry. Life circumstances, judging from the flat he'd visited earlier, that were far removed from Maddie's own.

Maddie glanced up at him. "What is it?" she asked. "Do the names mean anything to you?"

"Er." He blinked. "Sorry, let me have a look."

She held the list out to him. "Oh," she said, pulling it back, "and I think it's somehow connected to this bastard." She laid the sheet down and at the top wrote a name, underlining it twice.

Jack's stomach lurched. *Kayson Hart.* Time slowed as he stared at the two words, underlined. His father.

Maddie was saying something. "…Jack? Are you okay?"

Jack stood up suddenly, knocking Maddie's wine glass from the counter with his elbow. He lurched sideways to catch it but clipped it against the edge of the counter. The tumbler rang musically as a fragment of the crystal split away from the rim. Jack's hands, which were covered in Maddie's undrunk wine, trembled as he stared at the damage. He told himself that it was just a coincidence, that they were probably all chipped in sixty years from now…

"Jack?"

"Sorry, I'm being clumsy."

"But are you… was that another seizure?"

Jack moved to the sink, his back to Maddie, composing himself as he washed the red wine from his hands. "No, just one of the names is, well, I'd rather it wasn't there."

"Why? Which one?" asked Maddie anxiously.

Jack returned to her side and glanced down the list of names. "This guy, Tobias Keller" —he pointed— "was responsible for the attack on the East Hub in 2072. Not a nice character."

It wasn't a convincing explanation for Jack's reaction, but Maddie was too preoccupied with her fears for Suraya to query it, her mind filling with rumours about the torture that the captured volunteers had suffered.

Jack looked again at the top of the page where his father's name appeared all the more obscene for being written so beautifully. He realised then, that Kayson was the third figure in the photograph, the one with his back to the camera. He should have been in Brussels, so what was he doing here? And what was his involvement with the Republic?

Maddie took a shuddering breath. "Do you think Suraya's being tortured?" she asked, eyes wide.

Jack shook his head, wishing he was able to say 'no'. "I don't know. She's probably fine, just staying low to maintain her cover."

"Hart's a scumbag, but if she's with him then maybe no one will hurt her? After all, Hart has his political career to think about. He can't afford another scandal, right?"

"Maybe," Jack replied without conviction. "What do you know about Kayson Hart?"

"Not a huge amount. I mean, his politics are right-wing, but he's always been overtly pro-Europe, so I don't understand what he's doing with the RSG. Max told me that he's been in London for the last six weeks. It was Suraya's mission to find out what he was up to." She forcefully underlined the name for a third time, as though she could protect Suraya from him with a barrier of ink.

Jack had a bad feeling that he knew the answer to his own question but asked anyway. "Why your sister? Wouldn't it have made sense to have sent an agent with more experience?"

Maddie fiddled with her fingernails; her eyes fixed on the work surface. "You must have heard of his reputation. Although maybe history's been forgiving?"

An image of his mother flashed through Jack's mind: she was dancing with friends at a party, her expression joyful, her smile dazzling. The photograph must have been taken some time around her graduation from university when her life had still been full of possibilities. He'd never really thought about it before but realised now how beautiful she'd been. Her fateful mission had taken place less than a year later. Why had *she* been chosen for that mission? No; Kayson Hart's reputation had not been forgotten.

Jack's chest tightened and he closed his eyes, feeling

sick at the thought that history was being repeated. "Did Suraya know why she'd been selected?" he asked quietly.

Maddie bit her lip to stop it from trembling and shrugged. She glanced up at Jack and saw the exhaustion and strain in his face. For a moment their eyes met, his grey like storm clouds, their surface glossy.

Jack blinked a few times then picked up the sheet of names and began to pace back and forth across the room, reading aloud to himself. "Were these names all listed together?" he asked, "because there's quite a mix here."

"Hang on," Maddie reached for the paper, circled three groups of names, and handed it back. "Each group was on a separate page."

Jack studied each group. On the first list, Adam Fairfax, Tobias Keller, June Simpson and Rudy Cox were all known agents for the Republic. Those on the second list were all members of the Government Enforcement Agency, while those on the third list, including Dr Kingsley, had no connection to one another that Jack could make out.

"Was Hart's name on any of these lists?" he asked.

"No, I only know about him because Max told me. But this name was circled and had a big question mark next to it if that means anything to you?" She pointed at Aubrey Martin, on the list of government agents.

Jack narrowed his eyes in thought. In Jack's own time, Candice Martin was a Member of Parliament for the British Patriotic Party. She had led a back-benchers revolt against the EU, which had gained some traction amongst voters whose traditional allegiance had been on the right. Martin had eventually been charged with inciting violence and was forced to resign in 2147 after a group of her followers stormed the parliament buildings in Manchester, injuring dozens of people. However, Candice had remained a powerful voice for the British far right. Her father, Benedict Martin, had briefly served in parliament some decades earlier, and Jack was fairly sure that he was the son of Aubrey Martin, whose own role supporting the government of 2069-2074 had never been disclosed.

Jack glanced at Maddie. "I think that Aubrey Martin's legacy will be his son and granddaughter, both of whom work hard to push their right-wing agenda in the next century. I'm not aware of any connection to Kingsley or the Republic, but a connection to Hart is quite likely; they share much the same ideology."

"So, you're saying that this supremacist crap doesn't end with the war?" Maddie's nostrils flared. "Does the far right still control the country when you're from?" She thought of the slurs and abuse that she and Suraya had suffered, ridiculous given that they were British and born in London, and wondered if they were fighting and risking their lives for nothing.

"No, that's not what I meant," said Jack, sitting back down so that his eyes were level with hers. "In my own time, Europe and Britain have come together again, and whilst not free from the right-wing groups who currently hold power, the block more or less functions within the liberal ideals that will, ultimately, win this war."

Maddie clenched her jaw and released the tension with a sigh. "I'd really love to believe you, but I'm still not entirely convinced that you're sane."

Jack inclined his head, the left side of his mouth raised in a slight smile.

"So, what exactly leads Britain to re-join the EU, if that's what you mean?" Maddie asked.

"A common threat."

"The Republic?"

He nodded. "The ability to change time proves to be a very powerful bargaining chip, and quite a force of unification for those who're threatened."

"So, in the future, only the Republic can time travel?"

"No, Europe eventually develops its own programme, but it's way behind. The Republic has the advantage and given the affiliation between politics and fossil fuel, it also has the incentive to use time-technology for personal benefit, rather than the greater good. The acceleration of climate collapse is catastrophic."

"Well." Maddie shook her head. "I can't believe I'm

asking these questions… but can't Europe just go back and undo what the Republic's done?"

"Not without the risk of retaliation from the other side. It's a stalemate, a bit like the Cold War."

Maddie raised her eyebrows and cast Jack with a doubtful look. It all sounded like something from a bad sci-fi film. She thought back on pop-culture's take on the subject. "Isn't one of the premises of time travel, the fact that once a change has occurred nobody knows any different? You said that the Republic has manipulated the outcome of political legislation, but how do you know? How would anyone know?"

"They certainly didn't expect anybody to realise," Jack replied. "And it was quite a surprise to Republican leaders to learn just *how* much they'd tampered with time, just how thoroughly their good fortune was of their own making."

Maddie shot Jack a look of confused irritation.

Jack's gaze fell to the work surface where the fragment of the crystal tumbler caught his eye. He fiddled with it, moving it backwards and forwards with his thumb as he spoke. "One of the unanticipated consequences of time travel was the creation of a new kind of people – people whose parents come from different timelines. Someone might, for instance, have a mother born in the 20th century and a father who came from the 22nd, or a mother from the 22nd century who had a fling whilst on holiday in the early 21st. Officially, the children are known as Persons of Mixed Era Origin, though everyone calls them Cronods. A genetic abnormality in the way their brains process and store memory means that they can simultaneously remember more than one timeline."

"What?" Maddie's brow furrowed. "So, you're saying these people revealed what the Republic had done?"

"Those living through those changes, yes. And there are no doubt Cronods born prior to the 22nd century who have no idea what they are. Growing up before time-travel's invention means they'll continually struggle to explain conflicting memories, what we call polymorphic memories. No one will understand what's happening to them – they'll be dismissed as crazy."

Jack pushed down on the piece of glass, focussing on the sensation of its sharp edge pushing into his skin, and waited for the next question. But Maddie didn't seem to make the connection. He risked a sideways glance at her. She was staring at him, her expression frozen almost comically, with a look of disbelief, and Jack wondered why he couldn't have just come up with a credible cover story.

"Anyway." He cleared his throat. "Let's see what clues the rest of the documents on the phone give us."

§

15th August 2073
22 Bishopsgate

This wasn't the first time that Suraya had been in a scrape. Not the first night she'd spent in a cell. Though now, unlike then, her fear had an edge. This time, she had something to hide.

Her last boyfriend had made money on the black market selling stolen goods. He always needed a look-out, and she had dodged the police a few times as a result. Suraya smiled, recalling that Maddie couldn't stand him, but she couldn't help herself; she thrived on his attention, maybe even the danger. It beat sitting around, doing nothing, while your life just ebbed away.

Then Suraya had been arrested. It was the night before her seventeenth birthday and she'd decided to go clubbing, though the nightclub had no licence. Maddie had tried to stop her, but she'd been determined to have fun no matter the risk. Their argument had carried through the flat's thin walls and out on to the walkway.

"You're not my mum!" Suraya had shouted, knowing, even as the words were forming, just had badly they would sting. She'd sulked in her bedroom then snuck out while Maddie took a shower, confident that she knew how to slip the police.

But drones were another matter.

From inside her cell, Suraya had listened to the sound of other detainees come and go. Angry shouts and frightened cries, rowdy clashes followed by disconcerting silence. She'd hatched a plan, which involved flirting with the duty officer, and prayed that Maddie would hurry up.

And Maddie came to her rescue, as she always did. As she had when Suraya was caught smoking a vape at school. As she had the time Suraya hitched a lift to Wimbledon Common and got stranded. As she had when Suraya was caught trying to sell contraband holo-tech.

Suraya's freedom had required a bribe, costing Maddie

the last of her savings. And yet Suraya had never thanked her. To this day, she'd never once said sorry. She wasn't even sure why. Had she resented Maddie being right? Apologising meant admitting she'd been wrong, and the thought of that grated on her. But the truth was that if Suraya had done as Maddie asked, if she had been more like Maddie, she wouldn't have been in trouble.

But they couldn't both be like Maddie, could they? Maddie's role had been given to her by their parents. Suraya didn't have a role. But even as she envied Maddie's sense of purpose – their parents' final, parting gift – she knew that Maddie hadn't chosen it. It had been thrust upon her, and Suraya had done her best to make it difficult.

Suraya's chest tightened and she sighed into the darkness. This time, Maddie wasn't there to help, she didn't even know where Suraya was. But if she made it out, she vowed she would make things right. It was never too late to apologise... so people said.

Footsteps echoed outside. Suraya straightened, her muscles taut, her eyes wide in the gloom.

The door swung open, triggering the automatic overhead lights. Suraya winced and shielded her face from the worst of the glare. Head down, she watched the pairs of feet file into the room; two in well-worn boots, a third in polished black shoes. From the corner of her eye, she could see the open doorway, but even if she could reach it, where would she go? She had no idea where she was.

"Ah, there she is," crooned a smooth, low voice.

"Kayson!" Suraya sat forwards, her eyes at once wide, a smile of relief twitching the corners of her mouth.

"You have been causing me some concern, Suraya. I had to forego my Old-Fashioned tonight; Gemma doesn't make it quite like you do."

"I'm so sorry," Suraya gushed, looking up at Hart from beneath her long lashes and moving to her feet. "There's been some sort of misunderstanding, I really don't know..." she faltered as Tobias Keller entered the room and leant back casually against the wall, fixing her with a deeply unpleasant look that was half smile, half sneer. "I...don't know why I'm here."

"You don't?"

"No." Suraya risked a step towards Hart and reached out a slender hand to tentatively touch his lapel.

Hart looked down at her outstretched fingers and took a small step backwards. "Then we have a problem, don't we."

"What do you mean? If there's something I've done to offend you or anyone else for that—"

"We have a problem," interrupted Hart, "because my colleague, Mr Keller, tells me that you in fact work for the resistance group, LEFA."

Suraya's mouth formed several words without sound, and her hands began to tremble. "What?" she managed at last, glancing at Tobias who grinned broadly, filling his wide mouth with a row of crooked teeth.

"So perhaps we'd better have the truth? What have LEFA sent you to find out?"

"They haven't...I'm not part of LEFA."

Hart's face darkened. He considered Suraya with a long stare and then, before she could react, he struck her across the face. Suraya cried out and clutched her cheek, her eyes instantly brimming with tears, her heart pounding with shock.

"Don't. Lie. To me." Hart's voice was quiet, but each word rang clear. "I will not tolerate lies." He took a step closer and lifted Suraya's chin. "Such a beautiful face," he whispered, before shaking his head with frustration.

Suraya raised her eyes to his, hoping perhaps to see remorse, but his expression, thick with desire, frightened her, and she squirmed free from his grasp.

"I have a meeting," Hart announced briskly, stepping away and to the door. "Tobias, see what you can find out. Try not to damage her."

"No!" Suraya sprang forwards and made for the door, but Keller was already there.

"Let's see what it takes to have you cooperate, shall we?" he asked with a grin.

§

Richborne Terrace

After hours poring over documents, Maddie lay exhausted, but unable to sleep, staring at the sloped ceiling at the top of the house. Jack had suggested she take the master bedroom on the floor below, with its comfortable bed and ensuite, but she'd insisted she'd feel more at ease in one of the spare rooms. Jack's family would return to this house at some point and she was sure they wouldn't like the idea of a stranger sleeping in their bed.

Jack wanted to spend some more time examining the photographs, so Maddie had climbed the stairs to the top bedroom, leaving him alone, hunched over her phone in a halo of illusory candlelight.

She'd pulled off her top and jeans and wriggled down beneath the sheets, her limbs heavy but tense. She'd hoped that she would sleep easily after the exhaustion of the evening's anxiety and anger, but here she was, hours later, staring at the beam of moonlight that glanced off the ceiling.

When she heard Jack creep up and into the bedroom below, Maddie realised that she'd been listening out for him. She didn't know what to make of his story. Certainly, some of the details he'd shared that morning, before she'd returned to the Hub, were corroborated by the documents that she'd photographed. But that didn't make him a time traveller, it just made him well-informed.

A part of her had expected him to take the information and run the minute her back was turned, and as she heard him close the bedroom door below, she wondered why he hadn't done so. Did he need her help in some way? Or was he an enemy agent putting on a good act?

Jack still had her phone and SIM. Was he searching it for information on her? Her pulse quickened and she almost resolved to go and retrieve it, before reasoning that it held little of interest. The risk of being hacked was so great these days that she barely ever used it.

Her mind worked over and over the things Jack had said, but it was the things he *hadn't* said that she kept coming back to. There was something unspoken, something behind the look in his eyes when he'd asked about Suraya, about why she'd been chosen. Had he really known who Suraya was all along, but not the nature of her mission? Suraya hadn't mentioned a partner, but they could have been working together. After all, Suraya had stopped confiding in Maddie the way she once had. Maybe they'd even been lovers. Maddie shook away the image of Suraya and Jack together, the conflicting emotions of irritation and disloyalty making her uncomfortable.

When had Suraya stopped needing her? When had she morphed from the little girl who shared everything, sometimes to the point of excess, to the grown woman who hid things? Had Suraya known she was in danger, but not felt able to tell her? Maddie swallowed but the lump in her throat held fast. It was her fault. She'd trusted Sarah blindly, and in doing so she'd failed both her sister and her parents. But she would atone. She would set things right.

Based on LEFA's records, and the intelligence that supposedly came from the future, Jack was sure that if Suraya was being held, she would be at the Republican base near Threadneedle Street. Maddie had immediately begun to map a route there, listing the potential obstacles on their way, but Jack had insisted that they first go to Spitalfields. She'd been angry, arguing against any delay in finding her sister, but he maintained that the supplies stored there were worth the detour.

Jack had also suggested a different route to the one she proposed. Maddie had pointed out that it would take longer and lead them close to several government checkpoints, but he'd insisted that crossing the river at Blackfriars wasn't an option. When she'd asked why he'd been reluctant to explain, eventually revealing that the

Fringe Army, a militant offshoot of the Liberal Party, were planning to destroy the railway bridge.

"But most of the city's food comes through Blackfriars," she'd responded, shocked.

"That's what the government wants you to think," Jack had replied.

She wondered if Jack was a member of the Fringe Army. But then surely he would have just said that, rather than his crazy time-traveller story?

She sat up, pushed off the sheet, and brought her knees up to her chest, hugging them to herself like she used to when she was little. She missed her parents and their counsel, especially the humour that they always found, even when issues were grey and thorny. Her mother, Dembe, had always been an excellent judge of character.

What would she have made of Jack?

Maddie recalled an occasion when she'd been eleven or twelve years old. She'd caught Suraya, who could have only been three or four at the time, helping herself to a plate of cooling dumplings that their mother had cooked for a family new to the block. Dembe had found Maddie scolding Suraya, who, with a smear of food round her mouth and wide eyes filled with tears, was insisting that she hadn't taken any. Maddie had expected their mother to chastise Ray as well, but she'd put her hands on her hips, laughed a full-bellied laugh, then scooped them both into her warm embrace.

"Do you know," Dembe said, "my mother always said, 'he who tells no lies will not grow up'."

She'd given them both a kiss on the nose and taken the dumplings next door. Maddie had thought over her mother's words, taking from them the idea that rules were not necessarily as black and white as she'd thought. Suraya's take on the experience was that it was further proof that she could get away with anything.

One way or another, Jack was either hiding truths or telling lies. But as long as she found Suraya what would it matter? And she wasn't without fault. She hadn't exactly been honest with Jack.

Her dad had also been fond of a good proverb, often adding one of his own to compliment something her mother had said. Didn't he used to say that 'one never accuses without a little bit of lying'?

Maddie smiled to herself, remembering the banter and laughter that had been the lifeblood and glue of their family. She lay back down, pulled the sheet up to her chin, closed her eyes, and finally slept.

§

Jack stared at the ceiling and wondered if Maddie was asleep. He wasn't sure why her scepticism bothered him. He'd hardly expected her to believe him, but when she'd looked at him like he was crazy… To be fair, he had *felt* crazy at times, being able to remember things that other people couldn't.

His earliest polymorphic memory was from when he was four and had lived with his grandparents in a large semi-detached house in East Dulwich. The neighbours' children, two boys called Harry and Ted, were considerably older, and Jack spent hours watching them play from the far side of the garden fence, longing to be included in their games.

A breakthrough came one summer's day, with the arrival of the neighbours' new puppy, Rufus, who managed to squeeze through a gap in the fence to wreak havoc in his grandparents' flowerbeds.

Harry and Ted had clambered over the fence and, with Jack's help, captured the over-excited pup and led it back next door. The older boys said nothing when Jack returned to their garden with them, and the three of them had spent a happy afternoon throwing a ball for Rufus, chasing him round the synth-lawn and laughing as he licked them and rolled for treats.

For Jack, the afternoon's companionship made it one of the best days of his young life, and he could barely wait for the next chance to play together. But the changeable weather brought terrible thunders storms, and for the rest of the week Jack had to content himself with glimpses of Rufus being led out for walks down the water-logged road.

The storms had broken with the arrival of the weekend, giving way to the crackle of summer heat. From early on Saturday morning, Jack kept vigil in the garden, following the shade as it moved from east to west, listening for Rufus and the boys. Hours into his watchful wait, Jack had scrambled to look over the fence and was struck by a sudden and terrible headache. Nauseous and unbalanced, he had fallen and grazed his cheek on the rough wooden panels.

As he'd steadied himself, Jack finally heard Harry and Ted in the garden beyond. He had hauled himself up and called to them, asking if Rufus was coming out to play. The older boys had given him a funny look before turning away to play football. Jack had tried again, asking how Rufus was, explaining that he'd thought of a new game the puppy might like.

Ted had walked to the fence and frowned. "I don't have a clue what you're on about," he'd said.

Harry had rudely advised his brother to "stay away from that little weirdo."

Jack felt his eyes prickle with tears as he'd pleaded with them, asking them what they meant, insisting that they'd all been playing with the puppy the week before.

"He's crazy!" Harry had whispered conspiratorially to Ted, though plainly loud enough for Jack to hear.

Jack had run inside to his room, crying with frustration and disappointment. He pulled everything inside his bedroom, his clothes, toys, pens and pencils, out from drawers and shelves and onto the floor. The clatter and commotion had brought his grandmother running, whose first instinct had been to shout and scold him for the mess he'd made. She watched him replace all his clothes in his chest of drawers before she'd noticed the bloody graze on his forehead and asked how it had happened.

The story of his funny headache, the neighbours' dog and the mean brothers came tumbling out of Jack through sobs. He had expected his grandmother to say the usual things such as, 'it's just a scratch' and 'take no notice', but she'd gone pale and very quiet. She'd stood up stiffly and told him that the neighbours had been planning to get a dog, but the mother had unexpectedly lost her job and they were concerned about the cost. Then she told Jack to tidy his room and wash his hands for lunch.

At the end of the meal, while still seated at the table, Robert had explained bluntly that Jack's father came from a different time to their own. As a Person of Mixed Era Origin, Jack could recall parallel versions of time, and any changes made to his own timeline or those of people around him would unfortunately be painful and disorientating. He offered no words of comfort, he didn't hold Jack or reassure him, but simply stated that it was regrettable and something that he'd 'just have to get used to'. Jack had been left bewildered, frightened and angry.

Thinking back, he could see that his grandmother, in her own way, had tried to help him through those first few months after he'd learned what he was. She'd given him extra-large helpings of pudding for the whole of the following week. What he'd really needed, though, was someone to hold him, to tell him that they loved him and that it would all be okay.

Years later, Jack had learned that Ted and Harry's mother had been an investigative journalist who had fallen foul of her editor for revealing the newspaper's ties to Republican fuel lobbyists.

Jack pushed the bed covers back and moved to the window, pulling the curtains apart slightly and peering out into the street. In the distance he could hear sirens wailing. A movement on the opposite side of the road caught his eye. His pulse quickened. He mentally located the items he needed, and began to plan his escape route from the back of the house…

A fox emerged from the shadows.

Jack took a deep breath and closed his eyes, exhaling slowly to steady his nerves.

As he turned away from the window, his gaze fell on a

framed photograph on the dressing table. He picked it up and sat down on the foot of the bed so that the pale light creeping through the gap in the curtains lit the surface. It was Robert, who, with a rounded face and golden curls, looked here to be about four or five years old. His appearance was very different to Jack's at that age, although Jack could see something of his mother in him.

He recalled Mary's better days, when there were glimpses of who she'd once been. He'd combined those memories with the stories told by Howard to create an image of her, a translation of who she was. She was so unlike her parents, and Jack wondered, as he often did, what kind of person he would have been had his mother been able to care for him herself.

Jack replaced the photograph and lay down on the bed. He pictured Maddie in the room above, worrying for her sister, ready to fight for her. Maddie's love for Suraya was powerful and Jack felt a tinge of jealousy, a yearning to not feel so alone.

Would Robert have been a kinder, more empathic father and grandfather had he not been an only child? All Jack knew was that without Howard he would have been wholly lost, and while a part of him was still rankled by the knowledge that, for five years, Howard had abandoned him and his mother, he couldn't put a value on the affection and support that Howard had given since. Howard had tried endlessly to help Jack believe in his own worth. What there was of it was being well and truly tested now.

It had occurred to Jack, earlier that evening, that if his mission was successful then his and Maddie's efforts to rescue Suraya would effectively be in vain: time would be re-written and, in the latest update, Jack wouldn't be around to help. It was possible that LEFA would free Suraya. Or maybe this war would never happen. Either way, Jack would never know. The only thing certain was that if he succeeded, he would not play any part in these events.

Jack felt the gulf opening, a chill that crept up his

spine, the fear he'd spent months refusing to acknowledge. To have never existed was inconceivable, yet this was both the root of the fear and its salve – there was no sense in fearing something that he couldn't even picture. Jack had spent a lifetime building walls to protect himself, and instinctively he pulled within them now, forcing his mind to focus on his present dilemma.

He was torn. Logically, he should concentrate on finding Dr Kingsley, and not be distracted by Maddie or her sister. But he couldn't walk away from it. It involved Kayson Hart, and so it was personal.

All people were born with a finite amount of time, but his own existence was less than finite, more intangible. In this moment, however, he *did* exist, he *was* living, and he desperately wanted to give that life every ounce of worth he could while it was still possible.

The weight of the events of the following day sat heavily on his mind. He had given Maddie a brief outline of what would happen, but had avoided the details: the train that would plunge into the river, the deaths… She would know soon enough.

Jack thought about those who would soon be boarding the train, how they would never know the pivotal role they played in the final year of war. Until this moment, he'd had the relative comfort of viewing events from an historical perspective, but now they added another layer to his sense of anguish. As with Suraya, once time was rewritten, any intervention on his part would be undone. But even if he were able to save those lives, he understood why he couldn't. He wasn't convinced, however, that Maddie would see it that way.

Jack sighed and closed his eyes, knowing that once again, sleep would be a long time in coming.

§

Thames Barrier, London

Damn it, what was he missing?

For some reason, Dr Kingsley had not been able to recreate the time jump from yesterday's test, and the hours sitting, poring over the calibrations had begun to numb more than his buttocks.

Noah laid down his notes and stood up, stooping a little as he edged his way around the table and up the steps. Once standing on the well deck he stretched his back and stifled a yawn. It was still early, and the city upstream possessed that still quality that only the pale pink light of this hour could bestow. The morning tide had been particularly high, and the hydro-electric generator that Noah had attached to the Thames barrier had delivered more than enough power. Noah moved to the edge of the boat and peered down to where the ebb current sucked at the peeling bitumen as it continued its passage back out to sea. No, power was not the problem.

A previous owner had welded an oversized mooring stud to the side of the cockpit, and Noah used it now to help him up and onto the roof above the galley where, despite the protesting creak of his knees, he lowered himself to sit. He laid his hands flat on the bubbling paintwork and closed his eyes to focus on the rhythmic rocking of the vessel, Diana.

Diana, like most of the barges on the Thames, had seen better days. Those houseboats that had seen investment, the proud bearers of solar powered hot showers, flushing toilets and underfloor heating, had been motored upstream and out of London with the first whiff of war. The barges that remained were either immobile or slum-like, crude and rusting. But Noah didn't mind; the old barge reminded him a little of his uncle's shrimp boat, Betsie. And as for the wear and tear? Well, he reflected, his own framework was going much the same way. None of it mattered so long as his mind stayed sharp: there was still so much to do.

Noah turned to look downstream and his eye was caught by a gull, high above, soaring in and out of the thick clouds. He watched it a while, then slowly straightened. His pulse began to quicken. He had an idea.

§

Richborne Terrace

Jack was already in the kitchen when Maddie padded down the stairs early the following morning. He looked tired, worse than she did, and she wondered whether they'd managed five hours sleep between them.

"I just made some coffee," he offered. "It was years past its use-by date but vacuum sealed so…" He shrugged.

She nodded mutely and took a seat at the counter, stifling a yawn as Jack poured the hot black liquid into a mug and pushed it towards her. She took a sip. "Thanks."

The first light, blazing through the kitchen windows, was already hot and Maddie began considering whether to adjust their route to optimise the shade afforded by the most built-up areas. She made a mental note to look for some more water containers to fill before they left. There were shops and supermarkets open, of course, but they were closely monitored, all fitted with government surveillance.

"Are we coming back here?" she asked, noticing Jack's backpack on the floor, to which he'd added some cans of food.

"Possibly." Jack shook his head. "I don't know. There's space to bunk down at the storeroom in Spitalfields if we have to but, here…" He pulled a key from his pocket and slid it across the work surface. "If something happens and we get separated then come back here, it'll be safer than going back to your flat."

"What about you?"

"I've still got my key, that's a spare I found upstairs."

Maddie slipped it into her pocket.

The lid on a pan behind him began to rattle and Jack turned round and switched off the hob. "Are you hungry?" he asked, glancing back over his shoulder.

"Not really," she confessed.

He brought the pan over and set it down next to two

bowls. "Me neither, but it's a good idea to eat something, though I can't promise it will be nice." He screwed up his face and Maddie couldn't help but laugh, breaking some of the tension from the night before. Jack made a flourish and lifted the lid from the pan. "Rice porridge," he declared. "It was the best I could come up with."

"Congee!" exclaimed Maddie, beaming.

"Absolutely." Jack nodded slowly. "And that is?"

Maddie rolled her eyes and pulled over a bowl. "Congee. It's a traditional Chinese rice porridge. Did I tell you my dad was Chinese? He used to make it for us before school." She took a mouthful, chewing it slowly before offering her verdict. "It could be worse."

"I'll take that." Jack smiled and sat down to tuck into his own bowl. "You didn't tell me about your dad," he said, "but I saw the photo of him and your mum. I guessed they were your parents; I can see them in you."

"I'm more like my mum," Maddie said. "She was Ugandan. That's where that photo was taken, not long before she and my dad came to England."

"And they left because of the climate crisis?"

Maddie nodded. "Partly that, but also to escape the tension between Ugandans and the Chinese. I mean, I get that politically it was complicated, but my dad was Ugandan, he was born there, just like I was born here. For some people, where you're born or what you contribute amounts to nothing if you don't look the part." She sighed. "My dad's parents wanted them to move to China, while my mum's parents wanted them to stay, warning them that it would be the same wherever they went."

"The other photo was your maternal grandparents?" Jack asked.

"Yeah. Nana Ajeet, my grandfather, was Indian-Ugandan. He was born in the capital, Kampala, just after a dictator had expelled most of his countrymen." She shook her head sadly. "He struggled with it growing up, but by the time my mum arrived, he felt accepted. He understood my dad's feelings, but he was afraid that my parents might suffer worse in Britain."

"And was he right?"

Maddie thought about the stories her parents had told her, about their first years in England, and how they contrasted with those in which Maddie had grown up. "I guess to begin with it was better here, but as the number of climate refugees increased, so did the racism. There were kids at my school who used to taunt me, telling me to go back to where I'd come from, calling my family 'locusts'. We got that one a lot – families who looked like they were from Africa or the Middle East were nick-named 'the plague'." She pushed the porridge about her bowl, her appetite gone.

"I'm sorry," said Jack quietly.

Maddie shrugged, separating the grains of rice with her spoon and pushing them back together again. "It's okay."

"But it's not."

"No." Maddie's eyes met his. "It's not. But you say, in the future it's going to be better."

Her voice held a hint of derision, but Jack ignored it, replying quite seriously, "Yes, it is. And if I succeed in finding Dr Kingsley, if I can prevent time technology falling into the wrong hands, then we have a real chance to avoid the environmental collapse that created this war."

"But mass migration has been happening for the past thirty years, and you say time travel hasn't been invented yet?" She stared at him, her entire face a frown.

"You can't think of this in linear terms. That's both the beauty of it, and the problem." Jack held her stare until at last she turned away.

She took a deep breath. "Okay, nutcase…"

Jack raised an eyebrow and caught a glimmer of a smile from Maddie in return.

"…let's go over today's plan again."

Maddie and Jack set out a few hours later, having dismissed the option of leaving at dawn. While the idea of crossing London at its quietest time had its appeal, they would lose the relative cover given by the morning commute. Morning rush hour was a far-cry from the pre-war hustle and congestion, but from 8:00 onwards a steady stream of people made their way to places of work, to join the queues for rations, or to hurry their children to those schools that defiantly remained open. Even so, Maddie's planned route avoided the main roads as much as possible, where security cameras and police patrols constantly monitored the mood and motions of the populace.

Rummaging through his great-grandfather's wardrobe, Jack had found a couple of Panama hats which, besides affording them some relief from the glare of the sun, gave them a degree of anonymity from overhead drones. Maddie's hat was far too big for her, but with her thick black curls tucked up inside the brim it fitted well enough.

They'd set off in a wary silence, watchful of the few people they passed on the residential streets, but the volume of pedestrians increased as they neared the Oval, where the main road that ran around the edge of the cricket stadium was unavoidable. With two schools nearby, the pavements were busy with children, and Jack listened to their chatter as they passed, discussing toys, computer games, who'd fallen out with who yesterday and why they hated maths class. It felt timeless and disconnected from the hardships of living in London during wartime.

Jack turned to Maddie, his mouth opened to comment, when a loud bang shook the street. Children and parents scattered, running to shelter in doorways, behind walls and parked cars, with a speed which exposed the reality of their experience of these last few years.

Jack and Maddie crouched behind a car and peered around to see where the noise had come from. The culprit, in a dirty white van, lowered his window and hollered, "Sorry! I's awrigh', i's awrigh'! Jus' an 'ole in my exhaust!"

People emerged from their hiding places to resume their journeys. A couple of older boys yelled abuse at the driver as his van chugged up the road, spewing out black smoke. Unusually, the Society of Motor Manufacturers and Traders had failed to prevent the 2055 law that banned all but electric vehicles from central London, and the illegal vehicle had not gone unnoticed. Two drones converged on the driver when he stopped at the lights ahead, just in front of St Mark's Primary School. Jack began to turn back, but Maddie grabbed his arm and propelled him forwards.

"Keep moving and keep your head down," she hissed. "It's an MD6, their algorithms pick up on changes in movement suggestive of guilt."

From under the brim of his hat, Jack noted that parents and children alike kept their eyes fixed to the ground and maintained their progress, one foot in front of the other. As he and Maddie rounded the end of the stadium, the unlucky driver got out of his van and, in colourful language, began to remonstrate with the drone's controller.

"An' I said tha' the fuckin' Governmen' should mind i's own fuckin'—"

Pffip.

A dart struck the man in the neck and he stumbled before slumping forwards over the bonnet.

Maddie's sharp intake of breath disclosed her surprise and Jack gripped her arm and made sure that their pace didn't falter. Just beyond the school they turned left into an alleyway which, with flats to one side and tall hedges to the other, offered a degree of shelter. Maddie pulled away from Jack and shook her arms with agitation.

"I can't believe that!" she cried. "In front of a school for Christ's sake!" She took a shuddering breath. "And *darts* on those drones?"

"I take it they're a new addition?"

She nodded. "Where's it all going to stop?"

Jack leant against the wall and fished inside his backpack for his water bottle, taking a long draught of the already tepid water. He replaced the bottle in his bag. "As far as I know, drones in the 22nd century are no longer fitted with darts, guns, or any other kind of weapon."

Maddie opened her mouth to reply but closed it again when an elderly woman entered the alleyway, glancing at them nervously. Jack nodded a greeting and Maddie busied herself finding her own water bottle. They remained silent while the pensioner shuffled past then turned right and into the flats' inner courtyard.

"And that!" Maddie hissed. "When can we all stop being afraid of one another?"

The wail of a siren in the vicinity of the school spurred them to move on and they fell into step.

"The 22nd century sounds more appealing by the minute." Maddie shrugged sullenly. "Maybe I should hitch a ride back with you when you're done."

Jack smiled but said nothing.

They wound a path midway between Kennington Road and the Thames, staying west of Elephant and Castle before edging eastward as the railway track approached Waterloo. Their route avoided most of the local shopping streets and eateries, but those pubs and cafes that they did pass were either boarded up or broken into, and as they neared Lambeth Road the smell of acrid smoke filled the air. The housing estate on China Walk sported banner-filled windows, proclaiming a position that was neither in favour of the government, nor of tolerance to climate refugees. Maddie pushed her hat down a little lower and kept her eyes to the ground.

The view down the length of Lambeth Road revealed the debris of a recent riot, burnt-out cars, broken glass and improvised barriers, and the air hummed with drones, half a dozen of them circling and moving in and out of side streets. In the distance Jack could make out a group of people in high-visibility vests, labouring to pull apart a mangle of shopping trolleys and bedframes that blocked the crossroads. A group of policemen watched the spectacle, their weapons glinting in the bright morning sun.

Jack had slowed slightly while he'd crossed the street and sped up now to re-join Maddie whose own pace had quickened, leaving him behind. She lifted her eyes to him as he came alongside but continued to keep her head down.

"The riots were only a few days ago," she explained quietly. "I'd have taken us down the other side of the tracks but the police presence is higher along the river – part of the buffer zone around Westminster. This area isn't safe for someone who looks like me."

Jack's stomach twisted. He'd suggested this route without a thought of the danger it might place Maddie in. He touched the hilt of the knife that was tucked into his belt and glanced at the flats to their right.

"You know what sparked the riots?" she asked. "A group of migrant rights protesters were arrested for damaging the train tracks to Waterloo – the ones used to bring in supplies from Europe. The authorities had been using the line at St Pancras, of course, but the Fringe took that out after they discovered that most of the imports weren't food, as our government claimed, but armaments."

Jack said nothing, sensing her need to vent, but he knew all about the riots and the sabotage of St Pancras and Waterloo, both of which were precursors to this afternoon's events.

"Most of the protestors were just kids, sixteen, seventeen years old, one was only fourteen. They were taken to Kennington Police Station, then sent to Belmarsh – no trial, no hearing, nothing. Can you imagine that? Kids in Belmarsh." She shook her head. "Then Kenyatta Okoro, the tech investor – have you heard of him? He stepped in to bail them all out. No one knows exactly what happened, though I heard rumours that his grandson was one of the captured kids, but loads of people were angry that 'terrorists' had been set free. Or angry that a rich Black guy was 'allowed' to buy their freedom. 'Cos no white guy ever bought his freedom before." Her eyes narrowed and her face flushed. "Some people said the government should seize Okoro's assets to cover 'the cost to Britain for housing his kind'. Some people were just affronted by the fact that the government had accepted money from someone like him." Her face contorted with a bitter smile. "As though the wealth of this country wasn't built upon the labour of '*my kind*'."

Her voice had risen and she stopped, looking Jack in the eye as she all but spat the last words.

Jack struggled for how to respond, her anger was raw and justified, her life experience so different from his own. He wished he could offer some words of comfort but could think of nothing that she wouldn't already have heard. From him, words of recognition might be taken amiss.

A shout from a window above and the approaching buzz of a drone propelled them onwards. They walked side by side, watchful but equally engaged in their own thoughts. As a Cronod, Jack had known prejudice, the incident with the neighbour's children being just the first of many cruel reactions he'd experienced as a child and teenager. But his 'difference' wasn't outwardly visible and as an adult, he'd mostly been able to manage the pain and disorientation of temporal shifts so that those around him remained unaware. The fact that he felt the need to hide his identity was bad enough, but he'd experienced nothing comparable to what Maddie and her family had been through. He knew that the end of the war would bring a shift in ideology and a degree of reconciliation, but he questioned whether it was enough? Would it ever be enough?

Though still early, the sultry air was already oppressive, and Jack and Maddie paused for a while in the shade of a tree in Waterloo Millennium Park.

"This used to be a nice little park," Maddie remarked as she contemplated the sun-baked flowerbeds, now overrun with half-dead, straggling weeds and litter. She looked at Jack, half expecting him to describe the positive transformation worked here in the future, before thinking herself silly. It was just a tiny, obscure park, after all.

Jack surveyed the scene, picturing how close the waters

would come when the Thames Barrier was struck by temporal storms in the future. Few people had realised just how effectively it held back the river until it was critically damaged at the height of a surge tide. Perhaps that plastic bottle, thought Jack, or even the drink can by his feet, would remain here until the future flood water carried them away. He sensed Maddie's eyes on him but said nothing, hoping that particular future would never arrive. The weight of possibility rested heavily on his shoulders, as did the risk of failure.

With unspoken agreement they both stood, slung their bags over their shoulders and moved on, walking through the park so that they were hidden from the main road, only crossing once their path could lead directly into the smaller streets that branched off the other side. They wove their way towards Southwark Bridge Road, this time keeping well south of Southwark Street.

Their proximity to the Southbank and Tate Modern put Maddie on edge, and yet the events of the previous morning already felt distant and remote. It occurred to her that time, even within her own experience, was a pliable thing. One moment might feel like a lifetime, whilst a year could fly past, with barely a trace. She drew a finger across her cheek bone and knew that there were some moments she would never escape.

The railway arches on Redcross Way had seemed like the best place to access the track over the river, but nearing the bank of scaffolding abutting the arches, Maddie began to question her choice.

"You said this track hasn't been used in months," Jack reminded her. "And we can't risk crossing at any of the main bridges."

"I know," she reluctantly agreed. "Too many checkpoints on Southwark Bridge. But we'll be so exposed up there. What about drones?"

Jack ran his hand through his hair, considering the railway bridge above them and the distance between here and the far bank. If only he'd been cast north of the river, he thought with a sigh. He met Maddie's questioning gaze, then thought of his mother, of Suraya and Hart, and the tangled web he'd found himself in. No, meeting Maddie had happened for a reason.

"It's alright," he said. "We'll take it slowly." He crouched down and sifted through the debris, selecting half a dozen stones.

"What are those for?"

Jack pulled his makeshift catapult from his backpack and sent a stone flying into the distance. "There's more than one way to bring down a drone," he said with a smile.

Maddie raised an eyebrow and inclined her head in assent. She pulled herself up onto the scaffolding, climbing nimbly, pausing to look around from the top platform before she swung herself over and onto the tracks. Jack followed, pausing for a little longer as he listened for the sound of drones, before dropping down next to her.

It was still early enough to hug the shadow behind the wall on the eastern edge of the track and, with their hats removed, they were fairly well camouflaged. There wasn't much they could do about their heat signatures, given that the air temperature was edging in on thirty degrees. Jack hoped that Maddie's initial instinct was right – that this track was of little interest to either rebel groups or drone patrols.

They edged their way forwards then stopped where the bridge headed out across the water. Upriver, a queue of traffic had formed on Southwark Bridge, each vehicle waiting its turn to be searched before entering the historic City of London. A shorter line of pedestrians could be seen alongside, waiting for their own admittance. Above them all hovered a couple of drones, their humming lost, carried away by a hot southerly breeze. Excepting the occasional screech of a gull, it all was quiet down-river, both London Bridge and Tower Bridge having been closed to all but military vehicles for the past six months. Maddie scanned the tracks ahead with her binoculars then handed them to Jack.

After twenty minutes watching, with no discernible

change, Maddie caught Jack's eye. He nodded and they began to edge their way out and over the river, keeping as low to the tracks as they could.

They had reached the halfway point when the silence was broken by a flock of gulls, rising en-masse from the north bank railings with a sudden *whoosh*. Startled, Jack and Maddie froze. They listened, the birds calling to one another noisily whilst they soared above the bridge on warm gusts of air.

"Do you think something spooked them?" whispered Maddie.

"Maybe."

Jack pulled the catapult from his back pocket and fitted the sling with a stone, squinting as he looked along the length of the bridge to where it entered Cannon Street Station. He ran the back of his hand across his brow, wiping away the sweat that ran into his eyes while the sun pressed down from above and the tracks radiated heat from below. The longest of the train platforms was a short distance ahead to their left and the additional shade it offered was enticing. The platforms on the right were still a distance away though and, after straining their ears against the wind and detecting nothing but the gulls, Maddie pulled out her gun, nodded to Jack and led the way forwards.

They reached the end of the rightmost platform without incident and Maddie pressed her back against the concrete, appreciating the cool of its shadow that took the edge off the oppressive heat. Jack scanned the rooftop garden that looked down over the tracks, then peered along the platform to where the corner of the Victorian tower offered a way to scramble down to the river walk below.

"We might be hidden down here," said Jack, pushing himself back into the shade alongside Maddie, "but if we wait until the roof gives us cover, we'll have a wide section of platform to cross."

"Plus, the station will be under surveillance," Maddie added.

Agreed, they climbed a maintenance ladder up and onto

the platform and moved ahead quickly. They were just a couple of metres away from the tower when the distinctive thrum of a drone stopped them in their tracks.

Maddie and Jack pressed themselves into the diminishing shadow as the machine emerged from inside the cavern-like mouth of the station.

"MD5," Maddie mouthed.

Jack aimed his catapult, sending a stone clattering down the tracks midway across the river. The gyrocopter sped past them to the source of the noise.

"Go!" he hissed.

Maddie dashed to the corner while Jack, his eye on the drone, followed more slowly. Maddie lowered herself over the edge, fully exposed in the glare of the sun, when a second drone emerged. She froze, flinching when its siren emitted a short warning blast before heading straight for her. From the shadows, Jack sent another stone flying. It hit the opposite side of the tracks with a clang, but the distraction succeeded only in drawing back the first drone which whirred past to investigate.

From her position halfway over the parapet, Maddie struggled to see Jack. Keeping her head still, she strained her eyes sideways and finally found him. Jack nodded minutely then sent a third stone flying straight at the drone as Maddie dropped down over the edge.

Pfipp.

The stone struck, sending the dart wide. The gyrocopter crashed to the ground. Jack targeted the second machine, but it was too fast. Its laser hit the copper pipe leaving nothing but vapour. Jack's hand seared with pain.

Maddie shouted from below, drawing its attention. "Hey! Hey, down here!"

The drone rotated.

Jack pulled the knife from his belt and threw it hard. It caught the rotor blades, sending the drone into a spin. He vaulted over the side of the bridge, dropping down next to Maddie as the drone spun into the tower above them.

A third drone flew under the bridge – *pfipp* – releasing a dart that grazed Maddie's cheek.

"Shit!" Maddie dropped her gun. She stumbled backwards and clamped a hand to her face.

Jack stooped for the weapon, spinning up and around, and fired. The drone exploded sending the swooping gulls into a frenzy of agitated cries.

He knelt down and pulled Maddie's hand away from her face. The graze wasn't deep, but it was the quantity of sedative it contained that worried him. "Can you walk?" he asked, pulling her to her feet. She nodded. "We need cover and fast, tell me where to go."

"St Mary Abchurch. Down there." Maddie pointed at the lane that ran down the side of the station. She could see two images of her right hand, two forefingers pointing, and shook her head, trying to clear it. "I think the… the…" she struggled to think of the right word.

"I know. Come on." Jack jumped to the walkway below and helped Maddie clamber down. She held his arm for support as they hurried towards the main road which, with the desertion of most of the city's office blocks, was thankfully quiet. But when they entered Suffolk Lane, Maddie began to stumble. From somewhere to their left a siren wailed. Jack pulled her arm over his shoulder and maintained their pace.

"I's not far," Maddie slurred. "Nex' left… right at Cannon Ss… sstreet… then… lef'."

"Come on, Maddie, stay awake."

On approach, Jack could tell that Cannon Street was busy, a couple of small supermarkets drawing those who did still live and work in the area. Maddie's head flopped forwards and jerked back up as she struggled to remain conscious, and Jack fretted that her jerky movements would draw attention. Near the junction, an empty beer bottle lay on the ground. Jack scooped it up and pushed it into Maddie's hand.

"Now you're just another drunk," he told her.

She managed a scowl.

They stumbled across Cannon Street, looking like a couple who'd spent the night in high spirits, and had almost reached the entrance to Abchurch Lane when Jack spotted a police car heading their way. The vehicle slowed and the driver shouted to a man hovering in a doorway. A Snag. Jack rounded the corner and could see the church ahead, the front of which was undergoing repairs, but they couldn't risk entering the building in full view of the policeman and his informant.

He leant Maddie against the wall and brought his face close to hers, like two lovers sharing a confidence, their warm breath circling between them. He took the bottle from her hand, pretending to take a swig so that he could glance backwards. The Snag sloped away down Cannon Street in the direction of the underground station. The police car's electric engine hummed gently, but it didn't move. Jack leaned into Maddie, his cheek brushing hers. Her eyes flickered open.

"Sorry about this," he whispered, before bringing his lips to meet hers.

Maddie tasted the salt of Jack's skin and heard the whine of an electric vehicle as it slowly moved away. She wasn't sure if her eyes were open or closed, she couldn't focus on anything other than the taste of salt.

Jack pulled away. "I think it's safe now."

He took her arm over his shoulder and led her towards the hoardings that fronted the church. The builder's gate was locked, but the panel to the side had been loosened enough for them to squeeze through and the padlock on the church door had been picked before. Inside, the air was blissfully cool, and Maddie revived enough to point towards the dais. "There…let me sit there."

The last visitor, perhaps Maddie herself or another member of LEFA, had left a pile of blankets and pillows against the low railings that enclosed the dais and altar. Jack eased Maddie down and she slumped back, her eyes half open, staring at the ceiling.

"Be nice, if it was like that," she mumbled, before giving into the power of the sedative and drifting into sleep.

Jack checked her pulse, wondering what she'd meant. He looked around the room which, given the building's exterior, was much brighter than he'd been expecting.

The dark varnished screen behind the altar, wooden panelling and pews should have been oppressive, but were lifted by the light flooding through a series of arched and round windows. It wasn't a vast room, and yet it felt deceptively spacious, the roof being so—

Jack glanced up and smiled, seeing what Maddie had. An image of heaven beamed luminously down from the fresco above.

"Yeah," he murmured. "Looks nice."

His eyes moved around the winged figures on the domed ceiling who smiled back at him from their seats of cloud. At the very centre, the 'Light of God' burst forth, bathing them all in 'His glory'. It was beautiful and, more so now than ever, otherworldly – like a fairytale. As an historian, Jack had visited many churches, but his interest was purely rational. He didn't believe in God, in any god. His own experience, after all, didn't sit well alongside religious doctrine. But Jack understood the power of belief and of belonging, though neither a man of his birth, nor a woman of Maddie's, would see themselves reflected in the faces of such angels.

Jack sat down on the front step of the dais and opened his bag. He took a long drink from his second bottle of water, then pulled out the pouch of medical supplies. It contained two syringes of the regenerative serum, and two that held a reversal agent: an antidote against a range of toxins, including sedatives. It was a potent drug, however, with its own potential side effects. He glanced over his shoulder at Maddie then down at his watch. A full dose of sedative would have knocked her out straight away, the fact that she'd managed to remain conscious until they'd reached St Mary's suggested that she'd only received a fraction of the dart's contents. He could use the reversal agent to wake her, but to what advantage? Right now, they couldn't possibly reach Spitalfields unnoticed, but at 13:12 they would have the advantage of a diversion. If Maddie hadn't come round in a couple of hours, he would use the drug to wake her; in the meantime, it was better that she sleep it off.

Jack got to his feet and explored the opposite end of the room, finding another exterior door with vast locks that were rusted shut. The only ready way in and out was the same way they'd come, which at least made keeping watch easy.

A plaque near the main entrance said that a church had existed on this site since the 12th century. Jack looked down at his feet, planted on the flagstone floor, and marvelled that between the foundations and himself stood almost a millennium of history.

Further along the wall, a carved board listed the names of all those who had been rector or vicar of St Mary Abchurch from 1323 onwards. Jack counted them. There were sixty-one names, just sixty-one men whose work here covered a span of seven hundred and fifty years. Why was it, he wondered, that people thought of time as slow moving, when here was the evidence that it flowed irrepressibly fast?

He thought of the lists that had held his own name: schools, university, medical records and local government. None had the gravitas of this carved wooden board, where the names were inlaid with gold, and if Alice had done her job well, his name would no longer be found on any of them. His erasure from the digital record was a precaution taken for the mission, but his success would result in something far deeper. Something permanent. He wondered if Maddie would make the connection between his mission's goal and his demise, and hoped that if she did, they would already have parted ways. Some realities, he thought, are better faced alone.

Maddie groaned as she shifted position on her makeshift bed, crying out, "No, no, Ray, no!"

"Maddie?" Jack ran and knelt beside her, but her eyes were closed and he could tell that she was dreaming, the sedative making her nightmares all the more difficult to escape. He checked her pulse – fast, but not dangerously so – and felt her forehead with the back of his hand, half expecting the heat of a fever.

Her face contorted as she murmured again, "No, no, no…" and her head jerked from side to side.

"Shh," Jack soothed. "It's alright, shh."

He stroked her hair away from her face which gradually softened, the furrow between her brows slowly smoothing before it disappeared. Her lips parted with a sudden, deep intake of breath which she held.

"Maddie?" Jack whispered. "It's alright, you're safe."

For a moment she seemed frozen, until Jack took her hand, squeezing it gently, and she at last released the air. Her breathing resumed its steady rhythm, her chest gently rose and fell, and the traces of tension left her face.

Jack remained where he was, with her hand in his, studying the very faint lines at the corner of her eyes. He pictured her smile which, when broad and spontaneous, flowed through into the creases that had left those lines, lines that here were softened in sleep. He noticed that the creases were more pronounced on her left side, where the scar she tried to keep hidden had left her skin taut and vulnerable. It wasn't a recent scar, not marks left by the war as he'd first assumed, and he wondered what had happened to her.

Jack's gaze travelled down to her parted mouth which revealed the tips of her white teeth. His attention earlier had been elsewhere, but now the recollection of pressing his lips to hers and the sensation of their softness, the memory of the scent of her skin, caught him by surprise. He released her hand, and moved back, aware that his own pulse had begun to beat faster. He thought back over the last twenty-four hours, over each conversation and exchange. He took a deep breath and rubbed his face with his hands. No, that was not part of the plan. He reasoned that she might not remember that he'd kissed her. She'd been sedated after all. Though God knows that made it worse.

Jack shifted back to lean against the altar and thought about the last time he'd kissed someone. It wasn't recently. He smiled wryly to himself, wondering whether he would have approached his life differently had he known it would be ending so soon. But then he had never really sought out relationships. He'd found himself in a few whilst at university and, having drifted into them, had allowed himself to drift out again. Poor Nesta, she'd always wanted more than he'd been able to give. They'd got together during his final year at UCL and had somehow muddled through two years before she'd given up on him. Jack suspected that if her post-graduate research hadn't required quite so many trips to Brussels, they wouldn't even have lasted that long.

He remembered the night she'd left him. She'd turned up at his flat on her way to the station, her suitcase larger than the one she usually took for an overnight stay. She told him that if he couldn't commit to something more then there was no point in her rushing back. Jack guessed that she'd hoped he would ask her to stay, hoped he would take her into his arms and tell her he loved her. But he couldn't. He'd always known that she would leave him at some point and had been prepared. Instead, he told her that he was sorry, that she would find someone else who would make her happier than he could. She'd yelled at him; told him he'd never make a real connection with anyone if he didn't let them in. She was right, of course; Howard was the person he was closest to, and Jack had avoided telling him about Nesta's departure for months.

Jack had mulled over Nesta's words, wondering what was wrong with him. Wondering whether his disconnection was a symptom of his heritage. But then, visiting his mother one day, he realised that it wasn't his conception through time travel that was the issue, but that his mother's adverse reaction to time travel – as he'd thought of it then – had robbed him of the most meaningful relationship he should have had. As a small child, his journeys to visit his mother had been full of hopeful anticipation, his mind preoccupied with the things he would tell her, the ways he would make her proud, but time and time again the visits had disappointed him. Each time she pulled away from him it felt like an abandonment. And so, he'd learned to maintain a degree of distance, a buffer against the fear and pain of rejection.

He'd not had a meaningful relationship since Nesta.

It was easier that way, and he was young enough to avoid being the subject of well-meant questions about settling down or starting a family. Jack hadn't been on a date in well over two years, not since he'd become involved in Howard's Temporal Stability Project. He'd rapidly become absorbed in, and essential to Howard's unofficial work and, as a Cronod, had been key to the development of Gaia. Not that he understood how it worked, but he didn't need to understand it to provide DNA or be a test subject.

As the project advanced it had dawned on him that the ability to recall alternative timelines could be an advantage to whichever agent was chosen for the mission, and without telling Howard, he'd put himself forward for consideration. Jack was a good choice. He had no family or significant connections, beside Howard, and the ample inheritance from his grandparents enabled him to reduce his workload and focus on training. A girlfriend, even a one-night stand, just wasn't on his radar.

Yet he must have missed it, the physical closeness, the sensation of touch in which it was possible to forget everything else. It was some sort of cruel trick, to feel desire now, even fleetingly. It was the body's way of reminding the head of the advantages of life over death, of gratification over sacrifice. But now was not the time for such thoughts. There would never again be such a time.

Jack closed his eyes and listened to the faint sound of Maddie's breathing and waited.

§

22 Bishopsgate

"No! I'm staying here. I won't go with you." Suraya tried

to pull free from the rough hands that held her; that pulled her from her cell, through a maze of corridors and into an empty office space. She caught sight of the view outside and fell silent. The height was dizzying. Where was she? It was the wrong location for the Shard. "Wait, I—"

She was pushed towards a door, but craned over her shoulder, trying to place herself. She could see the Gherkin – she must be in Bishopsgate. The guard withdrew and the door closed behind her, shutting out Bishopsgate and the city beyond.

"It's quite a view, isn't it?"

Suraya jumped and spun round to find Kayson Hart seated at a desk, watching her with a smile. Without thinking she touched her face. It was swollen beneath her left eye. Kayson seemed not to notice but pushed himself back from his desk and held aloft two canvases.

"What do you think?" he asked. "I need a fresh opinion."

Suraya's breath came in short, ragged gasps and her eyes jumped around the room, looking for something to fight with, unsure of whether she could overcome Hart, let alone escape the building.

"Yes, they're both pretty dire, aren't they," Kayson murmured. His lip curled in disdain as he set down the AI-generated art. "I'm tempted to move the desk out there." He smiled smoothly as though unaware of Suraya's silence, her terror. "Now *that,* out there, is a view that no painting, or computer can match. Don't you think, Suraya?"

He moved around the desk so that he was closer to her, then leant back on it, observing the effect of his proximity on the young woman before him, enjoying how she shrank away from him, her back against the door. But then she squared her shoulders and stuck out her chin. He smiled darkly. Her defiance was tantalising, and he wanted simultaneously to draw it out from her and crush it.

"There's nowhere in the world more magnificent than

Europe, don't you agree?" He prompted. "And London: the cultural cornucopia at its heart. I'm afraid that the aims of your terrorist organisation would lead to Europe's destruction. A Europe, 'for all', would not be Europe *at all.* And Europe must be protected at all costs."

"We're not a terrorist organisation."

"Ah, you've found your voice."

"You and your Republican cronies are the ones destroying the planet," Suraya continued, finding courage in speaking out. "You're the ones destroying Europe, yet you have the gall to blame the victims."

The corners of Hart's mouth twitched. "You misunderstand me, Suraya, as many people do. But believe me, when I have achieved my vision, the world will be a better place for all of us."

"Really?" Suraya scoffed. "Because you seem to me, to represent the worst of everyone – Europe and the Republic. But we won't be silenced. We won't allow you to shut out those in need. You'll be held to account."

"Are they your words or your sister, Madeeha's?" Kayson asked.

Suraya felt herself blanch.

"Oh, I know all about you, Miss Chung. Your parents' unfortunate deaths, the squalid flat that you call home, and your sister… She's made a bit of a splash recently, had a run-in with a drone. She would now be quite the asset for our friendly neighbourhood Snags."

"You've got it wrong; my sister has nothing to do with LEFA, she has no idea what I've been doing."

Hart stepped forwards so that his face was inches from hers. "Oh Suraya," he said softly, pushing a stray hair behind her ear. "You're quite a good actress…until you're scared."

Suraya lunged sideways and grabbed a lamp, swinging it towards him. But Hart was faster, grabbing both her free hand and that which held the weapon, crushing and twisting it until she cried out in pain. She dropped the metal base.

Hart pressed his weight against her. She felt the acid

tang of bile in the back of her throat. She told herself that it wasn't real, that it couldn't be happening, but her heart hammered inside her chest, and his scent, of bourbon and cigars, filled her nose.

His lips caressed her ear, and she thought her knees might give way. "Don't," she whispered raggedly. "Don't do this—"

Knock, knock.

Suraya jumped at the loud rapping on the metal panel behind her.

"Yes?" Hart responded curtly.

"We think we might have another positive identification, sir," replied a voice from behind the door.

Hart sighed heavily and pulled back, placing a finger beneath Suraya's chin, lifting her face to his. "We can continue this…conversation, a little later."

§

St Mary Abchurch

It had been hours before Maddie began to rouse, gradually opening her eyes and staring in silence at the fresco on the ceiling.

At first, she couldn't make sense of what she saw: gathered faces gazing benevolently down on her. She'd seen them before somewhere… at work? A jumble of memories faded in and out of focus: a line of customers, some smiling, some tetchy; trays of expensive cakes, the sight of which made her stomach rumble; columns, a dome, and lions – enormous lions; a stolen kiss in one of the storerooms… Ezra. Was that where she'd seen this painting before? Wasn't Ezra restoring it for display, even though it was only a copy of the original? Maddie's eyes closed and she smiled drowsily, unsure why, but somehow happy that this 'fake' had made it into the gallery.

Her mind drifted back to the kiss. She should have known better. She did know better, but Ezra fascinated her, his work was a window into another world. He trod the line between her world and theirs, the curators, the donors, customers with money to spare on sweet treats and teas. But had the kiss been worth it? She recalled the touch of his skin, the brush of his cheek against hers, the taste of salt. She hadn't known he would kiss her, she wasn't supposed to be there, but that kiss…

In her half-sleep, Maddie's brow furrowed. She'd lost that job years ago; she had no work. This wasn't the National Gallery, and the kiss she was recalling wasn't Ezra's. She breathed in sharply and her eyes flew open.

"Hey."

"Jack." She squeezed her eyes shut and opened them again, trying to focus on the figure lowering himself down alongside her.

"Take your time, don't try to sit up too fast."

"I… Oh god, my head."

"It's the sedative from the dart. You've been asleep a while. Here." Jack handed her a water bottle.

Maddie's head swam, but she pushed herself up on one elbow and took a mouthful of water. A drop of the liquid escaped the bottle neck, catching the light as it rolled slowly across her lower lip. She wiped it away with the back of her hand and caught Jack's eye. Her memories sharpened and she looked away.

"It will take a little while for your head to clear," said Jack. "And your memory might be a bit hazy."

She could hear the slight question in his voice. She took a moment to think back over their journey from Vauxhall – the crossing over the bridge, their encounter with the drones, how she'd led him here, or had he led her? They'd almost made it to St Mary's but then they'd stopped. She pictured his face close to hers. The taste of salt.

She glanced at him as he looked up at the painted ceiling. The silence felt weighted. Was he worried that she'd be angry? Worried she might get the wrong idea? She understood, there was no need to explain. And it had worked. She wasn't sure who they were trying to fool, by that point she hadn't been able to keep her eyes open. But whoever had been watching had moved on, uninterested in a young couple's public display of affection.

His slight discomfort embarrassed her. If she'd been Suraya, she would have blown it off with a flirtatious comment and a smile. But then, if she'd been Suraya, he wouldn't have kissed her just to provide a cover.

"I can remember crossing into Suffolk Lane, but everything after that is hazy." It wasn't exactly a lie.

Jack nodded, a little too emphatically, then indicated the pile of cushions beneath her. "You've been here before?"

"Once. I was helping track a suspect who worked at the County Court and ran into trouble. St Mary's has been a LEFA safehouse for a while." She ran her hand over the topmost cushion, leaving a trail across its faded velvet cover. "I think someone from the Central Hub is related to the last rector, though I'm not sure how they feel about it being used this way."

"It's a Christopher Wren building, built after the Great Fire of London."

She smiled and raised her eyebrows. "Were you reading the pamphlets whilst I was out?"

He laughed, thinking how he could add more than seventy years of history to the information sheets stored inside the building's entrance. "Did you know that the fire of 1666 destroyed most of the City of London. This whole area was razed to the ground, but from the ashes rose buildings like this one. And far grander ones of course, like St Pauls. Determination and money can achieve a lot."

"Like a phoenix," she murmured.

"What?"

"London is like a phoenix, always rising from the ashes."

Jack raised his eyebrows wistfully.

"And who is the Christopher Wren of the 22nd century?" Maddie asked. "Will the Shard and Millennium Bridge, Covent Garden and St Pauls all be rebuilt in a new style? Or restored as though this war never happened?"

Jack pictured his London – the city that had burned one too many times – where post-war wreckage was left uncleared and damaged buildings remained empty. The devastation was boarded off, out of sight and out of mind. The problem was that the country's financial heart no longer lay in London; the impetus to rebuild, which had been powerful and urgent after the Great Fire, just wasn't there. The phoenix hadn't risen, it had passed the baton to its offspring, who had set up shop elsewhere.

"Jack?"

Her expression was hopeful, and Jack couldn't bear to be the doomsayer. "The reality is that people stopped inventing new styles a long time ago." He smiled. "Would you believe that when I was a kid, we all wore seventies style flares and sported mullets?"

Maddie laughed then grimaced, massaging her throbbing forehead.

"Drink some more," urged Jack. "It will help."

The slam of a car door and raised voices from outside silenced them both. Maddie picked up her gun and edged into a crouch, but after a few minutes the voices faded away.

"What's been happening outside?" she asked. "The police must be looking for us."

"Lots of drones, but fortunately the church walls are thick. A few passing vehicles, but they've headed towards the station. I assume the police think we've gone underground."

"Okay, so it's best to move now, while they still think that."

Maddie reached behind her for her bag, but Jack shook his head. "The area will be crawling with Snags."

"Well, we can't just wait."

Jack checked the time. 12:21. "I told you that the Fringe will take out Blackfriars railway bridge today?"

Maddie nodded.

"Provided that our run-in by the river hasn't affected the timeline, that explosion should take place fifty-one minutes from now. In the aftermath, every drone, police patrol and Snag will be focussing on the bridge and surrounding streets. That's when we'll move."

Maddie waited but Jack said nothing more so she stood up and stretched her legs. "Alright." She still felt a little lightheaded, but the thumping pain was receding. She grabbed her bag and stepped carefully off the dais. "The drones will have footage of us. I'm going to change my clothes. You should too."

A tiny room with a toilet and wash basin was tucked into the back corner of the church. Maddie headed inside and shut the door. She could tell Jack was holding something back and it unnerved her, although she could chalk that up to the list. She hoped that whatever he had stored in Spitalfields would somehow help make sense of his story, whether it turned out to be a time machine, proof that he worked for the Fringe, or his committal letter to a mental hospital.

She peered in the mirror, moving her head back and forth to better see where the dart had skimmed her cheekbone, noting bitterly that it drew more attention to her scar. She pushed it from her mind, splashed her face and neck with water, then pulled off her t-shirt and swapped it for another from her bag. They were different enough. She pushed the discarded top to the bottom of the rucksack and pulled out the hat she was wearing that morning. Wearing it now would pose a risk; the drone footage would be analysed and hers and Jack's matching hats would mark them out straight away. The route she had planned for the rest of the journey to Spitalfields avoided the security cameras she knew of, but Snags could be anywhere, armed with real-time updates on the latest bounties.

She returned the hat back to the bag and pulled out a piece of blue, terracotta and ochre fabric, wrapping it around her head and tying a knot at the nape of her neck. Her fingers lingered on the twisted ends of the material, which had softened from years of use. She forgot, for a moment, that it was her own reflection staring back at her, instead seeing her mother's face beneath the scarf that had been as much a part of her being as her hair or smile. Maddie felt again the dull ache in her chest, the wrenching sensation left by the loss of her parents, but especially the loss of her mother. She still had dreams of such vividness that she awoke with the smell of her mother's cooking in her nose, expecting to find her parents as they had once been, setting the table for breakfast, hurrying Ray to get ready for school while smiling indulgently as she complained about her teachers and the homework they'd set.

Whilst infuriatingly lenient with her youngest daughter, Dembe had nonetheless understood the burden of being the older child, having been the eldest of two daughters herself. It was made quite clear that Maddie must set a good example, must be the responsible one, but Dembe granted her a degree of freedom in return for her efforts and, more significantly, entrusted her eldest daughter with her secret hopes and aspirations. Suraya had been too young to know their mother inside and out as Maddie did, and the bond that mother and daughter had shared served as a source of strength, bolstering Maddie to continue to fight and realise the dreams of, not only her mother, but both her parents. Yet it was also a burden, because now the responsibility was hers alone.

Her parents' dream had been simple: to live and work as equals, to contribute to – and so create – a fairer society in which their daughters could thrive. Since arriving in 2045, Dembe had volunteered for, then been employed by, charities working with and supporting refugees. She had been so proud of her last appointment, working with UNICEF UK. Her new job and their new flat should have been the turning point in all their lives, but it wasn't to be. In Maddie's opinion, her parents were as much the victims of climate change and xenophobia as those who had died in the Migrant Massacre a few years later. But their names would not go down in history. No future monument to the fallen would remember Lee and Dembe Chung.

Maddie took a shaky breath and returned her thoughts to the present, checking her backpack and pulling the zip closed. When she looked again in the mirror it was her own reflection that stared back. She pulled out some curls from the front of the scarf, looped them loosely and tucked the ends in around her ears. If she'd had the money, she could have had laser treatment on her skin, but that was a luxury beyond her imagination. And now here was a man carrying around a serum that could magically heal skin within hours, leaving only the faintest of scars. She arched one brow, wondering just how much money that must cost.

Jack was rolling up the sleeves on a fresh shirt when Maddie re-joined him. His eyes ran over her head scarf.

"Is that the same fabric as in your flat?" he asked.

"Yeah. Bibi, my grandmother, gave it to my parents when they left Uganda – something to remind them of home. She helped make it."

"I've never seen anything like it before. It's not cotton?"

"No." Maddie smiled. "It's made of bark from the mutuba tree, although this piece *is* backed onto cotton. Bark cloth was made by the Baganda People, from the south, where my great-grandfather came from. Bibi told me that it's one of the oldest forms of textile in history, older than anything that was woven. It was even added to the UNESCO World Heritage list."

Jack noted the pride in her voice and tilted his head to one side, taking in the colour and texture of the cloth as Maddie sat back down next to him. "And your grandmother made it?"

"Well, she helped at least. Lots of families made the cloth for export in the Twenties after it featured in fashion shows and magazines." She reached up to her neck, a faint smile across her lips as she ran her thumb backwards and forwards across the corner of the scarf. "Some people didn't like it being commercialised because they thought the cloth was sacred. My grandmother's family didn't object to the money, but they did believe in the old stories, that the cloth has a spiritual power and can transport the souls of the dead to the land of our ancestors." Her smile faltered. "My mum used to wear this piece all the time. Maybe it helped her find her way back home."

Jack waited a while, watching her smile fade. "Maddie, what happened to your parents?"

She glanced at him, then looked away. It wasn't something she spoke about; she didn't want to relive those moments or renew her pain. But now she considered, for the first time, that to not speak of it was a disservice to her parents' memory. Maddie pictured her mother's face, the way she could smile with just her eyes, and began.

"The flats on Rockingham Street were in a state well before the war started, and my parents wanted something better for us. They'd lived in that dump for over twenty years, saving every penny they could. When my mum got a new job, they finally had enough to move to a better area, in what should have been a better building." She drew in a jagged breath and wound the tail of the head scarf back and forth across her fingers. "They got the keys to the new flat a few days early, so they could fix it up a bit. That last morning, they waved Suraya off to school and I went to work with the promise to pick her up later and walk her to our new home. Mum told me they were planning a surprise…"

Her voice trailed off and Maddie smiled sadly, looking down at the stone floor where she traced her finger around the worn outline of a name. When she spoke again her voice was low and quiet, her throat thick with emotion. "I knew something was wrong from a block away. Maybe I sensed it." She shook her head. "Or maybe I smelled the smoke. I told Ray to stay outside and call the fire brigade. I tried to get to them, but the door to the kitchen was jammed, the ceiling tiles were on fire, starting to collapse…" She brushed her cheek with her fingertips, feeling the point where her smooth skin became ragged, and a small sob escaped her lips. "I could hear them shouting, and the last thing my dad said to me was 'take care of Suraya'."

She lifted her head to look at Jack and he understood the layers of her pain: her past loss, and her current fear that she would fail her father and sister.

"Do you know what the official report said?" she continued, her voice louder. "That it was 'an unfortunate accident for which the landlord could not be held accountable.' But I saw the state of the wiring in that place, the way the fire-escape was blocked. It was just as bad as Rockingham. There were so many people in London, so many refugee families desperate to make better lives for themselves and their children, and endless scope for exploitation."

Jack knew the history; knew that during this time, the charges levelled against councils and private landlords were rarely investigated, the plaintiffs treated as somehow less than human. As climate refugees flooded into Northern Europe, the demand for low-cost housing had risen exponentially, and criminal landlords had reaped the benefits.

"And you've been looking after Suraya ever since."

Maddie nodded. "Mum's parents were dead, and going to live with our Chinese relatives wasn't an option. I do have an aunt in Germany – my mum's sister – but at that point the whole of Europe was pushing back against migrants, and that's how we'd have been seen."

"How old were you?"

"I was twenty. Ray was only twelve; still a child."

Jack tried to imagine it. "I'm so sorry. It must have been so hard on you both, especially on you."

Maddie looked at him, surprised. People normally thought first of the impact on Suraya, of how hard it was for her to lose her parents so young. They tended to assume that since Maddie had been an adult, it had somehow mattered less.

But Jack had spent years considering and trying to understand the dynamics of his own loss, how it had shaped him. It wasn't hard for him to see the duality of Maddie's grief and burden. He could tell she was taken aback by his comment, and added kindly, "Maddie, you lost your mother *and* had to become one overnight…"

Maddie's eyes became glassy. A tear broke free and rolled down her cheek.

"…and nothing could have prepared you for that."

Maddie stood a while in silence, then returned to the dais, removed the contents of her rucksack and repacked it methodically. She drained the last of her water and took the empty bottles to the sink to refill them. Jack understood her need for occupation, the need to fill the mind with practical tasks in order to push away the past. After a while, she broke the silence, asking how they'd know it was time to leave.

"We'll know," was all Jack said.

Maddie looked the other way, his restlessness and agitation putting her on edge, and lifted her face to gaze up at the frescoed ceiling. Her mind drifted back to Ezra.

Before it had closed, Ezra worked in the conservation department at the National Gallery, where paintings were cleaned and restored. Maddie had met him when she was working in one of the museum cafes. He came from Kenya but had lived and studied in North America and Europe, and Maddie had been as dazzled by his experiences and learning as much as by his handsome face.

For a short while Ezra had showered her with attention, seducing her with whispered secrets about the museum's artworks. At just nineteen, she had fancied herself in love, and it had stung her badly when he passed her over in search of a new conquest. She had been older then than Suraya was now, and yet, she realised with a pang, in many ways she had been more immature than her sister. Their loss, and the war, had altered them both.

She touched her scars and considered how a man like Ezra would no longer give her a second glance. He sought perfection almost as much as an easy lay.

Thinking about him made her feel uneasy, ashamed, but she recalled what she had learned through him with pleasure. Paintings, she had discovered, were full of hidden symbolism and each artwork told a story if you knew how to read it. The paintings in the National Gallery had inspired her. Even now, she sometimes thought that if only she could paint, she would create a canvas that wove the history of her family and their many homelands into one glorious image.

Maddie smiled a little to herself then, feeling Jack's gaze, looked up. She opened her mouth to speak—

The first set of explosives on the Blackfriars line detonated.

She froze, listening to the blast echo around the city streets and rattle the windows of the church. She checked her watch. 13:12.

Jack caught her eye. "Two more."

She stationed herself at Jack's side, her bag slung over her shoulder, ready to leave.

The second bomb went off, prompting shouts and commotion in the street outside. Maddie's heart thudded against her ribcage and she held her breath in anticipation of the final explosion, its loud boom reverberating across the lofty, domed ceiling.

They moved to the exit. Jack pressed his ear against the heavy wooden door, listening to the immediate sounds of frightened pedestrians, cars and passing drones, while in the distance the squalling cry of sirens bloomed. Once sure it was safe, he gently slid back the bolt and pushed the door ajar. They edged out under the cover of the hoardings and, after peering around the road and surrounding area, squeezed out through the gap in the fence.

Suppressing the urge to run, they moved at pace along their agreed route. Maddie steered Jack when he faltered, when his instinctive movements reflected the city from his own time rather than that of 21st century, and Jack found himself grateful for her guiding hand. The small lanes and alleyways led to Gracechurch Street, one of the larger avenues they would have to cross. They hung back in the cover of a yard and watched the road ahead.

Just out of sight, a woman's voice shouted news of what had happened. "Whole bloody train's gone in the river," she cried. "They'll tighten the rations after this…whole bloody train!"

Maddie and Jack pressed themselves into the shadows as the woman, who was wringing her hands, walked past the entrance to the alleyway. She was in her forties or fifties, her face pale with worry, and Maddie wondered if she had children. The past year's rationing had been hard on the youngest of London's residents.

While Jack checked the street, Maddie thought she heard a slight scrape from further back in the yard. They were under an archway and she took a few steps back, scouring the windows and doorways behind. Ahead, Jack beckoned to her.

They hurried across the main road and entered Bull's Head Passage on the opposite side.

"I think somebody was watching us," she hissed.

Jack glanced back over his shoulder and felt for the hilt of his knife. "Okay, at the end of the passage we'll double back on ourselves, go down…"

"Ship Tavern Passage," Maddie supplied.

"…then find a route further south."

"We need to avoid the Walkie Talkie – too many cameras – but it's safe enough south of Eastcheap."

They reached the end of the alleyway, glancing behind them and out as far as they could see, before turning right, only managing a couple of steps before Maddie grabbed Jack's arm and pulled him into a run towards Leadenhall Market.

"Drone," she mouthed.

They sprinted towards the Victorian market, ducked into the smaller arcade on their right, and followed it round to its opening opposite Lloyds of London. The faint whir of a drone echoed through the passageway behind them, but ahead all was quiet. Jack edged around the corner and crumpled when an iron bar met his stomach.

"Jack!"

Maddie pulled her gun but was struck from behind, the weapon knocked from her hand. Her arms were wrenched behind her and she was lifted from the ground, kicking and struggling furiously.

The blow to Jack's stomach had missed his ribs, but he was badly winded, his diaphragm in spasm. Footsteps closed in. His head swam and he sucked and gasped for air. His knuckles whitened, readied to swing.

Click.

Jack froze at the sound of the gun.

"Steady on, mate!" Jack's assailant kicked him down, then stepped forwards, planting his right foot on Jack's back and brushing the barrel of his gun across the base of Jack's skull. With his free hand, the man pushed his hood back, revealing a shaved and heavily tattooed scalp. He grinned at Maddie. "Well?" he demanded of his friend.

Maddie stilled, her eyes fixed on Jack. Her captor shifted his grip on her arms, pulled a scanner from his pocket and held it up to her face. "Bingo! I told you it was her!" He turned the device to his friend, giving Maddie a glimpse of her likeness and the bounty for information.

Maddie felt the man appraise her. She willed herself not to react as he leaned his head over her shoulder to whisper in her ear.

"You're gonna buy me a nice steak supper. *Real* steak, not any of that preserved crap." He breathed in deeply, inhaling her scent and Maddie's flesh crawled. "Shame really, pretty thing like you…"

The tattooed man cocked his head to one side and smiled. "Yeah, reckon they'll mess your face up good and proper." His eyes fell on her scar. "Though it may not be the first time, eh?" He laughed.

Maddie could still hear the drone – it would arrive within seconds once the Snags logged their find. But the tattooed man was young and cocky, his accomplice maybe new to the game, and not calling in the drone immediately was a big mistake.

Maddie caught Jack's eye.

He nodded.

She threw her weight backwards with as much force as she could, cracking her skull into the Snag's jaw. He roared with pain and released his grip. She lunged for her gun.

The tattooed companion faltered, directing his weapon towards Maddie. Jack swung his fist and caught him squarely in the side of the head, sending him sprawling to the ground. As the Snag groped for the dropped gun, Jack followed through with his knife.

Bang.

Jack spun around. Maddie was on the ground, the Snag slumped on top, both of them still. Fear fluttered in his stomach. "Maddie?"

Her eyes flickered open. She coughed and gasped for air. Jack ran to her, heaved off the man's body, and helped her to sit. Her hands, still holding the gun, trembled violently, and Jack eased it from her fingers.

"Is he dead? Did I...?" Her eyes fell on the body but quickly looked away.

"Yes." Jack straightened up and listened, expecting to hear the drone, but there was no sound. Something else must have drawn it away. He glanced up at the Lloyds of London building – no longer there in his own time. With its exterior ducts, lifts and curved metallic stairwells, it had been known as the Inside-Out Building, and security cameras dotted its façade.

"Can you move?" he asked. "The cameras will have caught everything."

Maddie followed his gaze and shook her head. "They're all out. A bomb, three days ago, destroyed part of the Gherkin and the surveillance circuits within a half mile radius."

"That's lucky." He took a deep breath. "We need to hide the bodies. Better that they're not found straight away."

Jack closed the fallen men's eyes, then removed their weapons and the scanner and stashed them in his backpack. He took advantage of the Lloyds building, pushing the bodies down into one of its exterior lift shafts.

Maddie had helped shift them, lifting them by the ankles, careful not to look at their faces, pushing down the rising hysteria and the voice that repeated, over and over, *you killed that man,* you *did...* Desperately countering each time, *I had to, he would have killed me, I had to...*

Jack watched Maddie as they walked on and away from Leadenhall. Her face was pale, her jaw clenched, her hands stuffed into her pockets to try to hide the trembling. This might be a war, those thugs and their deaths an act of self-defence, but he guessed that none of that would take away the horror or remove her self-reproach.

Jack pictured Maddie's image, the one displayed on the scanner, certain that it had come from the drone they'd encountered by Tate Modern two days earlier. A pang of guilt twisted his insides. He'd led Maddie into trouble, but the worst was yet to come. He tried to remind himself that it was her own choice, that he would help her to find her sister. Besides, if his own mission was a success, history would be re-written and Maddie would be free of him. But then what would become of Suraya?

In his mind's eye, Suraya's image interplayed with that of his mother. He caught his reflection in an empty shop window and for a moment saw, not himself, but his father, Kayson Hart. Was that what his mother had seen when she looked at him? Had she really pushed him away for his own safety? Or had she kept him at a distance because she couldn't bear to see in him the man who had snatched away her life?

His mother had warned against changing the past, and Jack wondered how many had tried and failed to undo the damage mankind had done. But what if sacrifice was the key to success? Maybe those who'd come before him had played it safe, attempting to make changes that would avoid personal loss. Jack considered the sacrifice he was preparing to make, and hoped that soon his mother's pain, and his own, would finally be worth something.

§

Jack and Maddie arrived at Brune Street an hour after they'd left the sanctuary of St Mary Abchurch and stopped outside a red brick building, the facade of which had seen better days. Its windows and doors, however, remained intact, with a series of bars and heavy padlocks helping to secure the entrance. Jack pulled off his backpack and knelt to look at them.

A gust of warm air stirred a cluster of dandelions that grew from a crack in the brickwork, sending a flurry of white seeds sailing along the road. Maddie's eyes trailed them as they danced into the distance, then fell upon the neighbouring building. It was dated 1902 and was solidly built, faced in a decorative sandstone into which was carved, *Soup Kitchen for the Jewish Poor*. The word 'poor' had been circled several times in bright red spray paint and below it a verse was scrawled across the glass, proclaiming that, '*The 'haves' have it all, we 'have-nots' have nowt, but we took our kitchen back, while you were out!*'

Other graffiti competed for attention, colourfully decorating the doorway and windows with a range of obscenities. Spray paint had been used to obscure the lenses of the block's security devices and, in one case, the artist had worked the camera into a cartoon depiction of a drone, below which, *Big Brother's Watching You,* was written. One of the windows closest to Maddie had been smashed, exposing the internal latch, and she noticed that the nearest door was splintered where the two halves met, kicked open from the inside. So many historic properties had been converted into upscale apartments in the last seventy or eighty years. Given this building's origins as a soup kitchen for the poor, Maddie guessed that the area's destitute had taken especial pleasure in plundering the possessions of its wealthy, but absent, tenants.

"Got it," Jack said, prising open the final padlock. He

pushed the door back, releasing the musty air trapped within. The whitewashed hallway was dotted with doors every three to four metres. Discreet signs on each revealed the services offered, and Maddie read them as she passed. *Samuel Jarrett, Accountancy; Michelle Busuttil, Nutritionist; Susan Softley, Crisis Counsellor…* Maddie pushed her hands deeper into her pockets, thinking how she could do with that about now.

Jack stopped at the first door on the second floor and ran his thumb over the digits on its keypad. He hesitated a moment, then tapped in a series of numbers: 15, 08, 73, 14. Maddie took a step, expecting the door to click and release but it didn't. Jack held up his wrist so that he could see his watch, his other hand hovering for a moment over the buttons, then tapped in two more digits: 16. The door popped open.

"It's a perpetual code-lock," he explained. "Day, month, year, hour and minute. If your watch doesn't keep good time, you'll never get in."

Maddie nodded and stepped past Jack, taking in the office with disappointment. A functional corner sofa and coffee table sat beneath the window where Venetian blinds did their best to cut out the afternoon's light. A large desk and chair were placed against the wall ahead. In the far-right corner, a bathroom door stood ajar, and on her right, a small kitchen counter and cupboard sat next to a fridge. She wasn't sure what she'd been expecting. H. G. Wells' Time Machine? A control room? A weapon or two at least, and she feared that her companion really was deluded.

Jack opened the fridge and began to rummage through the contents.

"Jack?"

"Here, it's cold." He handed her a bottle of water.

Maddie looked down at the plastic bottle in her hand, her eyebrows raised and shook her head. "Please tell me we haven't come all this way for nothing."

"I hope not." Jack crouched and peered beneath the lowest shelf. "Ah, there…"

Click.

Jack shut the fridge door, grasped the side, and swung the whole thing forwards, exposing a hidden opening. He stepped past the threshold, his presence triggering an overhead light, into a small room lined with parcel-laden shelves. Against the right-hand wall a generator hummed. On the left a computer and holo-TV sat atop a dusty desk. Jack took a parcel from the shelf and used his knife to slice through the brown tape that held it shut. He pulled away the packaging material, checked the contents briefly, and moved onto the next.

Maddie peered over his shoulder. "What's in them?"

"Tools, drones, holo-tech; things that will come in handy." He tilted a box towards her and she caught the gleam from the barrel of a small pistol. "Dig in," he said. "Do you want my knife?"

Maddie stepped back but said nothing.

Jack glanced at her as he opened another box, pulling back a layer of foam to reveal a set of projectors. "I'm sorry," he said, as her silence weighed in on him. "You were probably expecting something more impressive, but we'll need this stuff."

Maddie looked around the room and shrugged, her disappointment and fatigue washing away the last of her energy. She sat down heavily on the chair by the desk and watched Jack open the parcels. "So, you have someone in London working with you," she commented.

"What? Oh, not in that sense. We had a solicitor carry out our instructions: to make purchases and have them delivered here. Those instructions were written six months ago, in my own time, but delivered to the solicitor five years ago in yours. Neither she, nor this building's caretaker – who was paid well for his discretion – had any idea who the purchases were for. They're not in London anymore."

"Oh."

Maddie's voice was flat, and yet there was something accusatory in that one syllable. Jack stopped again and met her gaze, taking in her slumped shoulders and tired face. "Why don't you lie down for a bit?" he suggested gently. "You must be tired."

"I'm fine. I'm no more tired than you. And if something in those boxes will help us find Suraya then I want to know straight away."

Jack felt her bristle, her shoulders squared defiantly. He could tell she was questioning her decision to trust him, rekindling his sense of guilt. But alongside guilt there was something else. Anxiety. Perhaps fear that he would fail her. He sighed, frustrated that his emotions should undermine his focus so easily, risk undermining his primary goal. He reminded himself that she wasn't the reason he was there. This was bigger than Maddie and Suraya, or himself.

He moved towards her, but her expression stopped him short. "This equipment makes all the difference," he said at last. "And once we know what we've got to work with we can make a plan."

Maddie nodded in reply and Jack returned to his task. She watched him for a while in silence, allowing herself to wallow in her anger and frustration. Those were safe emotions, safer than the others that clamoured for her attention. Fear and self-doubt: those needed to be kept at bay.

Restlessly, she swivelled the chair back and forth, until the holo-TV behind caught her interest. She wondered about the train crash. Her stomach twisted at the thought that people had died and that she had known this before it had even happened. Who were those people?

A glowing red dot in the corner of the TV screen told her it was working. She stared at it, considering the distance to the office window and the thickness of the walls. Holo-tech emitted very little heat and wasn't likely to be detected by a passing drone.

"Holo-on," she instructed.

Jack glanced over his shoulder as the unit flickered into life, bringing characters from a vaguely familiar soap opera into the room with them, suspended in three-dimensional form above the desk. Jack watched a moment as the legless bodies of the man and woman circled one another and shouted angrily without volume. The closer the camera zoomed in on the actors, the more disturbing their partial forms appeared. Jack had always disliked holo-TVs, even as a child.

Maddie pushed her chair backwards, away from the desk and the actors who, now kissing passionately, were uncomfortably close. She stared through them before coming to a decision. "Channel 2 News."

The actors vanished and were replaced by a newsreader at her desk.

Jack's chest tightened. He knew her at once, every detail; the way she tapped a pen twice on her desk before her eyes lifted to the camera, her cream silk shirt, offset by a red beaded necklace, and each word that she would say. Jenny Cates, whose broadcast was known to every post-war generation.

"Volume 10," Maddie instructed, leaning forwards a little on her chair.

Jack took a step closer to the news desk, where Cates announced that their drones should, *"soon be bringing footage live from the Thames, where divers are hoping to recover the body of the missing train driver."*

"It's unclear why," said Jack in a hushed voice, "but government officials have restricted media access at the riverside."

"What?" said Maddie, turning to him.

Behind her, Cates told viewers that, *"it's unclear why, but government officials have restricted media access at the riverside."*

Maddie frowned as she turned back to the screen. "Did you—"

"We're now joining our correspondent, Raymond Stannard, from the roof of the South Bank Centre," Jack continued.

"We're now joining our correspondent, Raymond Stannard..."

Maddie looked from the newsreader to Jack and back again as the newsreaders seemingly copied Jack's words.

"Raymond, what can you tell us?"

"Well Jenny," said the correspondent, *"the restriction of media again calls into question the government's claim that trains arriving from the continent are carrying food and essential supplies. The initial indication is that this may be another Fringe attack, and that this train may have in fact been carrying armaments. The implications for the government, if this is proven to be correct, are serious. We have already witnessed a dispute here between the RNLI, who were first on the scene, and the government dive and rescue team who arrived shortly after. We believe that... ah, Jenny, we can now bring you the live feed from our drone..."*

The holographic figures vanished as the flat screen lit up with footage shot from high above the Thames. Half a dozen rescue vessels spanned the width of the river.

"We understand that government divers are assessing the wreckage in the hopes of salvaging and – this is from the official statement – 'salvaging any food supplies that remain undamaged'."

Jack had seen this footage before, twenty, thirty times at least, but realised now, as the camera zoomed in on bubbles breaking on the river's surface, that he was desperately hoping his memory would be proved wrong, that history had been rewritten. But he saw what he had always seen. Amidst the frothing brown water, a diver emerged, and as he reached for the hand proffered from the lifeboat, a head became visible, lolling across his arm.

"It looks as though the body of the missing train driver has been located," said Jack, as in front of him, Jenny Cates' voice echoed his words.

Jack took another step forwards and, as though to himself, whispered, "it looks like the body of a child."

"It looks like the body of a child," the newsreader repeated.

Maddie turned to Jack. His skin was pale, his expression pained.

"Raymond are you able to see this?" Cates asked.

"Jenny, we've been asked to move further back, but we

saw what appeared to be a child just before... Hey! Hey! We're members of the press, we have freedom of..." The figure of Raymond Stannard became blurred as the camera man was jostled. *"We're from Channel Two!"* The screen went blank as Stannard's voice cried out, *"You can't... Jenny we're—"* The audio fell silent.

Cates re-materialised in front of Jack, her mouth momentarily open in an expression of shock. *"That was our correspondent, Raymond Stannard, with whom we appear to have lost contact. I believe that we can bring you more footage live from our drone, as..."*

The screen cut once more to the drone's camera, revealing a diver cradling a young boy in a yellow shirt.

"Oh..."

Maddie drew in a breath. Her hand flew to her mouth.

"They're all children," whispered Jack.

"They're all children," confirmed the voice of Jenny Cates.

Jack turned from the screen and left the room.

Maddie watched in horror while bodies were brought to the surface. Even from a distance she could see they were fragile and malnourished. A small boy with pale skin, five, maybe six years old. A teenage boy in a football shirt. And then a young girl who, with long hair and dark skin, looked so like Suraya as a child.

Maddie found her phone with trembling hands and brought up Suraya's number. Her thumb hovered over the 'call' button. She stared at the screen, with its web of cracks, and thought how Suraya's name appeared to be trapped within them. A butterfly trapped in a spider's web. She took a shaky breath and hit the back button. She screwed her eyes shut, sending a rush of tears down her cheeks.

Jack stood at the window, staring through a crack in the blind, unnerved by his reaction, trying but failing to block out the image of a small child in a yellow shirt, cradled in the cold waters of the Thames. Jack knew the significance of this moment. He had grown up with it and had known exactly what would happen. He was watching history. But he hadn't been prepared for how it would feel, watching history unfold before him without the buffer of time, that safeguard against the brutal impact of emotion. He heard Maddie approach.

"How did you know what she was going to say?" Maddie demanded.

On the opposite side of Brune Street, a block of flats disclosed small clues about the people who lived there. Jack's gaze fell on a simple painting of a tree and stick figure, taped to an upper floor window. A child's painting. He imagined a boy holding a paint brush, wearing a yellow shirt…

"Everyone in the future knows what she says," he replied. "Children grow up watching Jenny Cate's report, year after year in their classes at school. It's broadcast every Remembrance Day as a warning, 'lest we forget the real victims of war', and to remind us why extremism must never be allowed to rise again." Jack took a deep breath and rubbed his eyes, forcing himself to look away from the painting.

"So, it's true."

Jack turned to face her, unsure of her meaning. Her cheeks were tear-streaked, her voice cold.

"You really are from the future."

"Yes."

"And you knew what was going to happen, you knew that those children would die?"

There was a pause before he nodded. He knew where this was going.

"And you did nothing to stop it."

Jack raised his eyes to the ceiling. He told himself that this was history, that this had already happened. "I couldn't. This moment changes the course of the war, it will bring down the government and—"

"But they were just kids. And us? We used their deaths as a distraction to save our own lives."

"I didn't cause this. I'm not the enemy. Those children were used as political ballast, but that decision will be the government's undoing. Their lives will have meant something."

She took a step towards him, her hands raised, her knuckles blanched white. Her lips parted to speak but she shook her head and turned away. "Fuck you."

Maddie yanked open the door and fled up the stairs. She reached the top floor and threw herself against the fire escape, but it was locked. She took a step back and raised her foot to kick it open, before remembering that she was in hiding, a bounty on her head, her likeness in circulation amongst the government drones and their human informants. She was trapped and impotent.

The corridor in which she stood, with its clean banality, felt suddenly oppressive. Her foot caught the fire hydrant next to the door, and she stooped down, wrenched it from its fixtures and hurled it against the wall with all her strength. The plaster cracked, but the wall stood firm. She slid down, her back against the wall, and sobbed.

Jack remained rooted to the spot, listening to Maddie's footsteps disappear above him. Her accusation unsettled him. Was she right? Was he some kind of heartless monster? But she hadn't grasped yet that most of his actions would never come to pass. No, he wasn't heartless, but he was a hypocrite. He had pledged to help Suraya despite knowing that this too would be undone. He tried to justify this, telling himself that Suraya may have information on Kingsley, but in truth, the difference was that his connection to Suraya had, by a twist of fate, become personal. He didn't know Suraya; he didn't owe her anything. But he couldn't shake the idea that through helping her he might in some way make amends for all that his mother had endured, for which he had been the embodiment. Redemption was what he sought.

Jack thought of the Fringe members who had worked through the night, setting explosives on the bridge. They too would seek redemption for the unexpected consequences of their actions. Jack considered Maddie and, in some ways, envied her: how much easier it was to act in the moment, free from the burden of knowledge of what was to come. How could she understand the significance of the Blackfriars Bombing? He too would have taken the moral high ground, were he not weighed down by eighty years of historical hindsight. It brought to mind that occasion, a few months back, when Howard had tried, but failed, to dissuade him from his current path.

§

February 2150

London

As the date for the mission drew close, Jack threw himself into training. Howard was busy overseeing the preparations for Gaia, and so they'd not seen one another for a while.

Jack ought to have noticed the light seeping under the door, an amber flush across the tiles, but that day's combat training had taken its toll and Jack had arrived home dog-tired and bruised. He opened the front door, stepped into the living room, and startled as Howard rose from the sofa to greet him.

"Jesus, Howard! A bit of warning…I could have hurt you." He put down the lamp he'd snatched up from the console table.

Howard raised an eyebrow. "By the looks of you I wouldn't be so confident."

Jack laughed and took Howard's hand, wincing slightly at the older man's firm grasp.

"Christ! Are you sure you're going to make it through boot camp?" Howard asked, releasing Jack's bruised hand.

"It's good to see you, too. Make yourself comfortable. Help yourself to a drink," he added, heading for the bedroom. "I need a shower. I'll be five minutes."

"Of course."

"There's still a drop of the Glengoyne," he shouted through the open door.

Howard fetched a couple of glasses and picked up the bottle from Jack's desk, turning it over to read the label. Highland single malt, aged fifty years. Fifty years old when Jack's grandfather had bought it, and twenty more years in the bottle. He recalled the recent trial of two brothers who had attempted to access a time capsule for the purpose of sending their newly distilled whisky back in time. He could see their thought process: distil whisky now, send it back fifty years to be casked, then reap the benefits straight away.

Howard considered the bottle in his hand. In all honesty, the flavour rarely benefited from so long in the barrel. Sometimes older was better, but sometimes it was just older. Had this bottle been left unopened, however, it would have been worth a fortune.

"Robert would turn in his grave to see us drinking this," Howard called.

"Investment for investment's sake is pointless," Jack shouted back. "And I may as well enjoy it while I can."

Howard sighed and poured out two doubles. He swirled the liquid in his glass, raised it to his nose to savour the aroma, then sat himself at Jack's desk to wait. The desk was covered in printed maps of London, dated from the past few years back to the late 2060s. Jack's notes were scrawled across them. Howard smiled to himself; Jack was ever the historian, and his love of antiquated documentation had always amused him. And yet Jack's training reports had shown he was quite skilled with technology, demonstrating an instinctive ability with both software and hardware. That ability hadn't come from Mary's family, and Howard wondered if it was something Jack had inherited from his father.

He put the glass down and pulled an envelope from his jacket, on which Jack's name was written in one fluid line of ink. Mary had asked that he give it to Jack when the time was right. Howard hadn't read it, of course, and could only guess at how much Mary had revealed. Would it disclose the truth about Jack's father? Would that change Jack's decision, or simply increase his determination to be the one to end the affliction of time travel?

Howard leant forwards, rested his elbows on the desk, and massaged his forehead. He hadn't slept well since Jack's announcement. His wife, Joanne fretted and worried about him, which he hated, not least because the cause of his disquiet was something she knew nothing about. Of course, Joanne was aware that he and Mary had once been close, but not that they had been engaged. And Joanne had no idea that Mary had once asked him to care for her child.

Howard had failed Mary thirty years ago, turned his back on her and Jack. Five years later, both his love for Mary and his shame, had pulled him back to her and the boy. He'd tried his best to atone for having abandoned them, but now, here he was – with Jack teetering on the edge of oblivion – poised to fail Mary all over again.

Jack emerged from the bedroom, and Howard tucked the envelope back inside his pocket. There was still time.

Howard stood up and handed Jack a glass. "You know, I don't think the capsule's big enough for all these," Howard joked, gesturing at the maps.

Jack tilted his head to one side and narrowed his eyes while he considered them. "Good job I'm only going back to the 21st then, not sure what 19th century Londoners would make of an iHolo." He grinned and raised his glass to Howard then took a mouthful of the amber liquid, closing his eyes for a moment to lose himself in its heady aroma.

"In all seriousness Jack, you don't have to do this."

Jack sighed and sat down on the sofa. "I wondered when this was coming," he said, leaning back and resting his legs on the coffee table.

"This isn't what Mary would have wanted, whatever you may think. It's not too late to withdraw," Howard continued, taking the armchair opposite and leaning forwards, his elbows on his knees.

"I don't think my mother knew what she wanted," said Jack. "At least not until the end." He pictured that day: the sun glancing off the river, the book he had put down when his phone had begun to ring. He recalled the tremor in the voice of the young receptionist as she had sought to find the right words. His first thought had been that Mary was finally free…

"I wish that you'd discussed this with me."

"Why? I have no family, no one that relies on me. I'm the perfect choice."

"You know that's not true."

Jack shrugged and took another sip of whisky.

"Besides," Howard continued, "there are other

volunteers who may do…better than you. You weren't exactly built for this – it's a brutal time."

"Thanks for the vote of confidence, and if you mean Gunter, then you try having a conversation with him." Jack lowered his feet and sat forwards. "I may not be a soldier, but my background in history and my…let's say, birth abilities, give me an edge that the other candidates don't have. Besides, as it turns out, I'm not a bad shot." He rubbed his bruised ribs gingerly. "Bit more work on the hand-to-hand combat and I'm good to go."

"But Jack, I don't think you fully appreciate what you'll be facing, how witnessing historic events first-hand might affect you. You'll have difficult decisions to make, sacrifices, and yours won't be the only one. Jack, I know you, your kindness, your empathy. How on earth will you manage?"

"Empathy? Not sure Nesta would agree with that. Emotionally guarded, I think was the polite way she described me."

"Jack, don't joke about this."

"I'm sorry. Look, I was given a full psychological assessment and I passed. I'm an historian, Howard, viewing events objectively and dispassionately is what I'm trained to do. I'll have five, maybe six days to get through. I think I can put my own emotions on hold for that long."

Howard shook his head slightly and leant back in the armchair. Both men sat in silence, lost in their own thoughts. "Do you ever hear from Nesta?" Howard asked eventually.

"A couple of emails over the past few years."

Howard raised his eyebrows in enquiry.

"I don't read them," Jack responded, looking down at the tumbler in his hand.

"I'm sorry."

"Don't be, I couldn't give her what she wanted." Jack raised the glass and downed the liquid, blocking out everything but the sensation of its heat in his throat.

"Have you eaten anything this evening?"

Jack shook his head. "Not yet. I've got leftovers I can reheat."

Howard stood up and moved towards the kitchen. "I'll sort them out for you."

"It's fine, I can do it." He stood up.

"Letting people help you is not a weakness, Jack. Sit down. Please."

Jack drew in a breath, accepted defeat with a slight nod, and settled back down on the sofa.

For better or for worse, Jack's grandparents had instilled a firm sense of order into their grandson, but the state of the fridge, the dirty plates and glasses piled by the sink, revealed the toll that training had taken on him. Howard sifted through containers of half-eaten food, throwing out several that had seen better days, and located the microwave under a pile of takeaway bags. He stacked the dishwasher while the food warmed, found the last clean fork, then carried it into the living room.

"Here you go…"

The empty tumbler had slipped from Jack's fingers. His chest gently rose and fell.

Howard set the plate and glass down and fetched a blanket from the bedroom, laying it carefully across him so as not to wake him. He sat back down on the armchair and took another mouthful of the Glengoyne. Howard recognised something of the child Jack had once been in his face as he slept, bringing back memories of their earliest encounters with one another.

Their first meeting had been on Jack's fifth birthday, and Howard had arrived with a gift that the boy had sat and held, but not unwrapped. He'd answered every one of Howard's questions concisely and politely, but offered nothing more, nothing of himself.

The same cautious reserve had remained until about a year later, when Howard had managed to persuade Robert and Sophia to bring Jack along to a picnic he'd organised at Greenwich Park. Howard thought that Jack might enjoy playing with his daughter, but it was the buildings and their history that had fascinated the young boy, whose never ending questions had stumped him more often than not. Jack had still avoided answering any questions about himself or his home life, but Howard's willingness to follow Jack's lead in conversation had opened a door between them.

He wondered, as he often did, what that child, and this man, would be like if he had raised him himself. Outwardly, Jack was well-adjusted and successful enough in his chosen path, but the emotional scars of his childhood had held him back, or rather kept him apart from those that he might have been closer to.

Joanne was convinced that Jack was still in love with Nesta, and Howard thought she was probably right. But who could blame Nesta for moving on? Jack always held a part of himself back, and though he might love Nesta, he doubted that she knew it. He'd probably never admitted it, even to himself.

Yes, he could see how Nesta might not think Jack empathic, with academic objectivity that served as a protective barrier, but Howard was privileged to be one of the few people with whom Jack would let down his guard. Perhaps he was wrong? Perhaps Jack's empathy would serve him well in the past, ensure that his decisions were balanced and selfless. Like Mary.

Howard stood up and pulled the letter from his jacket. He bent down to place it on the coffee table, then hesitated. He ran his thumb across the letters, then straightened and replaced the envelope in his pocket. There was still time. He returned the plate of food to the kitchen, turned out the lights, and quietly let himself out.

§

15th August 2073
Spitalfields

It was hours since Maddie had stormed out and Jack had agonised over whether to follow her, eventually deciding that time and space would do more than any entreaty he could offer. He'd been afraid that she might leave the building, turn her back on his offer of help and look for Suraya alone. But she struck him as practical, more likely to place Suraya's needs above any feelings of her own.

Jack tried to distract himself, to forget the look of disgust in Maddie's eyes by busying himself sorting through his equipment. His efforts to mend the water-damaged iHolo had been in vain, and instead he'd transferred the data to an early model, found in a parcel post-marked 2071. The older technology wasn't as sophisticated as he'd hoped, but it would do.

The door handle turned.

Jack straightened. He lifted the smart pistol from the table, setting it to manual, but relaxed when he heard Maddie curse from the hall beyond. The lock clicked open and Maddie slid through, pushing her back against the door to close it.

Their eyes met but neither spoke, and Maddie remained where she was, her hands behind her back, holding the handle as though she might yet turn and run.

In the silence, Jack felt the gulf between them widening. Who was he, with his middle-class background, and his white male privilege, to tell her that he was sorry? He searched for the right words, for the right explanation, then caught the look in her eyes. Sometimes the simplest words were the only ones. "I'm sorry." He swallowed. "I should have told you what was going to happen."

Maddie nodded and lowered her eyes to the floor.

"Here." He held out the iHolo. "I've uploaded my files. They may not change your opinion of me, but they might help you understand why I didn't intervene."

Maddie remained where she was, staring at the small tablet in Jack's outstretched arm, stepping forwards to take it just as Jack began to pull back. She turned and ducked through the doorway to the darkened storeroom and sat down on the floor next to the now empty shelves. Legs crossed, she laid the iHolo in her lap and released a shuddering breath.

"Holo-on," she whispered, and a dozen icons materialised in the air, softly illuminating the corner of the room. There were academic papers as well as excerpts from memoires and news reports. "Open 'Fifty Year Anniversary' document," Maddie instructed. "Flat-screen mode."

The icons faded and left only the screen alight, displaying an editorial piece from the European Observer. It wove a picture of the human cost of climate change, London at war, and the descent of much of Europe into the grips of fear-led fascism. It discussed the rise of the far right in British politics which led to hundreds of political prisoners, most of them migrants, being held in the north of England, their families removed to France for 'safe-keeping'.

In the immediate aftermath of Blackfriars, the government was quick to condemn the Fringe. It was the terrorist organisation that had taken the lives of thirty-two children; the terrorist organisation whose wilful destruction of essential food supplies and their transport hub had undermined efforts to feed the city's population; the terrorist organisation who saw human suffering as acceptable collateral damage.

Just days later, an undercover journalist discovered government warehouses near Victoria Station, stockpiled with food, prompting a whistle-blower to leak documents confirming that the Blackfriars line had only ever been used to transport armaments.

The government blustered: they had no knowledge of the warehouses; the footage of government security surrounding it was fake news; the Fringe was responsible. But it was too late. Their earlier, public lamentation had backfired. How could the government justify starving the city of London in order to substantiate its lies?

The first domino had fallen.

The victims of the derailment were identified as the children of political prisoners in the North, all of whom had exchanged information, or submitted confessions, in return for their families' safety. The government tried to distance itself, suspending the Home Secretary pending an investigation, but it was too little, too late.

Angry demonstrators marched through the city, defying the police and their drones, to paint the names of the dead on the pavement outside Parliament. The Prime Minister was reminded of his own words, that 'in times of war, more extreme forms of persuasion may be sanctioned.' Proof, his opponents claimed, of his own culpability.

In 2076, two years after the end of the war, twin monuments were unveiled. One stood on the banks of the Thames, the other outside the Parliament buildings in Manchester. Both were inscribed with the names of all thirty-two children.

Maddie read down the list of names until they swam before her, her eyes filled with tears. She pushed them away with the heel of her hand, forcing herself to read on. The coverage of the Blackfriars Bombing and the revelations of cruelty that followed did, as Jack had said, mark a turning point in the war. Ordinary folk who'd kept their heads down out of fear, centre-right politicians, members of the armed forces and wartime opportunists found that they could no longer be complicit.

Shock turned to outrage, which transformed into a new wave of resistance. The government might yet have withstood the backlash if it weren't for the electrifying effect of the disaster on the Nordic countries, whose involvement until then had been limited to diplomacy. Bolstered by the Scandinavian Defence Union, the Liberal Coalition gained ground, and by the spring of 2074, Britain and Europe's far right had conceded defeat.

Maddie's breath caught in her throat. Spring of 2074.

Next spring, and this would all be over. She pushed herself up from the floor and ran through to Jack.

"Is this true?" she cried, thrusting the tablet at him. "Will the war be over by spring?" Her breathing was rapid, her eyes wide.

Jack raised his eyebrows and smiled faintly. "Yes."

Maddie's nostrils flared and she bit her lips as she turned from Jack, trying to hold back the flood of emotions. The war wasn't over yet, but it would be, and the cause for which she fought would be victorious.

Jack stood and took a step towards her.

Maddie turned to him, her face contorted. "It's so unfair," she cried, "that their lives must be sacrificed for a peace they'll never know."

"I know." Again, the image of a child in a yellow shirt filled his mind, and he felt his eyes begin to prickle.

Then Maddie was there in front of him, her head resting on his chest, her shoulders shaking with tangled sorrow and hope. Jack put his arms around her and, unseen, allowed his own tears to fall, unsure of whether they were for the lost children, or something else, something more. The dull weight Jack had carried those last few weeks lifted a little, falling away with his tears.

At last, Maddie's shoulders stilled, her grief spent. She felt Jack's body tense and stepped away from him, mumbling an apology.

Jack cleared his throat and gave a small shake of his head. His skin tingled where she had leant into him, but he forced himself to ignore it, to refocus on the items laid out on the table. "Um…" He swallowed. "We should work out how best to use these."

Maddie's face clouded, followed by the slightest shake of her head, then she stepped up to the table. "Okay. What have we got?"

Working through the assembled technology took time, but Jack quickly realised that without her he would never have understood the nuances of items he'd handled only as historical replicas. She had a natural ability when it came to explaining things, and Jack found himself thinking how she would make a good teacher.

"What did you do? Before the war that is," he asked.

"Mostly piecemeal work," she replied. "Job opportunities are limited for migrant families."

He pressed his lips together in a silent expression of empathy. "Would you ever consider teaching?"

"No," Maddie laughed. "Being responsible for one child was hard enough. What about you?" She glanced up at him. "You must work for the secret service or something like that."

"Believe it or not, when not saving the world, I'm a historian."

"What? Like a professor?" she raised one eyebrow doubtfully.

"Yep. I'm a modern-day Indiana Jones."

Maddie shrugged uncertainly, his historical reference obscure. "So," she wrinkled her nose. "You're not a solider, or from a military background?"

Jack shook his head.

"I guess there's an advantage in knowing your history, if you are going to travel back in time…"

"But?"

Maddie shifted back on her seat to consider him. "But why would a historian volunteer for something so dangerous? I'm not saying that you can't handle yourself, but I don't imagine there were many undercover operations in your day job. You won't have faced attack."

Jack inclined his head, the corner of his mouth raised in a faint smile. "Oh, I don't know. I did the occasional guest lecture at UCL; the students can be brutal."

Maddie rolled her eyes.

Jack turned to the window, his smile fading. He pictured London's landmarks, those threatened by floods even as vast tracts of the planet were reduced to dust. He thought about the nurse who had vanished from existence, midway through medicating him for time travel. And he thought about his mother, who had risked and lost everything in her own attempt to secure the planet's future. "I volunteered because I know how important it is to succeed." He turned back to Maddie. "And I believe that I will."

A smile flickered at the corners of her mouth. "Good."

She stood up and stretched, then caught sight of her own clothes, stained and filthy. Her stomach tightened when she realised the stains were blood, and not her own. "I don't think there's anything more I can do here," she said, indicating the drone that she'd assembled. "I'm going to clean up a bit."

She grabbed her bag from the sofa and made herself walk calmly into the bathroom, tearing her top off as soon at the door was closed and throwing it in the sink. The Snag's face filled her mind, and she forced herself to breathe deeply as the voice inside her head taunted her.

You killed that man. You did.

"No!" she silenced it. "I will *not* go there."

She pulled off her head scarf, stripped, then worked to wash away the blood and sweat of the past twelve hours, scrubbing her top and cleansing her skin, before finally bending her head over the sink and allowing the cool water to run through her hair.

She found the last of her clean tops, pulled it over her head, then twisted her hair back from her face. She gathered her wet things and headed out to hang them from the top of the blinds, hopeful that the residual heat of the day would soon dry them.

Jack stood at the small kitchen counter, considering an array of mismatched ingredients.

"Instant noodles with a choice of pulses?" he suggested when Maddie joined him. "And congee for dessert? Just don't ask how long the noodles have been in the back of these cupboards."

Maddie laughed and took a packet, turning it over in her hands to find the use-by date.

Jack leant his hip against the counter and watched while she picked up each item in turn. She had twisted her hair into a braid at either side of her head, but the shorter locks had escaped, their curls weighed down by the water collecting at the ends. A droplet was gathering size, seeming to defy gravity for an impossibly long time, before finally falling into the gentle dip above her collar bone. The sudden urge to brush it from her skin caught him by surprise, and he cleared his throat and pushed himself back a step.

"So, what's it to be?" he asked.

She shook her head and laughed. "I'm not sure I'm desperate enough to risk the noodles yet, so I think mixed pulses with tinned tomatoes will do. Shame we don't have any more of those anchovies."

"Or the wine," Jack added wistfully.

Maddie took a breath then held it in thought, turning to look at the door. "There might be useful stuff in the other offices?" she suggested.

Jack raised his eyebrows. "It won't hurt to look."

A window sat above the turn of the stairs, its blinds drawn to conceal them from the street outside. A break in the slats, however, revealed a glimpse of the rapidly darkening sky. Jack glanced at his watch. He hadn't realised how much time had passed, and it would soon be quite dark. Even so, something beyond the approaching night had made his stomach contract, and he eyed the small patch of sky warily.

A soft click, accompanied by Maddie's hum of satisfaction, drew him back to their task. "That didn't take you long," he remarked, impressed.

"The lock's old." She shrugged. "If you look closely, you can tell which keys have been pressed time and again."

Jack peered closer. The keypad was grimy with grease and dust, save for around four keys. "I never thought of that. But there are still, what, at least two hundred possible combinations?" he said, raising his eyebrows.

"I guess I got lucky."

Jack smiled but hung back as Maddie turned on her torch and entered the workspace of *David Han: Acupuncturist*. "I may as well make a start on the next lock," he called, "see if my luck's as good as yours."

Using Maddie's method, Jack set about finding the code for the next office – a tax consultant. The same approach would be no use on their own door, where the code never remained the same. Not to mention that the door and wall had been reinforced, protecting it against brute strength. Those precautions might be of benefit over the next few days but had been irrelevant until now; this building had been chosen partly for its proximity to the central Republican base but, more importantly, because historical records confirmed that it had never been broken into, at least until now.

Finally successful, Jack pushed the door wide. The last hues of dusk lit the corridor in shades of grey, but inside the windowless office it was pitch black. Jack turned on his torch and ran the beam of light across a sofa, desk and chairs, a coat rack, complete with a long winter coat, and finally the kitchenette which, with multiple mugs and jars looked promising. Jack opened the first jar. The aroma of coffee filled his nose, but it was stale, the instant granules welded together in a single lump at the bottom of the cannister. A second jar held tea bags and a third, sugar, both of which were welcome.

Maddie's shadow appeared in the doorway. "Jack?"

"I'm here," he called from behind the door. "Anything useful?"

"A couple of blankets and some herbal tea. I'll try the next room."

As she moved away, he heard a faint rumble. He froze on the spot and listened. Just a truck in the distance, he told himself, though his pulse had quickened.

He heard a click from the corridor – Maddie accessing another office – and turned his attention to the lowest cupboards. Sachets of long-life milk sat at the back of the unit, alongside a stack of magazines that had no connection whatsoever to tax. He shook his head and closed the door, standing up and pulling open the one in front of him. The hairs on the back of his arms rose to stand on end.

"Please, not again," he breathed.

The air grew thick with static charge, fizzing at the margins of his vision. Jack clenched his teeth as pain surged, seeping from his temples, around his jaw and brow, until it burned white behind his closed eyes.

A lightning bolt shook the building. Jack crashed forwards, colliding with the open cupboard door. He fell to his hands and knees, the wail of the wind fighting with the voices that raged in his head...

*Fuck you! Fuck all of this! ... I had to, Jack. I had to save her... **Get down!** ... I guess you were right, Jack... **pfipp** ... Go, be with them... **Shit! Stay awake, Jack**... We'll find a way to put this right... **I have a message for you about Hart**...*

"Jack!" Maddie's cry cut through the clamour.

The wailing gave way to a choking nausea, and Jack realised that it was not the cry of the wind he had heard, but his own howl of pain.

"Jack, what's happening?"

She was there, steadying him, the glint from the torch beam reflected in her wide, dark eyes.

"God, you're bleeding. Come on, can you stand?"

Jack focussed on the pressure of her hand on his arm, forcing himself to breath in deeply and exhale slowly, then nodded. Grasping the worktop with one hand, he pulled himself to his feet.

Back in their own office, Jack lowered himself to the sofa and leant forwards, digging his fingertips into his forehead. "Ah!" he sucked in sharply and pulled his hand away. Blood ran slick across his fingers.

"Here, sit back." Maddie perched next to him and pressed a towel to his head. They sat in silence as the minutes passed and Maddie watched Jack's pulse, visible beneath the skin of his neck, as it slowed and resumed a steady rhythm. The storm clouds had dissipated, the fleeting light of dusk replaced by that of the moon, whose pale glow filtered through the blinds, tracing silver lines across the room, the sofa and their bodies.

His memories were still racing to catch up with him, but in his mind, Jack heard the words repeating over and over – *a message for you about Hart... a message... about Hart.*

Maddie shifted next to him, bringing him back to the present, and pushed the towel more firmly against the gash on his forehead. "Was that the same thing that happened to you before?"

Jack winced a little and nodded, then risked a sideways glance.

Maddie's brow furrowed in thought. She took a breath, a question on her lips, but hesitated, breathing away the words. With her free hand she took Jack's chin and gently turned his head so that the moonlight fell across his face. She pulled herself up a little, her breath warm on his cheek, and lifted away the towel to inspect the wound.

"I think it's stopped bleeding," she said.

Jack waited.

She bit her lips, then sighed. "Jack, this isn't just a side effect from travelling through time, is it."

Jack stared at the blank wall ahead. "No."

"You said something before, something about your body responding to changes in your past?"

He nodded, knowing that she had made the connection.

"So, something just happened to you, a change in your past. Only, most people wouldn't have realised, right?"

Jack shook his head.

"Your parents then, they must have been from different times. You're a mixed, uh, mixed-time—"

"Person of Mixed-Era Origin – a Cronod," he added with a hint of derision.

"Cronod?"

"It's slang for chronological oddity."

"I'm sorry," she replied. "Not for that," she added quickly, "but, I mean, I told you about my parents, but never asked you about yours."

"It's a complicated story," he said. "And I only know part of it."

"What time are they from?"

Jack felt his stomach tighten; the truth was new to him. Raw and painful. The words came out as a whisper. "My mum is from my own time; my father is from yours."

"Really? How did they meet?"

Jack sat forwards, avoiding Maddie's gaze. It was going to come out at some point, as soon as he saw Hart's name on that list, he had known it. But how could he tell Maddie the truth of his conception? The truth of who his father was? And what good would it do to tell her?

Maddie felt his hesitancy. "I'm sorry, it's none of my business."

"My mother was a member of Earth Revolution. She travelled back to 2070, hoping to change the future, but her mission didn't go to plan." He sighed and stared at the floor, watching the way the beam of moonlight fell across his boots. "I've never met my father. He doesn't know that I exist."

Maddie waited, unsure whether or not to ask more. "Does your mum still work for ER?" she asked at last.

Jack shook his head. "She was left very unwell. Complications from her mission. She died a couple of years ago."

"I'm so sorry. And that's what makes this so important for you." Maddie caught the change in his expression. His eyes, one moment haunted, were the next moment blank.

Jack turned to her. "Climate change is spiralling out of control. What I'm doing is important for everyone."

Maddie nodded. He didn't want to discuss his parents, that was clear. But his seizures were different. What if one occurred when they were at the Republican base?

"Do you have any warning, before a seizure happens?" she asked.

"A few moments," he replied, leaning back again. "I've been experiencing the effects of polymorphic memories since I was a child, but the past few have been different, more intense."

"Why? What do you remember?"

Jack studied the ceiling, the smooth, white-washed plaster. In his own time, it was yellowed and cracked, and at some unknown point in the future it would simply no longer be. He was sure now that the changes to his past were connected to his mission, and replied at last, "Someone's attempting to kill me."

Maddie's mouth opened but she didn't speak.

"I suspect it's the Republic, it's in their interests to prevent me from completing my mission."

"How many attempts have they made?" asked Maddie, her eyes wide.

"That was the third one."

"And what happened?"

Jack shook his head. "The timeline's been shaken up – it takes a while for the dust to settle, for the changes to become clear." He closed his eyes and tried to decipher the images that had flashed through his mind. His hand. Had he hurt his hand? He raised his left arm into a shaft of light to examine it, turning it over to discover thick scars across his palm. They'd been there for three years. But also, they hadn't.

Maddie reached for his hand and drew it on to her lap. The back was broad, his veins raised in the heat of the room. She turned it over, holding his wrist with one hand and gently tracing a finger down the pale line of the longest scar. "I noticed these the first night we met," she said softly, "when you'd passed out in the bathroom." She felt Jack's pulse beneath her fingers and, as her eyes met his, it quickened slightly.

"They weren't there," said Jack. "In one strand of memory at least." He followed the trail of moonlight across her face, from where it brushed her cheek, to its curve across her parted lips. "But you were there... in both."

Maddie's chest rose and fell rapidly as she felt his gaze move across her face and settle on her mouth. He sat forwards, and she leant in towards him, but a clatter from the hallway below brought her to her feet.

Jack flew to the door, drawing his gun, and pressed his ear to the wood.

"Inside?" Maddie asked in a whisper.

"First floor," Jack mouthed back, pointing down.

Maddie dashed silently to the storeroom, returning with the scanner that they had taken from the Snag. She flicked it on and glanced down the list of active drone locations. None of them were within a half-mile radius. She caught Jack's eye and shook her head. If it was a Snag, then at least he didn't have back-up.

She joined Jack at the door and loaded her own weapon. "It could be anyone from the neighbourhood," she whispered. "People still living here are bound to notice that the door's been disturbed."

They heard another clatter from the floor below. Jack tilted his head and raised an eyebrow.

"I came across the cleaning cupboard earlier," she confessed, "and might have left the odd broom and mop lying about."

A look of amusement flashed across Jack's face, cut short by the creak of the staircase.

"We need to be sure," he whispered.

Maddie swallowed and nodded, gently pushing down the catch on the door as they heard the footsteps mount the stairs. They both strained to listen. As the footsteps moved past, Maddie yanked back the door.

Jack stepped out and took aim. "Don't move," he warned.

"I... I'm looking for Maddie," the figured stammered.

"Max?" Maddie rushed from the door and grabbed the man's shoulder, turning him to face the pale glow from the window. His appearance shocked her. Dark shadows made hollows beneath his eyes and his jaw was swollen and red. "God, you look awful!" she exclaimed.

Max squinted at the shadowy figure standing behind her, arms still raised and weapon aimed. "You can thank you friend for that," he said, a hint of resentment in his voice.

Maddie glanced over her shoulder. "You can put that down," she said, "it's only Max."

She took him by the elbow and headed towards the door.

Jack didn't move. "Why are you here?" he asked. "And on whose authority?"

"For God's sake, Jack."

"Are we expecting other agents?" Jack continued.

"Jack!" Maddie protested.

"I need to know if we can trust him."

"I helped you escape before, didn't I? And got this for my troubles." He pointed to his bruised face. "Not to mention hours of interrogation."

Maddie touched his arm. "I'm so sorry, Max."

Jack lowered the gun slightly. "So why are you here?"

Max looked from Maddie to Jack and back again. "To help you find Suraya."

It was the truth; it was written all over his face. Jack sighed and relaxed his arms, tilting his head towards the office. "Go in."

Maddie led Max into the room and sat him down on the sofa.

He raised his eyebrows, taking in the array of technology that covered the coffee table, then pushed his glasses up his nose. "Wow, you've been busy."

"I'll get you some water," said Maddie, heading for the fridge.

Jack followed her, taking the bottles she handed him, whispering, "How the hell did he find us?"

Maddie shrugged. "I don't know, I didn't…" The colour drained from her face as she realised her mistake. "I dialled his number." She caught the look on Jack's face. "I was upset! But it didn't connect. I didn't speak to him."

"But he's your tech expert," said Jack.

Maddie nodded.

"I can hear you, you know," called Max. "And don't worry, I'm not an idiot."

Maddie returned to the sofa and handed him a bottle. Jack moved to the window, peering through a gap in the blind to the street beyond.

"No one else knows our location?" Maddie asked.

"Of course not." Max screwed up his face. "Is that what you think? That I'd just turn you in?"

"I'm sorry." Maddie sat down and rubbed a hand over her face. "A lot's happened in the past few days. Are you sure that no one's followed you?"

"When Sarah discovers I'm gone, she'll track my phone. I sent it for a ride on a drone, so it should keep her guessing."

"Your iPhone 65?" asked Maddie with surprise, remembering how proud Max had been after his dodgy contact came good and delivered the latest model.

Max shrugged. "It's just circuitry. Some things can be replaced."

A chill crept through Maddie's skin. She leant towards Max. "Has there been any news?"

"I don't know," he replied with a shake of the head. "I'm not sure that Sarah would tell me now anyway – she's not convinced by my claim that you coerced me into helping you."

"Is she okay?" Maddie pictured her fist flying towards Sarah's face in rage.

"Well, she looks marginally better than I do."

Maddie sighed with frustration. "It's all such a mess." She bit her lips, then considered Max. "How did you even get here anyway? The bridges must be blocked off."

"You can still cross upriver. I took the long way round on my bike. Have you heard what they're saying about the train that fell into the Thames?"

Maddie felt Jack's gaze and her face darkened as she glanced in his direction. "Yes, we heard."

Something in Maddie's expression stopped Max from saying anything more. His attention turned on Jack, though his words were still directed to Maddie. "And was your hunch, right?"

Jack folded his arms and eyed them both, bemused and irritated in equal measure to be subject to their assessment. He raised his eyebrows, waiting.

"Yes," Maddie replied. "It was."

"So, who are you then?" said Max, at last addressing Jack.

"I am a man who really needs to eat something, before

I can even think of explaining and justifying myself all over again."

Nonplussed, Max looked to Maddie for an explanation.

She rolled her eyes. "How do instant noodles sound?"

§

Jack let the cool water flow over his hands until it filled the sink, then pulled off his shirt and plunged it into the basin, pummelling it against the enamel with more force than was required. Max had gone with Maddie to collect items she'd spotted in the neighbouring offices, and Jack was grateful for the silence, for a pause in the endless questioning and disbelief. As with Maddie, he didn't blame Max for his doubt, but he hadn't appreciated the hour-long tirade on the implausibility, if not impossibility, of time-travel, the arguments for which belied Jack's very existence.

He leant forwards, a hand on either side of the basin, staring into his own eyes which saw beyond the confines of this moment in time. Was that why it bothered him? Was Max's scepticism a reminder of every time his word had been questioned? Of every occasion in his childhood where he had fought to be believed. His grandparents had remained silent on the subject of his mixed-era heritage and, with a mother who was known to be receiving psychiatric care, most people put the confusion of polymorphic memories down to a 'mental imbalance'. Jack was in his late teens before he began to see that the stigma his grandparents attached to his genetics was far less damaging than the misunderstanding that grew in its place.

Maddie had struggled to believe him at first and yet she had been open to the truth. He raised an eyebrow, recalling that she had accused him of being crazy. But she enquired, rather than denied, and listened when others might have turned away. He thought of Nesta. She had never doubted him: in fact she'd known what he was long before he'd confided in her. But her interest in his ability to remember multiple timelines had always made him a little uncomfortable. He agreed with her that there was an unspoken discrimination against Cronods that needed to be addressed, but he didn't share her belief that he was 'special'. It was not a status that he sought.

Gingerly, he touched the purple bruises that ran across his stomach. He'd been lucky; if the Snag had hit any higher, he'd have broken some ribs. He turned his left hand over, looking more closely at the scars that laced his palm. He tried to draw the memories forward but struggled to get past the recollection of Maddie's finger, trailing across his skin. He threw his head back, frustrated with himself and, giving up, changed tack.

He drained the sink, wrung out his shirt, then ran the tap to wash while thinking over their plan for the morning. They'd made some changes, now that Max was here, and in that at least, his presence wasn't a bad thing. Jack swept his hand over his face, pushing away the excess water, but making no attempt to dry himself. There was no need, the heat of the day had bled seamlessly into the night.

He left the bathroom and walked to the window, stretching to hang his shirt over the blinds. Behind him, the others returned from their forage.

Max went straight to the kitchen counter, dropping an assortment of boxes and containers, but Maddie paused just inside the door. She watched the moonlight ripple across Jack's skin as he turned. The droplets of water on his chest glinted silver, then disappeared one by one as he pulled a new shirt over his head and across his body. He looked up, their eyes meeting.

"So," Max announced from the kitchen. "We have every hot drink under the sun, which isn't particularly helpful right now, and one packet of custard creams." He waved the biscuits in the air. "Anyone?"

Maddie tore her eyes away from Jack. "Er... no. Thanks. I think I'm just going to try to get some sleep. Tomorrow's an early start."

Max's face fell, taking on again the strained look that she'd first seen back at the Hub. "Yeah," he said quietly.

"You're right. Me too." He looked around the room, sleeping arrangements not being a topic they'd discussed.

"I've made myself up a bed in the storeroom," said Jack. "You two take the sofa."

"No, you should take the sofa," said Max. "I can sleep in the chair."

"Really." Jack shook his head. "It's fine. Night."

Maddie watched him leave, swinging the door shut behind him, closing himself off. He didn't look back at her. She sighed, then turned to the sofa, which ran along two walls of the room. "I'll take this side," she said, shifting the cushions so that when she lay down, she was facing the storeroom door.

Max took off his glasses and laid them on the table, then stretched out on his back. He stared up at the ceiling. "Do you really believe him?" he asked quietly.

Maddie stared ahead, beyond the wall, picturing Jack on the other side. She wondered what thoughts were running through his mind. Would he have nightmares tonight, like he'd had at Richborne Terrace? Was that why he'd set himself apart from them, apart from her? Maybe this was his way of telling her she'd misunderstood. That moment they'd shared, or almost shared, was not about to be repeated. And what was she thinking anyway? Tomorrow, they would try to find Suraya, and nothing should distract her from that.

She pictured her sister the previous summer, confident and bubbly, flirting with boys and teasing Maddie for her own lack of interest. She smiled to herself, recalling how she'd joked that she was 'too old' to flirt. And then she remembered where Suraya was, where they thought she was, and prayed that they would find her – that confident, bubbly girl – and not just the shell of someone she used to be. She stopped before her thoughts spiralled.

"Maddie?"

"What?"

"Jack – do you really believe him?"

"Yes. I do." She shifted the cushion beneath her cheek, closed her eyes and slept.

§

Battersea Power Station

Kayson Hart replaced the oil painting on the wall and paused for a moment, as he always did, to admire the texture of the paint, the lines and shapes that echoed the iconic art deco structure in which he stood. Picasso may have set out to paint a man with a fireplace, but for Hart, the artist had rendered something that remained stubbornly reminiscent of the building which housed his London home.

Hart's holo-phone began to vibrate. He placed it in the centre of the granite dining table and leant forwards, his broad hands splayed, as the disembodied head and shoulders of Tobias Keller took shape. "Well?" Hart demanded.

"There's no match for the man she was travelling with," Keller replied with a hint of Boston accent. "Not on our database, nor on restricted records for the Republic, Europe, Russia or China."

Hart straightened and moved towards the window, looking out across the dull surface of the river. "Do you think it's him?" he asked as his eyes turned in the direction of Canon Street.

The holographic figure shrugged. "I guess we'll find out."

Hart turned back towards his accomplice, hopeful that this development would bring their collusion to an end sooner rather than later. Keller was little better than a mercenary, with no true passion for the Republic, or for anything besides his own thuggish gratification. That people suffered at Keller's hands didn't, in itself, bother Hart, but there was no purpose to it and the man's rudderless approach to life was something he could not abide. "The tracker's in place?"

"Yep. All precautions have been taken. She doesn't know a thing."

"Good. Handle this well, Keller, and you'll get everything you've asked for."

Keller's eyes glittered briefly then dissipated as the transmission ended.

Hart poured himself a whisky and reclined back on the sofa. "Everything you've asked for…and more."

§

2147

St Mary's Hospital, London

Jack screeched to a halt at the reception desk, his heart racing, not just from the shock of Howard's call, or from the run, but from the temporal storm that had brought him to his knees en route.

"Bonnie Palmer?" he asked, "I'm famil... I'm a close friend."

"Mr Elliot?"

"Yes."

"Mr Palmer's waiting for you." The receptionist checked her records. "Miss Palmer is in recovery in the Webb Suite, East Wing, First Floor."

"Thanks."

Jack's shoes squeaked on the polished floor as he hurried towards the private suite. The duty desk nurse was absent, and Jack peered through the window in the door, trying to catch the attention of the staff he could see beyond.

A shout from the consulting rooms behind caught his attention, and he turned to see a door swing open, held by a male nurse.

The man attempted a calm smile. "As the doctor has said, we will arrange an appointment for your scans, and in the meantime run full diagnostics on your blood samples."

"Fuck you! Fuck all of this!"

"Frits, please." It was a woman's voice. "I understand you're upset, but this won't help."

"*You* understand?"

"That's not what I mean. You knew we had concerns, but it was your choice to go."

"Well, I didn't notice you trying too hard to stop me, Feynman." The voice was almost a snarl. "Too good an opportunity for your research."

"David, can you close the door please."

"Don't bother." An elderly man in a long coat pushed his way past the nurse, pausing when he saw Jack. "Oh good," he spat. "You!" Then stormed off down the corridor.

Jack looked from the nurse, who was visibly shaken, to the retreating figure, completely at a loss. Noticing Jack at last, the other man hurried to his desk with an apology. "Sorry, can I help you?"

"Yes, I'm Jack Elliot, I'm here to enquire after Bonnie Palmer."

"Ah, yes, just a moment Mr Elliot." He vanished through the door behind.

Frits. Jack knew the name. Frits Janssen? The man *had* born a resemblance to the Danish Cronod that Howard had recently worked with. But that Frits was in his late twenties, early thirties at the most. Jack and Frits hadn't hit it off, their differing opinions on time-travel and the role of Cronods clear. Evidently, this older Frits, whoever he might be, wasn't a fan of his either.

The door behind him buzzed open and Jack hurried through.

"Howard!" He rushed to him and clasped his hand, which trembled inside his own.

"I've done something terrible," said Howard at once, looking over Jack's shoulder to the door through which he'd come. "But I had to, Jack. I had to save her."

Jack squeezed his arm reassuringly and peered through a window into the brightly lit treatment room. Howard's granddaughter, Bonnie, lay in the bed. Her mother, Emma, was stroking her hand. Joanne stood just behind her, her features pinched, listening attentively to a doctor.

"But she's okay?" Jack asked nervously.

Howard nodded. "She will be. I was right though, wasn't I?" He gripped Jack's hand harder. His eyes searched Jack's face. "I had to save her?"

Jack frowned, then breathed in sharply as understanding dawned. He shut his eyes and sought the memories and voices that he had heard earlier, during the storm. They were yet to form fully, but there was enough, and he knew now that it was Joanne's voice he'd heard, crying two words, over and over. *She's gone.* But that memory wasn't of this time. He breathed out slowly and nodded. "Yes, I think that in a different timeline, Bonnie died."

Howard reeled. Jack steadied him, drawing him towards a sofa and taking the seat opposite. "Howard, what happened?"

Howard glanced towards the treatment room. "She was hit by a car. She's so small, and we didn't find her until…" A small sob escaped his lips. "They'd just driven off and left her. By the time the medics reached her the damage was too severe." He hunched over, pushing his fingers into his eyes, trying to stem the horror of what might have been.

Jack looked again through the window, to where Howard's family were gathered, talking quietly, the staff attending them calm. His brow furrowed. "But she's in recovery. She's out of danger."

Howard nodded, his eyes on the floor.

"I don't understand. Did you change time? Try to prevent the accident?"

"I couldn't risk trying to prevent it. If I'd been found out I'd have lost my position, my access to T-tech and everything we're working towards. But going forwards, that could count as research."

"I'm still not following…"

Howard wrung his hands and stood, pacing back and forth, his eyes full of anguish. "Frits Janssen, he… *I* sent him *forwards* in time."

Jack's breath caught in his throat.

"You know that I've met travellers from the future, heard about regenerative serums in development. Frits brought back the medicine that saved her, but he…" Their eyes met.

"He aged," Jack breathed.

"You were right, Jack," said Howard, sitting back down. "He shouldn't have been allowed to travel forwards."

Jack opened his mouth, but no words came. Above them, the light flickered.

The door to the treatment room opened and the doctor called. "She's waking up, Mr Palmer."

Howard rose at once then stopped. "We'll find a way to put this right, Jack," he said, though without conviction. He took a step, then turned and held out his hand. "Join us?"

Jack followed Howard towards the open door. Howard's daughter was smiling through her tears, and Joanne beckoned her husband, holding out her arms to him. Jack hesitated. They were the closest thing to a family that he had, but that didn't make him a part of it. As he wavered, he felt the room darken. The weight of the air shifted around him.

Howard turned to him, eyebrows raised.

"Go. Be with them," said Jack. He forced a smile. The hair on the back of his neck stood on end.

Howard nodded and closed the door behind him.

Jack turned and ran for the exit, bursting through and down the corridor beyond. He made it to the atrium staircase before the pain began to swell, searing through his head and scorching the fibres of his body. He gasped when lightning hit the hospital roof, drawing cries from staff and patients in the waiting area below. Dazzled, he reached out for the banister, missed it, and tumbled down the steps. He thought he glimpsed a man in a long coat, stalking away. He dragged himself to his feet, the main doors in sight, determined to put a distance between his suffering and Howard.

Another crack of lightning split the air.

…

Silence.

…

Howard paced back and forth, his eyes full of anguish. "He brought back the medicine that saved her, but he…" Their eyes met.

"He aged," Jack whispered.

"You were right, Jack, he shouldn't have been allowed to travel forwards."

Jack shook his head. He felt dizzy. He opened his mouth to speak, closing it when the light above flickered. He stood up abruptly, feeling the floor lurch beneath him.

"Jack? Are you alright?"

The door to the treatment room opened and the doctor appeared. "She's waking up, Mr Palmer."

Howard took a step, then turned back to Jack. He held out his hand. "Join us," he said.

Jack shook his head and forced himself to smile through the rising nausea. "It's alright. Go."

As soon as Howard turned, he ran for the door. He burst through, struggling to hold his balance as he ran down the stairs to the atrium below. Outside the hospital, the sky had grown dark. In the distance he could just make out a man in a long coat.

Jack stumbled towards the exit.

"Get down!" a voice yelled from behind.

Jack spun to discover the very same man behind him. The glass in the doorway imploded. He threw himself to the ground. People scattered, screaming and running for shelter, but beneath the noise, Jack heard the soft hum. He scrambled towards the cover of the reception desk...

Pfipp.

...too late. "Aargh!" He pulled the dart from his neck, tried to find his feet, but staggered and fell back onto the receptionist's chair. Shards of glass from a shattered display case sunk into the flesh of his hand. He heard a blast, the thud of metal, and footsteps running...

"Shit!" An old man in a long coat and bowtie swam in and out of Jack's vision. "Stay awake, Jack."

Jack felt the warmth leeching from his flesh, ice creeping from his neck and spreading through his veins.

"Jack, can you hear me?"

More footsteps across the crunch of glass... "Who are you? What are you doing?"

"Saving him."

The sharp bite of a needle in his thigh.

"Jack, I have a message for you about Hart."

"What did you give him? You can't just...give me that!"

Sounds of a scuffle.

Darkness.

"Jack!"

§

16th August 2073

Spitafields

"Aargh!"

Jack woke, gasping. His hand flew to his neck to tear away the dart but it wasn't there. He must have pulled it out. He'd managed to pull it out… He pushed himself up to sit and looked about the darkened room, his memories slowly falling into place, and found that he wasn't alone.

Maddie let go of her knees and let her feet fall to the floor, pushing herself off the chair and lowering herself down, next to Jack. She reached forwards and pushed the hair from his face.

"How long have you been there?" he asked, catching her hand as it ran across his neck and over the scar left by the dart.

"A little while," she answered gently. "I could hear you, in your sleep."

Jack released her hand and pushed his fingers into his forehead, easing the tension and anxiety of the events that took place yesterday, and three years before.

"What happened? Do you remember?"

Jack shifted, so that his back was resting against the wall and took a moment, inhaling deeply and releasing the air slowly through his mouth. "The Republic are getting desperate," he said at last. "To kill me," he clarified when Maddie's brow furrowed. "But why these occasions, I don't know. Maybe they're the only points in time that they can find me." He screwed up his face and rubbed at his temples. "I'm harder to pinpoint than most."

Maddie shook her head, "I don't understand."

"Every attempt on my life has been in a public place, which seems strange, and each time I've been with Howard."

"Howard?"

"A friend."

"Oh."

Jack caught the question in Maddie's expression and answered it. "He was a friend of my mother."

"Ah." She nodded, looking down and pulling at the frayed strands of wool that ran along the edge of the blanket on the floor.

"But there's been someone else each time," Jack continued, "someone I hadn't recognised until now."

Maddie looked up, the woollen fibres falling through her fingers. "Who?"

"Another Cronod, a man called Frits Janssen. I didn't recognise him at first because I still picture him as he had been when we first met."

Maddie waited patiently, trying to understand the connections between fragments of information on a subject that barely made sense to start with.

Jack thought back. "I've only met Frits properly once before; I spent an evening in his company at Howard's house, and that was enough. Howard has overseen the TSP, the Temporal Stability Project, for the last five years. He's approached a few Cronods along the way for help, and Frits leapt at the chance to get involved; an opportunity to time travel was all the incentive he needed."

"And you say he's changed since then?" Maddie asked.

Jack rested his head against the wall and looked up into the darkness overhead. "Oh yes, he's changed. Unlike me, he was keen to explore all the possibilities that time travel presented. He thought that our abilities were a 'gift', an advantage that should be celebrated and explored. And if our gifts proved useful, as Frits believed they would, then, he argued, Cronods deserved special status and benefits to match." Jack shook his head. "He would have got on well with my ex." He glanced at Maddie. "But that's another story. Anyway, one of the rules of time travel is that you don't move forwards beyond your own loop. Travelling back, within the past hundred to two-hundred years, is relatively easy, since digital records allow us to calibrate the location we cast in to."

"Cast?"

"Time travel is like fishing – we cast out a line and aim for a specific point to land. Without accurate historical records, casting can be hit or miss. A miscalculation could mean that your capsule ends up embedded in a wall. A miscast, a few minutes or even seconds earlier or later than intended, could have unfortunate consequences for people nearby."

"Urgh!" Maddie raised her hand to her mouth.

"Don't worry, it hasn't happened often. But you can see why travelling forwards in time is a far greater risk: we just don't have the information to cast safely."

"So, this guy, Frits, was injured during a cast?"

"Not exactly." Jack sighed. "One of our physicists, Dr Feynman, theorized that if a Cronod travelled forwards, their DNA would spontaneously modify to account for the accrued time."

Maddie raised an eyebrow in question.

"They'd rapidly age. Feynman also theorized that the process would revert when Cronods travelled back to their own time. Unfortunately for Janssen, only the first part of her theory proved correct."

"So, this man travelled forwards in time and aged?"

Jack nodded. "Frits cast forwards by forty-five years. He was twenty-seven years old when he left but returned as a seventy-two-year-old."

"Oh my God. And it couldn't be undone?"

Jack shook his head. "No one knows how."

Maddie blinked, trying to digest the information that was both bizarre and shocking, remembering at last that it was somehow connected to Jack himself. "So, what does this guy, Frits, have to do with the attacks made on you? Was he the attacker?"

"I wondered that at first, but now I think he's been trying to prevent the attacks. This time, if it wasn't for him, I wouldn't have made it."

Jack reached up and felt the ridges of the scar on his neck. Darts wouldn't normally leave a scar, but that dart had carried more than just sedative. When Jack came around the day following the attack, Frits was nowhere to be seen, but his doctor had confirmed that if Jack hadn't received the antidote when he did, he wouldn't have survived.

Maddie swallowed. "So, if they succeed in killing you in the past, you just... everything since just doesn't happen?"

"Exactly, time would be rewritten. Although with each change to my past, my own timeline branches out. Some scientists theorise that I could die in one timeline but continue to live in another. Like pruning the branches of a tree: you can remove a few, maybe even all the branches, but as long as the roots and trunk survive it will live."

"So why haven't you been targeted as a child? Or your parents, before you were born?"

"When I was selected for the mission, my digital record was erased: birth data, medical records, voter registration, stuff like that. Tracing me isn't easy."

Maddie puffed her cheeks out. "And I thought my life was complicated."

Jack smiled, the expression fading quickly as he recalled Janssen's final words. "There was something else though, about Frits. Something he said this time."

Maddie leant forwards.

"He said he had a message for me, about Hart."

Maddie's pulse quickened as her eyes locked on Jack's. "What was the message?"

Jack shook his head slowly. "I don't know."

§

Jack woke with a start, dream-like images of shattered glass and stormy skies fading, replaced by the soft glow of pre-dawn that crept around the edges of the storeroom door. He had fallen asleep sitting up, his back resting against the wall. Next to him, curled on top of the bed of blankets, Maddie slept, one hand tucked beneath her head, the other stretched out into the darkness. The fledgling light was not yet strong enough to pull her features from the shadows, but instead picked out the sharp angle of her shoulder, the curve of her thigh and gentle arc of her cheek. Her form, simplified that way, brought to mind sculptures that Jack had once seen in a museum – human forms stripped back to their essence, and all the more powerful and graceful for it. Over the past few days, Jack had seen many sides to Maddie: strength, determination, compassion and vulnerability, and there was power and grace in all those things.

Jack recalled that moment at Richborne Terrace, when Maddie had shown him the passport photograph of Suraya. She'd seemed uncomfortable at the prospect of being compared to her sister, and Jack wondered about the dynamic between them. Had Maddie put aside her own personal life when she assumed the role of parent alongside that of sibling? Had she sacrificed her right to be loved, to feel desired and beautiful? She was clearly self-conscious about the burn scars to her face; a painful reminder of how much her life had changed. Was it that which undermined her confidence? Or had she been hurt in other ways he didn't understand? Either way, Jack couldn't help thinking that she failed to truly see herself. Like power and grace, beauty ran deep, and in Maddie, Jack saw all three.

The memory of yesterday evening, the moonlight falling across her mouth, her face close to his, flooded his mind. It would be so easy to reach out to her, to wake her with the kiss that had been interrupted the night before. But then what? If his mission was a success, he would not even count amongst those who had hurt her. He wouldn't count at all. Jack knew that, but Maddie didn't, not yet, and so it felt wrong.

He closed his eyes and thought back. What was it he had told Howard? That he was sure that he could put his own emotions on hold for a few days? He laughed inwardly at his own folly, then carefully, so as not to disturb her, pushed himself up and slipped through the entrance into the room beyond.

Max looked up from where he sat, crossed-legged on the floor by the coffee table, his back resting against the sofa. He glanced at Jack, then at the door behind him, pointedly raising an eyebrow as his attention returned to the object in his hand. Max clearly imagined more had happened in the night than was the case.

Jack shook his head. "It's not what you think," he said, whilst wondering at his own need to set the record straight.

Max shrugged and continued with his work.

Jack bit down on his irritation and flicked on the kettle, leaning back against the counter. "Tea?" he asked.

"Er, thanks." Max glanced up from his work, pushed his glasses on to the top of his head and rubbed his eyes.

"How long have you been up?"

"A while." He yawned.

Jack brought over two cups and set one down in front of Max, taking his own to the window and peering through the blinds to the flats on the other side of the street. A lit window on an upper floor reminded him that they were not alone here. War did not prevent lives from being led. The rhythm of life continued with old days ending as new ones began.

He turned and watched Max's fingers deftly reassemble the components of a scanner, the one recovered from a dead man's pocket. Max's brow set in concentration while he connected the scanner to a laptop and scoured down the paths of data. Jack moved around to take a seat opposite, while Max tapped in new lines of code.

"I've managed to hack into the Snag network," he explained. "Which means that we should be able to misdirect any Snags in the area."

Jack inclined his head with a nod. "That would be a big help, thank you."

Max responded with a wary smile and considered the stranger before him. "Look, I don't really know what to make of you…"

Jack sighed.

"…but Maddie clearly trusts you, and I trust her." He

pushed the laptop onto the table, pulled himself onto the sofa to stretch out his legs, then remembered the mug of tea. A murmur of satisfaction escaped his lips as he drank.

Jack bit down on a few responses, then finally asked, "How long have you known each other?"

Max leant back, thinking. "About seven or eight years. My aunt worked with her mum for a few years, but I only got to know her after she joined LEFA."

"So, you knew Suraya from before the war too?"

Max felt his hands tremble and set the tea down. "Not exactly. I met her once or twice, but she was just a kid back then. It's only in the past year, since she's been involved with the resistance, that I got to know her." His shoulders sagged. "I shouldn't have let her go," he said quietly. "And I should have told Maddie."

Jack's annoyance melted away. He leant towards Max and spoke softly. "I don't think that anyone could have stopped her, even Maddie."

"Why? Do you know something?"

Jack shook his head. "No."

"Then why'd you say that? You've never even met her. Yeah, she's stubborn and high-spirited, but she listens to Maddie. If she'd warned her not to go..."

Jack thought about Suraya and what he knew of her, which admittedly wasn't much, and yet like her, and Maddie, he had suffered and been shaped by the contours of loss. He considered Maddie, who to Suraya was all things combined: sister, role model, and mother. Maddie was pained by her own comparison of herself to her younger and dazzling sister, but how might Suraya view herself when measured against Maddie? Didn't Jack also feel that he had something to prove? And even more so once he knew the depth of the sacrifice his mother had made. Wasn't that why he was here? To prove his worth, and give her sacrifice meaning?

"Suraya went to prove herself," he said at last. "To prove her worth."

Max frowned and opened his mouth to speak as Maddie slipped through the doorway into the room.

"Sorry," she apologised, "you should have woken me."

Max shook his head, dismissing Jack's opinion. He looked from Maddie and back again to Jack, the silence between them weighted with unspoken words. He cleared his throat and rose from his seat. "It's okay, it's still early," he said. "I'll make you some tea."

Maddie smiled gratefully and let herself into the bathroom.

Max turned as the kettle began to bubble, waiting until the weight of his stare claimed Jack's attention. "You know," he said, "we're like a family – everyone at the Hub."

Jack returned his stare, waiting.

"Don't hurt her, alright."

"I wouldn't worry." Jack paused, a wry smile on his lips. "I'm unlikely to leave a lasting impression on any of you."

§

Thames Barrier, London

There was nothing amiss in any of his vital signs. Arthur was in perfect health. Dr Kingsley gently placed the mouse back in his cage and rewarded him with a small slice of apple; a meagre prize in light of his achievement, for Arthur was the first living creature to have travelled through time.

Dr Kingsley returned to his computer desk, humming as he walked, and accessed the security camera feed for the courtyard just outside. He had to establish if his machine had arrived at the programmed destination or not: arriving in the past in an unsuitable location could lead to innumerable complications. He watched the footage in reverse, the long shadows of morning softening and blending into the growing dark of night. He frowned and tugged at the hairs of his beard and replayed the footage forwards. His machine did not appear.

He rewound the footage further into the previous day.

There.

Almost twelve hours before it was supposed to, the time capsule materialised in the courtyard, remained for a few minutes then vanished. Kingsley let out a low whistle of relief; he had cast accurately in terms of location. Now he just needed to work through the issue of timing.

§

Spitalfields

Jack locked the door to the building and adjusted the holo-projector so that it appeared undisturbed, exactly as it had before they'd arrived. It was still early, the streets empty, but that didn't stop Maddie from checking over her shoulder every few minutes or ease the constant strain of listening for the sound of rotor blades. Max carried the scanner in his pocket, pulling it out intermittently to check that the sighting he had planted in the system was still live, drawing any Snags who were awake at this hour north, towards Hackney and Victoria Park.

The oppressive heat of the previous day had given way to a fresh wind. It whipped up the dust and debris from bombed out buildings and carried away the crunch of their shoes on broken glass as they passed through the shadow of the Gherkin. The building's own security cameras were still out of operation, following the bombing a few days earlier, but those of most other buildings nearby were back online. Bishopsgate would be riddled with cameras. The Central Republican base was located in 22 Bishopsgate, known locally as Twentytwo. The vast glass tower had dominated the area for the past fifty years, and it was outside this building that LEFA had captured images of Kayson Hart.

As they moved towards their destination, Jack ran their plan over in his mind. The historical files from his iHolo revealed that Twentytwo had logged a faulty air conditioning unit early this morning, and security footage from the street had shown a scuffle outside the supermarket across the road from Twentytwo's entrance. Jack's background as a historian, his eye for small details, had its worth, and they would use those details to help them gain access to the building.

The guards in the lobby worked for Twentytwo, rather than the Republic, their digital records easily traced, their habits and tastes up for public review. Max wasn't entirely happy about the role Jack had asked him to play, but without the guard's face, they wouldn't make it onto the floor that the Republic occupied.

Jack re-ran each detail, the passcodes he'd recovered from redacted files, and tried to block out everything else. He couldn't allow himself to lose focus, couldn't risk his judgement being clouded by his feelings for the man who had fathered him through an act of violent abuse. He wasn't certain that Suraya was in the building and it was unlikely that Hart himself would be there at this time, but Jack couldn't deny that a part of him hoped that he would be. The chance to avenge his mother was dangerously tantalising.

Maddie pulled on a baseball cap and picked up her pace, moving ahead and away from Jack to lessen the chance of being matched to security footage from the previous day. Max hung back, allowing the space between himself and Jack to lengthen.

Though hours before the supermarket on Bishopsgate would open, a queue was beginning to form there. Maddie crossed the street and passed through clusters of waiting men and women, angling her head away from the camera above the shop door, catching a glimpse of Jack and Max as they too crossed the main road. She headed for the covered doorway of an old bank which faced the skyscraper's entrance, eyeing the security camera inside despite Max's assurance that, with the bank long decommissioned, no one had thought to reconnect it.

Twentytwo loomed, leviathan-like, on the opposite side of the street, and Maddie stared up at the sheer glass that stretched skywards, whole and unscathed, and thought that its very presence and completeness felt oppressive.

Was it really possible to find one person within such a space? Was she crazy to think she could find Suraya, let alone leave with her? She shelved her doubts as Max arrived, stepping silently into the shadow alongside her, his eyes likewise drawn upwards to where Twentytwo met the sky. Maddie felt the tension emanating from him. His face was ashen. She looked beyond him, her eyes searching for Jack, and found him on the opposite side of Threadneedle Street. He was leaning against a door frame, pretending to talk on his phone, whilst watching the guards through the windows at the skyscraper's base.

Max followed Maddie's gaze, and considered Jack with a mixture of anxiety, admiration and envy. "This is crazy," he breathed.

"You don't have to help," Maddie replied, not unkindly. "You can leave now."

Max bit his lip but remained where he was.

They watched the building in silence.

"Okay?" Jack slipped into the doorway behind them. "The guards just changed over, and the delivery is due any minute. Everyone ready?"

They nodded.

Max pulled a tiny drone from his backpack and flipped the switch on its base. Its body rippled, then became translucent, rising into the air to hover in front of him.

Jack checked his watch and glanced up the street as, on cue, a delivery lorry rumbled around the corner, prompting the men and women waiting outside the supermarket to exclaim and jostle for their place in line. The hum from the drone was barely audible above the human commotion and the guard outside Twentytwo was distracted, watching the tired and hungry with mild amusement as they bickered and cursed one another.

A few moments were all Max needed to guide the drone in a sweep of the grand entranceway before carefully lowering the holo-scanner it carried to the base of a pillar. "I'll make the call," Max said, and pulled a phone from his pocket.

"Internal office only," Maddie reminded him.

Max stifled a curt remark. "Yes. I know."

Inside the building, the guard left his desk and disappeared through the doorway behind.

"Good morning," Max spoke into his phone. "This is Steven from AirCo, just calling to let you know that our repair team will be with you shortly…"

Outside the supermarket, two women broke into a fight. Twentytwo's guard, grinning broadly, walked a little closer to get a better view of the spectacle. Jack hit 'project' on the holo's remote and, with Maddie, slipped out and across the street while the guard's attention was diverted. The air between the pillars rippled slightly as they passed through the holographic replication of the building's facade.

Across the road, the supermarket's manager put an end to the argument. Entertainment over, the security guard strolled back to his position. He glanced inside at the guard on the desk then edged around the outermost pillar, leaning against it so that his back faced the nearest security camera. Furtively, he pulled out his mobile phone to check his status on HookUp.

"It worked," Maddie breathed, when the guard outside disappeared from view. "He was looking straight through me."

Ahead of them, the reception desk sat empty, but the sound of a man talking was audible from the office behind. Jack dashed forwards and leant over the desk, applying a black disk, no bigger than a penny, to the side of the computer. Maddie peered into the lobby beyond. It was empty. They moved across its expanse briskly, through a far door, and into the service stairwell.

Jack tapped his ear and listened a moment before he spoke softly, "Max, you should have access now via the matrix key."

"I'm working on it," replied Max's voice.

Maddie pulled a dart gun from her pocket, checked it, then returned it to the folds of fabric. Jack pulled a toolbelt from his backpack, fixed it around his waist, then checked the building's schematics on his wristwatch.

"Alright, I'm in," Max informed them. *"Deleting the footage of you entering... holo-projection is off and... okay. I've frozen the feed from the service stairwell; as far as Twentytwo's concerned you were never there."*

"And the Republican base?"

"Nothing I can do to disable the biometrics, but I'll get the scan to you as soon as possible. You'd better be right about that guard."

"I am. Thanks." Jack leant over the edge of the rail and peered up the staircase which circled ever upwards. "Time to find out how fit we are."

Max opened the 5D scanner on his phone and again felt a rush of excitement. In the late 21st century, 5D hard light holograms were still just a theory, and yet here he was, the technology held in his own hands.

Jack had managed to prise it from his battered iHolo and, after a few adjustments, Max had fitted it to the most recent phone they had. The interface was glitchy, but it worked. Max pocketed the phone and slung his backpack over his shoulder. He slipped out of the shadow to his left, onto Threadneedle Street, and hurried around the block via Finch Lane and Cornhill, back up to Bishopsgate. Once on the main thoroughfare he reduced his pace, and as he neared Twentytwo he made a show of checking his phone, tapping the screen irritably, before catching the eye of the security guard, who was leaning against a pillar watching him.

"Excuse me," called Max, approaching him. "Are you any good with phones?"

The guard appraised him slowly.

Max shifted on his feet, aware of the bruises on his jaw. "It's just my friends..." he rubbed his eyes and flashed the guard what he hoped was a winning smile. "Man, I drank too much at the Ku Bar last night... They thought it would be funny to change all the settings. I don't even know what the time is."

The guard shook his head knowingly and the corner of his eyes crinkled. The Ku Bar was one of the few clubs still running, albeit not officially, and he'd met a few of his boyfriends there over the years. The man with the phone raised his eyebrows in a pleading expression. He was kind of cute, in a geeky sort of way.

"Let me see." The guard took the phone and peered at the screen. "Abtastung? What does that mean?"

"God knows, my friends set it to another language." Max watched nervously, relieved that the guard didn't understand the German word for 'scanning'.

"Nice phone," the guard said wistfully.

"Yeah, a present," Max replied, stuffing his hands into his pockets.

"Lucky. Er... okay, there." He handed the device back to Max. "Reset to English."

"Thanks, really appreciate it." Max smiled and turned to continue up the road.

"Hey!"

Max's stomach tightened. He turned back, shoving his hands deeper into his pockets to hide the trembling.

"You at the Ku Bar often?"

"Sometimes," Max lied.

"Maybe I'll see you there?"

"Sure." Max smiled and, forcing himself not to move too quickly, turned and walked away.

Maddie was not unfit, but the relentless climb was gruelling. She tried to ignore the ache in her legs by focusing on Suraya. She was near, she knew it. Ahead of her Jack rounded the corner, bringing them up to the fifty-second floor. He paused and turned to her.

"Next level," he murmured.

Maddie's heart fluttered in her chest with hope and fear combined. She leant back against the wall, feeling the cold concrete beneath her outstretched palms, hoping that its solidity would be an anchor, that despite its height, the building might yet ground her.

Jack tapped his ear. "How's it coming, Max?"

"Nearly there." His voice was grainy. *"Just trying to smooth out a few flaws in the scan."*

Jack nodded, though Max couldn't see him, then clicked open the panel on the side of his watch, uncovering a tiny projector. It had picked up their test transmission, back at Brune Street, which they'd sent from the ground floor to the roof, but this distance was something else.

"Okay, you should be receiving it now."

Maddie and Jack climbed the final flight of steps and stopped beside a service door's access panel. It required a facial recognition scan as well as the passcode. Jack tapped the face of the watch and instructed it to project the file.

Maddie took a step closer and held her breath while an image of the guard's face began to build. It was translucent at first, flickering and glitchy, but it slowly gained substance until it looked as real as her own, every pore, hair and blemish perfectly recreated. It was so real to be gruesome, as though they'd severed it from the man's body.

Jack tilted his hand from side to side, watching the shadows change as the projection interacted with the stairwell lights. He nodded, satisfied, and moved closer to the security panel beside the door. The guard's face flickered when Jack moved, then re-solidified as he steadied his arm, resting his elbow against the wall.

Jack glanced sideways at Maddie. "Ready?"

"Yes."

He entered an eight-digit code onto the touchscreen, activating the 3D biometric scanner. Jack held his breath. The screen flared green, tracing lines across the holographic surface of the guard's face.

The door clicked open.

Jack put his ear to the gap and listened, then pressed his eye to the opening, peering into the corridor that cut through the heart of Twentytwo's central, concrete core. Light spilled through a window at the eastern end as the rising sun flooded the glass clad space beyond. Offices, laboratories, interrogation rooms and cells: those lay at the opposite end, where the glass door drew a blank against an inner whitewashed wall. The security hub was based in the room immediately to their left, and someone would soon question why a guard had accessed the door, but not yet appeared.

Jack pulled a holo-scanner from his tool belt. He crouched down to activate it and pushed it into the gap at the base of the door. He stepped back, nodding to Maddie, who slipped down the hallway to the far side of the security hub's door. She pressed her back to the concrete wall and eyed the security camera opposite. She was invisible to it, hidden behind the holographic replication of the wall.

Jack wedged the service door open, then pulled a shirt from his bag, laying it across the threshold. He stepped back into the shadowy space behind the entrance, pulled a dart gun from his belt and waited. In the silence he could hear the thudding of his own heart. What if the guards weren't in the hub? What if they saw Maddie? The distant creak silenced his doubts.

The door swung out towards Maddie, hiding her from the figure behind, whose deep Republican drawl filled the corridor. "What the…? What's that asshole, Franco, playing at?"

Maddie slid a key card into the gap above the door's hinge, her breath held, hand trembling, holding it in place. The man stepped into view and the door swung back, exposing her. Maddie felt her knees weaken and bit down hard on her lower lip, focusing on the pain rather than her terror. But the guard's attention remained on the service doorway. He moved towards it, pulling out his gun as he took a step through.

"Franco?"

Behind the door Jack forced himself to wait. He needed a clear shot.

The guard nudged the shirt with his foot, took a step forwards and peered up into the stairwell. He took another step and leant over the handrail to peer down the spiralling flights of stairs.

Jack fired the dart.

Pfipp.

"What the hell!" The guard's hand flew to his neck and he spun around.

Jack's fist met its mark and the man fell to the ground. Jack dragged him into the shadow behind the door then edged out into the corridor, catching the look of relief that flooded Maddie's face.

He slid along the wall, behind the holo-projection, until he reached the door. The key card hadn't stopped it from closing, but had prevented the lock from aligning properly, something, from the scrape of the chair on the inside, that the second guard had just realised. Maddie gently took hold of the handle.

Footsteps sounded behind the door.

Jack took a step back and raised the dart gun. His pulse thundered in his ears and his vision briefly blurred... He shook his head and steadied his hands.

Maddie felt the door begin to move and yanked the handle back as hard as she could.

The guard fell forwards into the corridor and Jack fired.

Pfipp.

Jack raised his fist to strike, but the guard was fast, lunging forwards to deflect Jack's blow, his own fist connecting with the side of Jack's head. The man drew back his arm to strike again and reeled when the sedative began to take hold. Maddie cracked the barrel of her gun against his skull and he crumpled to the floor. She grabbed his arms, Jack his legs, and together they lifted him back inside the control room.

"Arg." Pain shot through Jack's head. He dropped the guard's body.

"Are you okay?" Maddie dropped the man's feet and grasped Jack's arm. "It's not another—"

"No." Jack shook his head and touched his left temple gingerly. "No, just the effects of a powerful right hook."

Maddie turned Jack's head to the side. An angry red mark was beginning to bloom.

"It's fine," Jack insisted.

Maddie nodded, stepped across the prostrate guard, but

froze when the rumble of thunder echoed in the distance. Her eyes flew back to Jack whose skin had paled.

Jack forced a shrug. "Storms are forecast for today. Come on, we need to find Suraya and access the hard drive."

"Suraya." Maddie's head spun back towards the other side of the control room, where a bank of screens displayed every room and its occupants on the fifty-fourth floor. She stepped closer and scoured them for her sister.

Jack produced another small, black disk and stuck it on to the side of the main computer. He tapped just below his ear. "Max ... Max? Can you hear me?"

"I can't see her! I can't see Suraya!" Maddie's voice was shrill.

"It doesn't mean she's not here, just not in range of a camera. She'll be somewhere small, no window, maybe guarded, try looking for..." Jack's head began to swim. He paused and cursed under his breath.

"Look for what? ... Jack?"

Jack leant forwards and took a deep breath, willing the sensation to pass, trying to straighten when Maddie noticed his silence.

"Jack?"

The door flew open.

A man in a long coat and bowtie burst through, pushing the door closed with his back and pulling a gun as Jack and Maddie did the same.

"Shoot me and you're fucking dead!" he hissed. He pushed some strands of white hair from his face.

"Frits?"

"Surprise," he snarled. He relaxed his arms and fixed Maddie with a look. "You gonna shoot the messenger?"

"You're...you're the other time traveller."

"Smuk og smart," he replied in his native Danish. "Top marks."

Maddie lowered her weapon, looking from the bemused, age-lined face of Frits Janssen back to Jack.

"Who sent you?" demanded Jack, his gun still aimed.

"You did."

"What?" Jack's brow furrowed. "Every time I've seen you?"

"Oh, no, just this once, but since we're currently upstream, so to speak, you'll have to take my word for it."

"And the other times? Parliament Square, Greenwich, the hospital?"

"Feynman. Trust me, it took some persuasion to get me to help that bitch." He looked Jack up and down with disdain. "And you."

Jack's mind raced with questions, but Janssen's very presence panicked him. "Where is it? Your time-capsule? Frits, it can't be found."

"Calm down. I'll be leaving with it. I've a nice set-up in Gaia, in exchange for my troubles. But time's tight, so you need to listen—" A red light on the control panel began to flash. "Shit!" Frits dived forwards and peeled the black disk from the side of the main computer. "Should have done that first." He shook his head with irritation. "You!" He jabbed a finger at Maddie. "Your sister's in there." He pointed to a screen that appeared to show an empty room. "There's only one guard, outside. Here." He handed her a gun with a silencer. "No time to mess around. Take the south lifts down."

"But we haven't taken out the cameras."

"It's your funeral." Frits shrugged. "But the stairs didn't work out well for you last time I was here."

Maddie's mouth formed the shape of a question and she looked to Jack for confirmation, her mind spinning. Jack in turn stared at Frits. Could he trust him?

Frits tapped his watch theatrically. "The matrix key triggered an alarm; we don't have all day."

"Fine." Jack nodded at Maddie. "Let's go." He took a step towards the door but Frits blocked him.

"*We* need to get Hart's passcode from the mainframe, then the contents of his safe. Everything the Republic knows about Kingsley has been catalogued by Hart. She'll be fine."

Jack's chest tightened at his father's name, but his face remained blank. His eyes met with Maddie.

She swallowed, but her voice was steady. "I'll be fine." She inclined her head to the bank of computers. "Do it. It's what you're here for."

Jack watched her leave, aware of the sinking feeling deep in his stomach. He tapped the comms device in his ear. "Max?" A few snatches of words punctuated the low hiss of static. "Shit." He swiped a finger across the face of his watch. "Message to Max: Maddie and Suraya coming down south lifts, be prepared to help. Diversion may be necessary… Send."

Jack turned at last to Frits. "So how do we do this without the matrix key? And how is Hart mixed up with the Republic?"

Frits lifted his head from the keyboard he was examining and ran to the fallen guard. "Biometric keypad," he explained. "Give me a hand." He laughed at his own joke and Jack helped him haul the comatose guard over to the desk, slumping him into a chair. Frits picked up the man's right hand, pulling his index finger straight, then used it to punch in a line of code. The screen erupted with sequences of numbers which rapidly filled the space. Frits leant forwards, concentrating, his eyes followed the sequence, narrowing occasionally before a slight shake of the head, then widening again as another possibility presented itself.

Jack bit down on his impatience, on the unanswered question. What was the message about Hart? What was Hart's involvement with the Republic and T-tech? And what had happened in the future? Had he really sent Frits back? The monitor on the far-left caught Jack's eye. It showed the entrance lobby, into which four heavily armed men had just walked. "We've got to go. Let me try again with the matrix key – they know we're here anyway."

"It won't work." Frits grabbed a paper and pen and scrawled down a sequence of numbers. "Come on, we need to find Hart's office."

Maddie slipped from the control hub into the corridor. An oily light was filtering through the glass door at the eastern end. She strained to see through the room beyond, through the outer glass wall, and caught a glimpse of thunderous clouds gathering above the city. Unpredictable weather had become the norm in recent years, but right now she wasn't sure what was due to climate change, and what was being caused by changes in time.

She approached the other doorway and paused, trying to formulate a plan. Her uniform suggested she worked in maintenance and it might yet fool someone, so she pushed the gun into the overall's ample pocket, her fingers still tight about its handle. This weapon wasn't loaded with sedative, but she decided Frits was right: there was no time to mess about, she only had one chance.

The corridor on the other side was empty, and she exhaled slowly, turning right to head towards a cell block at the far end. She neared an office and ducked low as she passed the window. The sound of conversation rose and fell inside and its door drew open. Maddie raced forwards, pushing her way through doors to her right, finding herself facing a bank of lifts. She hit the call button on the first lift and it started climbing from thirty floors below. Behind her, the door she'd come through whooshed open.

"Hey?"

Maddie stared ahead, ignoring the man behind her. The lift was twenty floors away.

"Hey!" The man tapped her shoulder. "I wasn't informed that maintenance was in."

Maddie turned and flashed a smile, hoping that the Republican wouldn't see the tremble in her lips. Her fingers tightened on the gun. "Oh, I was servicing air-con a few floors down. Pressed the wrong button in the lift."

The man frowned at her. "You came through biometrics?"

Maddie shook her head and held his gaze, but from the corner of her eye she saw his right hand slip towards the back of his belt. "Think there's a fault on your system," she replied.

The man took a step closer and Maddie glanced back round at the lift.

"You look familiar," he asserted.

She swallowed. "I get that a lot."

Behind her the lift bell chimed and the doors slid open. They both drew their weapons. There was no time to hesitate.

Pht.

The bullet lodged in the man's forehead. His legs crumpled beneath him. Maddie grabbed him beneath the arms and stumbled with him into the lift, letting his body slump into the corner. She dashed back through the doors, hitting the button for the twenty-fifth floor as she left.

"This way," said Frits, pulling back the door.

Jack pushed past into the empty space beyond. He took a few steps then stopped, arrested by the panorama before him. Towering cumulonimbus rose vertically, taunting the static skyscraper with their motion as they billowed and swelled. Their underside formed a lowering ceiling, weighing down on the city below, where the diminutive buildings looked fragile, their bricks and mortar vulnerable to the energy of water and wind.

Jack drew in a ragged breath. The air felt thick. "Are we causing this?" he asked.

Frits tugged at his sleeve, drawing him back towards the other side of the cavernous space where a room had been built out from the building's core. "Yes, and no."

"Damn-it, Frits, what's going on? You know something I don't, and I will fail, apparently *again*, if you don't tell me!"

Frits ignored him. He pulled the slip of paper from his pocket and punched the digits into a code-lock. The door clicked open, and he studied Jack with curiosity as they stepped inside.

Given the office's location, on the fifty-fourth floor of a glass behemoth, it was unremarkable. A wooden desk, inlaid with leather, was scattered with papers:

procurement documents, copies of mid-21st century legislation, a draft proposal for a post-war trade agreement, but nothing that shed light on Hart himself.

Jack scanned the desk and the office walls, hung with soulless mass-produced canvases: the worst kind of corporate art. No photographs. Nothing personal. Jack felt the heat rise beneath his skin: the hatred that he'd not had time to examine, only time to contain and subdue. There was no outlet for it here, nothing to vent upon. He leant forwards, resting his hands on the desk, trying to clear his mind, to refocus on the reason he was here.

"Nice to see where Daddy works," Frits remarked, joining him behind the desk.

"What the hell?" Jack grabbed the collar of Frits' coat and slammed him back against the wall. "What did you say?"

Frits gasped as the impact forced the air from his lungs, remembering a little late that his body was that of an old man, with flesh and bones that bruised too easily. "No need to get touchy." He winced. "Just helpful, you know, to understand the background of both your parents."

"No one knows who my father is."

"Howard did. And he told Feynman... and she told me."

Jack clenched his jaw and leant harder against Frits, his arm pushing up and into his throat. "You're enjoying this, aren't you."

Frits smiled sadistically.

Jack released him and walked away, trying to force down his anger. "Well?"

Frits rubbed his neck gingerly. "Did you know you're a quarter Republican?" He smirked and resumed searching the office. "Hart kept that one close to his chest. His mother's affair wasn't exactly advantageous to the family brand – hard to sell yourself as the champion of the EU if everybody knows your daddy's a Republican politician."

"Who Hart was, or is, has *nothing* to do with who I am."

"Never said it did," said Frits innocently.

239

Jack clenched and unclenched his fists. Why Frits? Of everyone Feynman could have sent... "So," he said at last. "Kayson Hart's working for the Republic, using his government connections to help them find Kingsley?"

"Oh no, it's better than that." Frits grinned. "Candice Martin, remember her? Lost her seat in Parliament in 2147? Well, she's been busy creating a web of informants in the years since – came across Howard's project. Don't know how she got her hands on the T-Tech, but one of her agents tipped off Hart. Not so hard for him to convince the Republic that he'd turned coat. His fucking ridiculous name was probably enough to persuade them he was pro-Republic all along."

"And if he gets to Kingsley first—"

"The British government will be the first to possess T-Tech. They'll have the upper hand." Frits shrugged. "Maybe in our own time there'll be no temporal war."

"But they'll use T-Tech to ensure that the liberal coalition lose *this* war. The far right will retain its grip over Europe." Jack shook his head, imagining the exchange of one broken future for another that was equally damaged, where British leaders altered the past to remove 'undesirables' in the same way that the Republic had done. "And this government will do nothing to stop the destruction of the planet – they're as corrupt as the Republic."

"So quit standing there gawping and help me find Hart's safe. I've fucking been here once already. I didn't enjoy your company the first time and I really don't want a third round."

Jack's nostrils flared and he bit down on his response. He was unaccustomed to featuring in other people's memories, without the accompanying information in his own. He turned to the walls, lifting the edges of paintings, looking for a safe or somewhere Hart would store sensitive information. "So, Candice Martin's agents are the ones targeting me in the past. How did you find them? Know when to stop them?"

"I've spent more fucking time than you'd believe

tracing them, hours poring over Howard's bloody diaries." Frits shook his head with irritation. "Was tempted to let you die once or twice, would have been easier to figure it out that way."

"Thank you," said Jack, "for saving my life."

"Don't get sentimental." Frits lifted a cigar from the desk and clicked his tongue in appreciation. "I've no personal interest in your well-being, it's just part of the deal."

"So how does it connect to Howard? He was there every time I... ah!" Jack levered the front panel off the air conditioning unit, revealing a safe hidden within. It was unlike any he'd seen before, with an imprinted panel on which to lay your hand, inside a small iatric chamber lined with sensors.

From the other side of the building, Jack heard the dull echo of a gunshot and the crash of glass. "Maddie!" He made for the door but Frits grabbed his arm.

"This is more important than her."

Jack hesitated. "Just get what's inside and meet us back at the stairwell."

"I can't open it without you."

"What?"

"It's a DNA code-lock. Reads a code embedded at a cellular level."

"But it's Hart's..." Jack's voice trailed off as he understood.

"There it is. The penny drops. Feynman thinks the code is replicated in your DNA. Shouldn't be, but this genetic engineered shit is strange. So, besides Hart, you're the only one with a chance to open this."

Jack clenched his jaw and told himself Maddie was okay, that *this* was the mission he came here for, not Suraya. *This* was what mattered most. He shoved his hand into the opening and aligned his fingers with the imprint. At once the chamber began to glow, sending pulses up his arm and into his body. A series of readings began to flash on the panel above – body temperature, heart rate, neural function.

Jack stared at the readings. "What are those for?"

Frits had moved to the office door and pulled it ajar, cautiously scanning the space beyond. "It's checking that you're alive and conscious, other stuff too, otherwise all we'd need is Hart's corpse."

"How did you find out about it? The DNA. And Hart working with Candice Martin?"

"Howard did." Frits returned to peer into the iatric chamber.

Jack frowned. "He never said anything. Never mentioned her or the British Patriotic Party."

"He didn't know until after you'd cast."

"Why didn't you travel back to before I'd cast? If I'd known, even the day before I'd left, it would have helped."

"Seriously?" Frits flung his head back in exasperation. "I was already stretched, tracking Martin's agents while they targeted your past, and that was a bloody nightmare since I didn't share their information."

"What information?"

"And as for the here and now." Frits shook his head. "Your time stream is seriously messed up. I only managed to find you after you died here the first time. Piss me off, and you might end up dead a second time."

Jack felt a chill creep up his spine. He opened his mouth to speak, but no words came. A scream rang out from the far side of the building. Jack tried to pull away but Frits was on him, his gun at Jack's temple.

"Finish the job. If you're determined to kill yourself for her, again, that's fine by me, but get what we came for first. Then at least someone else can finish what you started."

Jack's eyes narrowed. Frits, how he loathed him. But if Jack did carry the code in his DNA, then the man was right; he couldn't risk throwing his life away. Not even for Maddie. Every muscle in his body trembled while he forced himself to hold still, resisting the urge to run to her. Howard had been right too. Under pressure Jack had cracked, been swayed by emotion rather than reason, and

Jack wondered whether someone else would have been a better choice. He glanced at Frits. "Is the capsule programmed to return to Feynman's location?"

"Yes, why?"

"Whatever's in here – you need to make a copy and take it back in case—"

The safe beeped softly and a low clunk told them that the lock had disengaged. Jack swung the door open with his left hand and pulled his right from the chamber. The safe was empty. He felt inside, along the walls and ceiling, but there were no hidden compartments, just a dark void. His stomach dropped.

"For helvede! Forpulet Røvhul!" Frits cursed in his mother tongue and smashed his fist against the wall.

"Shit. Where else would Hart keep the documents? He'd use another Republican base or, he has an apartment here in, in…" Images of newspaper articles flashed through his mind, everything he'd read on Hart the night before the mission.

"Battersea," supplied Frits. "In the power station."

"Yes, Battersea." Jack took a deep breath. "Now we find the others and get out of here."

They slipped out into the vast, empty office space. Outside, the sky encircling Twentytwo was almost black, creating a mirror of the windows and reflecting the two men. Jack held still and listened. There had been no sound since that scream, but the silence was somehow worse. It might have been Maddie or Suraya, but Jack told himself that it was someone else.

"This way," said Jack, moving back towards the building's core. The corridor leading to the control hub was reflected in the sheet glass window and Jack caught a flash of an unfamiliar face, realising at once that just as he saw them, they too could see him.

"Get back!" he yelled to Frits.

The door burst open and bullets scudded across the concrete walls. They retreated past Hart's office and entered a maze of corridors in the north-western end of the building. They hugged the walls, Frits watching behind, Jack peering into every room they passed, searching for Maddie.

"There," Frits whispered. He raised a finger to point. "That door leads to the northern stairwell. You need to take it down to floor forty-two, where the lift shafts change. I wired a signal from the time capsule to disrupt the security cameras in the northern-most shaft."

"But you told Maddie to take the southern lift shaft."

"And she'll be fine, but it's safer for you to go this way."

Jack seethed and spun around, the barrel of his gun directed at Frits' head. "What have you done?"

Frits scowled. "Didn't you listen? Last time this played out, you died trying to save her life. And as it turns out I *can't* let you die, Jack. Not yet."

"Where is she?" Jack's finger tightened on the trigger.

"Are you really going to make me do this a third time?"

"You've already changed the odds, so that's a chance I'm willing to take. And if you need to do it again, then do it again."

"So, it's back to Feynman for me, round and round like a fucking dog with a stick!"

"I guess whatever's waiting for you in Gaia is worth it," Jack countered.

The corners of Frits' mouth turned down. "And *she's* not even special," he sneered. "Not like me. Not like you. Ha! You could have been something... fucking waste." He shoved Jack away. "Last time, you found her over there, in the toilet block."

Pht.

Plaster exploded above Jack's head. He ducked and twisted to see down the corridor. Behind him, Frits edged forwards, the doorway to the stairwell in his sights. Jack adjusted his grip on his gun, his eyes straining for movement. A figure flashed across his line of vision. He fired but missed.

"See you in round three," Frits hissed. He sprang forwards, propelling himself across the hallway and through the doors, followed by a spray of bullets.

Jack dived forwards and fired at their pursuer. The guard tumbled backwards, a look of surprise etched on his face, having presumed both men had fled together. Shouts now rang out from behind him, from where Frits said he'd find Maddie; from where Jack had died trying to save her.

Jack's heart hammered inside his chest and for a moment his doubts got the better of him. Who was he to think he could change time? Who was he to believe that he could save her? In his mind, Maddie's face mixed with that of Suraya and his mother. He squeezed his eyes shut and forced himself to focus. If he could just work out what his mistake had been… Frits may have been lying, but instinct told Jack that the south stairwell and lifts were best avoided. He inched towards the building's core, trusting in those instincts and praying that he wasn't too late.

Splinters of wood burst from the cubicle door. Suraya flinched beneath Maddie's protective embrace and her eyes flickered open, her brows raised in a silent apology.

Tears spilled from Maddie's eyes. Vigorously, she shook her head; she wouldn't have Suraya blame herself. Her gaze fell to her sister's stomach – crimson soaked and glistening – and her skin crawled with icy fear.

There's only one guard, Frits had said, and like a fool, Maddie had believed him. The man outside the cell hadn't seen her coming, but the one inside had. Those moments were all a blur: the guard wrestling Maddie for the gun; Suraya kicking his legs from beneath him; two shots; the thud of the fallen man and Ray's scream of pain.

Which one of them had shot Suraya? Maddie didn't know. Her insides twisted and she stifled a sob. Damn-it, Ray was losing too much blood and Jack had the serum. She needed to get to him.

Maddie's eyes scoured the small space. Behind her, at head height, was a shelf. It was exposed, but from there she could edge onto the right-hand wall of the cubicle. It was a few centimetres thick at most and abutted the main wall, not much to get a purchase on. But she might be able to get a hold on the air vent above.

Maddie heard the gravelly crunch of feet on shattered tiles. She crouched and fired a shot in their direction, forcing them to retreat. She hooked her foot over the toilet roll dispenser, pulled herself up and onto the ledge, and slid her foot along the side of the cubicle. She leant forwards, the thud of her heart loud in her ears, pushed her fingers into the vent, and pulled herself into the wall and out of view.

The guard slipped through the doorway and Maddie raised her gun. The grip, in her left hand, felt awkward, but the range was short. The man ducked down to look beneath the doors. When he stood, Maddie took her shot.

Pht.

She dropped back down into the cubicle and closed her eyes, blocking the sight of red against white, only for the negative after-image to dance treacherously behind her eyelids. She breathed in sharply, telling herself to hold it together.

"I'm sorry, this might hurt," she told Suraya, sliding her arm beneath her, bracing to lift her. A sharp scrape told her that someone was at the outer door. Maddie froze, waiting. If it was Jack, if it was safe, he would call out to her.

In the stillness she detected the slightest hum.

Jack raised his weapon, the black-clad figure in his sights, but just as his finger tightened on the trigger, the guard moved out of view. Jack cursed under his breath and edged forwards until the entrance to the toilets was visible. The man had vanished. Jack crossed the hallway, pressed his body to the wall, then heard it: the hum of an approaching drone. There was little time.

He raced forwards, through the doors and into the tiled room, slipping on fragments of shattered glass and porcelain, almost tripping over the body slumped on the floor.

"Maddie?"

"Jack!" Maddie burst from her hiding place and flung her arms around his neck.

He stepped back and lifted her chin. There was a cut across her brow, bruises developing along her cheekbone and neck, but she was whole. "We need to go – drones. Did you find her?"

"Yes. Help me." Maddie pushed back the cubicle door, revealing Suraya slumped and bloody. "She needs the serum, you have enough, right?"

Jack slid to his knees in front of Suraya and placed a hand on her neck. Her pulse was weak. He unhooked one strap of his backpack but the hum from outside grew louder. "We need to get out of here first." He looked around, considering their options. "Turn on all the hot taps."

"What?" Maddie cried.

"Just do it!"

Maddie frowned but did as he asked, twisting the taps to full flow, releasing plumes of steam as the hot liquid spewed into the basins below. Jack switched on their last holo-projector and placed it at the base of the central cubicle door.

"Get behind," Jack whispered. "Keep your line of sight."

Maddie retreated into the cubicle with Suraya. The holograph rippled and understanding dawned on her – the holo-projection would screen them whilst the steam would confuse the drone's heat sensors. It wasn't much, but it gave them a chance. She pulled the door back, holding it open with one leg, lifted her weapon, and steadied her arms.

Jack took out the first drone as it rounded the doorway, Maddie the second, the dart it had fired falling harmlessly into the furthest basin. But there was no reprieve. Gyrocopters swarmed through the door. They shot down one each, while a third spun towards them, sensing their rising body heat despite the swell of steam on the opposite side of the room. Jack aimed and caught a blade.

It plummeted to the floor, colliding with the projector. The hologram disappeared.

Jack's eyes remained fixed on the entrance as he reloaded his gun. "We need another way out of here. Watch the door."

"I think they've gone," Maddie whispered. "Listen."

Jack cocked his head, straining to hear over the sound of gurgling water. Maddie was right, the whir of rotor blades had stopped.

Maddie glanced over her shoulder at Suraya. "If we go now—"

A chill crept up Jack's spine. "No. This has happened before and we didn't make it."

Maddie's eyes widened. "But we're trapped!"

Jack pushed the fallen drones up against the door, wedging their blades into the slim gap beneath it. He stepped back, aware of the dull thud of running feet in the corridor outside. "There's got to be another way out." Jack searched the room with his eyes and tapped his wristwatch, bringing up the building's schematics. "Project," he instructed, and a holographic diagram of the building formed in the air. "Enlarge section G11, fifty percent. Rotate vertical axis one-eighty. Enlarge twenty percent." He squinted at the criss-crossed lines before him. "Maybe here..." He ran to the back wall. "The plumbing connects to the toilet block on the other side of the building, and there's an access hatch."

Jack tore away the wooden panel below the sinks, revealing a small hatch in the wall. He tugged it open, slid his foot through a gap between the pipes and kicked sharply. The wooden panel on the far side toppled to reveal another set of toilets, replicated in mirror-image. If he could widen the opening they could get through. Jack wrenched at the first pipe, easily pulling the plastic connections apart.

From outside they heard the *click clack* of weapons being loaded.

"Jack?"

"Get Suraya." Jack wrenched a second pipe from the

opening, unleashing a flood of gushing water. He pulled away a third pipe then spun around. The door scraped shrilly against the fallen drones as someone attempted to open it. Jack fired a shot in its direction, then ran to help Maddie with Suraya. He pulled her arm across his shoulders and lifted her towards the back of the room. Her feet slipped on the floor as she tried to help, her warm blood soaking into Jack's top.

"Can you get through that?" he asked urgently.

Maddie ducked her head under the sink. "Yes, I think so."

"Good. Go! You'll have to pull Suraya through."

Again, the door behind scraped against the floor. Jack fired another shot but the door remained open. Beneath the sound of gurgling water, he made out the hum of more rotor blades.

"I'm through," Maddie called. She reached through the gap, grasped her sister's shoulders and heaved. Suraya cried out in pain.

Jack lifted Suraya's hips and she slipped across the threshold, her cries drowned out by the rising hum behind him. He seized the discarded panel from the sink, raising it above his head as darts rained down.

Pfipp. Pfipp. Pfipp.

Jack lowered the panel just enough to take a shot. The machine careened upwards, hit the ceiling, and crashed onto the floor in front of him, cracking open its casing. He wrestled the dart cartridge from its undercarriage, shoved it into his pocket and grabbed the wooden panel, shielding himself from a spray of bullets.

Jack wedged the panel in place, thrust his backpack through the gap and scrambled to pull himself through. The ruptured pipes caught on his belt. The wooden shield shuddered and splintered, on the verge of collapse. Jack wrestled to unhook his belt, his fingers fumbling over the pipe, and spotted an electricity cable inside the wall's cavity.

With a sharp *crack*, the wooden shield gave way.

Pht, pht, pht.

"Aargh!" A bullet tore through Jack's left thigh. He gritted his teeth, yanked his belt free, then grasped the wire and wrenched it from the wall. He pulled himself through the opening, swivelled around, and thrust the severed wire into the flood water. Sparks hissed and flew, accompanied by a strangled cry of pain.

Jack scrambled to his feet, took Suraya's weight from Maddie and stumbled with her to the door.

"You okay?" Maddie's eyes flashed with fear.

"Fine. Turn left. We need to take the northern staircase." Maddie tried to take Suraya's other arm, but Jack shook his head. "I need you to cover us."

A crack of lightning shook the building and Jack stumbled. From behind them, the thrum of motors grew into a pressing whine. "We can't access the stairs from this side," Jack shouted. "But if we go back past the control room—"

Three drones rounded the corner and bore down on them.

Pfipp, pfipp, pfipp.

Jack reached the door on his left and fell behind it with Suraya. Darts cracked against the glass. Maddie raced to join them. She heaved the door shut, grabbed the fire extinguisher that was mounted to the wall and wedged it behind the door's handle. She bent down to take Suraya's arm, touching skin that was cold and clammy, and saw the bloom of red blood that was growing across Jack's leg.

"Oh no." Her words were a whisper. Her stomach twisted tight. She needed him. She needed his help to get Suraya out.

"It's nothing," said Jack firmly, pushing himself up from the floor and taking Suraya's other arm. He tried not to wince as he put one foot in front of the other.

The lights cut out, plunging the corridor into shades of murky grey. Shadows masked the hand that struck out from the entrance to the control room and grabbed Jack's ankle. Jack crashed to his knees, his gun spinning out of reach. Hands clawed and pulled at his leg. He twisted round to see the guard, half-drunk with sedative, his expression an ugly mix of anger and confusion. Jack lifted his right foot and kicked down hard on the man's hand. Maddie raised her gun to fire—

Crash.

The door to the corridor shattered, spraying them with fragments of glass. Drones were gathering beyond it like a swarm of angry wasps, their soaring hum growing louder. Maddie reloaded her gun and shot at those closest, forcing the others back.

The guard, still disorientated, struggled to his knees and tried to steady himself. Jack ran his hands across the floor, searching for his gun, then remembered the darts. He pulled the cartridge from his pocket and prised two clear. The guard threw himself forwards, his fist connecting with Jack's jaw. Jack's head hit the wall but he grasped the man's collar, plunged the darts into his neck and shoved him back. The man reeled and toppled sideways.

Beyond the guard, beside the service door that led to the southern stairwell, was the holo-projector Jack had used earlier. Jack scrambled for it, placed it just in front of the guard's warm body, and pulled off his watch. "Record," he instructed. Maddie fired at another drone. "Stop. Play back on repeat. Insert loop interval – random duration, range 0.5 to 2 seconds. Start." He set the watch down and switched the holo-projector on, causing the air to ripple in front of them. "Come on!" He tugged at Maddie's arm. They pulled Suraya from the floor, through murmured words of protest, and made their way towards the far end of the corridor.

Maddie stopped at the door. Behind her, the sound of her gunfire echoed from Jack's watch. "Is this door really clear?" she hissed.

Pfipp. Pfipp. Pfipp.

Two darts hit the unconscious guard, while a third struck the wall just clear of Maddie's arm.

Jack shrugged and pushed it open a fraction with his foot.

The anticipated barrage of darts and bullets didn't arrive, but the sound of muted gunshot did, from somewhere to their right. A flash of lightning pierced the darkness, its harsh white light searing into Jack's skull, its pressure forcing the breath from his lungs. He gasped for air, felt his pulse race, while thunder rolled around the building. From their right came a shout and more gunfire. "Oh no," Jack groaned. "It's Frits."

Jack forced his legs to move, though pain erupted with every footstep and a dull numbness was beginning to spread outwards and into his hip. Where was Frits' time capsule? He had to get to him.

Angry shouts, the crack and crash of plaster, grew louder as they found the stairwell. They edged awkwardly down the first flight, Maddie struggling with Suraya's almost dead weight, Jack grimacing at the strain on his leg.

Jack risked a glimpse over the balustrade. Two flights below, a middle-aged man in a grey jacket and jeans sat just above the turn in the steps. Further down, a pool of blood suggested where Jack might find Frits. But Frits wasn't dead yet.

"Come on," the man in grey chided. He smiled, flashing a set of crooked teeth. "Wouldn't you rather be on the winning side, Frits? It is Frits, isn't it?"

"Fuck you!" came the reply from below.

The man's face came into view, and Jack recognised it as Tobias Keller, the man responsible for the attack on LEFA's East Hub the year before. Jack motioned for Maddie to hold back, then continued his descent.

Unaware of those above, Keller laughed. "Aubrey Martin did say you were stubborn."

"Never met him," Frits snarled.

"No, but I think you've met his granddaughter, Candice, a generous donor to the cause. Surprised you didn't take her up on her offer."

"So, you're working for her now," Frits scoffed. "Same as Hart? Pair of fucking turncoats. You won't last long once the Republic finds out." He broke into a fit of coughing.

"Well, I don't *need* long. Afterall, *you've* just delivered a fully functioning time machine to my door." Keller flicked out the cartridge from his gun and returned it with a loud *clack*. "All you need to do, is decide whether you die before or after I find it."

"Oh, I love a choice," Frits sneered, though his voice had less venom. He was weakening.

"Ah, but it is a choice, Frits, because you can choose whether to die quickly and efficiently, or slowly and painfully."

"Quick and efficient…"

Keller's head whipped round. Behind him, Jack pulled the trigger.

Pht.

"…is always best."

Keller's body crumpled forwards.

Jack yelled for Maddie to follow, running past Keller to the floor below, where Frits had tucked himself into the recess of the service door. Jack's feet slid on the slick floor. He winced, lowering into a crouch. Frits' eyes were closed, his chest rose and fell rapidly and sweat beaded his brow. Blood was seeping from multiple wounds across his legs and chest.

Jack swallowed, surprised by the swell of emotion sweeping through him. "Frits, I…"

Frits' eyes flew open. He seized Jack's wrist with surprising strength. "Give me the serum!" he hissed. "I know you have it – you're Feynman's favourite."

"I'm sorry," Jack breathed. "You're not gonna make it."

Frits' lips curled down and he opened his mouth to speak, issuing only another round of bloody coughs. "Need it for *her*, do you?" he managed at last, as Suraya, supported by Maddie, moved into view. His other hand flew up to press the barrel of his gun to Jack's head. His eyes darted from Jack to Maddie, wild and frightened. From above they heard the crash of glass.

"They're through the first door." Maddie touched Jack's shoulder. "We have to keep moving."

"Where is it, Frits? I *have* to destroy the capsule."

Their eyes locked.

"Give me the serum and I'll tell you." The corners of Frits' mouth twitched.

Jack pushed the gun away and leant in, his voice a whisper. "You told me that I'm the only one who can open Hart's safe." He turned his leg slightly, so that Frits could see the darkening fabric of his trousers, the severity of his wound.

Frits' eyes widened, returning to Jack's face. The confidence in Jack's eyes was gone, and Frits saw through the front that Jack was putting on for Maddie's sake. Jack's expression was dark and hollow, his eyes pleading.

"Fuck." Frits wiped a trickle of blood from his mouth.

"Even if I gave you the serum," continued Jack, "I couldn't get you out of here."

The low groan of twisting metal echoed down the steps.

Frits understood the stakes. He sucked air through clenched teeth and pressed his lips together in bitter resignation. "It's on floor forty-eight," he wheezed. "Here." He pulled a small device from his pocket. "This detonates it remotely."

"Thank you." Jack smiled grimly. "I will remember this."

Frits' face creased and he convulsed. "Don't make me laugh." He pulled himself up a little. "Now go! Fucking do-gooders. I'll hold them off."

Jack nodded and stood. The fire alarm trigger was in front of him. Not everyone needed to die. He punched the glass, setting off a high-pitched wail, then ran to the stairs, following Maddie who was making slow progress with Suraya.

"And Jack?" Frits called, his voice thick.

Jack paused mid-step.

"You asked how Candice Martin found you? How it connects to Howard?" he coughed and wiped away the bloody spittle with his sleeve. "They've got him. Martin's men took him before he made it to Gaia."

"What?" Jack's heart skipped a beat and the world around him clouded. Dully, he registered a crash above – the guards had broken through the second door – but he found he couldn't move.

"Jack, we need to go!" Maddie cried.

"They're tracking you through Howard, through his memories…"

Maddie dropped Suraya and ran back, grabbing Jack's arm, forcing him forwards.

"…if you fail, he'll be killed…"

Maddie drove Jack on. Frits' face disappeared but his words echoed after them.

"…if you succeed, Howard's life will be rewritten, but he'll survive."

A low hum echoed from the top of the stairs. Bullets clanged against the metal railings above their heads, rousing Jack from his stupor. He helped lift Suraya then charged down the steps, his ears filled with Frits' final, defiant roar.

Jack felt lightheaded, but there was no time to stop, no moment to pause. "Next floor," he panted. "We take the lifts."

"Pssssh…Ja…psssh…no Ma…psssh…"

"Max! Max?" Jack tapped his ear and cursed when the static fizzled out.

"Take her," Maddie commanded, releasing Suraya's arm to tug at the service door. It didn't budge. Above the wail of the fire alarm, she heard a cry, the thump of boots on the steps. She ran her hand over the code lock, stood back and fired at it twice. She braced one foot against the wall and heaved the metal panel forwards, just enough for them to slip through. Jack stumbled with Suraya and Maddie stooped to help him, noticing his pallid colour, the beads of sweat that clung to the skin above his lips. "Jack?"

Jack ignored the question, the anxiety in her voice. "Through here, on the right."

They fell into the open lift doors, grateful that the threat of fire had not immobilised them. Jack leant heavily against the back wall and slid down to the floor, his eyes on the countdown as the lift descended. He pulled the detonator from his pocket and flipped the cover open.

Floor thirty-nine…floor thirty-eight…floor thirty-seven…

He pictured the extent of the devastation caused by his

own time-machine. He had to ensure that they were well-clear, but maybe he could catch the drones in the halo of the blast. Floor thirty-six...floor thirty-five...floor thirty-four...floor thirty-three...

He pushed the button and held his breath.

The explosion shook the building, cutting the lights and plunging them into darkness. Maddie gasped. The lift shuddered violently and the air inside swelled with heat. It was a miracle that it kept moving.

Floor twenty-nine... floor twenty-eight.

The lift shuddered to a halt and the doors slid open, flooding the interior with hazy light and the acrid smell of smoke. Overhead, the sounds of shattering glass and roaring flames were replaced by wails and shouts.

"Come on." Maddie lifted Suraya onto her shoulder. Her breathing was ragged and her eyes had nearly rolled back in her head. Dread stabbed at Maddie's heart. "It's just a short way to the other lifts, right?"

Jack nodded. He breathed deeply, gritted his teeth, and pushed himself up from the floor.

"Psssh...Jack...psssh   Maddi...psh...ar...psh...you there?"

"Max, we'll be coming..." Jack panted, "down the south lift shaft."

"No! The...psh...rescu...psh...police and f...psssh."

"Damn it! Max, I can't make you out."

"Pssssh...I can...psh...son Hart...psh...in the...pssssh."

"Shit!" Maddie tried. "Max? Max? Can we take the south lifts?"

"Psssh...no it's...psh ...people evacuating fro...psh ...north entrance...psssh."

Maddie lowered Suraya onto a chair, raced through a maze of desks to the vast window beyond, and tried to make out the activity on the ground below. She hurried back, forming a decision. She reached for the bag on Jack's back. "We'll give her the serum now, and—" Above them the floor bulged and groaned ominously. "Fuck."

Jack was already attempting to lift Suraya, but Maddie pushed him aside and somehow heaved her sister's body over her shoulder. "We need to take the stairs." She headed for the doorway. "Can you manage it?"

The air in the stairwell was thick with smoke, blurring their vision and burning their throats as they stumbled downwards. Jack forced himself on, his mind and his body locked in a battle of will. Frits' words echoed in his mind: *you're the only one who can open Hart's safe... the only one.*

Maddie had taken charge now, shouting instructions, keeping Jack focussed, and all the while carrying Suraya with strength born of desperate determination. They reached the fourth floor, where the wail of the fire alarm was joined by that of sirens, raised voices and the clatter of feet. Fire and Rescue officers had entered the building.

"Pssssh... I've got a... psh... silver, registration LN63... psssh... avoid the... psssh."

"Max? Max? Damn it!" Maddie cried. The service door ahead swung open, and two firefighters burst through. The first ran to Suraya, lifting her from Maddie's shoulder before she could protest, examining her wounds and feeling for her pulse, as the second took out his radio. "We've got three people on the northern stairwell," he reported. His expert eyes quickly assessed the state of their injuries. "Two with severe lacerations and blood loss."

"Copy that," came the reply.

"Have you passed anyone else on the stairs?" he asked.

"No," replied Maddie, trying not to panic. "And we're fine, we just need some air."

"It's alright, you're in shock," the fireman spoke gently. He took Jack's arm and steered them through the door. His colleague, just behind, carried Suraya. "But you're safe now, and we're here to help."

Maddie and Jack had no choice. They were led out into the atrium and down the steps towards the lobby, both searching the street beyond for a silver vehicle, registration year sixty-three. Maddie spotted it, just beyond the police cordon, at the corner of Threadneedle Street. They emerged from the building and were led towards a row of ambulances.

Jack caught at Maddie's sleeve. "If we go to hospital… we'll be arrested…" He struggled with the words; his breathing heavy. "I don't know… what will happen to Suraya… but she needs this." He pulled out the pouch containing the last two syringes of serum. "She's too far gone."

Suraya was lifted onto a wheeled stretcher. Maddie reached out for the pouch. Behind her, Jack saw a flash of metal in the sky. "Get down!" he yelled, pulling her sideways. They crashed to the ground as a dart clattered off the side of the ambulance. A drone buzzed into view. The gathered spectators and evacuees screamed and ran.

In the commotion, Maddie seized her chance. She sprang from the ground and seized the stretcher, propelling it towards Max and the car. "Come on!" she screamed at Jack, who struggled up from the asphalt, clutching the pouch, limping after her.

"Wait, miss? Miss!" A paramedic ran towards Maddie.

Jack reached into his pocket and retrieved a dart, bearing down on the medic before she could reach Maddie, sinking the tip into her leg. "Sorry," he mumbled, and lurched on.

Max was out of the car, lifting and pulling Suraya into the back seat. Jack swayed and Maddie shoved him into the passenger seat. She scrambled into the back with Suraya as Max screeched forwards. The vehicle raced away, but not before Jack caught a glimpse of two soldiers, clad in black, behind a dark-haired man in a suit. His eyes closed on the man's twisted smile.

"Where is it?" Maddie cried, hysteria rising as she leant over from the back seat and pulled at Jack's hands. "Jack? The serum!"

Jack tried to open his eyes, tried to speak, but he couldn't find the strength.

"Max, you need to pull over."

"But the police, they're…"

"Now!" she shouted.

Max slammed on the brakes and reversed, backing the car into a covered archway.

"There, that's it." Maddie pointed frantically at the small fabric case in the foot-well. "There are two syringes, one each."

Max snatched it up, ripped back the zip and pulled out a syringe, handing it to Maddie.

"And the other one?"

"I think, this is it." Max replied. His trembling fingers held fragments of glass, their surface wet and glistening.

"Oh god, when we fell…"

Jack forced his eyes open to watch their lips, to better understand their words.

"Give it to Suraya," said Max.

"But Jack will die!"

"So will Suraya without it."

Jack tried to speak, but the words remained in his head. *I'm the only one who can open Hart's safe…the only one.*

Maddie's lips trembled. She looked from her sister to the man who had helped save her. "There must be something," she stammered, "some way we can—"

"We can't save them both," said Max. He snatched the syringe from Maddie's hand and plunged it into Suraya's leg. "I'm sorry."

Jack's eyes closed and surrendered to the darkness.

§

From beyond the shadows, words filtered through. Raised voices. Snatches of conversation. Soft, whispered pleas. But the cocoon-like darkness was comforting, and so for a time it held him, a refuge through which the voices ebbed and flowed.

"You have to let him go."

"I can't!"

…

"Down there, that's it, the clinic where Leroy's nephew works. Pull over. Pick up, Ben, pick up."

"Are you sure that's his number?"

"I'm certain. Leroy said he—Hello? Ben? This is Maddie…"

…

"I don't understand, Maddie. What you're telling me isn't possible."

"Ben, I need you to trust me. You have to do the transfusion now."

…

"Lala mtoto, lala lala, lala lala; lala sinzia lala.

Lala mpendwa, lala lala, lala lala; lala sinzia lala…

Do you remember that song, Suraya? Mama used to sing it to us. Suraya…please don't leave me."

…

"The transfusion may not have contained enough of the serum."

"But Suraya's started to heal, maybe it's just taking longer for Jack?"

"I'm sorry Maddie, I simply don't know."

…

"I'm sorry folks. The police were on the phone, asking all kinds of questions. You can't stay here."

"Just a little bit longer, Ben, please? She's stabilising now, but what if something goes wrong? And what about Jack?"

"Look, why don't you go to Sarah. LEFA has a medic, they can help you—"

"No. Not now."

"It's your call, but there's something else. We found this implanted under Suraya's skin."

"A tracker?"

"Yep. Someone knows she's here."

"Maddie, we need to move her."

"I know, Max, I know."

"I'll call Leroy."

…

"Oh Maddie, w'at a mess you got yourself into."
　"Leroy. I'm sorry, I—"
　"D'ere now, calm yourself. It gonna be alright."
　…

"Jack, can you hear me? We did it. Suraya's going to be fine. But we need to move now – they know where we are. Jack? You've still got a job to do, remember, so you need to wake up now. Okay?"
　"Maddie, come on. There's time for that later."
　…

"If they're in pain, give them these. If they get worse, then please try Sarah. She's not a monster."
　"Okay."
　"I'll do my best to stall them."
　"Please be careful. And Ben? Thank you."
　…

"You sure dis is the place?"
　"It's what he kept saying, over and over, there's got to be a reason."
　"Well, we've no time to argue, dat's t'ree times I seen that drone, and I can feel it's beady eyes watchin' me."
　…

"There, can you get through that? Mind his head. Ray, this way, hold on to me."
　"All t'rough?"
　"Yes. You've got the tracker?"
　"Mm-hm. Gonna go play me some cat an' mouse!"
　"Be careful, Leroy."
　"Always, baby girl. Always."
　…

§

16th August 2073

Mark Lane, Disused Underground Station

The storm had released a torrent of water upon the city of London, turning streets into rivers, underpasses into waterlogged caverns. For years, the underground system had been poorly maintained, and the tunnels echoed with the sound of water, filtering through cracks and fissures to drip onto the sodden rails below. The emergency lights in the disused station emitted a languid glow, their warm colour at odds with the damp and draughty space. It was a far cry from the bleached and brightly lit Jewry Street Clinic, where Leroy's nephew, Ben had done his best to patch Jack and Suraya's wounds.

Since escaping Twentytwo, Suraya had barely roused, and Maddie would have worried, save for Ben's reassurance that sleep was what she needed. Maddie sat between Jack, laid on the stretcher he'd been carried on, and Suraya, sleeping on an old wooden bench. If only Maddie could sleep, she might wake up and find that it had all been a bad dream. But she couldn't sleep, only wait, hidden below ground, desperately hoping that Jack would survive.

Suraya stirred.

Maddie's stomach fluttered and she leaned close to stroke her sister's face. "It's okay, I'm here."

Suraya's eyes opened. Her mind felt heavy and the view above her made no sense. She couldn't place where she was or where she'd been. Where had she been? Her eyes widened and she sat bolt upright. "Maddie," she croaked. "We're in danger."

"No, it's okay, we're safe." Maddie drew Suraya into her arms, her sister's head briefly resting on her shoulder.

"Oh God, it's him!" Suraya lurched backwards, sliding across the bench and away from the other person in the room. "It's Hart!"

"What? No. That's Jack, he helped rescue you, remember?"

But Suraya wasn't listening. Her eyes flew wildly about the room, searching for a weapon. She lunged forwards and snatched up a length of wood, part of the original staircase, and brandished it above her head.

"Ray that's not Hart, I promise. He's a friend." Maddie gently, but firmly, removed the wooden baton from her sister's hands.

Fear. Maddie had never seen Suraya afraid of anything before, and yet it was etched clearly across her face now. Maddie pulled her into a protective embrace and felt the tremble of her sister's slight frame.

Suraya fought against the rush of memories, whose cold weight threatened to drag her down. Overcome, she buried her face in Maddie's shoulder and wept, her tears a mixture of fear and shame as she strove to find her courage, the confidence that defined her. In Hart's presence, even with Tobias Keller, she had held herself together, she'd stayed strong. Why now, when at last she was safe, did she feel herself quake?

She focussed on the feel of Maddie's arms, their warm, reassuring solidity. On the words Maddie murmured in her ear, the words their mother once used to comfort them.

"Mukwano, mukwano," *My love, my love.* "Si kikulu." *It is not important.*

Suraya tried to recall the feel of their mother's embrace, the springy softness of her body, her scent, faintly spiced and warm, like cardamom. Or was it cinnamon? Maddie would know; she'd had longer with their mother, after all. Suraya squeezed her eyes tight and bit her lips. It felt so long along, when Maddie had stepped into that void, the space their mother had left behind.

Suraya sniffed back her tears and lifted her head to look at Maddie, her capable, reliable older sister who had never let her down. The shadows beneath Maddie's eyes, the deep-set creases on her brow, revealed how Maddie had suffered. Suraya was responsible; her impetuous character once again a source of grief to those she loved most. She opened her mouth to speak, her voice breaking as she tried to find the words to apologise. "Maddie, I'm, I didn't mean…"

"Ssh, it's okay, I know. It's not your fault."

The man on the trestle bed stirred, startling Suraya, and Maddie flew to his side. He murmured something in his sleep, his face contorting with pain. Maddie took his hand in her own and pressed it gently, softly speaking words Suraya couldn't make out.

Maddie's concern for this man, her affection even, left Suraya shaken, as though the ground had shifted beneath her. It was only a week and a half since the sisters' last meeting, on the shadowed embankment beside Somerset House. Maddie hadn't mentioned anyone then. Who was this person who had come to mean so much in such a short space of time?

Suraya edged forwards to better see him. He was younger than she'd first thought, fair haired, rather than dark, but there was a similarity in the shape of his face, the way his hair parted and fell at the front of his forehead. "I thought he was Hart," she said quietly, moving to just behind Maddie's elbow. "He looks like him, a bit."

"Hart?" Maddie asked in surprise. "He's nothing like him, he doesn't…" But her sentence was left hanging. She tilted her head slightly to one side.

Suraya watched the emotions flash across her sister's face, the slight widening of her eyes, but Maddie volunteered nothing.

"Who is he?" Suraya asked at last, gingerly lowering herself to sit on the bench.

Maddie sighed. "Honestly, I don't really know."

"What?"

"Well, I know his name, where he's from, sort of, and what he's trying to do. But there's much more that I don't know or understand."

"But you seem… I thought—"

"Oh, no." Maddie flushed. "It's not like that. I've only known him a few days." She wondered whose benefit those words were for. She sighed and raised an eyebrow. "Though God knows, it feels longer."

"I am completely at a loss."

A low scraping sound from the top of the staircase brought them both to their feet.

"It's me," called Max, returning from a foray into the building above where a bar, now long deserted, occupied the former Mark Lane Station building. He made his way down the staircase, pausing mid-step when his gaze fell on Suraya.

"Hey," he said quietly, setting his backpack down on the bench. His fingers fumbled with the zip, and his words caught in his throat. He was convinced Suraya could hear the roaring thud of his heart in his chest. He risked a glance, looking away quickly when their eyes met, and pushed his glasses up his nose. "How are you feeling?"

She stepped a little closer to him. "Could be worse. Hungry."

"There wasn't much," he apologised, unpacking some bags of peanuts, a bottle of water and a catering sized jar of olives.

Suraya picked up the jar and wrinkled her nose.

Maddie laughed.

"What?" Suraya demanded.

"Nothing," Maddie shook her head. "I guess beggars can't be choosers, especially when they're last in line."

Suraya pulled a disdainful face and Maddie swooped in on her, hugging her tightly.

"It's so good to see you're still you," Maddie whispered into Suraya's hair.

"What? Picky?" Suraya replied peevishly.

"Yes." Maddie grinned. She leant back a little to look at her sister. "Just like you've always been."

Suraya's eyes glazed with the threat of more tears, but she smiled and brought her forehead to rest against Maddie's. She'd always drawn strength from her sister, from their similarities, but even more so from their differences. For better or for worse, they were a part of how she knew and understood herself, and to hear Maddie laugh at her, to poke fun at her faults, was oddly reassuring.

They stood a moment, heads touching, until Suraya remembered Max, standing awkwardly to one side. Maddie released her and took the bottle of water. Suraya picked up a packet of peanuts, ripped open the sachet and tipped a few into the palm of her hand. She glanced up through her eyelashes. "Thank you, Max... for helping find me."

"I shouldn't have let them send you," Max responded at once, words flowing from him with his guilt. "I should have made Sarah ask someone else. Told you not to do it."

"But it wasn't up to you." Suraya looked down, her lips pushed together, half grimace, half smile. "I wanted to go. I wanted to help." She took a shuddering breath and shook her head, clearing away images that only she was a party to. "Anyway, you found me." She smiled shyly.

Max felt his cheeks flush again and nodded mutely.

"You should sit down," Maddie cut in, directing Suraya to sit on the bench. Out of sight, she gave Max's arm a quick, reassuring squeeze.

Suraya winced as she lowered herself down.

"Is it still very painful?" Max asked.

"Not too bad." Suraya lifted her blood-stained top to see the bandage on her stomach. "Which is weird. I still don't get it. I almost bled to death earlier and now it's as though it never happened." She peeled back the dressing and drew in a short, sharp breath. "Oh my God."

Maddie pulled away Suraya's hand, revealing a bruised and reddened area of skin – skin that was whole and unbroken. Max raised his eyebrows and blew out a long, low whistle.

"How is this even possible?" asked Suraya.

Maddie spun around to Jack, lifted the trouser fabric from his thigh, and crouched down to gently free the blood-caked bandages. The wound beneath had shrunk. "It's working," she breathed.

"Can somebody please tell me what's going on!" wailed Suraya.

Maddie eased herself onto the bench beside her. "Okay, but you're probably not going to believe me."

"I still can't believe that you punched Sarah in the face!"

Maddie's laugh echoed from inside the darkened tunnel. "I know, I was so angry." She bit her lower lip and glanced at Suraya. "And scared. I don't know what I would have done if you'd…"

"Been killed?"

"Or, you know…" Maddie swallowed and reached for her sister's hand. "Ray, did Hart, did he hurt you? Force you to do anything?"

Suraya's stomach tightened and she looked away. For a moment she thought she could smell him, a mix of bourbon and cigar.

Maddie squeezed her hands. "Ray, I'm so sorry, I—"

"No." Suraya's voice was firm. "He didn't. He might have, or maybe that's just what he wanted me to think. Everything was a game to him."

Maddie pulled Suraya into her arms and rocked her, murmuring, "You've been through so much."

Suraya allowed herself to be comforted a while, settling into her sister's embrace, but her thoughts refused to be silenced. She squeezed her eyes shut, desperate to block out the truth, but it curdled in her stomach. She drew a shuddering breath and broke free from Maddie, wiping her eyes with the heel of her hand. "And what about you?" she demanded, her voice unexpectedly harsh "How much have I put you through?"

Maddie frowned. "Suraya, you were following orders, you can't hold yourself responsible for that."

"But…" Suraya fought to reconcile her emotions; was she angry with her sister, or angry with herself? "It's not just that, is it?" Suraya lifted her hand to Maddie's face and touched the damaged skin in a tender caress. "I…I always wished I was like you."

"What?" Maddie's expression hardened. "Scarred and ugly?"

"Don't say that. It's not true."

Maddie shrugged and caught Suraya's hand, lowering it to her lap.

"You are beautiful and kind and...and the bravest person I know."

"Now I know you're being silly," Maddie said, rolling her eyes. "*You* have always been the beautiful one and the brave one, whereas I was the sensible one."

"You're wrong. When you tried to save mum and dad..." Suraya's chin trembled and she drew a breath to steady herself. "You were more courageous than anyone I know. And I... did nothing."

Memories flooded Maddie's mind. Her throat constricted. Her words were little more than a whisper. "You were just a child."

"And you were barely an adult, not much older than I am now. Look at everything you took on, everything you gave up for me, for my sake." Suraya cast her eyes down and picked at the brittle tape that held together the broken bench on which they sat. "I can never live up to that," she mumbled.

Silence descended, broken only by the distant drip of water from deep within the tunnel. Maddie contemplated her, the sister she'd envied and admired, nurtured and chastised, but always cherished with every cell of her body. She had never considered that her dazzling sister might also feel inadequate, might worry that she would never measure-up next to herself.

"Look at me." Maddie said, gently lifting Suraya's head. "We are not in competition." She laughed inwardly and sighed. "We *shouldn't* be in competition. We're sisters; we're part of each other. There is nothing for you to live up to, and nothing that I haven't willingly done."

Suraya shrugged and tore back a strip of tape, twisting and untwisting it around her finger.

Maddie reached into the backpack by her feet and pulled out their mother's blue and terracotta headscarf. "Here." She wrapped the material around Suraya's head, twisted the ends together, and tucked them under to secure it.

Suraya raised her brows uncertainly.

Maddie smoothed a thumb over the lines on her sister's forehead and thought a moment, conjuring an image of their mother, of what she would say. "You and I are born from a long line of strong women," she said at last. "Our grandmother, our mother, and now you and I. Mama once said that this is the cloth of our motherland and the strength of our people is carried in its strands; when you wear it, you will always know yourself and have the courage to be yourself."

Suraya's lower lip trembled. "I miss her."

Emotion swelled in Maddie's chest and she nodded. She missed her too. More than anything she missed her mother's guidance, her reassurance. What would she give to see her mother again? If she could travel in time, like Jack had, that would be where she would go, no question: to a time and place where her parents were still alive.

Suraya watched her, waiting. Maddie pressed her lips together and placed her hand gently over Suraya's heart. "She's in here," she said, feeling it, knowing it was true. "And now"—she smiled— "you look just like her."

"Really?" asked Suraya with childlike eagerness.

"Really."

Suraya leant into her sister's warm embrace. Their tears and laughter wove in and out of murmured recollections, filling them both with the warmth of shared memory. Together, in the darkness, their voices rose and fell like the counterparts of a melody.

Jack dreamt of his mother. Mary was young, maybe his own age, and she was walking in Greenwich Park with a man whose stance was familiar, but whose face Jack couldn't see. Two children, a boy and a girl, ran to-and-fro with dizzying energy, skidding on the dewy ground, slipping between the adults' feet whilst laughing and throwing autumn leaves at one another.

Mary's nose and cheeks were flushed pink from the cold autumn breeze, and tendrils of golden hair escaped her woollen hat to dance across her face. She was relaxed and contented. Free. Jack had never seen her that way.

He could have watched her for hours, but she moved past him and up the hill towards the observatory. He tried to follow her, to step past the ancient chestnut tree where he stood, but his feet were anchored to the spot. He called out her name and she heard him, turned towards him even, but she looked straight through him to the river beyond.

Mary turned away and stooped down to snatch up the boy. She threw him into the air while he giggled and squealed, then planted a kiss on his cheek before he squirmed free to chase his sister with a playful roar.

Jack's eyes trailed after him; the boy and Jack looked nothing alike. But Mary, she was the picture of what he had always longed for, the doting mother Jack had craved. She was joyful. And she was out of reach.

Jack stirred a little as the images began to recede, overlaid by the low murmur of voices in conversation. Jack recognised one of the voices, a cadence that felt familiar, and listened, not to the words, but to the inflections as they rose and fell like music.

Jack pulled his mind forward thickly, through the syrupy refuge of sleep and back to the present moment. The dull ache in his thigh triggered memories of smoke and drones, of desperate voices and anxious words. But he was alive.

He opened his eyes to the sight of riveted girders, pale arching bricks and thick shadows which sucked at the torpid, yellow light. He grimaced and pushed himself up on to his elbows, triggering a scrape of feet and an end to the lyrical flow of conversation.

"Jack?" Maddie appeared beside him.

Jack suppressed a sob and reached for her, clasping her head in his hand, pulling her forwards until their heads touched. He took a moment to ground himself, to sense her wholeness and his own. But his mind raced, recalling that there had only been one syringe of serum. His brow furrowed as he searched her face. "Suraya?" he asked, fearful of the answer.

"She's okay." Maddie smiled.

The rush of relief left Jack lightheaded. He closed his eyes briefly, and an image of Mary danced behind his lids.

"Jack?" Maddie felt his forehead, fearful.

"I'm fine." A shift in the light caught his eye, and he raised himself up to sit.

Suraya stood, a little awkwardly, a few feet back from Maddie, watching Jack uncertainly.

He smiled faintly while snatches of conversation returned to him. "You gave one of us the serum, then did a transfusion?" he asked.

Maddie nodded. "Our friend – a nurse – works near here, but we had to move on before the police found us."

Jack looked about the dim-lit space, aware of a void that stretched away on either side where any normal room would require walls. "Mark Lane?" he asked.

Maddie took a deep breath and puffed out her cheeks. "You kept saying it in your sleep, over and over so…" She shrugged.

"This is good. Thank you." Jack lifted the fabric from his injured leg, then eased his feet to the floor. The wound was healing well, though it felt hot, smarting each time he moved. The rest of his body was one low, dull ache. Jack looked around. "Where's Max?"

"He's scouting out the tunnels, looking for a way around the commotion outside. Figured that's why you suggested this place."

Jack smiled. Max was growing on him.

"He's been gone a long time though," Suraya said, twisting to look over her shoulder, a trace of anxiety in her voice.

The last time Jack had seen Suraya, she'd been bloodied and bruised, her cheek red and swollen. Thanks to the serum, there was little evidence of her physical trauma, but as she turned to discover Jack watching her, and blanched in response, Jack knew that other, less tangible damage, might yet leave its mark. She moved towards the countertop, picked up the plastic bottle of water and held it out towards him with a trembling hand.

"Thank you," she mumbled. "For helping to find me."

Jack took the water with a grateful nod. Suraya's watchful expression was uneasy, and it was familiar. He'd seen it many times on his mother's face, and it wrenched at him to see it again, on the face of a woman he didn't even know. Had his mother looked at him, as Suraya did now, and seen the face of her abuser?

He wondered what Maddie and Suraya had discussed while he was sleeping. Did Maddie already know who Kayson Hart really was? Maddie's attention had returned to her sister and Jack noted the shadow of concern that flittered across her face. No matter how much he willed it, the connection to Hart would never go away.

"Listen," Jack began, "there's something I need to—"

"What was that?" Maddie spun towards the tunnel and drew her gun, targeting a faint glow in the distance. She sighed and relaxed her arms when a whistle echoed in the darkness.

"Max?" Suraya called.

A light bobbed up and down in time to the faint crunch of footsteps, gradually unveiling Max from the sweep of shadow as he neared the old station platform. His eyes fell on Jack as Maddie reached down to help him up. "You're awake," he remarked. "How d'you feel?"

Jack narrowed his eyes in thought. "Like I'd rather not nearly die for a third time this week."

The others stared at him awkwardly.

"Yeah," Max managed at last.

"Thanks though, for getting us out of there."

"No problem." Max nodded.

Jack looked at the others, deciding that there was nothing to explain. It would soon all be irrelevant. He took a breath and changed tack. "We need to get south of the river. From there, the Northern Line is our best bet. How far did you get up the tunnel? Any patrols, or drones?"

"There's no problem getting to Monument," Max replied. "But the connection to Bank is impossible. Unless there's a maintenance shaft or something that connects the lines there, we'll have to go up to Liverpool Street."

"That's fine. We can get through from Monument."

"To the Northern Line?" asked Maddie, confused.

"LEFA and the Fringe both used the ventilation shafts that run between deep level lines and the surface; they moved equipment around right under the government's nose." He caught the look of confusion on their faces. "Or they *will* do, next year; it's well-documented. Anyway, once we're on the Northern Line we can cross beneath the Thames and from there..." Jack looked down. "From there, you can all get to the Hub. Get to safety."

Maddie waited for something more, but Jack remained silent. She struggled to breathe evenly, at last asking, "And you?"

"I'll follow the Northern Line to Battersea, it's where Har—" Jack caught Suraya's eye and bit off the name. "It's where I'll find the next piece of the puzzle."

In the heavy silence, Max shifted his feet, the soft scrape of his boots making trails across the ancient dusty tiles.

Suraya looked around their group, feeling lost. Only Max met her eye, but she didn't have to look at her sister to feel the swell of conflict within her. She forced down her reflexive urge to draw Maddie close, to claim her, and instead suggested that she help Max check upstairs for supplies one last time.

Jack watched them climb the steps, aware of Maddie beside him but unable to look at her. He could feel her stare, feel the hurt emanating from her like a sudden heat. But what could he do or say? He had fulfilled his promise to her, and now he had another that he had to keep.

Maddie slipped down in front of him, forcing him to look at her. The air felt charged, the contours of the space around them blurred, but there was no pain in his head, no overwhelming nausea. Just a dull ache in the pit of his stomach.

"You're going to find Hart." Maddie searched his face.

Jack nodded.

"Because he knows where Dr Kinglsey is? Or because he's your father?"

Jack's stomach lurched. He looked away, down at the floor, anywhere to avoid the truth now that it was upon him. "Maddie... I'm sorry, I should have told you."

Maddie pulled herself up to sit on the stretcher beside him. "I get it. I'm not sure I'd want to share that connection either." Maddie frowned into the heavy pause. "Was he different when your mum knew him? I mean, were they in a relationship?"

"No, it wasn't like that."

Maddie noted the tension in his face, his muscles coiled tight.

"Listen," his voice was strained. "Did he...is Suraya okay?"

"I think so."

The muscles in his neck relaxed a little, and he ran a hand over his face.

"Is that why you agreed to help me find Suraya? Did Hart hurt your mum?"

Jack's nod was barely perceptible.

"Does he know about you? Does he know that he has a son?"

"He raped her," Jack whispered into the space between his knees. "But she escaped. He never knew."

Maddie reached forwards and took his hand.

A memory from that morning returned to him. Frits, gleeful and mocking, Jack insisting that no one knew who his father was. Then Frits had replied, 'Howard did, and he told Feynman, and she told me.'

Howard. The truth settled in Jack's stomach, bringing a fresh wave of anguish. Howard's life hung in the balance – their enemies had captured him and were using his memories to target Jack. Led by Candice Martin, those same people had recruited Hart, tasked him with finding

Kingsley before the Republic. Before Jack. Had Candice discovered the connection yet? Did Hart in fact know exactly who he was competing against in the race to reach Kingsley first? Jack sighed, unsure whether such a thing would matter or not.

The faint clink of water on metal reverberated from the west-bound tunnel, the conduit to Hart with whom Jack's path must reconnect. It was as though the universe demanded that the very man whose cruelty had given rise to Jack's life, must also be present at his death. Some might call it fate, but with luck, Jack would call it justice.

§

Battersea Power Station

Hart flicked through the photographs on his desk. His lips curled down at the edges. "It's definitely him?"

"The DNA trace confirms it."

"Good."

"Shall I inform Mr Martin, sir?"

Hart leant back in his seat, his eyes flicked to the Picasso painting and back again. "No, I'll call him myself. Ensure that this is removed from the reports."

"Very well. I'll be gettin' back to the station then – loose ends to tie up."

"Thank you, Noakes."

The police officer remained where he was. Hart peered up at him from below his brow, sighed, and pulled out his desk drawer. He withdrew a fat envelope and held it out.

The envelope disappeared inside the man's jacket and he turned and strode towards the door. "'Ave a good day, sir."

Hart's phone began to vibrate. It was the Republican Charge D'affaires, Steve Dalton, a cool and discreet figure who, unlike the ambassador himself, had made it his business to distrust everyone, Kayson Hart included.

The Republic was naturally concerned that the police investigation, following the explosion at Twentytwo, might uncover sensitive data; the wartime relationship between the Republic and the UK was fragile, the scale of Republican activity in London underplayed. Dalton would be seeking an assurance from Hart to intercede on the Republic's behalf, if it became necessary.

Hart watched the phone, patient, his breaths slow and steady, until it once again fell silent. He glanced out the window. Images of blue flame and the thunderous split of steel and glass, played across his mind. He had never seen destruction like it and he doubted that there was anything left on the upper floors of Twentytwo to give Dalton cause for concern.

He glanced again at the photographs on his desk: the charred remains of two figures, found in the stairwell not far from one another. As far as Hart was concerned, Keller's demise was propitious, if a little premature. But who was the second figure? The second victim for whom there was no DNA match. Keller's final message had simply read, '*he's cornered*'.

If it was the same man Hart had seen in yesterday's drone footage – an undocumented male in his late twenties to early thirties, seen travelling with Suraya's older sister – then the explosion had succeeded where Candice Martin's agents had failed. That might be a boon for Martin, who was, in Hart's opinion, unimaginative in her methods.

He pictured the group that had emerged from Twentytwo. Somehow, the sisters had survived the explosion, though Suraya had looked close to death. Dead or alive, the tracker they'd implanted had been removed and discarded into the Thames, and so LEFA's secrets looked to remain just that.

But there had also been a man, trailing, half-dead in their wake. He might yet prove to be the one Hart was looking for. Hart frowned, trying to picture the smoke-stained face he'd glimpsed through the window of a retreating car. If that man was the time traveller, if Hart could find him and use his knowledge, then he would surely discover Dr Kingsley before the Republic did.

Hart swivelled his seat towards the glass and watched the river as it swept downstream. His phone, reflected in the window, glowed red; someone was approaching the door. Hart turned back to his desk and flicked on the surveillance camera.

"Noakes? Don't tell me that your price has gone up."

The policeman shifted foot and leant in towards the camera. "One of my boys down the docks had a match on the fella you're lookin' for. He's been brought in for tresspassin'."

Hart felt the air around him thicken. "The Republican?"

Noakes nodded at the camera.

"Wipe the records and bring him here."

"Sir." Noakes hastened away.

For a brief moment, Hart felt dizzy. He sat down heavily and poured a drink, all thoughts of the time traveller forgotten. This was it. His chance to prove himself.

Hart had been an only child. An unhappy child. No matter how hard he'd sought approval, there had always been a distance between himself and his father. He was in his teens before he'd learned the reason why, his parents' argument loud, his ear unnecessarily pressed to the study door. He wasn't his father's son, that was the shameful truth, and his father's anger had been wrought that day across his mother's face.

As a young child, Kayson's relationship with his mother had been affectionate, but as he grew older, she, too became distant. He recalled how she was always drawn to Republicans, her polite enquiries that commenced with hope, concluded, always, with despair. She was searching for him, Kayson knew, and he hated her for it. He loathed his mother's disloyalty to the man who ought to have been his father and he thought her pathetic, searching for a man who clearly wanted nothing to do with her.

Kayson may not be his father's flesh and blood, but he vowed to prove his right to the family name. He would never allow himself to be treated the way his father had.

Affection was frivolous and weak, and marriage and children were neither desirable nor necessary. He would carve out his own legacy.

When he experienced his first premonition he'd been drunk, and he'd put the sensations down to the excessive quantity of alcohol coursing through his blood. The second time had frightened him. He'd cut back on the whiskey and curtailed his visits to the club. But the premonitions hadn't stopped, and as he pieced together the world he saw through them, he began to wonder if they might be a gift, a clue as to how he might leave his mark on the world.

But the world of his visions was at odds with the world that provided his family fortune, ensuring status as well as a luxurious lifestyle. And so, Hart bade his time, trusting that one day his path would become clear.

When Aubrey Martin approached him with proof of the existence and power of time travel, Hart knew that his opportunity had arrived. He would claim the technology for himself and fulfil the promise of his vision. He would arrest the progress of climate change, reverse it, and in doing so Hart would rid Europe of refugees and restore its essential character. The changes would cost his family fortune, but time technology would provide endless means of compensation.

Hart could be everything: rich, powerful, and righteous.

§

Northern Line Underground Tunnel

Maddie stopped again to listen, but there was no low-lying hum, not even the drip of water this far down, only the sound of their steady movement along the track.

"Are you in love with him?" asked Suraya as Maddie fell back into step beside her.

"What? No." Maddie felt a warm flush spread across her face and neck and silently thanked the darkness.

"But you like him, don't you."

Maddie glanced at her sister and rolled her eyes. "We're not kids in the playground, Ray."

"I've seen the way you look at him."

"Oh, come on. Whatever you think you may or may not have seen is irrelevant, there's a bigger picture here."

Suraya turned her sister's words over in her mind. "Hm. Not relevant…"

Maddie flashed her a scowl.

"Okay, fine, you're right." She shrugged. "There is a bigger picture. But we're all a part of it. Each one of us is like, is like…" Suraya struggled for the right words. "Well, this," she said at last, touching the cloth on her head. "We each weave our own thread through time, entwined with those of other people, and together those threads form the cloth."

"You do know that bark cloth isn't woven right?" Maddie replied. "The bark is pounded out until it's thin enough to be used as a fabric."

"God, you're infuriating." Suraya pulled the cloth from her head and cuffed Maddie with it.

Maddie laughed.

"I'm serious," Suraya replied plaintively. "You always play yourself down and push aside the things you want. But you shouldn't have to. Yes, there's a bigger picture, but without the pieces of the puzzle there's no picture at all."

They walked in silence for a while, Maddie watching the light from Jack's torch as it bobbed in the distance ahead. She could feel Suraya's gaze, sense her frustration. She considered how Suraya's words were all very well, but the reality was that her own desires might as well be irrelevant. She'd worked it out.

During the long wait below ground, Maddie had gone back over everything Jack had said, every detail of his life he'd shared. There wasn't that much, but enough to realise that his was a suicide mission. For Jack, the bigger picture had to take precedence, and beyond that there would be nothing. Even if that weren't the case, hadn't Jack demonstrated that he didn't feel the same way?

There was friendship, yes, but he'd kept his distance every time that it might have become something more.

Knowingly, Suraya reached out to brush Maddie's hand. "You know, I think he likes you too."

"You would conjure up a love story between a tramp and a movie star," Maddie replied with a sigh.

"Does he know how you feel?"

"Urgh! That's enough now, okay? Just stop. We're just people, thrown together by a crazy situation. He's focussed on his goal and I'm focussed on mine, which, of course, was to find you. Now that's done, we can just—"

"You should tell him, you know, how you feel."

"Oh, shut up. Anyway, what about Max?"

"Max?"

"Yes, *Max.* He's clearly head over heels. But how do you feel?"

Suraya drew her head back as though shocked. The movement had a studied air to it which faltered as her gaze travelled from Maddie to the silhouettes moving against the torchlight further up the tunnel. "Max is kind…" Her voice trailed off and her expression softened. "But he's such a nerd." She shook her head dismissively. "Not my type."

But Maddie noticed that Suraya's eyes slid back to where the men were walking, how she pulled her lower lip between her teeth in thought. "If you say so," she mumbled under her breath.

A long, low whistle from ahead silenced them, and they quickened their pace to reach the others.

"We're coming up on Elephant and Castle," Jack explained. "There's a maintenance shaft just before the platform, which leads to the rear of the station. We can use our drone to scope it out and, if need be, use sedative darts to clear the exit. The Hub isn't far, and it's the safest place for you all." Jack glanced at Maddie, his expression apologetic. "Save for the wrath of Sarah."

Maddie shook her head. "Ray and I have talked it over, and we don't think going to the Hub is a good idea." Max opened his mouth to protest. "Not yet anyway. It might put Jack at risk, and Sarah will want to make an example of me."

"I know that you're going to see Hart." Suraya forced herself to meet Jack's stare. "That he's got something you need." She stuffed her hands into her pockets and looked down, shrugging as though it were no big deal. Her hands, clenched tight within the folds of the fabric, told another story. "I might know something that could help."

"So, it makes no sense to split up now." Maddie's tone was resolute. "Also, we just lost most of our tech – but Max can help repurpose some of the stuff at your grandparents' place."

Jack didn't speak. His head was a turmoil of conflicted emotions. He turned to Maddie, noting the way that she folded her arms, challenging him to withstand her determination. It wasn't supposed to be a group mission, and Jack's chest tightened at the thought of placing Maddie in more danger. But truthfully, he didn't want her to leave. Not yet.

"Your place is much more comfortable than the Hub," Maddie persisted. "And we're all exhausted, and hungry." The last two words were almost a question.

Jack relented. "Fine. We'll all go to Richborne Terrace."

Maddie shot him a triumphant look. "May as well make the most of your family's cornucopia," she quipped.

The corner of Jack's mouth raised in recollection.

Max shot Suraya a quizzical look and she shrugged in reply.

"Come on then." Maddie set off down the southbound tunnel. "Oval might be the closest, but we'll be safer coming up at Stockwell."

They resurfaced without event at Stockwell Station and emerged into a disconcertingly quiet Clapham Road. Even so, they stuck to backstreets and small paths, cutting across South Lambeth Road on a residential stretch to avoid commercial buildings and their security cameras.

Jack's thoughts returned to Howard. Fail his mission or succeed, Jack had no way of knowing what would become of his friend. Without time travel, millions of lives would be re-written, their pathways unrecognisable from what they had been. But succeed or fail, Howard's wife, daughter and granddaughter would live on without him, sealed within Gaia's temporal bubble. Jack would never face them, never see the loss reflected in their eyes, and he was sorry for that. He would neither share in their loss, nor their memories.

Max nudged Jack's arm and held out the scanner. "Look at this. I've never seen so many Snags gathered that close. They're all in the City."

"Looking for the Bishopsgate Bombers," said Jack, drawing on memories that were filtering backwards from the future he had shaped. "No Snag ever found them, though their bounty was one of the most coveted of the war. Us," he explained, and registered the looks of shock. "The Ku Bar will be under surveillance for the next six months. Just as well you're not really a regular," he added to Max.

"Fuck," Max breathed.

"Yeah, it's a lot to take in." Jack rubbed a hand across his face. His fingertips massaged his temples. "Anyway, if I'm lucky, our notoriety may yet be fleeting. Come on, we're nearly there."

Approaching the house, Jack searched for signs of interference, a discreet camera embedded in the brickwork, a blind left closed that now stood open, but it was unchanged. It shouldn't have been surprising, given that they'd only been gone two days. But time was deceptive and treacherous. For Jack it was running out, only not in the way that he had anticipated.

§

North Woolwich Police Station
Canning Town

Noah sat upright, his back pressed against the chipped plaster of the cell wall. Though anxious, he was outwardly calm, having occupied the indeterminate wait with a methodical review of each scenario he might face and its likely outcome. His hands rested in his lap, and every now and then he pulled them apart, to feel the tension of the shoelace held between them. It was a mediocre weapon, hampered by muscle atrophy and brittle bones, but also by his own character. Noah was not an aggressive man. Not anymore.

Visions of his past, his youth, interplayed with Noah's analysis of his immediate future. He, of all people, knew how much he'd changed. Once, he'd been a god, a giant of a man, both physically and intellectually. But Noah had been hot-headed, impatient with the unhurried rate of social change. He was an easy target for the cops who maintained 'public safety' at the marches. Noah's size, his aura of authority and his refusal to back down, riled them every time. That refusal to cower, to look the other way, had set his life on a path he'd detested, and wrestled to be free of ever since.

Kill or be killed? It wasn't a choice, it was self-defence. But either way, Noah had blood on his hands. The authorities weren't interested in why that was, but on how it could be used to their advantage. Life imprisonment would be a waste of the young scientist's talents. Better that Noah atone for his 'crime' through working for the authorities, by serving those who had pushed him to commit it.

Noah had refused, of course. He would rather a lifetime in prison than make weapons for those who would put him there. But it was made clear that non-compliance would have consequences: did Noah value the freedom of his family? The life of his sister and her children?

Noah leant his head back against the wall and pictured the twins, dark-eyed and chubby-cheeked, with wild shocks of curly black hair. With luck, they were now grown men with families of their own. But Noah remembered them as they had been, and the vow that he had made them, to right the wrongs that he was about to commit.

Working for DARPA had put Noah in a unique position. He became his own double agent, learning and refining his skills, biding his time. As Noah aged, that part of him which sought revenge grew quieter, replaced by a more methodical approach to how he might best serve his family. The world he'd been born into was vanishing, the bayous lost beneath the sea, the toxicity of the climate more fearful than the venom of the diamondback serpent. And so Noah began to investigate how he might reverse the effects of global warming. He couldn't have imagined where his research would lead, and now here he was, so close to achieving the means to fulfil his promise.

The timing of the last cast had been perfect, but somehow the time capsule's return had gone awry. Noah had traced the capsule as far as the river's north bank, but he'd been out of place and his search had exposed him. The capsule was still there, somewhere in the vicinity of the Victoria Docks, and he silently prayed that it wouldn't be found.

The bolt on the door drew back, its rusted metal scraping loudly.

Noah pocketed the shoelace, hopeful that violence would not be necessary. Two officers, of differing age, entered the room. The older man was heavy and muscular, fit for his late forties, with a glint in his eye that was disconcerting rather than friendly.

"Get up," he instructed, with a kick of a highly polished boot.

The other man was shorter and baby-faced, a junior officer. He hovered at the edge of the room, and looked through Noah, rather than at him. He held a sedative gun in both hands, as though it were too heavy for his slight frame.

"I don't think that will be necessary," said Noah, rising to his feet. "Can I ask why I am being detained? I do not believe that I have broken any rules." Noah spoke the same way that he thought; considered, methodical.

"That's not for me to comment on," replied the senior officer and he grabbed Noah's wrists to cuff them. He rested his hand on the baton that dangled from his belt and inclined his head towards the door.

Noah moved through it slowly.

"We haven't got all day," said the policeman. He jabbed the baton between Noah's shoulder blades and pushed him towards the station's back door.

"May I at least have my personal effects?" Noah asked, turning to the baby-faced officer.

A slight sheen spread across the younger man's forehead. Not every police officer towed the government line willingly. He turned to his colleague and gave a slight shrug. "There's nothing that's dangerous. Not even a phone. Just a little notebook and one of them old fashioned watches."

The senior officer sighed and nodded his assent. "Give him his watch, I'll take the notebook."

Noah smiled as the junior officer pressed the watch into his hand. "Thank you, son. My grandpa gave me that."

The senior officer yawned theatrically then shoved Noah out of the door and into the back of a windowless van.

As the soft whine of the electric motor rose and the vehicle moved forwards, Noah pushed his fingertips against the back of the watch. The rhythm of the vibrations was unaltered; the location of the capsule was unchanged. He breathed out deeply. DARPA might reclaim him, but he'd be damned before he'd hand them his work.

§

Richborne Terrace

Max, standing on tiptoe to see over Jack's shoulder, let out a long, low whistle. "Wow, you weren't kidding about your family, were you. That's a lot of food and... wine! Christ, what's that? Thirty, forty bottles? That one's even Italian."

Jack stooped to pick up the bottle Max had spotted. "It's a Borolo," said Jack. "Ages well."

"Well, it's had a while," Max remarked. He turned the bottle over to inspect the label. "Nothing's come out of Italy for years – olive oil, cheese, wine – nothing."

The floorboards overhead creaked and Suraya peered over the top of the stair rail.

"Hey," Jack called. "How did you get on?"

Suraya rounded the foot of the stairs, rubbing at her wet hair with a towel. "Not exactly my style," she said, glancing down at herself. Like other teens, Suraya's own clothes were either overly tight, or overly baggy, whereas the trousers and top she'd settled for had a ministerial air. "But not bad if, as you say, they belong to your great-grandmother."

Jack smiled. "Well, technically, she's still a way off that status."

Suraya shrugged. "Maddie might need a nudge – she's feeling a bit weird about it."

"I'll talk to her. Why don't you see what you can cook up with these." Jack held out two tins of vegetables.

Suraya screwed up her face. Cooking wasn't her forte.

"Let me." Max took them from Jack's outstretched hand. "I owe you a meal." He turned to Suraya, eyebrows raised, hoping that she remembered that conversation in the Hub. "A burger, right?"

Suraya smiled. "Right." She felt a blush creep across her face and hid it, stooping to pick up another can. "Though god knows how you're gonna make a burger out of these."

Jack left them to it and headed upstairs, pausing outside the door to the master bedroom. He heard the shuffle of

Maddie's feet, her soft sigh. His pulse quickened, and he was at once both reluctant and eager to be inside the room with her. He took a deep breath, tapped his knuckles on the wood and called, "Can I come in?"

"Um, just a minute…yeh."

Maddie clutched the top of the towel that was wrapped around her and glanced at the mess of clothes on the bed. "Sorry," she said, with an apologetic grimace. "Suraya got a bit carried away." She crouched down to retrieve a couple of tops from the floor and draped them over a chair. The back of her neck and shoulders were bruised – purple-black marks against burnished bronze.

"They're a bit conservative." Jack dragged his eyes away from her and to the mound of clothes. "But hopefully something fits."

"Oh, you know…" Her voice trailed off and she glanced towards the window, where the late afternoon sun slipped through the gaps in the blinds. That morning's storm already felt like a dream. "I'm sure my own clothes will be dry soon enough."

"They're full of holes," Jack pointed out. "And besides, you've borrowed clothes before."

Maddie pictured the woman who'd once lived in the Southbank apartment, whose clothes Maddie had 'borrowed' on more than one occasion. She'd been killed while protesting for migrant rights. "Those people weren't coming back."

"Well, my family isn't due back for a while," said Jack. He moved around the bed to sift through a pile of tops. "And even then," he added quietly, "they may yet find this place as they left it."

Maddie said nothing, holding back the question that had been forming in her mind.

"Here." Jack, held out a top and trousers. "These aren't so bad."

Maddie raised an eyebrow but relented. She reached out for them and winced.

"You're bleeding," said Jack, seeing the cut on her neck.

"Oh, yeah, I pulled the stitch. I'll put something on it." Maddie gestured to a first aid kit on the dressing table.

"Let me." Jack pushed the clothes away. "Here, sit down."

She did as instructed, conscious that her heart beat faster as Jack knelt down before her and gently turned her head to one side. Her skin tingled at the touch of his fingers.

"It's not too deep," he said, catching her eye. "Just needs a steri-strip."

She nodded and watched their reflection in the mirror behind him. Felt the warmth of his breath on her neck as he leant in towards her.

Jack smoothed the strip across her neck, once, twice... trailing his fingers across her skin for longer than required. "There." He swallowed. "Better. Though I can't promise it won't leave a scar."

Maddie shrugged dismissively. "What's another scar?" She lowered her head and pulled the damp curls of her hair forwards so that they fell across the side of her face. "Doesn't matter how I look."

Jack placed a finger beneath her chin, lifting it so that their eyes met. The arch of her brows was defiant. Defensive. He brushed the strands of hair back behind her ear and gently ran his thumb along a faint, silvery scar. "Maddie, you are beautiful."

She felt the intensity of his gaze, the swell of her shallow, rapid breaths as she placed her own hand over his, the dizzying warmth of his proximity. She raised her other hand to draw him closer, but he stood and turned, fumbling with the first aid kit on the dressing table.

"So... We should go and join the others," he said, his back to her.

Her eyes filled with tears.

"I'll see you downstairs."

Jack fled from the room and pulled the door shut. He stood a moment, his hand behind him, his fingers still clasping the handle. His deep breaths did nothing to ease the agony of indecision and he grimaced and turned back to the doorway, laying a hand on either side. He held back, even now, but for what? Was it fear of hurting her? Or his own fear of being hurt.

From below, Max called him. Jack took a deep breath and turned to head downstairs.

They gathered to eat, the cool atmosphere at odds with the mounting heat of the night. Max did his best to fill the silence, supplying what LEFA knew about Hart and Battersea Power Station, and the Republican Embassy that lay in its shadow.

Jack tried to concentrate, but with each pause his gaze slid to Maddie. Her own eyes looked anywhere but at him.

Suraya sat back in her chair, her arms curled protectively about her, and shook her head. "That's all I can think of." Her body made a slight, involuntary shudder.

Jack's mind clouded in thought. When he glanced up, Suraya was watching him. A flash of pity crossed her eyes. Jack knew that when she looked at him, a part of her saw Hart, and no doubt she now understood why. He placed his elbows on the table and leant forwards, the words of Suraya's account running back and forth through his mind. "But what did Hart mean by *visions*? Did he explain or say what they were about?"

"Not exactly," Suraya replied.

"Even the smallest detail could be useful," Jack prompted.

Suraya pulled her feet up and onto the seat, so that her arms now wrapped around her legs, and her chin rested on her knees. She looked smaller, vulnerable, and Jack noticed the dark shadows that grazed the space beneath her eyes.

"Come on," Maddie bristled. "She's tired, she needs to rest." She rose to her feet and gathered the empty dishes, pointedly depositing them in the sink with a clatter.

Jack felt a stab of guilt. "I'm sorry."

"I can speak for myself you know," said Suraya sharply.

Maddie raised her palms in the air. Max shifted uncomfortably on his seat.

Suraya sighed. She slipped her feet to the floor and leant against the table with her hands tucked beneath her legs. "Hart told me that the Republic were making mistakes, and that he could see a 'better way' for Europe. He said he had *seen* it, that he would 'realise his vision' or something like that. I don't know, it didn't make sense. I think he was drunk or something, he was definitely off balance that night."

Jack frowned. "Does he drink a lot?"

"Not usually. He'd have a drink or two each evening. I'd try to get him to have more, you know, to loosen his tongue." She shrugged. "But he rarely did. Anyway…" She yawned. "That really is everything I can think of."

Jack nodded. "Thank you, I know that wasn't easy for you. And you must be tired. We all are," he added with a glance at Maddie.

Max shifted backwards off his seat. "Yeah, well, I'll see what I can do with the projector in this." He lifted the holo-candle from the centre of the table.

"Thanks." Jack smiled.

"Come on." Maddie spoke to Suraya. "I'll come up with you."

Jack stood and followed them to the foot of the staircase. "Maddie?" he called after her.

She squared her shoulders and twisted to look down on him.

His words withered on his tongue and all he managed was, "I'm sorry."

"For what?" she replied curtly, then turned on her heel and headed upstairs.

§

Battersea Power Station

"My apologies, Dr Kingsley, for the uncomfortable nature of your arrival."

Noah rubbed his wrists and sat down in the chair Kayson Hart indicated. The apartment was elegantly furnished, revealing both the owner's taste and wealth. Though it was dark outside, the glass wall revealed that they were high up, set apart from other, nearby buildings.

"Can I get you something to drink?" Hart asked. He placed the handcuffs on top of a bronze and parchment cabinet and lifted a bottle from a tray. "Perhaps a taste of home? A bourbon from Baton Rouge? Though I don't rate it so well as those from Kentucky."

The fake pleasantries grated on him, but Noah's face retained a studied neutrality. "Thank you, no."

Hart gave a shrug of indifference and sat down opposite. "It must be tiresome," he remarked. "Running and hiding. Cut off from your own people, your own country. I spent several years working in China. So much to admire – an undeniably rich culture – but it wasn't home." Hart smiled at his guest, but Noah made no response. "It's quite some time since you last saw your family," Hart continued. "You had a sister, I believe."

Noah's hands gave an involuntary jerk. It had been four, no, five years since his sister had been laid to rest, and still he hadn't been able to pay his last respects.

"And nephews too? I understand that one is a father himself now, with twins. It must run in the family."

"You can dispense with the small talk, Mr Hart, and get to the point."

Hart raised one hand in the air and waved it vaguely, before bringing it to his mouth. He tapped his thumb against his lips as if in thought, then shook his head with a smile. "Very well. The truth is that I don't care for the institutions of the Republic any more than you do. I am, however, sufficiently well connected to understand the lengths the Republic will go to, to retrieve you and your expertise. They are close to discovering where you've been working which, I would guess, is not far from where my men picked you up."

Hart paused to measure Kingsley's reaction, but his face remained impassive. "Fortunately for you, DARPA doesn't know the nature of what it's looking for, and bereft of that information, they're a little slow to see the larger picture."

Noah frowned slightly. "I've never cared for riddles, Mr Hart."

Hart laughed and leant forwards in his seat. "Your invention, Dr Kingsley."

No response.

"I understand it requires a great deal of power. I've been wondering where you might source that power without it being detected. The grid is monitored, is it not? A precaution against the illegal manufacture of armaments. But yesterday, something of mine was retrieved from the river, and that got me to thinking. The river appears sluggish, and yet the distance that object had travelled suggests otherwise. For a scientist of your calibre, it might not be so difficult to channel the river's power, the hydro-electric capabilities of the Thames, effectively enough to, for example"—he paused, enjoying his own theatricality— "power a journey through time?"

Noah blinked rapidly, two, three times, and reflexively pushed his fingers against the face of his watch, conscious of the contrast between his own rapid pulse and the idling vibrations within the mechanism; the capsule hadn't been moved.

How did Hart know of his work? He sat forwards, his eyebrows raised in scepticism. "You understand the drawings, the equations in my notebook, Mr Hart?"

"Oh no, I specialise in the interaction of power and politics on a human scale; the interactions of matter and energy are beyond me I'm afraid." Hart's eyes flicked to the Picasso painting in the far corner of the room. "But there are many others who understand your work. Some of them have been specialists for many years." He paused, thinking. "Or they will be, as it were." Hart shifted forwards on his seat, his expression earnest. "Dr Kingsley, I'm afraid that the Republic has, or will, abuse your technology for its own benefit. I have *seen* how this has already injured Europe, damaged London, and disrupted the natural order of the world. The effects of time travel are manifold.

"When events first take place, we, none of us, can do more than react to them. But I'm here to offer you a second chance, the opportunity to determine *who* will be in control of your technology. With my help, it need not be the Republic."

Noah sat back. His mind reeled at Hart's words: time travel worked; it was a future reality. But Hart implied that his research would be seized by DARPA, that it would be used for the wrong reasons. "Are you telling me that you have travelled through time, Mr Hart? That you have come here from the future?"

"Ah, no." Hart laughed. "Though I've been in communication with those that have. I've been working with them to find you, and now that I have, you and I can realise *our* vision of a better future."

Noah knew a little of the man before him, and he doubted that Hart's vision would align with his own. He was aware of his heart beating fast, his fingers twitched with the adrenaline coursing through his veins. He took slow, steadying breaths, and channelled his thoughts.

If the time capsule did work, if Noah was a few minor alterations away from perfecting his prototype, then the capsule itself was expendable. He had the remnants of an earlier model, and he could build another. Yes, it would take time and resources, but so long as he had his designs, his records, and the calculations in his notebook, it could be done. The working capsule, which sat exposed and vulnerable somewhere in the Docklands, was now a liability. Finding where Hart had hidden his notebook was Noah's priority.

From the corner of his eye, Noah scanned the room. There was no sign of anybody else, and Hart appeared unarmed: something that was either carefully staged or an indication of the man's arrogance. Noah considered him. "I assume that those I may choose between are the Republic, and the people you are working for?"

Hart bristled. He stood up and walked a few paces

towards the glass wall. "Do not be confused, Dr Kingsley. I've been working with others in order to locate you, but I do not work *for* them. Indeed, and albeit unwittingly, they have been working for me."

"I see. And would you enlighten me as to your intentions for my work?"

Hart sighed and glanced out beyond the darkened river towards the heart of the city. "The climate crisis has cost many people their homes. Even their countries. But what we're seeing is only the beginning. Already, Europe is overburdened, but before long, the influx of the displaced will break it. As I've said, it is a terrible thing to live apart from one's own people, one's homeland. If used properly, your technology could rectify the Republic's mistakes and everyone can return to where they're meant to be." Hart turned to his guest. "Is that not what you also want?"

The notebook was forgotten. Noah narrowed his eyes. "We are increasingly forced to live cheek to jowl, in a world that is shrinking before our eyes, but people should have a choice about where they live, not be told where it is *appropriate* that they should live. I know all about your politics, Mr Hart, and I doubt very much that our aims are the same."

"Perhaps not exactly, but surely preferable to the alternative?" Hart shook his head with mock resignation and turned away, opening a drawer at the top of the cabinet.

Noah pushed his hand into his pocket and found the shoelace. He leant forwards with his hands between his knees to wind the ends around his fists.

Hart sensed the movement and turned sharply, a gun aimed at Noah's chest. "I wouldn't do anything rash, Dr Kingsley."

Noah's eye ran over the weapon. It wasn't anything he recognised, and whether it fired a bullet or a dart he couldn't be sure. "You may kill me if you like, but my knowledge will die with me."

"Yes, that would be inconvenient, but given the records that you would leave behind, not insurmountable. As future history stands, however, DARPA would be the first to find your laboratory. I can't imagine you want that. So perhaps you had better think again about who you will entrust your work to?"

Noah loosened his left hand from the lace and raised his watch to his mouth. "Protocol thirty, eighty-eight, ninety-three, thirteen—"

"Stop!" Hart leapt forwards and struck Noah across the face. He prised the watch from his wrist. "What is this? What did you do?"

A trickle of blood ran from Noah's temple into the wiry hairs of his beard.

Hart's eyes flicked from the watch in his hand back to Noah. His lips curled at the edges, his words enunciated, clear and precise. "You will tell me the location of your laboratory, or I will be forced to reveal the details of a domestic terrorist threat in Louisiana. A *twin* threat."

Noah twisted the lace around his left hand. "Authorisation Kingsley," he murmured.

Down river, seven miles away, the time capsule exploded in a halo of blue fire.

Hart's smile faltered and pain seared through his head.

Dr Kingsley lunged towards him.

Hart pulled back, lurched into the cabinet, and sent bottles crashing to the floor. Hart fell amongst the slivers of glass, Kingsley's weight on his back, the lace tightening around his neck.

The gun had fallen beneath the cabinet. If Hart could just reach it... The fingers of one hand clasped the stock of the gun, whilst the others clawed above his head and found a drawer handle. Hart wrenched it open, into Kingsley's shoulder, knocking him sideways. Gasping for breath, he twisted and pulled the trigger.

Pfpp.

Noah looked down at the dart in his side. His knuckles whitened. He drew his fist back... and slowly crumpled to the ground.

§

17th August 2073
Richborne Terrace

Jack awoke with a start, his heart pounding in his chest. The air felt heavy, its taste almost metallic. Something had changed. His memories morphed and coiled, refusing to settle in any one clear form. Jack didn't think the change was connected to him, not directly, but still the discomfort flowed through him, a dull undercurrent that barred him from sleep.

The heat inside the room was oppressive and Jack slid from the bed and crossed towards the window. He reached out for the latch then hesitated. An open window might be noticed from the road below, but from the living room he could easily slip out and into the back garden.

He opened the door to the landing, where a slight draught caught at the hair on his arms. He reached back inside the door frame and found the handle of his grandfather's cricket bat, then crept towards the source of the breeze – the small back bedroom that overlooked the garden. He raised the bat and pushed at the door with his foot.

The door swung open.

Maddie startled.

"I'm sorry," Jack murmured, lowering the bat. "I thought you were upstairs with Suraya."

"I couldn't sleep," she said, turning her back to him, returning her gaze to the window.

She'd pushed up the bottom half of the sash and sat on the sill, one arm resting on her bent knee, her other foot lowered to the floor. Jack hovered uncertainly, aware from the set of her shoulders that he was intruding, but unable to turn away. Her coldness to him that evening, her refusal to accept his apology, troubled him. He wasn't sure that he could face what came next knowing that he had hurt her.

"I was trying to spot a constellation," she said at last, almost to herself. "But the window faces the wrong way."

"Oh?" Jack crossed the room, sliding round the bed to stand behind her. His eyes hovered on her a moment, then moved to the view outside.

"I'm no astronomer," Maddie clarified. "I wouldn't know the Big Dipper from Orion's Belt. But every summer my mum would point out this constellation – Scorpius. She said it was one of the few visible both from the north and the south. She claimed she knew if she was looking at it at the same time as my grandmother… said she could feel it." Maddie drew in a ragged breath. "I'm always looking for that constellation. No one I know is in the Southern Hemisphere anymore, least of all my mum. Yet there's still this silly part of me thinking that if I could just find it, then maybe I'll find her. Maybe I'll feel her looking back at me."

Outside, the stars glinted in the darkness, their light's odyssey as old as time itself. They were a glimpse of the past and of other worlds, and yet, thought Jack, the stars had forged connections between people since the beginning of human history. Through mythology and religion, navigation and discovery, man's relationship with the stars had helped shape who we were. Jack thought of Howard and the Observatory at Greenwich, how that place had somehow been an anchor throughout their relationship.

"That's not silly," he said at last.

Maddie's posture softened and she swivelled round to face him. The moonlight shifted across her skin, lending her an ethereal glow.

"There are times when I would give anything to have one more moment with my parents…" Maddie's voice trailed off and she sighed. "But it's not possible, not for me. I think about them all the time. Imagine their advice. Imagine making them proud. Picture myself back when I was a child and times were simpler. It would be so easy to lose myself in the past, but my parents wouldn't want that." She raised her brows a little and caught his eye. "They wouldn't want me looking backwards in order to feel happy."

Jack lowered himself to sit on the bed. His body ached. Not from that day's bruises, but from the effort of holding back, from years of burying his feelings deep inside. He wanted to give her everything, but all he had to give was the truth.

"Maddie… I can't give you what you want."

She huffed out sharply, though somehow the expression wasn't unkind. "And how do you presume to know what I want?"

Jack closed his eyes for a moment, wishing that it didn't have to be so hard. "You must know by now that I won't make it out of this. I won't even be a memory. Not for you, not for anyone."

Maddie nodded, almost imperceptibly. She knew.

She leant forwards to take Jack's hand and turned it over so that the moonlight fell on his palm. She ran a fingertip across the silvery trail of his scars and it occurred to her that she and Jack were the same, both resigned to something less, both hiding behind their scars. But she was tired of treading lightly, of settling for what was safe, instead of reaching for the stars.

"There's no more certainty to my future than there is to yours," she said. "All we really have is the moment we're in, and if there's even the slightest chance to feel happy here and now, then shouldn't we seize that with both hands?"

"But I don't want—" He paused, his pulse racing. "I can't allow myself to feel that, not now." His eyes found hers. "To love, knowing I must give that up… It hurts too much."

"To feel pain is to be alive. And don't you want to feel alive, even if just for a moment?" She raised his hand and pressed her lips to his palm.

Jack shivered at the touch of her mouth, though his hand, held in hers, tingled with heat. He wanted so badly to feel that warmth spread across him, but he was torn. He looked away, and his eye caught the flash of a shooting star. It burned brightly, then was gone. But for that brief moment, it was glorious.

So, Jack let go.

He pulled Maddie into his arms and felt the heat of her encircle him. His fingers tangled in her hair. His lips pressed against hers. Both lost and found in the sensation of skin against skin.

Maddie stirred, rousing Jack from a dreamless sleep. Beneath the blanket of her body, he felt a sense of safety, an immunity from the realities of past, present and future, all of which demanded something from him. In this moment, there was only her.

But the dawn advanced, its soft glow creeping across Maddie's skin. Jack willed it to stop, to allow them more time. Jack's relationship with time had been indifferent for so long, but now its passing was a torment.

Jack felt the flutter of Maddie's eyelashes on his chest and knew that she was awake. He wondered if she felt the same mixture of joy and grief which made his heart both falter and soar. He'd not felt that way for such a long time. She was right, it made him feel alive.

He watched the pale light grow warm and glossy, claiming Maddie from the last of the shadows. Once again, Jack recalled the sculptures he'd once seen, organic forms with an almost primal beauty. What was it about Maddie that kept bringing them to mind? He saw their shapes reflected in the curve of her shoulder, the dip in the small of her back, but perhaps the connection was something less tangible.

Like a figure cast in bronze, Maddie had a substance, a presence to which Jack was drawn. In the whirlwind of fluctuating time and memory, she had remained constant, real. Her presence had a weight, a certainty to it that Jack felt he'd never possessed. Where she was solid, he was insubstantial. If she were cast in bronze, then he was cast in time. Transience was an affliction they all faced, just some more than others.

He trailed his fingers down her back, and she nestled closer, her face turned into his neck. She murmured something he couldn't quite make out.

"What was that?"

"I said, I'm coming with you today."

"What?" Jack freed his fingers from hers and lifted her chin to better see her face. "No, I've put you in enough danger already. This is my battle, not yours."

Maddie raised herself on her elbows to look at him. She was aware of pain – yesterday's cuts and bruises, the strain of carrying her sister – but she leant into Jack and her discomfort softened. She brushed her lips against his, felt the sharp intake of his breath as it drew cool, across her mouth. He still tasted of salt.

With an effort, she pulled away and took a long, steadying breath. "If all that you've told me is true, then this battle belongs to us all. Ssh." She pressed a finger to his lips to silence his protest. "If we succeed, we'll make a better world for everyone, create a second chance for those who never had one. I'm not going to walk away from that."

Jack's heart and mind raced. There were the familiar sensations of guilt and fear, but also something else, something new that felt good. He studied her, the way her jaw set as she steeled herself for the fight, her dark eyes that stared levelly into his, daring him to challenge her resolve. This particular battle, at least, was lost. "Okay," he breathed.

Maddie nodded, a slight smile on her lips. "And..." She leant in to whisper in his ear. "If you fucking injure yourself in the leg again, I will kill you myself."

Jack laughed. "Understood."

§

Battersea Power Station

Kayson Hart watched the paramedic enter the lift on the security feed. "Can she be trusted?" he asked.

Noakes nodded. "She knows it wouldn't pay to put my nose out of joint."

Hart narrowed his eyes as he watched her check her phone, then glance up at the security camera. He sighed and flicked off the screen. "All the same, I think this is one loose end that had better be cut."

Noakes raised his eyebrows. "Sir, my resources have been reduced considerably in the past few weeks. You might come to regret that."

"We are not in parliament, Noakes and this is not a matter for debate." Hart flicked on an iHolo and scrolled through the files that hung in the air. "Is your compensation insufficient?" His finger paused over one file longer than the others. "Do I have any cause to doubt *your* loyalty?"

Noakes dropped his eyes to the floor. "No sir."

"Good. See to her." Hart smiled smoothly, noting how the muscles in the policeman's face twitched as he nodded and left. Just as Keller had been Hart's Republican informant, Noakes was his puppet within the British police. Hart hoped that he hadn't misjudged the sergeant's motivation. But then that was why he kept the files, just in case.

Hart stood up, walked to the room the paramedic had just left, and turned up the dimmed light to better see his guest. The monitor beeped rhythmically. Dr Kingsley stirred in his sleep, twisting, even in his dreams, against the restraints that held him.

Hart picked up the medic's notes. 'Allergic reaction to sedative. Bed rest required. Possible memory impairment for the next twenty-four hours.' His face darkened and he screwed up the sheet of paper to hurl it against the wall. He ran his fingers across the bruising on his neck. He'd underestimated Noah Kingsley. It had almost cost him his life, and still it might cost him the advantage he had worked tirelessly to gain.

Hart didn't know the exact date the Republic would find Kingsley's workshop – it had never been recorded – and so Hart guessed that he had two days, maybe three at most. He had men searching the Docklands and drones watching Republican bases, but it was clumsy and slow. If he was going to find Dr Kingsley's laboratory first, he needed Kingsley alive and cooperative.

§

Richborne Terrace

Suraya stifled a yawn and descended the last of the steps into the kitchen where Jack and Maddie sat side by side at the kitchen island. She sensed the shift, even before she saw the evidence; her sister's shoulder touching his, a sideways glance and responding smile that spoke of a new familiarity that hadn't been there the day before.

On the one hand she felt a sense of satisfaction: she had been right about her sister's feelings. But on the other, she felt the same agitation that had unsettled her the previous day. The prospect of sharing Maddie's affection was not something she had faced before. She shook her head as though she might shake off the feeling and took a deep breath to relieve the tightness in her chest.

Maddie looked over her shoulder. "Ray." She stood up, took Suraya's arms, and looked over her with concern. "You don't look so good. Did you sleep?"

"I'm fine," said Suraya. "Don't fuss." She batted Maddie aside and turned to the sink to fill a glass, allowing herself a private, satisfied smile.

"You do look pale," Maddie persisted. She pulled out a stool for Suraya, then sat back down next to Jack.

"Well, I did almost die yesterday," Suraya retorted with a theatrical flick of her hair. "And then I gave half of my blood to your boyfriend in order to stop him from dying too." Maddie flushed. Suraya raised her eyebrows and turned to Jack.

He smiled to himself before meeting her stare. "If you *had* given me half your blood you really would have died." His face became serious. "But I'm grateful. Thank you."

"I guess we're even then." She shrugged and took her seat.

Jack nodded.

"What time are you leaving?"

Jack glanced sideways at Maddie. "Within the hour."

Suraya caught the look that passed between them. Her stomach clenched.

Jack touched Maddie's hand lightly, then pushed back his stool. "I'll go and see how Max is getting on."

Suraya waited until his feet had disappeared around the top of the staircase then rounded on Maddie, her voice loud. "You're going with him?"

Maddie opened her mouth, then closed it, biting her lips instead. She nodded.

"But you can't! It's not safe. What if you die?" Suraya stood abruptly, her stool scraping the tiles.

"I won't die." A cold shiver crept up Maddie's spine. She ignored it and moved around the island, pulling Suraya's stool back and perching on the one beside it.

"You don't know that." Suraya sank back onto the seat, still but for the rapid rise and fall of her chest. Once again, she was the little girl who had lost her parents too young.

Maddie's resolve faltered. But then she thought about Jack, what he would face, and knew that she wouldn't let him face it alone. "Jack and I will watch out for each other."

"And what if he dies? And then it's just you and Hart. What if he hurts you? Maddie, you don't know what he's like."

"Ssh, it will be okay." Maddie tried to draw Suraya into her arms, but her sister wouldn't be held.

"Maddie, I can't lose you, you're all I have. Please, don't leave me."

"You know," said Maddie, smiling at the irony. "I said the very same thing to you yesterday." She smoothed the hair away from Suraya's face. "But—"

"You've made up your mind." Suraya sagged forwards and allowed Maddie's arms to enfold her. "Is he worth it?" Her voice was muffled, her face pressed against Maddie's shoulder. "Worth more than me?"

"Oh Ray..." Maddie's voiced cracked and she squeezed her sister tight. How often had she soothed away Suraya's fears whilst fiercely suppressing her own?

How often had she longed to have someone hold her and tell her she would be alright, that she was doing great, that they were proud of her? But that wasn't what she sought from Jack.

Maddie sighed. "Nobody is more important to me than you. But this isn't about you, or even Jack. This is a chance to do something that might actually make a difference."

Suraya pulled herself free and fixed Maddie with a doubtful stare, her eyes red-rimmed and doleful.

"You look like you did that time when you were six and Mama caught you opening the presents on Christmas Eve," laughed Maddie.

"She told me that Father Christmas would take everything away in the night for being naughty," Suraya said plaintively. "I was desperate not to lose that tea-set… But losing you!"

"I need to do this. Believe it or not, this is me, for once, choosing to put what I want first."

Suraya took in the familiar stance that said, without words, that her sister would not be moved. It was their grandfather, Nana, to a tee. "You're as stubborn as Nana Ajeet was."

"So, there's no point trying to dissuade me."

Suraya laughed, though tears welled up and spilled over her cheeks. "I can help you get ready?" she suggested. She drew in a jagged breath and managed a smile.

Maddie leant forwards so that their foreheads touched. "I'd like that."

Maddie pulled the door shut and forced herself to put one foot in front of the other as she walked away. She brushed her thumb against the headscarf that Suraya had pressed into her palm; the once rough fabric, now worn smooth. She had meant Suraya to keep it, but she was grateful now for this small connection to the women of her family, through which she might draw strength.

She caught up with Max, falling into step with him,

noticing his long backwards glance towards the house where Suraya had remained. Maddie considered how, after all, there were others Suraya could rely upon. Whatever Max was, or could be to Suraya, Maddie knew that he wouldn't let her down. "Max? Promise you'll get Ray to the Hub as soon as you can. If things don't go to plan, the house may not be safe."

Max gave a small, grim smile. "I promise." He pushed his glasses up his nose and surveyed the darkened house fronts warily. "And the files from Jack's computer?" he asked.

"If nothing's changed by tomorrow night then make sure Sarah, Castillo and Botha all receive them. It might not be too late to change the course of events."

"And how will I know if anything's changed or not?"

Maddie shrugged. "If your laptop is still full of news stories written fifty years from now, then nothing's changed."

Max shook his head. "And if Fuller thinks this is a load of bullshit?"

"Then you need to persuade her. Anyway, she doesn't need to believe in time travel, just understand that Dr Kingsley's work mustn't be found by either the Republic or the government."

Max looked ahead to where Jack was waiting in the shadowed alley between two blocks of flats. "I really hope he's right about this."

Maddie's eyes flicked north, as though she might see all the way to Parliament Square. "He usually is."

Jack looked up when the others arrived. The screen of the Snag's scanner shone bright in his hand.

"Well?" Max asked.

Jack nodded. "It's happening. And just about every Snag in central London is being drawn in." He turned the device towards them. A grid of live camera feeds revealed Westminster awash with protesters and police.

"All because of Blackfriars," Maddie murmured.

Jack nodded. "This is the turning point."

Maddie thought about the children on the train, about the monument that would one day stand where crowds now gathered to protest. She caught Jack's eye. "Let's make it count."

The backstreets that morning were quiet, everyone they saw heading the same way, towards Westminster. The hush receded on the approach to South Lambeth Road, where groups of people, some holding hands, others clasping placards, wound their way north. Larger, noisier groups owned the centre of the road, shouting their approval when new people emerged and joined them. Smaller, quieter groups hugged the pavements and the shadows, warily watching overhead for drones. But even those people, Maddie noticed, wore a look of conviction that drove them on.

Pressed into a shop doorway, Maddie, Jack and Max watched them pass.

"How did word spread so fast?" Maddie asked. "Media platforms are censored, texts and holo-mail constantly screened. A call to arms would never get off the ground."

"The Fringe went back to basics – sent out runners."

"It's all word of mouth?"

Jack nodded. "Passed between families and neighbours, by those who trust one another. By the time the government realises the scale of the response, it will be too big to suppress." He peered down the road, looking for a break in the flow, but if anything, the street was becoming busier. He pulled back, watching two families pass, and caught some of their conversation.

"We tried to cross at Chelsea," a middle-aged woman explained, waving vaguely behind her. "But they're not letting anyone over."

"What makes you think we can cross at Vauxhall then?" challenged a teenage boy. He carried a piece of board across his shoulders which bore the question, 'How many kids will die to cover their lies?'

"Vauxhall?" The woman looked surprised. "Haven't you heard? The Fringe has control of Lambeth Bridge. Already thousands of us in Westminster. This time we'll have our say."

Maddie turned to the others, a question on her lips and

saw a flicker of a light pulse amber, then red on the scanner. She snatched the device from Jack's hand and updated the feed. "Approaching drones," she breathed.

"It's okay," said Jack, leaning over to see the map. "They're heading for Lambeth."

"What?" Her face blanched. "That's not okay! The protesters... the Fringe, we need to warn them." She stepped onto the pavement but Jack grabbed her arm.

"They're prepared, they can take them. The Fringe intercepted the St Pancras line, remember? They've got quite the weapons stockpile." Maddie's expression remained uncertain. "Trust me, Lambeth Bridge is well protected."

"Weapons stockpile? How come LEFA didn't know about that?" Max frowned.

"They did, at command level anyway. Today, the North and Central Hubs will help safeguard protesters at Westminster, whilst the South Hub is working with the Fringe at Lambeth Bridge."

Max puffed out his cheeks. "Man, a lot happened in two days."

"Casualties?" Maddie asked in a whisper.

"Some," Jack held her gaze, steady.

Maddie's stomach dropped and she looked away, her eye following the wave of protestors. They were mostly young adults and teenagers, but there were pensioners, even a few children, their small hands clasped tightly as the march moved forwards. She picked out the teenager who'd passed them a few moments earlier. He looked about Suraya's age.

Maddie imagined an alternative version of events, one where she hadn't met Jack, but instead found herself, alongside Max and Sarah, defending the river crossing against government drones. Would Suraya be there? And who amongst them would survive? Was she meant to have been there, fighting alongside her friends? She shivered and wondered whether she was failing them.

Jack's hand found hers and drew her close. "They'll be okay."

She exchanged a glance with Max, who shifted uneasily, troubled by the same anxious thoughts.

"Come on." Jack pulled her forwards. "There's a lull. Let's go."

They crossed the path of the march, expecting to be called out and questioned, but they made it to the railway arches without reproach and were soon hidden from the main road. Once up on the tracks they moved at pace, clinging to the hint of a thin shadow on their right. It gave little cover from the windows of high-rise apartments that loomed over them, but the city's attention was focussed on those moving towards Westminster, rather than away from it.

They dropped onto the north-bound line just beyond Stewart's Road and pressed on, shielded by an overgrown tangle of brambles and buddleia. Up ahead, the four chimneys of the Power Station stood proud against the sky. As a child, Maddie had always liked them, imagining the Station as a bricks and mortar dog, lying on its back with its legs waving in the air. No doubt, the proximity of Battersea Dogs' and Cats' Home had given her the idea.

"I'm just going to check out the road," Max said, interrupting her thoughts. Maddie nodded and slowed her pace, watching the space grow between her and Jack, who was walking up ahead.

Maddie passed the kennel block, her ear cocked, listening for the sound of barking. But then she remembered that the animals had been evacuated to the West Country six months after the conflict had begun. She sighed, wondering how it was that animals had escaped the fighting, when so many children remained in the city, their safety far from assured. She realised, of course, that finding space for evacuees in the overcrowded counties posed its own problems, but where was the will to try?

Up ahead, Jack sank to his knees, peering through a gap in the hoardings – their way in. Fear trickled down Maddie's spine, but she was committed now. She wouldn't let Jack do this alone.

The sight of the Power Station took Jack's breath away. Though almost a century older, the Art Deco masterpiece still held court over its neighbours. Alongside it lay Foster's serpentine glass construction, and Gehry's fractured yet undulating apartments. Both buildings arresting, but neither able to match the quiet, powerful presence of the Station itself.

London, like all great cities of the world, was made from layer upon layer of ideas and design, restoration and progress, confidence that rose and fell, optimism against the odds. Jack drank in the view, knowing that the odds were not stacked in Battersea's favour. In his lifetime, the development would become a victim of temporal storms and the rising river. But those facts might yet be rewritten.

Memories of the future competed for his attention with what he faced now, here in the past. Somehow, at the centre of it all was Kayson Hart. For Hart, it had been three years since Jack's conception. Three years, during which Hart had continued to enjoy his privilege and position, with no thought for the consequences of his actions. The psychological damage caused by rape, caused by drugs that Hart had administered, had stolen Mary's life away just as Jack's had begun.

Jack wasn't sure how he would react to Hart's presence, and that worried him. To lose control would be dangerous. But in truth, Hart could be anywhere in the city: at the nearby Republican Embassy; rallying his cronies in Parliament; or directing his agents from beyond the city's limits. In many ways it would be better not to encounter him, yet Jack's mind raged against the possibility that he should come so close and not look Hart in the eye, not make him pay for the suffering he'd inflicted.

But Jack's mission must come first. He owed it to Howard, to Howard's family, who within the protective embrace of Gaia, would never know what had befallen him, seeking comfort from the belief that Howard's sacrifice was worthwhile.

Jack *had* to ensure that was the truth.

More importantly, this was his chance to finish what his mother had begun, and his chance to save her. He wondered again what new shape her life would take, if she would marry and have children. The knowledge that he would not be part of it hit him again as a physical pain. He struggled to breathe, to lessen the tightness in his chest, and tried to focus on the joy – her joy – that he was determined to restore.

Mary had travelled back in time, targeting Hart in the hope that her organisation, Earth Rebellion, could use him to lessen the impact of climate change. Even if she had succeeded, ER's scale of ambition was insufficient. Now, through the destruction of time travel itself, Jack could both accomplish his mother's goal and protect her from Hart. Provided he didn't die trying.

A movement drew Jack's gaze up the striated wash towers to the crest of the chimneys. Dark smudges sped across the sky in the direction of the protest. Drones. Beyond the river, dark clouds were forming. Jack's pulse surged, his hands aches. He looked down and found they were clenched tight, his knuckles white.

Maddie slipped down beside him. "You okay?"

"Fine," he lied, flexing his fingers to ease the tension.

Max joined them, tailed by a blast of wind that sent dust billowing off the tracks and whirling up into the darkening sky. He glanced back the way he'd come. "Something's happening along Nine Elms, maybe at the Republican Embassy. I hung back a while by the bridge but I didn't dare get any closer." He opened his backpack and pulled out a drone.

Jack closed his eyes and the slightest sensation of light-headedness washed over him. He ran through his memories, months studying war-time London, but it was no good. The timelines were unstable, but he couldn't predict changes, only remember them once they'd taken place.

Maddie watched him, her breaths shallow and uneasy.

Jack's eyes opened and locked with hers. He turned to Max. "Once we're inside, go back to Suraya."

"What?" Max paused in his work and frowned. "The plan was to stay until you're back out."

Jack squinted into the distance. "Something is changing, but I don't know what. If you don't go back soon, you might not be able to."

Maddie's heart fluttered at the thought of Suraya, alone and waiting. Lightly, she touched Max's arm. Her voice was a whisper, "Please."

Max chewed his lip. He'd screwed up before, allowed Suraya to be placed in danger, and he needed to know now that she was safe, for his own sake as well as Maddie's. But Maddie was his friend too, he'd known her for years. Besides, Maddie's wasn't the only promise being asked of him. His eyes flicked from Maddie to Jack, then back the direction they'd travelled from. "Fine. Let's get on with it then."

Max handed them each a headset, containing the adapted holo-projectors he'd salvaged from the candles at the house. "Remember that these are basic – the hologram may glitch when you're moving, and there's not enough power for continuous projection, so it will cycle in and out. They should give you cover from the security cameras though, provided they don't have heat sensors."

"We just need to reach the first one," affirmed Jack. "Then we can freeze the network."

Max nodded. "I'll scout the entrance using the drone."

Jack stood and held out his hand. "Thank you. For everything."

Max shook it, smiling grimly. "Good luck."

Maddie hugged Max tight. "Look after her for me," she whispered in his ear.

"I will." He disentangled her. "Until you're back."

Maddie kissed him on the cheek, then followed Jack through the hoardings and into the tangle of weeds below. They cut their way through the wire fence separating them from the development, drew their weapons, then edged towards Circus Road West and the Power Station's westerly entrance.

"There," Jack breathed. "Two o'clock, just to the left of the door."

"I see it." Maddie inched towards the camera as smoothly as possible, praying that the holo-projection, shielding her from view, wouldn't cut out at the wrong moment. She thought about what Suraya had said. According to one of the Power Station's maids, the building's residential security was surprisingly relaxed – a single network of cameras, monitored by one guard on the front desk. But that was before Suraya's identity had been discovered, before Jack had blown the top off Twentytwo. Maddie doubted that Hart would now entrust his safety to a single guard.

She fought the urge to dash the last few metres, inching forwards until she could easily reach the camera's base to which she attached a small round disk. "It's on," she whispered. "Let's hope you're right about the security platform they use."

"We'll soon find out."

A slight blurring in the air above their heads told them that their drone had passed.

"There's a car approaching from the north," Max's voice warned them.

Jack and Maddie hid in a restaurant doorway and watched a black vehicle with diplomatic plates pass. Jack's heart thudded as he strained to make out the figure in the back seat. The tinted windows revealed little besides the shadowy bulk of a large man. It could be anyone.

"You're clear. The good news is that I can only make out two guards in the lobby, one behind the desk, the other just inside the door."

"And the bad?" asked Jack.

"There's some sort of scanner in place just inside the entranceway. It's not on any of our schematics. Could be biometric? But it's likely linked to the internal security. If you set it off the whole building may lock down."

"So, we need to get inside the lobby legitimately and disable the system from the inside." Jack looked at Maddie, eyebrows raised.

"We know the names of Hart's Embassy associates and some of the lobbyists who work for him," Maddie mused. "Could you pose as one of them?"

Jack shook his head. "They'll be on the system. It needs to be someone with a connection to Hart, but who wouldn't be on the biometric database. Someone with a reason to remain off-grid, but with good reason to just show up." Jack ran a hand through his hair, thinking. "Hang on…" He freed the rucksack from his back and pulled out the scanner, bringing up the list of active targets. There'd been a flurry of new listings since yesterday, including the Bishopsgate Bombers.

Maddie's stomach lurched as her eyes fell on a blurry image that was, nonetheless, recognisably her. Below that was a head shot of Suraya.

"Here." Jack pointed to a code beside his own entry. "Every target has its own reference number, which includes the registration code of the police officer responsible for that case; it means they're automatically notified of any sightings, or the capture of those targets. We've all been uploaded by the same officer."

"But that's just logical."

"Yes, but look." Jack scrolled down the list until he found an image of Dr Kingsley. "Same code."

Maddie screwed up one side of her face, unconvinced.

Jack shrugged. "Hart will make sure he hears about any sightings first. He'll have an officer working for him, keeping him in the loop, I'm sure of it."

"I don't think Kingsley's listing is active anymore," said Maddie, pointing at the screen.

Jack's stomach felt cold. If Kingsley's listing was no longer active, he must have been found.

"If you click on a reference number, you'll get a full list of that officer's uploads. Provided no one's discovered my hack, you should get the officer's name."

Jack did as Max suggested. "Okay… He's called Noakes, Sergeant Noakes. Let's plant a sighting of the Bishopsgate Bombers north of the river." Jack tapped the screen. "That should keep the Sergeant busy. Now, given the commotion around Westminster, it's plausible that Noakes would ask Snags to bring their bounty straight to Hart. The Power Station staff won't risk interfering with a police directive." Jack and Maddie locked eyes. "Last chance to turn back," he said.

Maddie nodded towards the screen. "I'm a wanted woman one way or another." Her eyes rose up the vast building before them and she smiled coldly. "So, let's deliver."

Jack pulled the baseball cap down a little further, though his own image, logged by Noakes, was hard to distinguish.

"You guys ready?" came Max's voice.

Maddie adjusted the cable ties so that her hands, placed together, appeared as if bound. "Yep, ready."

"The same way you were when we approached St Mary's," said Jack.

A flash of memory, the taste of salt and the brush of his lips, surfaced in Maddie's mind. As though he sensed it, Jack paused mid-step, lifted Maddie's face to his own and kissed her.

Maddie felt herself tremble as they moved out and into the street, though she told herself it was due to the kiss, rather than her fear. She made a show of dragging her feet and stumbling, as she had done under the effects of sedation, and as they approached the west entrance, the doors swept open and a heavily built guard stepped outside.

"This area's access by appointment only," he warned. He placed his hand on the hilt of his gun. "I haven't been notified of any visitors."

"Can't get no one's fuckin' attention at the gate," said Jack coarsely. "Bloody chaos up there."

The guard's eyes flicked in the direction of Nine Elms and back again as Maddie made a sudden lurch sideways. Jack pulled her back towards him, tutting disapprovingly. The guard drew his weapon.

"Steady on," said Jack, holding his free arm in the air,

his palm raised. The action pulled his jacket back, revealing the blinking light on the Snag's scanner. He inclined his head towards it, to make certain the guard saw it too. "Noakes said your boss would wanna take delivery of this one directly," he said with a slight grin.

The guard's expression faltered, and an exasperated sigh escaped his lips. "Can you confirm your reference?" he asked.

"Yep, its…" Jack paused.

The guard raised his eyebrows, waiting.

"You don't wanna write it down or nothing?" The guard began to turn away. "Alright, no need to get testy, it's 9373 NO39424."

The guard touched his ear and spoke to his colleague inside. "Marek, can you check a code for me?" He repeated the numbers. After a short wait he nodded. "Okay, bring her inside and we'll patch you through."

Maddie's arm tensed beneath Jack's fingers and he made a show of pushing her forwards. The glass doors slid open and the guard passed through a biometric film that rippled green then vanished when Jack and Maddie entered.

"Make a call up to Mr Hart, tell him—"

Maddie swung her arms forwards and fired at the man behind the desk. Jack plunged an improvised taser into the other guard's stomach. Maddie sprinted, leapt across the desk, and knocked the young man to the floor. He struggled for a moment before the sedative took effect. Behind her, the first guard slumped to the ground with a thud. She pressed a small black disk to the side of the main computer and glanced nervously at the security feed. The screens flickered then reset with imagery captured a few minutes earlier.

"Guys?"

"We're alright, Max." Maddie replied.

Jack threw her a roll of tape and they set to work, binding the guards' arms and legs. Max sighed in relief. *"If you're sure then, I'll head back to Suraya."*

"We're sure," Jack replied.

"Okay, see you two on the other side."

Jack caught Maddie's eye, both aware of what Max was yet to grasp. Jack pressed his lips together, fighting the sudden, unexpected swell of emotion, and dragged the bound bodies of the guards across the lobby and into the men's room.

Maddie sat at the desk, cycling through camera feeds for the residential areas. "Here, this is it, Hart's apartment."

Jack returned from the door with their drone and leant in to see. The guard had confirmed it – Hart was here. Blood pounded inside Jack's ears.

"He won't just let us in," Maddie added.

"No, not together," Jack agreed. "But if he thinks it's just you…" He glanced back towards the men's' room. "I've got an idea."

The guard's uniform fit Jack well. Maddie stood back to appraise him. "Maybe if…" She ran her hands under the tap then smoothed Jack's hair into a side parting. "Better. Just stay behind me and keep your face down."

At the main desk, Jack's fingers hovered over the buttons. He took a deep breath and dialled. His body was tense, his heart pounding with each long, protracted ring. No answer. Hart wasn't there. Jack moved his hand to end the call.

"Yes?" The voice was low and gruff.

Jack forced out words, imitating the voice of the guard he'd tasered. "Good morning. We have a delivery for you in reception. With your permission, Marek will bring it up to you."

"No. It can be collected later." The line went dead.

Jack and Maddie exchanged looks. It was Hart, Jack was sure of it. His hands were clammy as he redialled. He forced himself to breath slowly.

Over and over, the ring tone sounded.

"What the hell is it that can't wait?"

"My apologies, Mr Hart, the er, courier is most insistent that the delivery is made straight away. I believe that he's waiting for payment?"

"Tell him that he—"

"He has a reference code, 9373 NO39424."

There was silence on the other end of the line, followed, after a while, by a dull clicking sound.

Why aren't your cameras working?"

"Just a system glitch, sir, they'll be online again shortly."

"Very well."

"I'll send Marek up with the"—Jack glanced at Maddie— "with the goods."

The line went dead, but Jack remained still, staring at the image of Hart's apartment door on the screen before him.

Maddie placed her hand on his. "You can do this. *We* can do this."

He ran his hand across his face and pushed his fingertips into his temples, the pressure a relief from the buzzing of his own mind. He nodded and handed her a holo-headset, then fixed on his own.

Jack and Maddie entered a glass lift at the base of the north-easterly wash tower and rose rapidly towards the sky garden, nestled in the Station's crown. Looking inward, they caught glimpses of the building's core, where deserted coffee shops and chichi perfumeries offered nothing but the scent of their former wares.

Looking outward and along Nine Elms, they could see the throng of protesters, pushing forwards and falling back as one, their movement creating an impression that the street itself, writhing and serpentine, was alive.

"Almost everyone I know is down there," breathed Maddie. She pressed her face to the glass, her eyes drawn to the flash of blue lights on the approach to Lambeth Bridge. "I feel like I've abandoned them."

"You're doing more to help them than they could ever imagine," Jack reassured her. He craned his neck to try to see the Embassy, wondering again about the diplomatic vehicle they'd seen earlier, but his view was obscured by apartment blocks. The lift passed the tenth floor. "Nearly there," he said.

Jack had reinstated the security cameras on the top floor, so as not to raise suspicion, and he and Maddie resumed their act of captive and captor. Jack lowered his head and pushed Maddie, her eyes half-closed, from the lift, around the corner, straight into a housekeeping trolley. The cleaning lady beside it shrieked in alarm as she stood up, duster in hand. She stared wide-eyed with horror at Maddie's lolling head.

"Delivery for Mr Hart," Jack explained. He side-stepped her mop and pushed Maddie away down the corridor.

"Do you think she'll say something?" Maddie hissed under her breath.

"Who to? Smart people don't get involved."

"Camera on your left," Maddie whispered.

Jack pulled her closer and turned his head to the right as he moved past.

"Ten steps ahead."

Jack pressed the buzzer and Maddie lurched closer to the security camera so that her face would fill the image. They heard the click of the intercom, a gentle intake of breath, then Hart's voice.

"Which one was it?"

"…Mr Hart?" Jack made a stab at a polish accent.

"The Snag, which one?"

"Ah…er, eet wos, *ow!*"

Maddie threw her head backwards and caught Jack on the chin, pushing him to the side of the camera as she struggled against her imaginary constraints. She flashed him a look of apology as she slid back in front of the camera.

"Sorree," Jack mumbled. "Sedative is wearing off."

Hart muttered something and the intercom switched off.

The door swung open. Jack's and Maddie's hands flew to their weapons. But there was no one there.

"Bring her in," Hart's voice called from inside.

Jack and Maddie stepped over the threshold. The apartment, whilst not the largest in the building, might well have been the most expensively furnished. Maddie stared, open mouthed at the canvases that dominated the walls of the open plan space: Mark Rothko, Paul Klee, even a Picasso. A column-like screen of thick, rippled glass created a divide between the dining area on the left and the living area ahead of them where a statement, mid-century sofa was as much a work of art as the sculptures arranged around it. The bold artwork was offset by neutral walls, and the pallid, grey light that oozed through floor to ceiling windows. A staircase to their right led to the floor above.

Jack searched the space with his eyes. "Mr Hart?"

"Yes, yes, you'd better collect the payment," came the impatient reply from a doorway just beyond the dining room.

Jack moved around the table until he saw, through the opening, the figure of Hart bent over a desk. He raised his gun and fired.

Pfipp.

But the dart flew straight through Hart, whose image rippled and flickered.

"It's a holo—"

Pfipp.

"—gram."

Maddie stumbled and reached for the dart embedded in her neck. Jack spun around, saw her sink to the floor, and fired at the glint of a weapon near the stairwell.

The sound of laughter echoed around the room and multiple versions of Hart appeared, one from the doorway through which they'd entered, another from the staircase and a third from the small office behind Jack. All were armed, and each had Jack in his sights. Jack slid his left hand towards his jacket, reaching for a second weapon, tucked inside, but stopped at the soft click of Hart's gun.

"Yes." The three Harts simultaneously sighed with satisfaction. "They sound different, don't they. I'm not really a fan of sedation guns, inelegant weapons, don't you think?"

A slight movement from the floor caught Jack's eye

and he glanced through the table legs. Maddie opened her palm to reveal a syringe which, a moment before, had contained the reversal agent.

Three pairs of eyes flicked towards her, but Hart remained oblivious to her communication, noting only the dart that she had pulled from her neck. "Oh yes, well… Let's just say that was an act of charity. Besides, she may yet have her uses."

Jack gritted his teeth and looked from one Hart to another. It was 5D hard light technology, with embedded audio projection – holograms almost indistinguishable from the real thing. He could even hear the one behind him breathing, but since he'd already shot a dart through it, he focussed on the other two.

The three Harts smiled at Jack with amusement. "And now you're wondering which one of us is real?" Their voices were slightly out of sync, the sound discordant. "Two of these weapons are nothing more than light, whilst the third could tear the flesh from your bones. Your chances of survival do not look good."

Jack's eyes fixed on the Hart in front of him. Inwardly he seethed, his impulse to wipe the smug smile from Hart's face so strong, he almost couldn't breathe. He blinked rapidly and forced himself to think. Hart was well-informed, with contacts in the police and the Republic as well as those from the future. Slowly, he shook his head. "No. I don't think you want to kill me. I think you've been waiting for me."

"And why would you think that?"

"Because we're both looking for Dr Kingsley, and together we stand a better chance of finding him."

Hart snorted. "So, you are the one then." His eyes and gun remained fixed on Jack as he drew a second lethal weapon from inside his jacket and took aim at Maddie. "I don't suppose I'll need her after all."

"Wait!" Jack's stomach flipped. "Let her go. I'll tell you what you want to know."

Hart laughed again. "Let her go?" he asked incredulously. "I can't do that. She knows too much."

"But who's going to believe her?" asked Jack. "The daughter of immigrants, a member of a terrorist organisation, spouting crazy stories about time travel? Is that really a threat to someone like you?"

"No." Hart turned slightly towards Maddie. "But I don't like loose ends."

Hart turned and Jack heard the slight scrape of his shoes as they pivoted against the wooden floor…

Three versions of Hart tightened their finger on the trigger.

Jack swung around towards the source of the sound. The *only* source of the sound: the Hart that stood behind him.

Pffip, pffip. Darts fired out from somewhere near the stairwell. Maddie twisted on to her back and shot at the red glint of an automated heat sensor.

Hart's bullet sliced through the shoulder of Jack's shirt and splintered fragments of granite from the kitchen worktop behind.

Jack threw himself sideways and fired a shot that grazed Hart's leg.

Hart cursed but lashed out, booting the weapon from Jack's hand. His finger tightened on the trigger of his gun…

"Stop!" Maddie screamed. "He's your son!"

The shock of the statement.

A split second's delay.

Jack swung his leg forwards and knocked Hart off his feet.

Hart fell, his face creased with confusion, words on his lips. "My son?"

Jack threw himself forwards, snatched Hart by his collar and brought his fist down with the fury of the wronged. His body shook as he roared into Hart's face, each word punctuated with a crashing blow. *"You… are… not… my… father!"*

"Jack!" Maddie seized his arm.

Jack stopped. Panting, trembling, dizzy from his frenzy. He released his grip and Hart dropped to the floor. Jack stood and reeled.

"Oh God." Maddie's voice was small, frightened. She knelt next to Hart. "If he dies, do you?" Blood covered Hart's face, his lip was burst open, his nose oozing blood, his left eye swelling shut.

"No." Jack panted. "I've…It already happened." His eyes flicked from Hart's bloodied face to an indistinct point ahead of him. "Is he?"

Maddie swallowed and leant over him, looking for signs of life, not wanting to touch him.

Hart groaned. His face creased and he erupted into a spasm of coughs. He gasped for air and began to twist onto his front, words forming under his breath. "Protocol… Noakes—"

A boot to his stomach silenced him. Jack hauled him from the floor and held him while Maddie located his phone, deftly removing its power cell. Jack pushed Hart onto a chair and bound his hands and feet.

A dull clunk sounded above their heads.

"What was that?" Maddie asked.

"The maid," Hart sneered.

Jack lifted an eyebrow. "Watch him," he told Maddie.

He retrieved his gun and mounted the stairs rapidly. A second lounge, minimal and empty, led him to the bedrooms. There was no maid, but from the last room Jack heard the level buzz of a heart monitor flatlining. His skin prickled. He crashed through the door, but the room, though recently occupied, now stood empty. He switched off the machine and listened, but all was still. The crumpled sheets gave no clue as to who had lain upon them.

Jack made his way back downstairs to where Hart sat with his head lowered. "Who are you hiding?" Jack demanded.

Panic flashed across Hart's face. He looked up and a blaze of light burst through the clouds, dazzling him and casting Jack in shadow. He squinted against the light but said nothing.

"Was it a Republican?" Jack noticed Hart's body stiffen, coiled as though ready, were he able, to spring. "You're still playing both sides."

Hart's laugh became a hacking cough. He spat out a mouthful of blood and smiled scornfully up at Jack. He craned his neck to see Maddie, wincing with the effort. "That was an interesting ploy," he sneered, changing the subject. "But I have no children, I make sure of it."

Jack bit down on his response. "Let's find the safe," he muttered. "We won't learn anything from him." He moved to a row of cabinets to begin his search. Maddie hesitated, then moved into the next room to do the same.

His captors distracted, Hart took the chance to scan the room, listening for any sound from the floor above. How had Kingsley got lose? And where was he? Hart racked his brain, desperately trying to think of a way to free himself. He could reveal the location of his safe; since only he could open it, they'd have to untie his hands. But it might risk giving them what they wanted.

He thought about what the girl, Madeeha, had said. His own reaction had surprised him, perhaps touching in a small way on his own past, but it was nothing compared to the raw nerve it had exposed in her companion. That was something Hart could exploit. Pushing Jack to, once again, lose control was dangerous, but those who lost control also made mistakes. With Kingsley free, Hart had no choice but to act quickly.

Hart twisted again to look over his shoulder. Trying, despite his swollen eye, to gauge the distance to the dining table, beneath which was a touch activated silent alarm. Hart's feet, bound to the chair legs, were unable to get a purchase on the ground. But if someone else pushed him backwards, he might be able to reach it.

Hart looked to where Jack knelt, his back to him, prising open a locked cabinet. There was no safe there, just cigars. "Don't misunderstand me," Hart began. "I've never suffered for lack of choice. So many women though...it all becomes a bit meaningless, just like the women themselves."

Jack's body tensed. He stood up slowly, but he didn't turn around. He was frozen, fists balled, his knuckles white.

"What are you?" Hart pressed on. "An orphan? A

fostered child? Abused and abandoned by your real parents, looking to connect yourself to someone of wealth and importance in order to validate your worthless existence. Did you think that if you travelled back in time, you could re-make yourself? Did your life, your future, really hold so little meaning? One thing's for sure, whatever sorry sort of a woman brought you into the world, I certainly wouldn't have fucked her."

"*Shut up!*" Jack swung around, his gun drawn.

Hart squinted against the light, trying to read Jack's expression, but his captor's face was no more than a silhouette.

"Jack?" Maddie emerged from Hart's office, her face taut, eyes wide. "Don't rise to it, it's what he wants."

"No, I won't let this lie. This can't be ignored. Remembering my mother will be the last thing you do, Hart. Your final moments will be spent knowing that you die because of her, because of what you did to her."

Hart forced a smile as Jack moved closer, hedging his bets on the knowledge that they needed him alive. Jack wouldn't shoot him, but if Jack shoved him backwards, closer to the table, he could reach the alarm. Madeeha was behind Hart somewhere, and Kingsley must be close by. Hart noted the spare gun in Jack's belt, the bulge of a phone in his pocket. Maybe he could persuade Kingsley to help him? Persuade him that Jack was his true enemy.

Gunfire echoed from outside the building and Jack glanced over his shoulder, towards the window. The light, though fading again, flowed across his face.

Hart stopped mid-thought and stared. He hadn't seen Jack's face properly until now, but it was there, a likeness that shocked him into silence. Jack turned back to him and began to speak.

"My mother cast back in time from 2119 to 2070, under orders to locate the politician who had driven the defeat of every emergency environmental policy put forward by the EU over the course of thirty years." Hart looked at him blankly. "That was you."

"I haven't *been* in politics for thirty years."

"You will be." Jack inclined his head. "Or at least, you were *going* to be."

"But I—"

"Shut up!" Jack raised his gun again and Hart fell silent. "My mother found you in Strasbourg. You were living in luxury, funded by the very fossil fuels that have wrecked this planet, whilst ignoring the pleas of those people you helped to displace. You—"

"Your apparent knowledge comes from a future that is yet to happen," Hart interrupted, "and my own perspective has changed. Yes, my mode of living in Strasbourg was privileged, but only as befitted my position. And as to recalling individual acquaintances, I can only say that it was a very busy time."

Jack paused and shook his head. The corners of his mouth turned down in disgust. "You must have drugged and abused a lot of women then, if you can forget them so easily afterwards."

"What?"

"Amorbarbital – a sedative and truth serum. Your personal charms must be overrated if you had to resort to drugging women."

"This is ridiculous, I…" A movement in the shadow behind the staircase caught Hart's eye. Dr Kingsley was still here. That changed things. He could help Hart, but only if Hart could turn the conversation around. "I've no idea where these notions came from, but I can assure you that they're nothing more than fanciful."

"Think, Hart. I'm sure that you, especially you, can remember the events of the Massacre – 29th March 2070 – and the people you saw that day. After all, you were at the centre of history being made."

Hart's eyes widened, only slightly, but it was enough for Jack.

"Yes. You do remember." Jack's voice became a cold whisper. "You destroyed her life and you deprived me of mine."

"I – it wasn't like that. The trauma of that day's events, the Massacre… Memories could easily be confused—"

"*Liar!*" Jack's hand was shaking. "*She was just twenty years old!*"

Outside the window, the clouds had turned black.

Jack gripped the gun with both hands to steady his aim. "Her name was Mary Elliot…" Jack's finger tightened on the trigger and the hairs on the back of his hand stood on end. "And it will be the last name you ever hear."

An explosion shook the building. The sky lit up, dousing the room with an amber glow.

"The Embassy!" Maddie gasped.

But Jack didn't hear. He dropped his gun and doubled over, pain surging through him.

"Jack?" Maddie ran to his side, caught him as he stumbled, and lowered him to the floor.

Jack cradled his head in his hands, willing the cacophony of voices, the contradiction of conflicting histories to subside. He was screaming with pain, the sound of his own voice disjointed as though it came from some other place, from beyond him… He forced his eyes open, gritting his teeth with the effort. Hart was writhing against his restraints, howling. And Jack realised that it wasn't him, it was Hart. The cries of pain came from Hart.

Maddie stood up, mouth open as the realisation hit. Her eyes jumped from Jack to Hart. "Oh my god." She ran to the kitchen, filled a glass with water, and brought it back. "Here, have some."

Jack grasped the glass in shaking hands, almost dropping it through fingers slick with sweat. He brought the rim to his mouth and focussed on the sensation of the cool liquid against his lips until his breathing steadied. On the chair in front of him, Hart whimpered softly, his eyes twitching beneath closed lids.

"Is he also a…?"

"It looks like it." Jack pushed himself up into a crouch, making sure he was steady before rising to stand.

"Did that happen before?" asked Maddie, looking through the window to where a tower of black smoke rose midway along Nine Elms. "Or was the explosion the change?"

"I think so. I'm not sure. The Republic…" Jack's words trailed off as his memories churned, sending another wave of nausea through him. "Dalton," he said at last. "Something happened to Steve Dalton. He was the Republican Charge D'Affaires. He was in…" Jack stopped, suddenly aware that Hart's eyes were open, fixed on him, a look of confusion and surprise, unfolding in their depths. "It was you," hissed Jack. "What did you do?"

The confusion cleared. "Is that really so unclear?" Hart asked. His face, beaded with sweat and slick with blood, was grotesque, out of kilter with the confidence Hart forced into his voice. "I'm ridding us of a mutual enemy. Neither of us want Kingsley's work to fall into Republican hands."

"But it didn't work," said Jack. "You've changed the narrative, but not the outcome."

Hart frowned.

Jack raised his eyebrows and exhaled a sharp breath of air. "And you don't even know."

"What?"

"What you are, you have no idea."

"What the hell are you talking about?"

Jack took a step closer, considering Hart and the strange paradox he presented. Proof that Hart knew nothing of his own nature.

Hart shifted uncomfortably under Jack's gaze.

"Despite your wealth and your connections," Jack began, "you don't have the means to stop the Republic. You might, if you were working with the government, with Aubrey Martin, but you're double crossing him too, aren't you? You want the technology for yourself."

Hart didn't respond.

"You knew that the Republic was close to finding Kingsley, and so you needed to distract them, to buy yourself a bit of time. You had a meeting here, with Dalton, planted a bomb, and sent him back to the Embassy. You removed a few key players, sowed some confusion and panic, but it didn't end the race. Your actions did, however, alter the course of history. And you *felt* it, as I *feel* it, because like me, *you* are a Person of Mixed Era Origin."

"I don't know what the hell you're talking about."

"We're chronological oddities – Cronods," Jack sneered, "and we never forget the past, even after it's been altered. And when it does change, it hurts like hell. There will have been other times you felt it: a prickling sensation in your skin, a rush of white light behind your eyes, searing pain and heat that thickens the air and knocks the breath from your body."

"No! No, that's not it," Hart cried. "I have *premonitions* of how the future could be, not the past. I've seen a better world, and I know that through time travel, that world can be made a reality."

Jack laughed. "Those aren't visions of how the world *could* be, they're memories of how it *was*, before time technology meddled with history. Time travel can't make the world a better place, it's only made our problems worse, controlled by those who lust for power and influence. Its mere existence is a temptation, and it will always, *always* fall into the hands of those who will abuse it for their own benefit."

Jack took a few paces towards the window, recalling what Frits had told him, about Hart's mother, her affair with a Republican. "Your father was a time traveller," said Jack. "A Republican politician from the twenty-second century."

Hart looked at Jack aghast.

"You never met him, did you? Not because he denied you, but because he didn't exist yet – not in your own time – and in his, your existence never even occurred to him. He came from the future, took his pleasure and was gone. But the funny thing is… the irony is, that in trying to prevent the Republic from discovering time technology, you're actively undermining your own existence."

Hart's face darkened. It was ridiculous. And yet, as memories flooded his mind, he could see the truth in

Jack's words. He thought about his mother who, for all her money and connections, never did find her Republican – Hart's real father.

But Jack's revelation, if it was true, changed everything. If Hart's life depended on the Republic discovering Kingsley's laboratory first, he must ensure that neither Aubrey Martin nor Jack Elliot interfered.

Hart had ensured that the explosive he'd planted on Steve Dalton would be traced back to the Fringe. But even so, he was one of the last people to see Dalton alive. Republican guards would pay him a visit, and soon. They could free him, and in return he could provide what both he needed and they wanted: Dr Kingsley and his notebook.

Hart just needed to stay alive until then.

Maddie lifted a large painting from the wall to reveal a safe. "Jack, look."

Hart twisted to see. "Good luck with that," he muttered.

Maddie ignored him and peered closely at the buttons. "It's a code-lock, but if we drill here and here, we—"

Jack placed a hand on her arm. "Let me try." His fingers hovered over the keypad and he closed his eyes, picturing Frits outside Hart's office in Twentytwo. He entered the same six digits that Frits had used. The lock gave a low clunk and opened.

Maddie smiled and swung open the door, only to discover a second safe within, unlike anything she'd seen before.

Behind her, Hart laughed. "Did you really think it would be that easy?"

Suraya's words rang in Maddie's mind – *everything's a game to him*. Rage pulsed through her. She reached Hart in two long strides and grabbed him by the collar. Pressing her gun to his temple, she brought her face close to his. "Oh, we can make this easy."

Hart remained still, but his broken face smiled. "I'm afraid you will need me alive if you want what's inside. And for that, you will have to untie me."

"You sure about that?" said Jack. He pulled back the

sleeve of his shirt and inserted his arm into the iatric chamber, aligning his fingers with the handprint inside. The sensors reacted at once, illuminating the chamber with a soft, green glow, sending pulses up Jack's arm and into his body.

Maddie returned to Jack's side, watching the readings flash across a small, embedded screen. Her brows drew together. "What's it doing?"

"Reading my DNA. Searching my genome for an embedded code." The safe door beeped softly and Jack removed his hand.

Hart's face darkened. He pulled at the restraints around his wrists, cursing under his breath when they didn't budge. Maddie glanced at him. "A code that came from Hart, from his DNA?"

Jack's face clouded. It was a reality that he despised, but that couldn't be denied. "Yes."

Maddie touched his hand lightly. "It's not what makes you who you are," she whispered. But she could see that Jack was troubled, his eyes the colour of the storm outside.

Jack pressed his lips together and reached into the safe, retrieving a bundle of documents and a small leather notebook. He took them to the dining table and scanned through each one, placing them in two piles: those things he already knew, and those that might help locate the laboratory.

Hart watched him. Seething. Silent.

Jack lifted the notebook last, opening it at a random page, covered in notes and equations. He turned the page, then another, his keen eyes absorbed in the details within. "What is it?" Maddie asked.

Jack closed the book to inspect the cover, then moved to stand in front of Hart, the notebook still in his hand. "This belongs to Kingsley."

"Does it?" Hart didn't look up.

"Where did you get it?"

"I don't recall."

But Jack didn't need to know. The information in Hart's dossiers, combined with Jack's own knowledge, would narrow his search to just a few locations on the Thames, either near a bridge or – Jack opened the notebook and found a diagram a few pages in – the Thames Barrier.

Jack rummaged through the drawers in the kitchen until he found a lighter, then gathered up the larger bundle of papers and handed them to Maddie along with the notebook. "Take these to the bathtub upstairs and burn them."

Maddie nodded then inclined her head towards Hart. "What about him?"

"He'll get what he deserves." Jack leant across the table and picked up his gun.

"Wait! Wait!" At once, Hart was animated. "Let's talk about this. You must have questions? Things you want to know about your family?"

"I have no family." Jack's voice was flat, matter of fact. "And no questions that *you* could answer. I came here with one purpose only – to erase time-technology for good. Now I have the added satisfaction of knowing that my actions will also erase you, and all the pain that you have caused."

"Jack?" Maddie's tone was apprehensive.

"Fine." Jack tucked the pistol into his belt and picked up a dart gun. "I don't need to kill him, just allow time to take its new course."

"Not that," Maddie replied urgently.

Jack turned to look over his shoulder. Hart craned his neck to see past him. Maddie took a step backwards off the bottom of the staircase.

A man was standing a few steps above her, weapon drawn. "I will take those," he said, holding out his hand.

"Dr Kingsley!" Hart cried. "You're better, thank God. Be careful, these terrorists will destroy your work. You heard them say so yourself." Kingsley redirected the gun towards him. If he was startled by Hart's bloodied appearance he didn't show it.

"Don't think I won't, Mr Hart. For as it has been said, no matter how much a snake sheds its skin, it *is* still a snake."

331

"Come now, Dr Kingsley. You and I want the same thing, remember?"

"No. We do not."

Hart's face darkened. "They'll kill you," he snarled, tilting his head towards Jack. "And destroy our last hope for this planet."

"You didn't listen to a thing we said!" Maddie cried.

Jack huffed out air. "Hart's not in the habit of listening, lest it undermines his own opinion."

Carefully, Jack placed his weapons on the table, then stepped away, his palms raised towards Dr Kingsley. The physicist was older, more fragile than Jack had expected. The only photographs he'd seen were of Kingsley as a young man. Jack knew that many years had passed, and yet he hadn't adjusted for it in his mind.

Jack had imagined this meeting, had expected to feel anger, even hatred. After all, Dr Kinglsey was ground zero – the route of all that was wrong in Jack's life. But anger wasn't what he felt now. There was sadness, yes, echoed in the face of Kingsley himself. But also awe. "It's an honour to meet you," Jack said at last. "Not many men can say they've come face to face with their maker."

"I'm not sure that is an honour I can lay claim to, Mr?"

"Elliot. Jack Elliot."

"Mr Elliot."

"Directly, no. But without you and your work I wouldn't exist."

Noah lowered his arm and blinked slowly. The things he had heard that day left him confused and weary. God-damned weary.

"What? Don't lower your weapon," Hart blustered.

"Mr Hart, I no longer take orders from those who would imprison me."

"Will you sit down, Dr Kingsley?" Maddie asked. "You don't look quite well."

Noah nodded and took the arm Maddie proffered. He lowered himself gratefully onto one of the dining chairs. "Thank you."

"How did you even get free?" Hart hissed.

"Just because you neither seek nor earn compassion, do not think others incapable of doing so."

"The paramedic?"

"It seems that she did not think an old man deserved to be so tightly bound."

Hart clenched his teeth and pictured the paramedic's face, her self-righteous judgement simmering beneath a few clipped words. She, at least, had paid the price. Now Hart had to rid himself of Jack and Madeeha, and the appearance of Dr Kingsley might be just the distraction he required. Republican guards would be on their way. The more time Jack and the girl wasted questioning Kingsley, the closer Hart's own liberation. And once the guards arrived, Hart would put a swift end to Jack and his claims. Hart's story wasn't over – he would restore his own narrative.

At the table, Noah flicked through the pages of his notebook, relieved to see that it was all still there. He looked up at the young man who claimed to have travelled in time, to indeed, be a product of time travel itself. "How did you know that this notebook belonged to me?" he asked.

"In the future that I'm from, your notebook was taken by DARPA, but a few years from now, Republican dissidents will smuggle out a few key pages. Europe will use them to kick-start its own Temporal Programme. There's a mark, a doodle, in the corner of one of the pages." Jack traced his finger over the surface of the table, forming a spiral, intersected by a straight line. "It's used on the insignia of the European Confederacy of Time Technology."

Noah opened the notebook near to the centre point and ran his fingertip across the very image Jack had just drawn. He laid the notebook down, placed his elbows on the table and steepled his hands, touching his fingertips to the bridge of his nose. He sighed. "This future you describe is not the future I hoped for."

"But we can change it," Maddie urged.

Noah glanced at her. The girl's eyes were bright, her

optimism touching, though from his own experience, misplaced. "By destroying my life's work?" The question was directed at Jack.

Jack nodded. "It's the only way to be sure."

"But perhaps, given your understanding of what will happen, we do not need to destroy it? You can help me to move my laboratory, protect what I have developed, and I can fulfil my original objective and put right the mistakes of the past."

Jack shook his head. "It's not that simple. The timelines have been tampered with hundreds of times already and they're highly unstable. Those clouds out there, the storms of the past few days, they're not the result of climate change, but temporal flux. And it gets a lot worse. The Thames Barrier where, if I'm not mistaken, you source your electricity, will be damaged by the temporal storms. You know how powerful a tidal surge can be. Without the barrier, all this…" he gestured to the window and the riverside streets below. "Well, it goes the same way as the bayous."

Noah stared blankly through the window. The bayous. How he wished he'd been able to take his nephews fishing on the bayous, as he had once done aboard his uncle's old boat. Or steer them through watery cypress avenues in a canoe, beneath a canopy of Spanish moss…

A wail of sirens broke the silence, drifting up from the streets below. Maddie moved to the window to watch.

"And what if it doesn't work?" asked Noah at last. "What if we destroy my records, my prototypes and my laboratory, but this world still continues its descent into irrevocable climate change?"

Jack shrugged. "I'm not saying this is a cure-all – it won't remove the environmental challenges we face. But taking time travel out of the equation will reset the clock, give people the chance to make the necessary changes."

"And do you recall a time when the bayous still existed, Mr Elliot?"

"No. There's no thread within my own lifetime, no strand of memory in which they exist. But I'll bet you that there are in his." He inclined his head in Hart's direction. "The world of his 'premonitions' is the world as it should be now; how the world was before the Republic began to meddle with time. *That* world is still within reach."

Maddie returned from the window, Jack's iHolo in hand, and opened up the security feed that they'd tapped into. "We can discuss all this later, but right now, we need to make a move. Jack, if you're right about Steve Dalton, then Republican guards will be on their way here."

Jack moved so that he could see across the Power Station development to Nine Elms. Blue lights glittered across the sea of glass – police vehicles drawn from the Westminster protests to the Embassy explosion. His eye fell on two unmarked, dark vans entering Pump House Lane.

"You're right. We need to go." Jack grabbed the pile of documents and Dr Kingsley's notebook and shoved them into his bag.

Hart twisted his head in their direction, wondering how to delay them. "How do you propose to get out of here? Just going to hop on a boat and travel down river?" He laughed. "The area will be crawling with police, and you're all on the wanted list."

"The Tideway tunnel," Noah suggested. "We can access it at Kirtling Street, just a few minutes' walk from here, and follow it all the way to Beckton."

"You won't make it to Kirtling Street!" Hart sneered.

Jack and Maddie exchanged a glance.

"That's why you're coming with us," said Jack.

Hart's good eye widened in surprise.

"Your life depends on the Republic being first to discover time-technology. It's not in your interests for Dr Kingsley to fall into the hands of the British police or Aubrey Martin so, if stopped, you will give us clearance."

"Why on earth should I cooperate? What you intend to do will destroy me."

"If you cooperate your odds improve. Otherwise, I'm

more than happy to kill you now." Jack's face hardened and he drew his gun. "It's your choice."

Hart cursed under his breath.

"Jack, can we talk in private?" Maddie asked. She climbed the stairs to the first floor and waited for Jack to follow. "This isn't going to work," she said, as soon as he joined her. "We can't restrain Hart in case we do run into the police. And restrained or not, he'll cross us as soon as he can, even if he dies in the attempt. He's got nothing to lose."

Jack paced the floorboards, thinking. She was right. He threw back his head, frustrated, then his eye fell on the room where Kingsley had been held. "What if we sedate him? Just enough to slow him down and inhibit his speech, and there are spare scrubs in that room."

Maddie frowned. "I'm not following you."

"We're up against Republican guards *and* the police, but we might get past them both if we present Hart as a victim of whoever bombed the Embassy. The roads are all jammed right now, so the river is the fastest, safest route to a hospital. That's where his personal guard"—he tapped a finger to his chest— "and medics"—he pointed at Maddie— "are taking him."

Maddie nodded slowly. "Okay, but you'll need to change too."

Jack grabbed a dark suit and tie from Hart's wardrobe and dressed quickly, avoiding his reflection, afraid of seeing Hart's image staring back. From the moment Jack learned the truth about his father, he'd tried to distance himself, to prove to himself how dissimilar they were. But the first chance Jack had got, he'd beaten Hart to a pulp, and now was using him to advance his own aims. Did that not make them both alike?

Jack had questioned his involvement in Howard's project many times, whether the end would justify the means? His actions would determine the fate of others like him, the lives of thousands of Cronods extinguished in an instant. But billions more would be spared because of them. Logically, the lives of the many outweighed those of the few. But how many people would be willing to step up and make that choice?

He pushed his thoughts aside and hurried back to where Maddie, clad in a set of scrubs, stood beside Hart, an empty syringe in her hand. Kingsley stood to one side, his expression that of studied calm.

"I gave him about a sixth of the dose," said Maddie. "I just hope it's not too much."

"Or too little," remarked Jack as he cut through the bindings and pulled Hart to his feet. "Dr Kingsley, are you ready?"

"I believe so."

They took the lift on the western wash tower. Its descent, as anticipated, drew the attention of drones, and the hunted turned their faces from the glass and prayed that the sky's reflection would obscure their identity. On the ground floor they doubled back towards the exit at the base of the eastern tower, avoiding the drones, but not the police officers approaching from Cringle Dock.

Hart struggled against Jack's grip on his arm. "Thhinn yuur sso clevrr," he slurred.

"Shut up."

"A'll yell fffur help."

"Be my guest."

Hart's face creased slowly with confusion.

Jack exhaled with weary irritation. "I *know* that the Republic makes a mess of the future, so if I must choose between the Republic and Aubrey Martin, I'll choose the latter. It can't be any worse. If you want to cry for help, go ahead, you're just hastening your own demise."

Hart said nothing and didn't resist when Jack put his arm around him and manoeuvred him through the exit.

The closest of the police officers, a sergeant, called to her colleague and advanced, weapon raised. "Stop where you are and put your hands in the air."

Maddie and Noah did so, but Jack kept his arm around Hart.

"I repeat—" she began.

"Please!" Maddie interrupted. "This man needs immediate medical attention."

The sergeant's eyes ran up and down Hart, taking in his bruised and bloodied face. "Constable Gibb," she shouted. "Call for an ambulance."

Maddie shook her head. "The journey by road will take too long, his injuries are too severe."

"He can take his chances, along with everyone else," the sergeant replied, unmoved.

Hart lurched, slurring words as he did so. Jack steadied him then spoke. "This is MEP Kayson Hart, British liaison to the Republican ambassador. According to his account, he came under attack from unidentified hostiles shortly before the explosion at the Republican Embassy. He has suspected internal bleeding and has imbibed some sort of poison. He may know who's responsible for that mess." Jack titled his head towards the plume of smoke rising from Nine Elms. "But if he dies, the knowledge dies with him. I have a boat arriving to take him to St Thomas's."

The police sergeant squinted at Hart, trying to recognise the man beneath the swollen flesh. Dr Kingsley took a small step forwards, and Jack caught the flick of his eyes to their right. The unmarked black vans were approaching the end of Pump House Road.

"The ambulance is on its way," Constable Gibb informed them.

"Tell it to go to the west entrance," said Maddie. "There are two Station guards, both injured but alive."

"Very well," the sergeant relented. "Gibb, go with them to the hospital."

Maddie's eyes darted towards Jack, but he smiled graciously and allowed the constable to take Hart's other arm.

"The boat's at Cringle Dock," said Jack, pushing ahead at a pace. He felt for the handle of his dart gun, ready for the moment their path wound around the corner of the dockside apartments, out of sight. But the squeal of brakes from behind stopped the constable in his tracks.

The group turned to see two vehicles, a silver Range Rover and a black van, their noses inches apart. The Range Rover's door swung open and a man in a suit and blue tie stepped out. It was Aubrey Martin.

"Go!" hissed Jack. He propelled Hart forwards.

Maddie and Kingsley broke into a run.

"Wait!" yelled the constable.

Pfipp.

Gibb lunged towards them, stumbling when Jack's dart struck his leg. He pulled his gun from his holster and aimed at Jack. "What the fuck do you think you're doing?"

Jack frowned. The sedative wasn't working.

The constable tapped his leg. "Prosthetic," he explained with a smirk. "But this ain't no dart gun, so put your fuckin' weapon down."

Jack's left hand tightened its grip on Hart and he slowly lowered his gun. At the base of the wash tower, the sergeant was negotiating with the drivers of the two vehicles, her palms raised as though to calm both men. Martin drew a weapon.

Unaware, Constable Gibbs tapped his comms device. "Unit Twelve, this is Unit Ten, requesting—"

Pht.

The constable flinched. He spun round to see the driver of the black van crumple to the ground. His sergeant's eyes were wide with shock. Martin strode towards him.

Pfipp.

A dart lodged in Gibb's neck. His arms flailed and he lurched backwards, grabbing hold of Jack as he fell.

Hart, released, tumbled to the ground. He tried to steady himself on hands and knees while the earth beneath him rose and fell. His vision was blurred but he made out the dark, black hulk of the Republican van and scrambled unsteadily towards it.

"Damn it," hissed Jack, freeing himself from the policeman, swapping his dart gun for his pistol. Hart was in his sights. Jack's finger tightened on the trigger.

But the air filled with the hum of drones, emerging

from behind the Station. Jack fired at the machines, sending the lead drone spiralling into the river.

Pht. Pht. Pht.

Bullets rained down. Jack threw himself behind the body of the constable.

"Stop your fire!" Martin was close now with Jack in his sights. "Sergeant, get your fucking drones to hold fire. Where are the sedation drones?"

The woman reddened then tapped her comms device furiously. "Unit Twelve, instruct your drones to stand down. We require MD5s with sedation. Repeat, sedation only."

Jack peered over the top of Gibb's body. To his left, Hart resumed his crawl towards the black van.

Martin glanced at Hart and shook his head. His tie flapped as the wind eddied around him. "Hello Kayson," he called.

Hart's head whipped around and he nearly lost his balance. "Aubr...? Mmartn, iss thaaa yyuo?"

"Christ! Look at the state of you, you're a mess."

Despite the fug of his mind, the desire to live gave Hart an unexpected clarity. Aubrey Martin might yet be his deliverance. Martin could protect him, and in return Hart would give him Jack and Madeeha. He could feed Martin false information about Kingsley, a breadcrumb trail that led nowhere, giving the Republic the time it needed to find the Doctor first.

Hart staggered to his feet, willing the words in his mind to form on his lips.

"It wss hm," Hart said. "Th' tra... th' taaem travlerr, hhirr...we mmus killl hm."

"The traveller. I see. And Dr Kingsley?" Martin asked. "Where is he now?"

Hart's brow furrowed. "Whha?"

"Oh, come on, I know how much you hate lies. Noakes told me about your 'arrangement'. Seems he wasn't very happy about your last set of instructions."

"I don' knnn-"

"You don't like liars, Hart, and I don't like turncoats. What did the Republic offer you? Must have been something spectacular to make you turn your back on your own country, on Europe."

Hart's jaw tensed. The Republic. If only Martin knew how much he hated the Republic and everything it represented. And now, to have his life bound to that very place. Anger seethed in the pit of Hart's stomach. His skin felt hot. The injustice of it, the injustice of it all. His flesh prickled and the sky, like his mood, darkened further.

Jack brought his legs up beneath him, poised to sprint, and felt the hairs lift on the back of his neck. "No, no, no," he murmured. "Not now."

A second black van raced towards the front of the Power Station, tyres spinning, a gun held out the window.

Pht. Pht.

Martin turned, half crouched, and saw the sergeant crumple to the ground.

Behind him, Hart was screaming.

"What the…"

Jack thrust himself forwards, away from the sound of gunshot, but stumbled and fell. Somewhere to his right he could hear voices. Kingsley. Maddie. He had to reach them. But the air was too thick, it bound him, its static charge flowing through him with a heat that seared white behind his eyes.

A savage gust of wind peppered Martin with dust and grit. He ran for the cover of a low wall and tapped his own comms device furiously. "Re-engage the drones. Repeat, re-engage!"

The van doors opened, spewing guards clad in body armour. Martin peered over the brickwork, he steadied his hands on the wall, taking aim.

Pht.

Martin's body toppled backwards, blood trickling from the centre of his forehead.

The sky erupted white. Lightning struck the Station with an ear-splitting crack, cleaving apart the chimney, sending a sonorous rumble down through the wash tower that radiated out through the ground. Jack was winded, unable to breathe. The whir of drones and gunshot interwound with the shrill whine of sirens drawing near.

Hart lurched to his feet, then doubled over with another wave of nausea. Aubrey Martin was dead. Hart needed to get to the van. He had to warn the Republic about Kingsley, about Jack. He forced his feet forwards. The air pressure shifted. He looked up and released a strangled cry.

A hand grabbed Jack's shoulder and hauled him to his feet.

"Move, Jack. Move!"

A strangled scream rang out from behind him. He twisted to see the Station's east chimney come crashing to the ground, hurling dust and debris, burying Hart.

"No!" Jack cried.

Hart was dead. He must be dead. But there was no time to pause. The whir of drones rose through the clamour and chaos. Hands pulled and pushed him onwards. His body stopped resisting and his feet fell into automated rhythm, pounding the last few metres to the tunnel entrance.

Kingsley went down first, followed by Jack. Maddie warned him to go slow, to take his time, then she stepped onto the ladder and heaved the hatch shut, plunging them into darkness.

§

Tideway Tunnel

Jack, Maddie and Dr Kingsley felt their way down six flights of steps, putting space between themselves and the drones above, before they dared pause. Dank air clung to their skin, hinting at what they would face below. The darkness enclosed them, reducing their surroundings to the stairwell and the metal rungs beneath fingertips and feet. Yet the dull reverberating echo of their footsteps revealed that the gulf above and below was unimaginably vast.

Jack sat down heavily on the metal landing and pressed his back to the shaft wall. The cool of the concrete numbed his nerves, still throbbing with the heat of temporal flux, from the ripping of realities and the overthrow of one memory for another.

He ran his fingers over his neck. The scar was still there, as was the one on his chest. He placed his hands together and felt the scars on his palms… It didn't make sense. If Aubrey Martin was dead, then his son would never be born, and nor would his granddaughter, Candice.

He muttered to himself under his breath, tracing the connections in his mind. "Aubrey Martin can't have been contacted by his granddaughter; he can't have involved Hart; Candice Martin can't have captured Howard or sent agents to kill me. The scars, I should remember them, but they shouldn't be visible. This thread should no longer be the dominant one."

He sat forwards and clasped his head, pushing the heels of his hands into his temples as though he could squeeze out the truth. There was movement in the darkness and he felt Maddie's hands on top of his own.

"Jack? Are you okay?"

He released his head and shook it slowly, "No, I'm not. It should be different, all of it. Candice Martin, Aubrey, Hart. I don't understand." He tapped his watch so that it cast a pale light over Maddie, revealing eyes wide with concern. Beyond her stood Dr Kingsley, brow furrowed in thought.

"Who?" Maddie crouched down in front of Jack.

"What?"

"Who are Candice and Aubrey?"

Jack's stomach tightened. He drew breath in short,

shallow gasps. He felt as though he'd been cut adrift. "Back at the Power Station, there was a man in a suit, a dark blue suit with a pale blue tie. He was maybe in his early thirties?" Jack tried to focus on the memory. "He arrived in a silver car. Does that ring any bells?"

Maddie screwed up one side of her face. "Maybe."

"And was he shot? Did you see that?"

"Yes, I think so, by one of the Republican agents."

"And you didn't recognise him. You don't know who he was?"

She shook her head. "No."

He thrust his hand towards her, palm up. "Have you seen these before?" he demanded. "The scars?"

"Yes. I saw them the first night we met on the Southbank, when you were hurt."

Jack frowned. "That memory, these scars, they should have been supplanted by something else. Candice Martin sent her agents back in time to kill me. *They* left me with these. But now she'll never be born."

"Don't you mean Adrian Fairclough? The leader of the British Patriotic Party. You told me he's the grandson of Henry Fairclough, who works for the Government Enforcement Agency – the one that Hart double-crossed."

"Fuck." The tightness in Jack's stomach fell away, replaced a hollow emptiness. "Different reality, same shit."

"Jack, you're not making sense."

"I'm sorry. It doesn't matter." Jack exhaled slowly and pushed his neck against the cool skin of the concrete wall. He thought back to the final words Frits had spoken, back in the stairwell of Twentytwo. Frits had told Jack that Candice Martin had captured Howard, that she was tracking Jack through Howard's memories. But now another recollection came into focus alongside it, in which Frits told him that it was Adrian Fairclough who held his friend. Aubrey Martin's death had altered the future, but one family had simply been replaced by another.

"Forgive me for interrupting." Dr Kingsley shuffled

towards the edge of the platform. "But by my calculations we have a further thirty-five metres to descend and twelve point eight kilometres to walk. Once aerial footage establishes that we neither left the area on foot, nor by vehicle, it will not take long for the Republic to determine our whereabouts." He pulled a small flashlight from his pocket and shone it over the edge of the railings. The floor of the shaft rippled and shifted beneath the puddle of light.

Maddie peered down at it and swallowed. "And if it rains?"

"Let us hope that it is not a storm."

She glanced at Jack who shrugged in reply. What other option did they have?

The Tideway Tunnel had been completed fifty years earlier and had, for some time, dramatically improved the water quality in the Thames. Otter sightings became common place, migrating Atlantic salmon returned in large numbers and even the population of short-snouted sea horses flourished. But then time travel undermined climate policy, and the nation's waterways began to heat at breakneck speed. Native species had no time to adapt, and over a few short years the ecosystem fell apart.

But the super-sewer was still that, and in heavy rain, the polluted overflow that once spewed directly into the Thames was carried through tunnels, more than fifty metres below ground, towards Beckton, East London, to be processed and cleaned.

Just a few days earlier, the stench of London's streets had taken Jack by surprise, but the smell as they gingerly lowered their feet into ankle deep effluence made his eyes water. Behind him, Maddie retched and coughed. Only Kingsley seemed unaffected, although whether down to a lack of smell, or an incredible degree of self-control, Jack couldn't tell.

They took the eastward tunnel and set off at a steady pace, sliding their feet forwards to lessen the splashing of slurry. Jack should have been chilled by the water, but it did nothing to dampen the simmering heat beneath his skin. Again and again, Hart's death replayed in his mind. Jack had told Hart that he would die because of what he had done to Mary, but in the end, the opportunity to avenge his mother had been snatched away. Without revenge, there was no closure, and Jack would have to live with that in the brief time that remained.

Jack's bitter train of thought was pushed aside by the mounting effects of the rank air. He and Kingsley fashioned masks from the lining of Jack's jacket and Maddie wrapped her mother's scarf around her face, but they succeeded only in delaying their reaction to the sewer gasses, which Maddie felt most keenly. There was nothing left in her stomach now. She straightened and wiped her mouth, accepting a bottle of water from Jack with a grateful nod. "How much further do we have to go?"

"We must be about a quarter of the way. Though we've slowed down a bit."

Maddie pulled her headscarf back over her mouth and nose and massaged her forehead.

"Are you okay?" Jack peered at her, concerned.

"It's just a headache," she replied, then stopped. Behind them, the splash of Kingsley's footsteps had paused. "Dr Kingsley?"

He was standing very still, seven or eight metres back along the tunnel. "Can you hear that?" he asked.

Jack and Maddie listened. The silence was deep and unnerving. It conveyed a sense of their depth, of the great weight of earth and mud and clay, of concrete and asphalt high above them.

Maddie shook her head. "I can't hear—"

"Sh…" Jack raised his hand in the air. "I hear it."

"What?"

Jack peered down at their feet. Maddie followed his gaze. "The water's rising."

The effect on Maddie was electric. "We should go back to the last shaft," she declared, at once turning back the way they'd come.

Jack stopped her. "We'd come out near Blackfriars, it's too dangerous."

"I suggest we push ahead," said Dr Kingsley, splashing past them. "We can assess the risk as we near Shad Pumping Station."

Maddie looked at Jack, her eyes imploring, and he realised that she was trembling. "Come on, it'll be fine."

"Jack... I can't swim."

He bit down on his surprise, pulled her closer and squeezed her hands. "You won't need to. This pipe is seven metres wide – it would take a full-blown storm to fill it."

"Yeah, and those don't have a habit of following you around or anything," she muttered as Jack moved on, her hand still in his. Reluctantly, she fell into step. She glanced nervously over her shoulder, as though expecting a subterranean tsunami at any moment. Guilt churned Jack's stomach; of course she couldn't swim. The mid-21st century had seen the cost of food, utilities, clothing – everything – soar. The costs of running a pool were exorbitant and swimming became an experience and skill beyond the means of most families.

Jack felt responsible for Maddie's terror, her fear of being trapped and drowning underground. He reminded himself that she'd chosen to come, she wanted to help. But what of Suraya, awaiting the return of her sister and protector? She hadn't chosen this. And every other Cronod, those he knew, and those he didn't, all condemned by the actions he was undertaking – people who hadn't been given a choice.

Right now, though, Jack felt far from success, watching the noxious water rise and push ahead, swirling around his legs, taunting him as it raced past, towards his destination.

The distant hiss of falling water signalled that they were nearing the shaft at Shad Pumping Station and an escape route up to the surface. Maddie powered forwards, fearful that water would be cascading down the shaft, but the overflow was channelled through a smaller, internal pipe leaving the access stairwell clear and dry. She stretched to grab the bottom rung of the ladder and hauled herself out of the torrent, then reached down towards Dr Kingsley. She froze.

The hatch, far above, clanged opened. The light shifted, and voices echoed down.

"It's them," Jack hissed.

"What do we do?"

"Keep moving forwards." Jack's eyes darted around the space. "Misdirection." A length of loose pipe on the stairwell gave him an idea. "Maddie, have you got your phone?" He pulled the rucksack from his back, fished out the drone and handed it to Kingsley.

Maddie dropped back down into knee-high water and pulled her phone from her pocket.

"Set it to audio record," Jack instructed. He grasped the pipe and moved back into the westbound tunnel. "Now." He scraped the pipe against the concrete walls, then tossed it aside. He splashed back and grabbed the phone from Maddie's hand. "We need to find a way to attach it to—"

"It is done." Kingsley pointed to the drone's belly, where he had fashioned a rudimentary pocket with his facemask and a shoelace, his mind one step ahead.

Jack nodded. "Now, if we set the audio playback—"

"On a loop, yes." Kingsley exchanged the gyrocopter for the phone, his fingers moving deftly across the screen. He slipped it into the pocket, then flew the drone back down the tunnel in the direction from which they'd come from. The sound of metal scraping against concrete echoed in its wake.

They raced to catch up with Maddie who had pushed ahead. "It's not far to the next shaft," she whispered.

"It's too close to this one," cautioned Jack.

"Too close?" her voice rose a notch. "We don't have a choice, look at the water." It was true, the water had risen fast and now reached Maddie's thigh. "If it gets much higher it'll pull us over, and if we breathe that in, or swallow it we—"

"We can make it to the north bank," Dr Kingsley interrupted. "It is not far—" he broke off with a sudden fit of coughs. "Not far from there to Poplar. I know of somewhere we can rest."

"Dr Kinglsey, what if we can't make it?" Maddie asked, wide-eyed.

"Given our situation, you may call me Noah," he replied with a smile. He and Maddie looked to Jack.

The call of voices was clear now, above the bubble of water, the scrapes of the pipe. Jack weighed the threat of their adversary against that posed by the toxic waste. "We'll exit on the north bank," he decided.

Maddie clenched her jaw and stared sullenly ahead, remaining silent when they passed the shaft at Chambers Wharf. It was soon far behind them, their forwards motion requiring little effort now that the water was hip height and propelling them along. Fear and adrenaline had helped negate the effects of the sewer gas on Maddie, but their toll on Noah was now clear. His lungs wheezed and rattled, and he slipped so often that Jack and Maddie took an arm each to prevent him from going under.

"Not far now," Jack murmured, feeling the water creep a little higher. "We'll be fine."

Maddie abruptly stopped. She swayed precariously as the waist height water buffered against her. "Listen," she said. "Behind us."

There, like a bass note beneath the alto-hum of flowing water, was the drone of rotor blades.

"Is it ours?" she whispered.

"That is an MD5 or MD6," Noah wheezed. His chest heaved with the effort.

"Come on," said Jack. "Don't run! You'll lose your footing."

"I'm not running," Maddie snapped. "It's the current."

"I'm sorry." Jack shook his head. "Can you reach the wall if you stretch out your arm? Get a hold on the ridges between the concrete rings."

Maddie tried. "I think so."

"Okay. I'll help Noah. Stay behind us and keep a hold on the wall. We're nearly there."

"I think I can hear it! The overflow pipe up ahead."

Maddie rushed forwards and lost her balance. Her feet flew out from under her and she scrambled to dig her fingers into the ridge. Jack spun around, sloshing water across Noah, grabbing Maddie's waist to steady her.

"Sorry, I'm sorry, I'm so sorry." Her teeth chattered with cold and fear.

"Ssh, it's okay. I've got you."

"What's that?" Noah pointed back along the tunnel.

Jack and Maddie turned to look. A flash of sparks illuminated the space, just long enough to see a drone consumed by a rushing wave of dark water.

"Shit. Go!" Jack yelled. The water rose to his chest. "Maddie, hold onto my backpack. Noah, don't let go of my arm!" Jack felt his feet lift off the floor as they were hurled forwards by the oncoming wave.

"We need... to move... to the other side," Noah gasped.

Jack strained to see. The bottom of the shaft was approaching fast. If they failed to catch hold of the stairwell they'd be lost to the current.

"Maddie, you need to push against the wall. As hard as you can."

Maddie leant out and shoved. Noah stretched his arm wide. Jack held his breath and swam strong strokes towards the far wall.

"A bit more," Noah yelled. "It is coming, coming...got it!" One hand closed tight around a metal upright, the other tightened on the strap of Jack's backpack.

The current swung Jack forwards in an arc, smashing him into the balustrade of the stairwell. Jack gasped, spat the water from his mouth, and reached behind him to push Maddie up and out. She grabbed hold of Noah and helped drag him onto the platform where he collapsed, coughing and retching on the metal grille.

"I think I swallowed some," Maddie cried, as Jack hauled himself out beside her.

"Think we all did," he replied. They were filthy with the slick liquid, but somewhere above was the means to get clean. "Come on."

Their exhausted bodies struggled up the stairs,

shivering and wet, pausing to retch and vomit. Sharp pain stabbed at Jack's shoulder and ribs where he'd been smashed into the steps, and his hands fumbled, struggling to open the hatch into the maintenance building above.

The building was little more than a control room – claustrophobically small – filled with gauges and basic maintenance equipment. Thankfully, it was empty, and a small basin in a recess allowed them to wash off the worst of the sludge. Jack finished last, washing his rucksack clean as best he could before carefully opening the watertight packet that contained what remained of his medical supplies. He pulled out the last syringe of reversal agent. It hadn't been designed with sewage in mind, but many of the toxins they'd ingested were found in the engineered chemical and biological weapons it did neutralise. Jack hoped that a small dose would be enough. Sharing a needle risked cross-contamination but given the circumstances, it wasn't worth worrying about.

Maddie sat on the floor of the control room, her back against the wall.

Jack knelt next to her. "Here, give me your arm."

She raised her eyebrows, looked down at the syringe, and nodded.

Jack gave a third to Maddie, then Dr Kingsley, who was slumped on the single swivel chair, before finally plunging the last of the serum into his own arm. He settled on the floor beside Maddie and allowed himself a moment to be still.

"Dr Kingsley? Noah?" Jack leant forwards at last and touched the doctor's arm.

Noah's eyes flickered open. His chest wheezed ominously.

"Where is the place you mentioned? The safe house?"

"Maureen's," he murmured. "Go to Maureen's." His eyes shut again.

"Dr Kingsley? I need an address."

"Market Square, Poplar. Not far."

§

Poplar

The journey to the safe house exposed them, but the rain fell in sheets so hard and fast that security cameras were rendered blind. The shifting wind, the weight of the sky, the oily smell of the sodden ground and the constant prickling sensation in Jack's skin all played on his nerves. Jack had always been a barometer for temporal change, but this time it felt different. The change wasn't upon him, not yet, but Jack could sense it coming. This was it, the moment before the end of time. His own time, at least.

The occasional clash of thunder mingled with the distant crackle and boom from upriver where the people's protest pushed on, undeterred by the downpour or the river that lapped over the edges of the Embankment and submerged the Thames Path.

"There, it's just around that corner," said Noah. He reached out to point and tripped over a submerged kerb.

Jack caught and steadied him, felt the tremble in the older man's body before his helping hands were shrugged away. Noah's frailty was evident, but his spirit was galvanised by obstinate determination, and he delivered them at last to the back entrance of the flat above Maureen's Pie and Mash Shop.

"Pie and Mash," Jack commented with a flicker of a smile. "That's a relic of the past."

"Somehow makes me think of home," Noah responded as he wiped the rain from his face and disabled a series of digital locks.

They entered a neglected room, cluttered with catering equipment – packets of wooden cutlery, boxes of flyers and sachets of mustard – strewn across a peeling lino floor. The internal door, which had looked flimsy, turned out to be steel-reinforced. It slid back, following a retinal scan, to unveil the remains of a small workshop and laboratory.

"I was here a while, at the outbreak of the war," Noah explained. He flicked some switches and pressed his thumb to a biometric touchpad. He sat down with a squelch at a small table and nodded towards a door. "You can shower in there. The water is hot."

"Oh my god." Maddie smiled. "Hot water! But we can't risk it – a heat spike might attract drones."

"The entire apartment is thermo-insulated, including the photovoltaic glazing." Noah indicated the windows. "It is quite safe."

"Then you go first," Maddie said, noting the goosebumps on Dr Kinglsey's arms.

"I need to rest my legs a while first. Please, I insist." He raised his palm towards the door. Maddie all but ran into the bathroom, closing the door behind her.

"Do you have any spare clothes?" Jack asked.

"Garments belonging to former residents are in the room behind me," Noah replied. "After you have chosen something, we must talk."

Jack paused, hand on the door handle and turned to find Kingsley watching him, studying him, his face unreadable. Jack realised that he was holding his breath, and raised his eyebrows, inviting Kingsley to expand.

"I wish to know why you have chosen *this* path of action. From what I have heard, it does not end well for yourself, or for others like you."

Jack's skin felt cold. "No."

"Then I must understand your story. I have not brought you here simply to keep you safe, Mr Elliot—"

"Jack, call me Jack."

"Jack." Noah tilted his head to one side and considered the man before him. "This was my home for two years, its security measures designed to my own specifications. You and your friend will only leave if I choose to allow it. I appreciate your assistance today, but what you are asking of me is a great deal. If I am to comply, then I must know for myself, *feel* for myself, that it is the right thing to do."

Jack nodded. "I understand."

Noah sat at the table, staring at the film on the surface of his now cold tea. The discussion with Jack had not been positive, though it had been illuminating, and he wondered just how far-reaching the effects of his work had been. Were it not for accelerated climate collapse, mankind might have had time to rethink how and where populations were fed and sheltered. Was he responsible for the mass-migration that had ultimately led to war? Had he played a hand in the demise of his beloved bayous, caught within an abhorrent loop of his own making?

Noah's work had grown from a promise made to his nephews, though they never knew. He had not been there for them. He had never told them stories of the bayous, never taught them to catch crawfish as his own uncle had. And he hadn't been able to hold them, to help shoulder the burden of grief when their mother died.

Instead, he had built weapons for those who had enslaved him. For his own family's safety, he had endangered others. He had tried not to think about how the weapons were used – covert wars waged on 'troublemakers' both home and abroad, a sweeping definition for those who refused to look the other way, those who resolutely stood their ground.

Noah could not right every wrong he had committed, but he knew that nothing he did would matter if human life became unsustainable, if nothing was done to prevent total, ecological collapse. So, he had focussed on creating a future for his nephews, and for their children to come.

Noah's dream of time travel had been born and, as he inched closer to making it a reality, he believed he could change the course of events. He believed he could heal the world. But Noah was wrong. In the future, his captors, as they would again become, waged war with his technology, blinded by greed to the true damage they were doing.

Now, Noah had placed his trust in a stranger, choosing to believe that Jack offered a solution, a chance for his nephews to experience the wilds of Louisiana, the bayous of his own youth. Noah had questioned his trust, but there was an honesty in Jack that he recognised, that he respected. The voice of a man who was willing to give up everything to help others could never be denied.

The luxury of hot water kept Maddie in the bathroom for longer than she'd intended. The flats at Rockingham Street had no form of heat, destined as they were for demolition, and the only hot water available at the Hub had been from a boiled kettle.

Maddie scrubbed at her skin until it chafed and stung, but the stench of the sewer still lingered. She took some of the soap foam and cleaned out her nose, then a little more, swished it around her mouth and spat it down the drain. She recalled a time, when she was little, when she had sworn, and her mother had threatened to wash her mouth out with soap and water. Her seven-year-old self would have never believed how pleasant the taste would one day be.

Maddie finally emerged, wearing fresh clothes Jack had tucked around the door, and felt a shift, a new weight in the atmosphere.

Jack turned at the sound of her voice but didn't meet her eye. Dr Kingsley sat at the table, his hands folded in front of him next to a half-drunk cup of tea. He eased himself up, ready to take his turn in the bathroom. Maddie watched him shuffle past, then turned back to Jack. Still, he didn't look at her. She moved around to see his face, the slight crease between his brows, his eyes cast down.

"It's alright," Jack said at last. "It's not the first time my arrival's been the death of someone's dream." An image of his mother flashed through his mind. "But it's hard for other people – learning that their good intentions have ruinous consequences."

Maddie reached out to him, but he jerked away.

"Don't, you're clean."

Simple words. On the surface they referred to his soiled clothes and skin, but Maddie sensed there was more to them than that. "Jack? Do you want to talk about it?"

"No. The sewer is something I'd rather not recall."

"That's not what I mean."

Jack exhaled heavily then stood up. "I know."

"Jack, it's okay to not be okay. You just met your father for the first time…and then watched him die."

But Jack didn't want to talk about it, he didn't want to think about it. The weight of his memories, the events of that day, the burden of his task was too much. He was drowning. "Really, I'm fine. I need to clean this up." He jabbed a finger towards the puddles of grey water on the floor and began to search for a cloth.

Maddie's eyes glistened as though she might shed Jack's tears for him. "I can do that."

"No." Jack's voice was harsh. He bit his lips, annoyed with himself. "Why don't you check the other room, see if there's something we can eat. We could do with a hot meal."

It took a while to find anything more substantial than tartar sauce, but Maddie finally returned to the kitchen clutching a large bag of rice. The floor and table were clean and dry, the room empty.

She set the bag down and peeped into the bedroom. Dr Kingsley was asleep, his hands folded in that same neat way atop his chest. She crossed silently to the opposite door, resting her ear against the chipped wooden panel, listening to the patter of water on the other side.

Maddie thought about the night before, how Jack had opened up to her, had let her in. Now the barrier was back up and she wasn't sure what to do. She sighed and began to turn away, then paused. Her mother would tell her to try. If not, she might regret it, and this might be their last chance to talk alone. Maddie pushed the door open and slipped inside.

Jack didn't hear Maddie come in. He was leaning against the shower wall, lost in thought, rivulets of water flowing down his back. He imagined that the water had begun the process of removing him, little by little, washing away first his body, then all imprint that he had ever made. In some ways he was glad. With him would go Kayson Hart.

In the end, death had come to Hart suddenly and without warning. Jack thought he should feel relieved, but instead he felt deflated. It had been too easy, Hart's suffering too brief, and Jack resented that. After all, his own suffering continued.

Jack had spent his whole life blaming himself for his mother's illness, holding back from people lest they reject him, as she had. He had studied the past, rather than look forwards to the future. But Jack had been wrong; he wasn't at fault, and his mother's distance wasn't rejection, but her attempt to keep him safe. Jack knew that now. But the freedom that knowledge gave him was already lost. He'd relinquished his right to a future before he'd known his mother's story. Before he'd come to know Maddie. Months ago, Jack had made peace with his choice, but now that peace had been disturbed.

A sound from behind roused Jack from his thoughts, and he twisted to discover that Maddie was there. He turned off the tap and stepped, dripping from the shower, onto the tiles. Maddie handed him a towel and he wrapped it around his waist. She directed him to a stool and made him sit, took another towel and rubbed at his hair, then gently pushed the mussed-up strands back from his forehead.

Jack eyes began to prickle and he squeezed them shut.

Maddie laid the towel down and took his face in her hands. "I wish we had more time," she whispered and pressed her lips to his forehead. "Jack, you're not alone."

A teardrop swelled then broke free, rolling across Jack's cheek to fall silently to the floor. It was followed by another, and another.

Maddie pulled Jack's head to her stomach and wrapped her arms around his shoulders which heaved and shook as everything Jack was holding back spilled forth. She didn't speak, but simply held him until the shuddering subsided and his warm breath against the inside of her arm had steadied and softened.

Jack rubbed a hand across his face and looked up at her through red-rimmed eyes. Life hadn't been kind to

Maddie and yet here she stood, resilient and determined, lifting Jack as he faltered, pouring into him her strength. Her expression held neither pity nor contempt, no fear nor bitterness, just an open acceptance of him as he was: emotionally bruised, with a clock close to zero.

The events of the past three days had shaken him, challenged his resolve to do what he had promised. Jack had never pictured his future before, just taken each day as it came, moving one step at a time. But with Maddie he felt alive. With her, he wished he could imagine a future.

But Maddie's future was rendered uncertain by the same invention that made Jack's life possible. If Jack were to live, what kind of life would they have? Could Jack stand to watch the planet die, through drought, and floods, and disease, knowing that he might have made a difference?

No. It was simple. Through giving his life, he could change the past and the future, and give everyone more time. Tomorrow was beautiful once, and it could be again, and the right choice for Jack's future could ensure that Maddie's own held something more.

He took a deep, shuddering breath and with it blew out the last of his uncertainty. He looked at her, a slight smile at the corners of his mouth. "Time was never mine for the keeping," he said. "But perhaps it's within my gift."

§

18th August 2073

Docklands

It was just after midnight when Jack, Maddie and Dr Kingsley left the safety of the flat, slipping through the dark, hopeful that even the most fervent of Snags had enjoyed their fill of action for the day. The rain had petered out, replaced by a thick, low-lying mist that cloaked their movements and muffled their footsteps. They headed towards the point where the East India Dock Road crossed the river Lea, where Noah, a year earlier, had hidden a small boat beneath the arch of the bridge.

"The boat is solar powered," Noah explained whilst probing the undergrowth. He found the edge of a protective oil cloth, dragged it out and unwrapped a pair of wooden paddles which he handed up to Jack. "But she's been under cover too long for any residual charge, so we will have to do this the old way."

Jack's shoulders slumped a little, he couldn't help it, but then no part of his journey had been easy. His bruised ribs sang with pain as he dragged the boat to the water's edge and tethered it to an elm that overhung the bank. He lowered it onto the water, sending a ripple out through the mist.

Maddie stepped alongside him and swallowed. The boat was rusty and weather worn, and she nervously searched for signs of a leak. "Are there any lifejackets?" she asked.

"Here." Noah joined them, handing Maddie a piece of rubbery fabric with a hole in the centre. "It works the same way as those from an airliner."

Maddie screwed up one side of her face and shrugged. She hadn't been on a plane before; for her, a childhood trip to Southend-on-Sea had been exotic.

Jack took the lifejacket and pulled it over her head, fastening the straps around her waist. "If you need to, which you won't, pull the toggle here and it will inflate."

Maddie pulled her lower lip between her teeth and nodded. Kingsley stepped into the vessel with ease, then held out his arm. She took a deep breath, grasped his hand, and stepped down into the hull.

Jack followed, freeing the rope and casting-off. The boat drifted to the centre of the river where she hung uncertainly, caught between the incoming, brackish tide and the outflow of fresh water.

Noah caught Jack's eye. "The timing is not ideal," he conceded. "The distance to the Barrier is not great, but we shall have to battle the tide."

Jack puffed out his cheeks, pulled the oars from the bottom of the boat and fixed them into the oarlocks. He swung the paddles back, bracing his feet as he pulled forwards, his strokes slow but strong, the mist eddying as the blades rose and fell. At first, the boat made good progress, but slowed as the counter current grew stronger. They were nearing the confluence, where the river Lea met the Thames.

Jack paused a moment to wipe his brow and adjust his grip, fighting against the leaden weariness spreading through his arms and legs. He'd undergone months of training, building his strength and stamina for the mission, but nothing could have prepared him for the assault his body had taken in the last few days.

"Let me help," said Maddie.

"I'm fine, really."

"Well, I'm not." She steadied her nerves and slid onto the bench beside him. "The sooner we're on dry land the better. We'll take an oar each… I can match you," she added, with an arch of her brows.

Jack drew up the paddles and smiled, absorbing the familiar, defiant expression, the challenge in Maddie's voice. If they'd been alone… But that time had passed. Instead, he handed her an oar, waited until she had set her grip, then a brief nod set them to motion. Her stroke, almost at once, matched his.

Dr Kingsley's back straightened. He looked past Maddie,

his eyes strained against the dark. Beams of light shone through the mist – a vehicle's headlights. And something else. He held up a hand.

"What is it?" Jack panted between strokes.

"Are we there?" Maddie turned to look. Her stomach tightened. Though still some distance away, softened by the mist, a red light glowed from the belly of a drone.

"Jack?" Her voice was a whisper.

He glanced behind and clenched his jaw, then pointed a finger towards the bank.

They steered the boat in under the cover of a derelict pier. Maddie slumped forwards over her oar, her palms were raw and blistered, her breath came hard and fast. Jack's back and arms were on fire, his hands stiff and cramped, but he was focussed on the sound of voices, drifting from the darkness ahead.

"Republicans." Noah frowned. His bushy brows masked the hard set of his eyes. "It seems that we are late after all."

Jack shook his head. "There must be another way in besides the main door?"

"There are two access points on the far side of the warehouse, via Herringham Road. The delivery bay is one, but it is exposed. The former caretaker's office is another, but his biometric security remains intact."

Jack exhaled slowly, thinking, aware of the river tugging against the side of the boat. He had held his own against the current, fought the tide to reach his destination, yet still the water did not relent, never paused in its efforts to carry him away. Perhaps time was the same, resisting those who pushed against it, who moved against the flow. It just needed a nudge, in the right place, at the right moment, and the current would do the rest.

Jack checked the gun Kingsley had given him, then hauled himself from the boat, up onto the footpath. He felt it again, that conviction that he was it – he was the nudge – and time was only waiting for him to be in place. He held his hand out to Maddie. "Come on, we'll find a way."

They approached the west side of the warehouse through the neighbouring construction site. The mist had begun to clear, improving their visibility but making them vulnerable. Jack tightened his grip on the gun. It was now their only firearm and he wondered that a man being pursued for his skill in designing weapons should have kept at his former base only one very simple pistol for his protection.

Overgrown shrubs, interwoven by brambles, ran the length of the perimeter fence, giving just enough cover to gain sight of the loading bay doors. A team of six men were attempting to disable the locking mechanism, while a seventh radioed instructions to those on the building's riverside.

"There are too many," Jack whispered. "We need to—"

A cry and flash of sparks from the compound cut him off.

"They have discovered my additions to the building's security," Noah pronounced, a hum of satisfaction beneath his words. "The structure is an excellent conductor."

Jack snatched a glance at the chaos. Prone men clutched their burnt and blistered limbs, a soldier had been knocked out cold – or worse – while others ran back and forth to commands and counter commands. "Come on," he whispered, edging back from the fence. "This should draw them away from the other side."

Jack set off at a sprint – the others would catch up – racing up the west flank of the warehouse, slowing as he neared the river path. Ahead, to the left, a light flickered and went out. Jack ducked low into the shadows. Was it another guard? Or even a Snag? Whoever it was, they were hidden in the gateway that led onto the construction site.

Behind him, Maddie and Kingsley rounded the corner. Jack raised his arm, signalling them to slow down. He crawled forwards, to where moonlight cast a shadow over the narrow road and dashed across. He inched along the wall. Closer. Closer.

Shoes scraped on rough ground. A word was muttered beneath someone's breath.

Jack reached the brick gatepost, raised his gun, and slipped into the shadow beyond it. "Turn around slowly. Hands in the air."

The figure flinched and went rigid, then twisted to face the gun.

"Max?"

"God! You scared the shit out of me." Max pushed his glasses up his nose with trembling fingers.

Jack took a small step closer, the gun still aimed. "Why are you here? *How* are you here?"

Max blanched. "Are you fucking being serious?"

"Max?" Maddie arrived behind Jack. Her brow furrowed. "What… What's going on?"

Jack's head inclined with the slightest shake. "How did you know where to find us, Max?"

Maddie blinked. Uncertain, fearful. "How *did* you find us?"

Max shook his head. "Thanks for the trust, guys." He scuffed at the ground with his foot. "I took Suraya back to the Hub, as you asked me to, then—" Max looked up. "Is that him?" His eyebrows rose. "Dr Kingsley?"

Jack took a step, in front of the doctor.

"Alright," snapped Max, "don't get your knickers in a twist, I'm not a spy."

Maddie, her eyes wide and urgent, raised a finger to her lips.

Max took a calming breath and lowered his voice.

"We saw Sarah. She was getting supplies for the others at Lambeth Bridge. Suraya filled her in on Hart's involvement with the Republic."

Maddie bristled but said nothing.

"For what it's worth, Sarah did apologise to Suraya. And she showed me a transmission, sent to the Republican Embassy maybe five, ten minutes before the place went up in smoke. It confirmed that Kingsley had been snagged near the Thames Barrier. I've been mapping the city's energy use, and when I collated the data from last week, I found that there were five massive power surges in this location."

Jack lowered the gun.

Max's shoulders relaxed. "You told me that the capsules need an impressive injection of energy, so…"

"You deduced correctly," said Noah, moving into view. "As, perhaps, have others," he added with a glance towards the warehouse.

"I figured that if you were still alive," said Max, "this is where you'd come."

Maddie touched him on the arm. "Is Ray safe? Is she okay?"

"She's fine, just worried about you. *That's* why I'm here," he added, with a pointed glance at Jack.

"I'm sorry," said Jack. "I had to be sure."

Max shrugged off his own terse response. "Yeah, I get it. Anyway, Leroy's at the Hub – said he'll keep an eye on Suraya, and Sarah's re-joined the others at Lambeth Bridge."

"Did Sarah" —Maddie drew a breath— "mention me?"

Max screwed up one side of his face. "Kind of. She said if I saw you, to give you these." He opened a bag, revealing a couple of guns and a handful of micro-explosives. "A peace offering?"

Maddie nodded, a flicker of a smile about her lips.

"Any drones?" Jack asked hopefully.

Max shook his head. "Sarah took them all."

"Shame. But these are good." Jack picked up one of the tiny explosive discs and turned it over in his hand. "We need to get inside, but the perimeter's crawling with Republican guards. If we can distract them—"

"I'll help," said Max.

"Thanks. I need to get a look at the front of the building. Dr Kingsley, would you come with me? Max and Maddie, watch our backs."

Maddie turned on Max the moment they'd gone, her voice a harsh whisper. "You shouldn't be here."

"And you should?" he replied.

"You promised me you'd look after Suraya."

Max threw his head back, frustrated. "This *is* me

looking after her. She was going out of her mind worrying about you – she almost set out herself. I promised to make sure you were safe."

Maddie opened her mouth to remonstrate but stopped, realising Max was caught between what she and Suraya wanted, how neither of them had considered his feelings. Maddie's stomach twisted. "Oh, Max…I'm sorry."

He shuffled his feet, avoiding her eye. "Yeah, well. Let's just focus on what we need to do."

Jack and Kingsley returned, gathering close within the shadows of the gateway.

"There are only four guards at the front now," said Jack. "But while this helps even the playing field" —he handed Maddie a gun from the bag— "we'd be swamped as soon as we attack. We need a diversion, something to give us more time."

"I could stagger a series of explosions, radiating out, to draw off the guards?" Max suggested.

"You will need to work quickly," Noah warned. "The electric field in the loading bay was invented for DARPA – it will not take long to disable it, now that they know it is there."

"I'll help set the explosives," said Maddie, but Max shook his head. She set her hands on her hips, waiting.

Max pressed his lips together, weighing up the dangers and his promise to Suraya. "Okay. I'll set up those closest." He pointed at the building site behind them. "You do those on the far side." He dug in the bag and pulled out two earpieces. "Take this – we'll need to coordinate the detonations."

"Do you have another?" asked Jack.

"Only two I'm afraid."

Jack caught Maddie's eye. "Set the charges so that they move away from the river, and then loop back around to us. You should be able to see the entrance from over there." Jack pointed to the river-end of the road. "If there's a problem, get back to the boat."

Maddie held Jack's gaze, her heart thumping, her stomach knotted. She wondered if this was the last time she'd see him, the last chance to tell him how she felt. Words formed silently on her tongue. She gave a small nod, then disappeared into the darkness with Max.

Jack stared at the point where she'd vanished, momentarily adrift, until Kingsley reminded him that they must take cover. They returned to the bramble-swamped perimeter fence, ignoring the thorns that caught on their clothes and scraped at their skin, pushing into the shadows between the plant's spiny stems.

Jack's sense of foreboding grew. His mission had veered off course since the moment he'd miscast. He'd fought off thugs, met Maddie, rescued Suraya, learnt from Frits that he'd died, and watched his father – and justice – slip between his fingers. If that was anything to go by, then it was unlikely that his journey would end in the way he'd anticipated.

Kingsley was speaking, his melodic, methodical voice describing the building's interior, but his words were hard to hear. Jack replayed Maddie disappearing into the darkness. If he failed now, what would happen to her? Maddie, Howard, his mother. Their futures all depended on him, on this moment. He exhaled slowly, searching again for that sense of conviction. The belief that he would not fail.

An explosion lit the sky, sucked in air and spat it out with a boom. The cry of the river-gulls, shocked from their sleep, echoed about the water – high notes underlaid by the staccato crunch of boots on asphalt. Drones whooshed overhead. Jack and Kingsley pulled deeper into the brambles, counting the guards who ran towards the disturbance – two from the north side of the building, four from the south. A second explosion, further inland, drew away more men and another drone.

Jack checked his gun then nudged Kingsley. "It's now or never."

They raced to the end of the warehouse, peering around the corner to find the guards gone, their tools on the ground at the base of the doors. Kingsley ran to the entrance and began reconnecting severed wires, tutting under his breath at the damage, the inconvenience. Jack scanned along the river front, his eyes lingering at the point where he hoped Maddie would appear.

The flash and boom of another explosion shook the warehouse walls. Fragments of dust, captured by the damp air, drifted down like ash.

"Come on, Maddie," Jack murmured. "Where are you?"

A shout from the opposite direction brought Jack to a crouch. "Get down!" he hissed.

"I'm very nearly there," Noah insisted.

"Down! Or you'll be very nearly dead."

Kingsley slid to the ground and Jack took aim as two men moved into sight. A fourth explosion, more distant this time, sent the guards back the way they'd come, and Kingsley scrambled to his feet to continue.

There was a movement at the corner of the construction site. Maddie. She glanced around her, slipped out from the shadow of the wall and raced a few steps before the thrum of rotor blades sent her skidding to a halt.

A drone swept over the wall and hung in the air above her. Jack's flesh turned cold. He raised his gun, but the distance was too far, the machine too close to Maddie. He twisted and shot at the wall behind him, his bullet clanging loudly against the metal panels. The drone spun towards the source of the noise and Maddie fired, sending it crashing to the ground.

"Come on, Noah," Jack hissed. "We need that door open now."

Maddie sped towards them.

"Just one more connection...there."

There was a soft clunk and hiss of air. Kingsley disappeared inside. Maddie was running towards Jack, almost there. He held out his hand for her, ready to pull her inside. In the distance behind her, Max appeared.

Maddie saw Jack's focus shift. She stopped, not yet at the door and turned. Max was moving, but something was wrong. His steps were slow and awkward – he was injured.

Maddie started to head back to him—

Bang.

Max fell to the ground, his arms flung wide. A guard emerged from the side street. "Max!" Maddie scrambled forwards, but Jack leapt from the doorway and seized her around the waist, hauling her towards the building. "No! No! We have to help him!" She wrestled against Jack's grip, tears streaming down her face. "We've got to help him!"

Bullets clipped the edge of the door as Jack pulled Maddie through and slammed it shut. Kingsley, his face grave, reactivated the lock.

"No!" Maddie cried. She tugged furiously at the handle. "We can't just leave him."

"Maddie, listen. Maddie!" Jack grabbed her shoulders, forcing her to face him. "The only way to help Max now is to finish what we've started."

She squirmed free from his grasp and wiped a hand savagely across her face, pushing away her tears. A clang and scrape on the far side of the door made them jump.

"We do not have long," Noah warned.

Jack turned again to Maddie. "We succeed, and none of this happens. It will all be rewritten." He squeezed his eyes shut and tried to steady his own breathing, then held out his hand to her. "Please, I need your help."

Maddie stared at him, her eyes wet with tears, her mind replaying Max fall, over, and over again. She clenched her jaw to stop it from shaking and lifted her chin. "For Max," she said.

Jack nodded. "For Max, and Mary, and Howard."

"This way," Noah called. He hurried along a corridor flanked by storerooms, then out into the cavernous space of the warehouse. Metal chains and machinery clanked ominously from outside of the loading bay doors. He dashed towards a bank of computers and hit a switch, illuminating the space with a soft glow. "I will wipe my digital files and records, but those" —Noah pointed to shelves of paper files— "will need to be destroyed with everything over there."

Jack recognised the skeletal structure of a time capsule, perhaps an early prototype, its wires and controls laid bare, like a body without its skin. "Does it contain the caesium core?" he asked. "Can we use it to—"

"Yes, we can use it to set off a chain reaction. It will vaporise anything within six yards. Do you know how to activate it?"

Jack ran towards the workstation, shifted through the tools on Kingsley's bench, and found the one he was after. "Yes," he shouted. "I know what to do. Maddie, I need you to bring the paperwork over here."

Maddie spotted a platform trolley, pulled it to the shelves and began to load it up with files. "Please tell me we can set that thing off remotely?" she asked, dumping the first lot on the floor near Jack.

"Well," Jack mumbled, a screwdriver between his teeth, "from behind that fire screen at least."

Maddie dragged the trolley back to Dr Kingsley and realised that his computers were banked up behind a tall fire-retardant screen. "Great," she muttered, with a glance at the ceiling. "That will be really useful when the building crashes down on us."

A short, high pitched wail brought Maddie's hands to her ears and the room was plunged into darkness.

"They have disabled the electric field," said Noah, his face illuminated by the glow of the screens.

"They can get in?" Maddie's voice rose as fear constricted her throat. Frantically, she felt her way in the darkness, pulling the remaining files on to the trolley.

"The building's infrastructure is steel-reinforced, but their drones will scan it to reveal the weak spots."

"Where? Where will they come through?"

"Most likely opposite the river, four yards down from the north-eastern corner."

Maddie heaved the laden trolley across to where Jack worked, a torch now held between his teeth, his brow creased with concentration. She scanned the bench, grabbed some tape and a roll of wire and ran back towards the storerooms. "Be rude not to give them a good welcome, don't you think?"

Maddie felt her way back down the corridor, her eyes

adjusting to the dark, her pulse thudding loud in her ears. The main entrance lay ahead, undisturbed, but a faint red glow shone through an internal door on her right. Maddie wove through the storeroom towards the light, and the growing roar of a heat gun, carving its way through the wall. Red hot globules cascaded to the floor, dangerously close to the room's flammable contents. Metal vapour filled the air, stinging Maddie's eyes and catching at her throat.

Back at Maureen's, she'd carefully cleaned her mother's headscarf, and she pulled it now from her pocket, fixed it back around her mouth and nose, and set to work placing the remaining micro-explosives. She left two where the wall would most likely fall in and another at the entrance to the corridor, connected to a trip wire. The wire wasn't subtle but, given the heat gun's progress, there wasn't time to rig up something more sophisticated.

Maddie stepped over the wire into the corridor where she got down on her hands and knees to feel along the ground. The floor tiles were cheap lino and easily lifted. She hid two more explosives beneath them, then fixed the final one to the door that led into the main warehouse. She slipped through and closed it gently, taping a wire from the explosive to the inside wall.

"Nobody open this door," she warned. "We don't have much time – how can I help?"

Jack looked up from the detonator he was screwing back together. "Nearly there. Help Kingsley bring all the hardware over here. The drives are wiped, but better safe than sorry."

Boom.

The first of Maddie's devices went off, shaking the warehouse walls.

"They're in!" Maddie raced across the room to help Kingsley. She heaved the trolley towards the piled papers and hardware, passing Jack who was unspooling a coil of wire towards the fire screen.

Noah joined her and placed the final piece of equipment on top of the pile. His eyes clouded, taking in his life's work, disorganised, carelessly heaped. Hours, weeks, and years of toil all amounting to nothing. His empty hands clutched together at his breast.

"Is that everything?" Maddie asked.

Deep in thought, Noah made no reply.

"Dr Kingsley! Is that everything?"

Noah startled, his brief surprise soon hidden. "Yes," he replied calmly. "That is all."

"Come *on* then." Maddie grabbed his hand and pulled him back towards the fire screen.

Boom.

The walls groaned. Wailing cries from an injured man in the corridor were joined by the rise and fall of sirens outside.

"Police?" Maddie, wide eyed, slid down beside Jack.

"They may assist us in occupying our Republican friends," Noah suggested. He sank down against the fire screen.

Jack barely heard their words. His skin was electric. There was buzzing in his ears. He brushed his thumb across the detonator and lifted his eyes to Maddie. "Are you ready?"

Maddie drew in a sharp breath. This was it. The moment had arrived. "Jack, I…"

He lifted his hand to touch the side of her face. "It's okay, we—"

Boom.

The door to the hallway blew in, spewing smoke and fragments of glass across the room.

"Get down!" Jack yelled, and hit the button.

Nothing happened.

Beyond the settling smoke, a clamour of accents hurled insults and commands.

Jack tugged on the wire. It slid towards him without resistance. "Shit. It's severed. Cover me." He crawled across the floor, trailing the wire through his fingers until he found the break.

Pht. Pht.

Maddie ran across the room, ducking behind a workbench. She drew her gun and fired at the shadows in the doorway, Republican or police, they were all the same now.

Pht. Pht.

"Aargh!" A bullet clipped Maddie's arm.

Noah flew to her side. "Get back!" he shouted. He exchanged fire with the encroaching figures, grateful that the loading bay doors had yet to budge.

Pht. Pht.

"I'm fine." Maddie took aim again, wincing as she raised her arm.

"All this is happening because of me. Now do as I say and get back!"

"Go!" Jack yelled. "I'm nearly done."

Maddie raced back and fired shots from behind the screen.

Pht. Pht.

"There are too many," Noah cried.

"Go now!" Jack shouted. "I'll cover you."

Pht. Pht.

Bullets bounced and clanged off the metal walls. Jack sprang from the floor and raced towards the others, determined to take one last look at Maddie. He slid behind the fire screen, locked his gaze with hers, and slammed his fist down on the detonator.

The air erupted in a ball of blue flame. It rolled outwards, vaporising the time capsule's framework, the glass and circuitry of the computers and hard drives. Sheets of paper swept upwards, burst into flame, and rained down as ash. Guards who'd fought their way in were barrelled over, their bodies desiccated by the heat. The walls of the building heaved and groaned as the metal expanded and ruptured.

Scorching air savaged the surface of the fire screen until it rippled and glowed. Maddie's ears were ringing, the acrid smell of burnt hair filled her nostrils, the skin on her hands, on the back of her neck, was blistering. She squeezed her eyes tight and pictured herself standing with her mother and grandmother, ready to join them.

But the heat began to lift, the ringing subsided, and for a moment there was a deathly hush. Maddie uncurled her hands from around her head and looked up. Ceiling panels, hanging precariously by a single corner, groaned and swayed. Her lungs were on fire and her throat was raw. Dr Kingsley was slumped against the wall. He blinked, once, twice.

A wrenching howl of pain broke the silence. Jack, curled into a ball beside her, screamed and clutched his head, his knuckles white, his hair singed and ashy.

Tears rolled down Maddie's cheeks as she wrapped her arms around him, waiting for that moment, any moment now, when he would simply disappear. Her touch soothed him, and she stroked his back, silencing his cries, steadying his breathing. And still, he was there.

"Jack?"

Jack mumbled something she couldn't hear.

Maddie sat up. "It didn't work," she croaked. She caught Kingsley's eye. "Why didn't it work?"

Jack struggled to his knees, shaking and retching with the effort. He scanned the devastation for something he'd missed, but there was nothing. "I failed."

"No." Maddie took his face in her hands. "Maybe there's a… a time glitch, or something. Maybe you get to live?" Her eyes widened, daring to hope.

Jack shook his head.

"I am the problem," Noah wheezed. His hand fumbled for the edge of the fire screen. He grasped it and winced – it was still hot – but clenched his teeth and pulled himself to his feet.

Noah shuffled towards the mounds of dust – all that remained of his invention – kicking up ash and smoke which billowed around him. "In order to reset time, I need to die, otherwise my ideas will remain a latent reality." Noah pictured his nephews – two bright eyed babes with their lives yet to live.

"No." Maddie frowned. "You wouldn't… you know now what's at stake." She struggled to her feet then helped Jack to stand.

Noah looked over his shoulder. He held Jack's eye until he discerned the slightest of nods. He thought of the bayous, almost smelling their briny tang, and pictured the grand cypresses draped in Spanish moss. "I will hope for a better ending, on the second time around." He placed his gun to his head and pulled the trigger.

Pht.

"No!" Maddie flew forwards, too late.

Kingsley's body crumpled to the ground.

Maddie spun back to Jack. She was shaking, her eyes wide with tears.

Jack's throat was tight, the words difficult to form. "It takes a minute," he said.

Maddie ran to him, grasped hold of him, feeling his solidity. She told herself that it wouldn't work – it didn't before, it wouldn't now – and searched his face for signs of pain.

Jack had expected it to hurt, as it always had when time shifted and realigned. But this time he felt no pain, and that was how he knew. There was no searing heat, no white light behind his eyes. Just light-headedness, a lifting of weight.

A thousand anecdotes insist that when you die, your life will flash before your eyes. But death, and what Jack faced, were not the same. There were images filling his mind, but they were not of the past, nor of his own life, but of the future, of what it might now become. There was Mary, walking in Greenwich Park, two children skipping by her side. And then, there was Maddie. Again, and again, there was Maddie. Defiant. Brave. And happy. Perhaps Jack would leave a legacy after all, and this, Maddie's happiness, would be it.

He pushed his fingers into her hair and pulled her towards him so that their foreheads touched. "Thank you," he breathed.

Maddie dug her fingers deeper into the folds of his shirt and pushed her lips against his, willing him to remain.

Jack took her face in his hands and smiled. "I love you," he whispered.

Then he was gone.

§

Epilogue
October 2073
Trafalgar Square

Maddie had an early finish that day, but rather than rush home, she bought a coffee and cake from the gallery cafe and sat down to enjoy them in the sunlight that cascaded down the steps.

Tourists gathered, as they always did, to admire the bronze lions guarding Nelson's Column, and puzzle at the meaning behind the latest sculpture topping the Fourth Plinth. Maddie smiled to herself, knowing, as she did, that the artist was poking fun at the tourists themselves.

She pulled out her iHolo and rang Suraya. Her sister didn't answer, but pinged back a message that hung in the air – *Meet me on your way home, at the Southbank?* – followed by a winking monkey holo-emoji. Maddie licked a crumb of cake from her finger and replied, *30 mins xx*

She stood up and stretched, then headed for The Strand. Up ahead, she spotted Ezra, returning from his lunch break with his latest squeeze. He'd moved on from the cafe staff to the girls who manned the gift shop.

"Maddie!" he called out. "You leaving early today?"

"Yeah, the school bus broke down. They've rearranged their workshop for next week."

"Oh." His face fell. "That's a shame, a few of us are having drinks after work."

The girl on his arm eyed Maddie jealously.

"Oh no." Maddie shook her head. "It's fine – I'll get a bit more studio time. Have a good one." She smiled brightly and walked on. She had no space in her life for a playboy like Ezra.

Maddie glanced in the shop windows as she passed, her own face briefly replicated on those of the holo-mannequins, but her eyes looked through them. She was thinking about last night's conversation with her mum; she couldn't wait for the bark cloth to arrive. True, the yield hadn't been as high as her mum had hoped – the drought that year had been harsh – but the wastewater management scheme and new rainwater reservoirs were making a difference. In time, she was sure, the harvest would improve.

Maddie visualised the artwork she was making, the layers of cloth, the colours, and the textures, and felt the pleasurable tingle of anticipation for that afternoon's work. And today, the National Gallery had agreed a date for her textile heritage talk, and a wall where her artwork would be hung. Yes, it was a bit of a back-corridor, but it was still more than she'd dared to dream of.

Maddie reached the Embankment and set out over Waterloo Bridge. A driverless taxi crawled past, carrying a mother and child. Maddie caught the look of horror on the woman's face when she discovered her son drawing on the side window with her lipstick. The 'artist' grinned at Maddie as the vehicle sped away.

Maddie narrowed her eyes at the delivery drones that hummed back and forth on either side of the bridge like some species of giant, domesticated wasp. She didn't like them, the drones, though she couldn't say why. Ray insisted she was being silly.

Maddie smiled to herself. Suraya had only been in London since the start of summer, yet she already knew the city inside-out, approaching every opportunity with the same gusto she'd always had.

Suraya was only twelve when Maddie had moved to London to study for her MA in Art History, and choosing to live so far away had been a tough decision. But Maddie was glad of it now. She'd had time to herself, to discover who she was and what she wanted. And now she was settled, she was better able to keep an eye on Suraya. Her baby sister was newly enrolled at UCL, and their parents, back home in Uganda, imagined all kinds of trouble. Maddie laughed to herself, knowing that she'd have her work cut out.

The Southbank was busy with street performers, tourists and families, people enjoying the mild autumn weather. Maddie spotted a guitarist, living statues, and a man blowing flurries of glistening bubbles. Some things never changed. Jubilant tots were shrieking with joy, chasing the soapy spheres along the path, popping them between their outstretched hands. A few bubbles escaped, wafting away across the river, and Maddie's eye followed their trail.

She saw that it was low tide and a small beach had appeared. Her neighbour, who'd lived in London for over seventy years, told her that tidal beaches on the Thames had once been common, even large enough to attract the odd sun-bather or spade-wielding youth. Now the sea level was higher and a glimpse of the riverbed quite rare, but at least it hadn't been necessary to raise the river wall, as London's Mayor had once predicted.

Maddie entered the pedestrian underpass beneath Blackfriars Bridge, and the sound of children's laughter was replaced by the echo of her footsteps. Though warm afternoon air flooded the tunnel, Maddie shivered. She always did when she passed this way. She wrapped her arms around herself and quickened her pace, smiling gratefully as she stepped back out into the sun, heading for the spot where she and Ray liked to meet, outside Bankside Gallery.

Suraya was already there, reclining on a bench with her eyes closed, catnapping to make up for another late-night party. Maddie noticed the way in which people couldn't help but stare at her sister as they passed, as though she were a beautiful statue rather than a hung-over teenager. Maddie shook her head, glad that she didn't have to endure the invasive nature of strangers' eyes.

She planted a kiss on Suraya's forehead and flopped down beside her.

Suraya's eyes popped open and she broke into a wide smile. She yawned theatrically and stretched, before seizing Maddie's cup. "Oh, it's empty," she complained.

Maddie laughed indulgently. "I can get you one?"

"No, it's okay. Caffeine isn't good for you, you know."

"Nor are late nights and alcohol." Maddie raised an eyebrow.

"Oh, I wasn't drinking... But it *was* a late night; everyone had so much to say. It was good though," she added. "I can learn a lot from the older students, including Max's best friend – he was there last night." Suraya was effervescent. "Did I tell you he's doing his thesis on environmental activism? He's promised to help with my petition to reinstate the environmental clause in the Bill of Human Rights." She sighed contentedly and laid her cheek on Maddie's shoulder.

Maddie shook her head in wonder. Who was this woman, and what had she done with her little sister? "Still Max then?" she asked.

Suraya linked her arm through Maddie's and squeezed it. "Yes," she grinned.

"I still can't believe you're dating an engineering nerd."

"Max is not a nerd, he's a genius! And anyway, you've only met him once, so you wouldn't know—"

"Okay, okay, it's just... it still surprises me, that's all. But in a good way," she added. "I like him."

"Me too." Suraya beamed and glanced at her iHolo. "Oh. I'd better go, I've got a lecture in half an hour." She squeezed Maddie's arm again. "Glad I caught you." She stood up and took two steps before she remembered something and stopped. "Hey, do you wanna know something crazy?"

Maddie raised her eyebrows.

"Max went to see some American astrophysicist give a talk the other day, and he said it's theoretically possible to time travel. Ha! Can you imagine?" She laughed and blew a kiss, then slipped off through the throng.

Maddie's chest tightened. She wasn't sure why. Perhaps it was the bitter-sweet sensation of seeing her little sister grow up before her eyes. Yes, that must be it. Her poor mum, how she must have felt it when first she, then Suraya left home.

She pushed herself up from the bench and crossed the

footpath to lean against the river railings. Simple acts of life played out all around her: a business woman side-stepped a kissing couple, hurrying to her next meeting; teenagers laughed and swore, performing skateboard tricks on the steps below the Tate; an elderly couple, holding hands, watched their dog sniff the grass at the base of a tree; and a young man, chatting with his girlfriend via iHolo, forgot himself and the technology's limitations, absent-mindedly reaching out to touch a wayward strand of her hair.

On the far side of the river, the latest construction projects carried on apace, dwarfing St Paul's, which still somehow sang out to Maddie and all those who stopped to take in the view.

She watched a gull float past on the current and thought to herself that she really ought to go for swimming lessons: after all, you never knew when they might come in handy. Perhaps her talk would be a great success. She'd go on a world tour, sharing her skills and her knowledge about bark cloth, and stay in fancy hotels with swimming pools of pure, azure blue.

The gull drifted under Millenium Bridge and bobbed out of sight. Maddie considered Suraya's parting words. Could time travel be possible? She didn't know.

When she thought about time, she imagined it as a river. But time, unlike the tidal mouth of the Thames, only flowed one way. Sometimes, life's current ran smooth, at other times it was treacherous. Either way, Maddie realised that she didn't fear it. She would ride the river of time to destinations as yet unknown, and her view, like herself, would always be changing.

Maddie turned her face to the sun and smiled.

If the future lay before her, fluid and unformed, then she had the power to shape it. She would take it and sculpt it into something with meaning. With time, she would make something beautiful.

Acknowledgements

There are so many people to thank, so here goes!

Thank you to Peter and Alison from Elsewhen for taking a chance on this story; to my editors, Sofia and Isobelle, who taught me so much; to Mike Ashley, for your generous words and perceptive comments; and to Alex for creating the stunning artwork gracing my cover.

Thank you to my high school English teacher, Sally – yours were the first words of encouragement and I still have them on the Post-it note you stuck to my pages.

Thank you to all my wonderful writing friends – Sarah, Steve, Isobelle, Rachel, Carly, David, Andrea, Olivia, Ness and Jessa. Thank you for cheering me on, offering advice, sharing your knowledge and inspiring me to keep going!

Thank you to my amazing friends and family – I could fill an entire page with your names – you know who you are and I love and appreciate you all. I'd particularly like to thank Elena, Flora and Emma who read the earliest versions of this story and persuaded me that I wasn't delusional! Thank you also to Cristobal and Maria for improving my understanding of genetics – I'm still pushing my luck, but knowingly so!

To my grandfather, Peter Phillips, and 'Uncle' Mick – your stories inspired me and I hope you would be proud.

To my brother, Oliver, and all the hours we spent watching *Star Trek* and *Red Dwarf*.

Thank you to my parents, Ann and Andrew – you taught me, by example, to follow dreams, to be creative, and believe that anything is possible.

Thank you to my boys, Hugh and Tobin – I love how you have cheered me on!

And finally, thank you to my husband, Simon, who read the manuscript as I was writing it, encouraging me, helping me navigate plot holes, and never once doubting my ability to make something of my ideas. I could never have done this without your support.

Elsewhen Press

delivering outstanding new talents in speculative fiction

Visit the Elsewhen Press website at elsewhen.press for the latest
information on all of our titles, authors and events; to read our blog;
find out where to buy our books and ebooks; or to place an order.

Sign up for the Elsewhen Press InFlight Newsletter at
elsewhen.press/newsletter

ONE MILLION TIMES

A Science Fiction Anthology Series
ROGELIO FOJO & R. JAMES DOYLE

Chronicles of time travellers among us

What happens when we hunt down elusive visitors from the future?

Discover a present where we invite, seduce, trap, love, hate, and even murder… our time-travelling twins.

Short stories by
R. JAMES DOYLE
ROGELIO FOJO
DAVID GERROLD
R.C. MATHESON
CHRISTOPHER PRIEST
TEIKA MARIJA SMITS
FERNANDO SORRENTINO
…and more!

cover art by FANGORN

ISBN: 9781915304902 (epub, kindle) / 9781915304603 (192pp paperback)

Visit bit.ly/OneMillionTimes

A TRUTH BEYOND FULL

ROSIE OLIVER

Don't dig deep lest you regret what you find

Miranda, an ice and rock moon of Uranus, has been a thriving mining colony. But recently there has been a rise in fatal accidents. Kylone has an ability to extrapolate patterns behind a rock face to determine where and how to dig. When his fiancée died in another accident, he blamed himself and his ability; a wreck, no longer able to mine, he became a priest with limited duties in the locally developed Priesthood. Assigned to officiate at a hero miner's funeral, the widow asks Kylone to investigate the spate of accidents and, along with some help from an unexpected source, he starts to suspect that they may have a more sinister cause, a suspicion which puts his own life in danger.

ISBN: 9781915304582 (epub, kindle) / 9781915304483 (326pp paperback)

Visit bit.ly/ATruthBeyondFull

RINK

Chris Matravers

The world is a nursery in which selves mature after multiple incarnations

What if some souls are not bound to a body but can exist in a 'between place' for years after death before 'shifting' into a new body.

Most people live as ephemeral humans, 'Phems', oblivious of any previous life. But a few become 'Rinks': fully aware of previous incarnations as selves of different genders and race and in diverse civilisations. Continuously re-incarnating they are unaware that eventually they could mature enough to evolve onto another plane of existence. Or, at least, that is what is supposed to happen but renegade Rinks are failing to mature. Running rampant as crime and war lords, they are intent on exploiting the Phems.

When Jay re-incarnates in London in 2026, he is shocked by their activities. He has endured too many lives: he's seen and done everything. Previously he's searched for a way to stop the seemingly endless cycle of life and death but now he finds himself compelled to try to restore order and so Jay enlists the help of like-minded Rinks to defeat the renegades.

But what will he do when he's forced to choose between the love of his life, and death...

ISBN: 9781915304735 (epub, kindle) / 9781915304636 (280pp paperback)

Visit bit.ly/Rink-Matravers

About Amy Orrell

Amy grew up in a family of artists and writers where discussions about dragons and leprechauns flowed on from debates on the existence of extraterrestrial life or the probability of time travel. Painting was Amy's first artistic calling – her artwork focused on narrative art – but the complexity of the stories she wanted to tell demanded something more, and naturally led her to writing.

Amy likes to write thought-provoking science fiction and fantasy, delving into her characters' emotional lives whilst delivering fast paced thrills, twists, and turns. She lives in Norwich, in the East of England (which contrary to popular opinion, is not flat) with her husband, two children and writer's support cat.